I0761866

A LOVE STORY BY PETER AARONS

***"Give her a chance, please, Bud.
I promise, you'll like her."***

Look For These Other Peter Aarons Books:

Glory Days

Home Again Home Again (Coming Soon)

The Converging Objects of the Universe (Coming Soon)

Oh, Baby! (Coming Soon)

Visit our website at

www.peteraarons.com

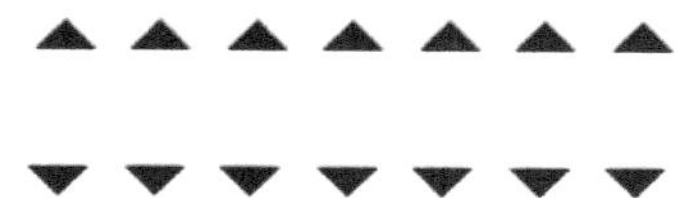

And This Author's Dragonhorse Tales Series:

Conscience of the King

Peace on Another's Terms (Coming Soon)

A Lopsided Colorwax Heart (Coming Soon)

Spirit in Motion (Coming Soon)

Dragonhorse Rising (Coming Soon)

Visit our website at

www.dragonhorserising.com

Showandah S. Terrill

ANOTHER MAN'S WIFE

A LOVE STORY

BOOK TWO OF THE PETER AARONS NOVELS

This book is a work of fiction, and any references to historical events, real people or real locales are used fictitiously. Other names, places, characters and incidents are products of the author's imagination, and any resemblance to actual events or locales or persons, living or dead, is purely coincidental.

Published 2020 by Short Horse Press.

Original Photography by Showandah
Book Design and Shorthorse Press Logo Design by Jeremy T. Hanke
The text for this book is set in times New Roman, 11 point
Manufactured in the United States of America
Library of Congress Control Number: 2019919241
ISBN 978-1-7328052-6-2 (hardcover)
ISBN 978-1-7328052-7-9 (paperback)
ISBN 978-1-7328052-8-6 (eBook)

For Jerda and Jeremy
Who found each other.

CHAPTER ONE

Glory caught my attention without trying to yell over the music, and indicated by the spread of thumb and little finger that someone was on the phone.

"Who?" I mouthed, reversing directions. I wondered momentarily if Mother or Dad was sick, but that couldn't be it. Glory would be yelling, not gesturing.

"Tommy," she mouthed back, measuring about chin high and drawing a slightly pudgy outline with both hands. She stepped further into the room and turned down the music.

"Really? I groaned. "He's starting already?"

"Seems so."

I tossed my jump rope and followed her into the kitchen.

"I figured you was about done anyway. That knee holdin' up?"

"It's fine," I muttered. "Coffee smells good." I told her both those things every morning, and every morning she asked about me, and looked after me. It had been a blessed and familiar routine for most of my adult life, and I considered myself a very lucky man.

I toweled off enough to handle the receiver and leaned back in one of the chairs at the breakfast bar. "This is an outrage," I growled. "It's not even light yet, and you're already calling people? I know your mother taught you better than that." I spent a moment trying to get my breath back, and Tommy leaped into the silence.

"Did you read it?" He asked, and I could hear his breath hissing quietly through that underbite of his. "Did you?"

"Yes, I did, as requested. Finished it about one O'clock this morning."

"Like it?"

"Absolutely." Not a lie. "Glory's been trying to get me to read it ever since I got home from London. It moved well. It had sensitivity and depth. A little sex. Quite a bit of sex, actually. A little adventure, great sense of social consciousness. I liked it very much. I can certainly see why it's hanging out at number one on the New York Times Best Seller List. Now, what exactly does this have to do with me?"

"Oh, come on, Bud. It's the part of a lifetime, and you know it."

"The part of my lifetime, is Sergei Rachmaninoff," I corrected. "This is an excellent book, but that's all it is. What do you mean, 'Part of a lifetime?' I don't see a screenplay here."

"Not yet," he enthused, "but it can be. The screenplay could be as good as the book if you help write it. And … if you'll play Mark Kincaid. This whole thing is riding on your answer, Bud. Will you play the part of Mark Kincaid? That is the question!"

"And here all these years I've thought the question was, 'to be, or not to be,'" I laughed. I chewed a little on the corner of my lip and studied the intricate detail in the molding which ran around the edge of the kitchen ceiling. "Tommy," I said at last, "I know this means a lot to you. I do. But I really don't want to get involved. How many months did I prepare just to try out for the part of Sergei Rachmaninoff? That's my dream part. If I should happen by some miracle to have it offered, I want to be open to take it, and it's the lead role in a major motion picture. I wouldn't have time to do one single other thing."

"The part of Rachmaninoff is already yours, and you know it. Stop worrying."

I made a deprecating sound with my lips. "Right."

"Everybody in Hollywood knows David Swift wants you in that part. He's wanted you in that part since he was six years old. He's practically having the damned thing written for you. Nobody knows why he's even having tryouts. It's yours. Relax."

"Oh, of course," I muttered. "I'll just assume I'm a shoo-in and see where it lands me."

"Bud, I know how hard you've worked," Tommy said, and there was no smile in his voice. "I promise we can shoot around it. I'd never get in the way of a part that good, you know that. But we both know that part will be slavery. This part," he paused for emphasis, "will be fun! This won't be a long shoot. Come on, Bud, put those bedroom eyes and those racehorse legs to good use."

I was getting nowhere with him. "Tommy, I spent four, long, hectic years playing Nathan Strauss in a series that feels like it ended about ten minutes ago. I've been doing King Lear for the last six months. Before that, it was a concert tour with GLAS. I need a rest."

"And most recently it was two weeks skiing in San Moritz. You've had your rest. Besides, we're not going to start shooting tomorrow," he said reasonably. "It's not even a screenplay yet."

"Stop! You know perfectly well that I play Indians, bad guys and space aliens. I'm a character actor, not some dashing lead. I'm sure I'd be miserably uncomfortable with it. Besides, many's the good novel I've seen ruined by a screenplay. I'm …" my final word, which was out, was cut off by his excited, annoying laughter.

"Stop yourself, you big sissy. Sergei Rachmaninoff is certainly a lead part as you well know, and that doesn't seem to be bothering you one bit, so just shut up and listen. The woman who wrote the novel has control of the screenplay. When you're number one on the New York Times Bestseller list, and when you have as much marketable charisma as P.K. Tyler, you can do that if you want to, which you would know if you'd pull your head out of your ... Steinway once in a while." There was a pause and the laughter was gone. "Bud, this is the chance of a lifetime for Bellwether, please don't throw it away for us. Please don't. She says if you'll do the part of Mark Kincaid, she'll write it with you, and for you, and give you final approval on your own character."

"Really?" I said aloud, and caught Glory smirking over by the toaster. I glared at her, and she chuckled deep in her chest. She and my dad both wanted to see me back in the flickers. Apparently, so did Tommy Sinclair. I took a deep breath and gave it some thought. Tommy was absolutely right about it being good for Bellwether – maybe not the chance of a lifetime, but if he saw it that way I wasn't going to argue with him. It would give me the opportunity to dabble with writing and maybe directing and some of the things I didn't often get to do. It was a good book. It was a very good book. And Mark Kincaid was an amazingly well-written character. He scared me, but the thought that I just might be able to pull him off was titillating.

Tommy finally lost patience. "Will you at least meet her? She's in town. I'll put a leash and a muzzle on her for you if that'll help. Hell, I'll put a bag over her head. I'll put a bag over your head in case hers falls off."

"Have you met the woman?" I asked suspiciously. "I mean, really met her?"

"Yes, I've really met her. How do you think I got the rights? Tentatively got the rights."

"Through her agent?" I drawled, looking absently around for a cigarette. There was no point asking Glory. She never helped me find cigarettes. Wouldn't buy them for me, either. She'd laid down the law on that twenty-six years ago, and never budged an inch. She said she wasn't into killing people she was fond of.

"No agent yet. Right now she's working alone with no big staff behind her. I get the sense that she'll be easy to deal with, but that will change if she gets a handler, and there are plenty of them out there clamoring for her attention. Bud, it could be us! Please, it could be us!"

I knew how much this meant to Tommy, and I was weakening, maybe because I loved the guy, or because I was beginning to realize he was right, or because my ego was beginning to get the best of me. "What's she like?" I asked, trying to sound casual. Glory touched my right shoulder to indicate she was there, set breakfast down in front of me, kissed my temple, and made a dash for the door. "Thank you," I called after her. "Hey, weren't you and Rafael heading out with the Teuferts today?"

"We are now," she laughed. "Lunch in the ice box. Dinner with you folks tonight. You be nice to Tommy, you hear me?" The back door closed behind her.

"You need to listen to her," Tommy said peevishly. "Can I tell you what she's like? Not that you'll believe me."

"Don't bother," I sighed. "She's five foot ten with bleached blonde hair, a Chanel suit, and two inch fingernails." I unbuckled the heavy brace on my right knee and let it drop to the floor.

"No. That would be your ex-wife."

I ignored the jab. Tommy had loathed Megan from day one, and the feeling had been mutual. Of course Megan had loathed all my friends, and, ultimately, me and everything I stood for. "P.K. Tyler. Four foot ten, two hundred pounds, blue hair, cookies in all her pockets. Don't get me wrong, that's better than the five foot ten thing."

"None of the above, I swear. She's nice. Not gorgeous, not voracious. Nice, and really quite shy, so you'll have to be a little less outspoken than usual. You'll like her, Bud."

"Meaning ... she fits the latter description?"

"Oh, for Godssake, what does it matter?" Tommy snapped. "Do you want to work with her or have sex with her?"

"I'm not sure," I grinned, "but, having read her book, I think I may need to keep my options open, especially if any of that sex makes its way into … the screenplay." Suddenly, I was no longer amused. My heart made a funny little thump like it does just before the curtain goes up or the conductor brings his baton down. "I'm … not sure."

"Right now, she wants you to play Mark Kincaid. That could change abruptly, my friend. You come on like the gun-shy misogynist Megan turned you into, and Mrs. Tyler will take her million dollar book and go elsewhere. Everybody wants the story, and a helluva lot of people want her, too."

"Sorry," I said, and I meant it. Bellwether was Tommy's whole life. He was the one who'd devoted himself to running the company, while Kit made movies and I made music. Bellwether was a successful production company because Tommy Sinclair had made it so, and I was brushing aside his efforts because I was scared of wearing a little less makeup.

"Mrs. Tyler will be in my office at eleven O'clock this morning. Can you be here?"

A shiver ran up my spine and I heard myself bleat, "Today? Now?" It was the oddest feeling.

"Oh, Jeez, Bud. Yes. Today. Just sit there and let her size you up. She also has a say in the casting. I thought she might like that, so I offered it to her. You don't have to say a word if you don't want to."

Again that shiver went up my spine. I was getting unnerved by something, like somebody was stepping on my grave, as my Grandmother used to say. I made one last attempt to squirm free. "Tommy, listen to me, I'm not the noble Mark Kincaid, who, having lost two wives, goes bravely on. I am not a leading man. I'm the villain. The loner. I only love my horse."

"She loves horses," Tommy said, and I could hear his smile. "Her name is Philippa, Latin, feminine of Philip, a lover of horses. Give her a chance, please, Bud. I promise, you'll like her."

"Oh, all right, I'll see you at eleven," I groused, and hung up the phone. I dabbed at the sweat trickling into my eyebrows, and realized it was still running down my back, cold, by now, and clammy. So much for premonition. It made me laugh.

Interesting, I thought, heading for the shower, that Kincaid was tall and dark and so was I. So were half the men in Hollywood, for that matter. Nevertheless, he fitted my description to the last detail - a bit to the flattering side, to say the least - and I had an inkling it was no coincidence. I looked at myself in the mirror and it was obvious; physically, I was Mark Kincaid. He'd been created for me, and I was impressed. He was deep, and kind, but three dimensional. Sexy. A little vulnerable and suspicious. A tad controlling. A great character. Extremely well written.

I was impressed and I was flattered, but I was also apprehensive. Maybe, self-conscious joking aside, she was dangerous. Maybe Mark resembled me because P.K. Tyler was a stalker. Maybe she'd get me alone and knife me or put Ipecac in my coffee. People get weirder and weirder as the century winds down. That's a fact. Even if she wasn't nuts, she was on top of the best seller list with a first novel. Pretty heady stuff for an ego to deal with. A woman's ego could be especially difficult, and God knows, I'd had my fill of difficult women.

I wondered about the character of Jean Whiteside in the book – the lover of horses. Did she reflect her creator? It seemed to me at the time that most women writers did one of two things, they wrote about women just like themselves, or women who were totally opposite. What, I wondered, would P.K. Tyler be like? Maybe she'd be Jean Whiteside, small, broad shouldered, full breasted with big green eyes and tons of dark auburn curls. Just about forty. Just about perfect.

I laughed, dried myself off, lit a cigarette, and realized I was getting caught up in the story. I decided I'd better sit down and really evaluate things before Thomas Ogden Sinclair got hold of me, so I got dressed and headed for my usual thinking spot. On a whim, I parked one hip on the freshly polished banister and slid down into the living room. I was blissfully unaware of it at the time, but that long, curving slide kind of set the tone for the day.

I sat at my beloved Steinway, wiggled my fingers to warm them up, and began to play. I could feel the tension slip out of my shoulders, and my mind began retracing P.K. Tyler's best seller, Petroglyphs in Sunlight. Even the name was evocative.

Mark Kincaid, documentary film maker, whose mission in life is to make historical documentaries more interesting, accessible, truthful, and powerful. So far, so good. I could relate. I loved documentaries - had since I was a kid. Had some half-baked plans of my own to make documentaries someday. Mark Kincaid, widower times two, his first wife lost in a filming accident in which he nearly loses his own life, and his second wife, lost to cancer. Excellent preface to a man with serious baggage. Did I have experience to transfer to this aspect of the character?

I'd lost my wife in the not too distant past to a much younger man. Very painful. Of course when my ego stopped smarting, I'd been vastly relieved to have her gone. Probably didn't qualify, but there were emotions sharply remembered that I could transfer and use. The merest thought of Esther brought her back to life. I could hear her laugh, smell her hair, feel her beside me on the piano bench, her head on my shoulder as I played for her. My beautiful sister. After all these years her death still brought tears to my eyes. I could do grief.

Jean Whiteside – fiery tempered, fiery haired – half Irish, half Cherokee, recently widowed high school history teacher who writes to Mark with an idea for a documentary. Bonny Jean of the gentle voice. God, did women like her really exist? I doubted it.

Mark, likes Jean's ideas, she likes his vision, they like each other's style. He invites her to help him with a documentary on the role Jim Bridger played in events leading up to the death of George Armstrong Custer, and they discover a mutual love of horses. That's the start of it all.

I could relate to that, too, I thought, modulating from a polka to one of Rachmaninoff's Symphonic Dances. I loved horses. P. K. Tyler must love horses, too. As she wrote of them, color and passion and eye popping imagery sprang off the page. I was beginning to relax a little mentally. Maybe I could do this, after all. Riding, I was good at. "I can do this," I said aloud.

But it wasn't all about riding and knowing how to operate a movie camera. The book was about relationships. About how, in developing a documentary concerning the third world conditions existing on various Indian reservations, and how that mindset is perpetuated, Mark and Jean explore their own prejudices and fears about being alone in a world that seems to have forgotten them, too.

A complex novel, but one that flowed as powerfully as the river beside which Jean and Mark finally fell in love. They did ... fall in love. I sighed. Of course they fell in love. It was part of the reassessment, reconciliation piece happy ending that Fay Weldon says gets the best and most lasting response from readers - a reconciliation of the self. In this case, a giving of the self, one last, precious time. I'd done some writing. I knew how it was supposed to go. I had to admit it, P.K. Tyler was a master wordsmith; far better than I ever thought of being. I could learn things from this woman.

I pounded my Steinway for a couple minutes, focusing on what I was playing, thinking only of the rhythm, the movement, the dynamics, the complexity that was Sergei Rachmaninoff. I was playing the last piece he ever wrote. What was I thinking? I wanted the part of Rachmaninoff more than I'd ever wanted anything in my life! I shouldn't let this miniseries thing even cross my mind. That was it. I was calling Tommy.

But my legs didn't move. The images in that book continued to play themselves in my unwilling mind. I wished Glory was home. She could help me sort this thing out. She knew me better than I knew myself. I got up without really realizing it, wandered over to my recliner, and picked up P.K. Tyler's novel. Just one more look, I promised. One more look.

At eleven O'clock I was where I said I'd be, but P.K. Tyler was not, nor was she at eleven-fifteen. At eleven-twenty, just as I was telling Tommy to forget the whole thing, Philippa Kate Tyler came breathlessly into my life.

"I am so sorry!" she exclaimed, and despite her flushed cheeks and slightly windblown appearance, her voice was dark and soft and slow. "I really and truly thought I knew where I was going."

She took Tommy's hand as he hurried to meet her, but I was just standing there, staring at Jean Whiteside. She was dressed like a college kid, in a powder blue sweater and plaid skirt, tiny penny loafers on her feet. The billows of hair were mostly captured in a long French braid that was doubled back on itself at the nape of her neck, and it was a soft golden brown, not auburn, and her eyes were a stunning deep blue with black rings around the irises, not green. Other than that, she hadn't changed a thing. If this was Tommy's definition of 'not gorgeous', he had all his taste in his mouth.

"Philippa Kate Tyler, Peter Aloysha Aarons," Tommy said, and I took her hand. "Hide your fingernails," Tommy warned, and she laughed, flashing a set of big white teeth my direction.

"Not much to hide. Why?"

"I have a fear of women with long fingernails", I smiled. "Yours, I see, are of an acceptable length. And most everybody calls me Bud."

She studied her hands, then grinned up at me with a twist of her lips and said, "These are my city fingernails, so they're longer than usual. They're also considerably cleaner than usual." She winked, and I knew she was teasing. "I have no idea how women accomplish anything with long nails."

I smiled handily over her head at Tommy and said, "You see? There is someone else in the world who feels like I do. Philippa, please sit down and catch your breath. Where have you been, or do you know?"

She was built on a sturdy, square shouldered frame that made her seem taller than she was; a fact which became apparent as she landed appreciatively in the chair I'd indicated. "Huh," she said, and found herself sinking. She grabbed the arms to keep herself from being swallowed, and shifted closer to the edge so her feet would touch the floor. "I haven't the vaguest notion where I was. I got chased into the left lane by a diesel rig and some lady in a pink Cadillac, and I saw my off ramp go by and it was all wilderness from there." She made an off-into-space gesture and a whimsical, goofy face to go with it, and I liked her instantly.

"I assume from the size of your eyes, and the rate of your pulse when I took your hand, that you don't live in the city," I said, still chuckling under my breath.

She blushed a little, and looked down, and shook her head. "No, not in the city, nor the state, and I'm not sure I recognize the planet, either."

"These people are in a hurry," I said, sensing her genuine fright and vulnerability. "This can be a pretty scary place until you get used to it. Can I fix you a drink? I know it's early."

"No, thanks," she said, and her smile was as honest and open, as any I'd ever seen. I realized I was rapidly becoming infatuated with this woman who had written such a lush and beautiful book, and who just might be gentle Jean Whiteside. Just hearing that voice – Jean's voice – was like sticking my fingers in a light socket, and I was totally unprepared for the sensation. It was almost as if her voice could set my skin tingling. I didn't know whether to enjoy it, or run like hell.

"I don't drink, and I'm glad I don't," she said, her voice rolling quietly into my thoughts, "If I did, I'd be drinking a lot right now."

"The price of success," I managed, and mentally gave myself a good shake. "Coffee?"

She nodded and said, "Thank you. A touch of sweetener, if you have it." She squirmed a little to adjust herself in the chair and went on. "The price of success seems to be homesickness, and restaurant food, and sleeping alone in motel beds. But hey," she laughed, gesturing outward with slender, work-worn hands that looked much older than she did, "I am, very literally, just an Okie from Muskogee. I admit it. I might as well," she shrugged, chuckling again, "The first time I open my mouth everybody knows anyway. I write for therapy, and because where I live it's too hot in the summer and too cold in the winter to do anything else. The idea that I'd actually sell a book never occurred to me. This success thing is totally unexpected, and I'm not in the least prepared to cope with it." She took the coffee, thanked me, and buried her nose in it so she didn't have to meet my gaze. "Sorry," she murmured. "I'm not used to talking so much."

She was wrong, at least about the accent. Her voice was creamy, but there was no immediately discernible inflection. It sounded superbly trained to me. To my unexplainable disappointment, there was an indentation on the third finger of her left hand. I tapped it and said, "No wedding ring, I see. All this big city touring and all these handsome men going to your head?"

"For Godssake, Bud," Tommy grimaced. "Please, P.K., don't mind him."

I watched her very closely as she waved Tommy's apology aside. "I agree with him. I think anyone who's married should wear a ring. Saves confusion and embarrassment." She looked at me, and she didn't smile. "I do have a ring that I wear when I'm not gardening or working with the horses, but the filthy air down here ... and there's salt in everything, even the water. Anyway, my hands swelled up so badly I had to soap my ring off and leave it off." Her tone changed and her eyes grew cool and challenging. "I assure you, the absence of a ring in no way reflects my feelings for Frank. I've been successfully married for nearly fourteen years. Not that I ever get to see the man, or talk to him for that matter. But I am married, and I intend to stay that way."

"Good for you," I smiled, feeling like an idiot. There was a sore spot in her life, and I'd hit it square on. Tommy was right. I needed to keep my mouth shut. Her expressive eyes registered hurt, and the set of her square jaw was intimidating, and suddenly, I didn't want to lose points with this lady, married or not. "Look, I know you've had a tough morning.

I didn't mean to add to it by saying something thoughtless. I'm sorry if I offended you."

"It's always best to know where things stand right off," she said in her deep, quiet voice, and her eyes softened again. "You were very kind to come here, and it's an honor to meet you. I'm one of your biggest fans."

"I'm flattered," I smiled, then looked at her straight on. "We're lucky to have made connections. This is a big town."

Philippa met my gaze for a few moments, the blue swirls in her eyes seeming almost kaleidoscopic, then she dropped them shyly away. "It gets smaller when you know exactly who you're looking for," she murmured, examining her coffee, "I did."

"So, Tommy didn't find you. You found Tommy, and he's the pipeline to me. Amazing. Why me?"

"I based Mark Kincaid on you," she smiled. She looked at me, realized she may well have said something inappropriate, and blushed deeply.

"I didn't realize women did that anymore," I smiled. Her eyebrows asked the question. "Blush. It's nice. Go on with what you were saying, Philippa." Her name was soft, like she was, and rolled gracefully off the tongue. If she was a stalker, I was game.

"Well, you are what I consider ... the ideal man ... at least to write about. You're easy to visualize. You're handsome, but not pretty. You come across as having more character than ... I dunno, charisma, I guess. I don't mean that unkindly."

"Not taken so. Go on."

"You have great eyebrows, Bud. Take it from someone who has none. You have great eyebrows. Black eyes, high cheekbones. Exceptionally nice Greco-Roman nose. That Russian bass of yours is rich as honey, nice teeth. Wonderful dimples when you smile." She laughed, very much the confident writer. "So much for the physical, which is cheap in your line of business, I guess. I like the way you present yourself on film. I mean, heck," she shrugged, "if you're going to spend a long, cold winter locked in your study with somebody, he might as well be ..." she searched for a word that was descriptive but impersonal, "agreeable. I mean, someone who is easy to visualize as you write ... whose actions are crisp and impressive enough in the mind to translate easily to paper ....” Her voice trailed off. She realized, as Tommy and I did, that she was beginning to flounder - trying to keep from revealing things that were intensely personal.

I was both flattered and intrigued. You could fry eggs on the love scenes she wrote, and I’d been there. Amazing. I was a talented pianist and a competent character actor. My Shakespeare got good reviews. But a sex object? It made me want to giggle nervously and preen. A couple of totally inappropriate images drifted unbidden into my mind, and I enjoyed them briefly before forcing them to move on.

She was gazing out Tommy’s fifth story window into the wintery Southern California sunshine, and I could see her tongue moving under her upper lip, scrubbing away at one of her canine teeth. She exhaled sharply, and with a movement that was obviously forced, she looked back at me. “Mr. Aarons, I’m sorry. It was a whim. I hope you can forgive me for stealing your body and doing intimate things to you without your permission. I swear to you, nobody else knows who Mark Kinkead is based on. I didn’t ... tell a soul.” She sighed and looked both sad and annoyed. Amazingly expressive face on this woman. “I’d take it back, but it’s a little late for that. I will try to make it right, though, I promise. Please give me the chance.”

She was squirming like a little kid in that chair, and I was delighted. Genuinely delighted. I could feel that my face was a little flushed. Luckily I had enough of a tan left to hide it. “You are going to have to make it up to me,” I grinned, “but I will do the film for you.” There was a whoosh out of Tommy, “Providing, as Tommy assures me, we write it together, and I have final say on my character.”

“I wouldn’t have it any other way,” she smiled, and the gush of her voice said she was vastly relieved. “I’m counting very heavily on your expertise. I did some writing for theater in college, but that’s been a few days ago.”

“So,” Tommy smiled, “We have an agreement?”

“Not quite,” I said. I finished my coffee and set the cup on the conference table, then leaned back, lit a cigarette, and contemplated them both.

What came out of my mouth next, I swear to Almighty God, fell unbidden from the wild blue yonder and sealed my fate. "I want to cast the part of Jean Whiteside."

There was silence. Tommy stared at me. I winked, and from the sudden slackness of his jaw I knew he realized what I was driving at. His eyes rolled back in his head, then turned with mine to look pointedly at Philippa.

"I don't know," she said finally, innocent of it all, "There are some things I'd like to see in Jean, that ... well, would be hard for a stranger to come up with."

"Like what?" I asked, baiting her just a tad.

She squirmed. She was fighting a losing battle with that chair, and, she also sensed, with me. I could see her beginning to wilt. Not a lot of stamina. I remembered her comments about the air, the food and the sleeping arrangements. And the absent husband. No support system, nothing comforting around her. I wanted to scoop her up and take her home to Glory's tender ministrations.

She straightened her chin with an exaggerated motion and said, "That's difficult to explain. She's going to be very hard to cast."

It's hard to let go of yourself, I know, I thought, but what I replied was, "I don't think so. I think she'll be a snap to cast, and since I have to make love to her, and I've never, ever done that in a film, or a miniseries, or whatever this is going to turn out to be, either I cast her so I'm comfortable with her, or I walk."

"Damn your hide, Peter Aarons!" Tommy shouted, pushing his chair away from the green, granite topped table, "This is just not like you. You already agreed to take the part. And put out that damned cigarette. I hate it when you smoke! Everybody hates it when you smoke!"

"I agreed on my terms," I said placidly. I stubbed out the cigarette, folded my hands across my chest and stretched my legs under the table - assuming my siege stance.

We spent a pregnant few minutes saying nothing - locked in one another's gaze - mentally circling in a game Tommy and I had played since high school, and more often than not, with good humor. Philippa was the newcomer to the arena, but the way her eyes moved unhurriedly from face to face, it was obvious she could play, and play well.

Tommy's eyes were green and readably annoyed, which had always been his weakness - that, and the way he set his mouth. He'd lost at chess that way, and poker, and a time or two at bridge, which annoyed hell out of Emily, his wife. Philippa's eyes were very blue and interested. Disturbingly and distractingly blue. Mine are so dark you can't see the pupils, which makes them a tad more inscrutable, but the woman's presence was rattling me. How could I work with somebody who had this effect on me? What was I thinking? Of course now it was out of my mouth, and I was committed. If I back-pedaled, Tommy would know it in a hot second. Plus, of course … deep down inside, in a place I didn't even know existed … I didn't want to backpedal.

"Tell you what," Philippa sighed after a bit, "It sounds like you have someone very special in mind, and you don't strike me as one to handicap yourself. Throw out a name, and please, please don't make it any twenty-five-year-old blonde Hollywood bimbo, and let's see what happens."

I took a deep breath. "You," I said.

There was a slight, slow cocking of the head to one side, nothing more. After a moment's pause she looked straight back at me and sighed, "That's not funny. You don't want to do this thing, you want to punish me. I said I was sorry and that is all I can do, Mr. Aarons."

"I'm serious," I said quietly. "I want you to play Jean to my Mark."

"And you don't think I'd be a handicap? Me, who has not a lick of training? Are you thinking at all?" she asked, and she still looked disbelieving. She still thought I was teasing, being mean.

Tommy's mouth came open and I gave him a gentle kick under the table. He shut it again, shaking his head slowly from side to side as though he were watching a very bad comedy. "Are you telling me I'm not discerning enough?" I smiled. "Who knows more about Jean Whiteside than you do? Who looks more like her?"

"Jean Whiteside is a much glamorized Philippa Kate Tyler, I assure you. Jean's supposed to be a very pretty woman." The tone was genuine. Either she had a poor self-image, or she was already a good actress. "I only gave her some of my physical characteristics, and my likes and dislikes because it's easier to work with at least one character you know. It gives you someone to play off of, like a sounding board. Besides, why should I stay home and let some other woman go off adventuring with the man of my ..." She stopped abruptly, glanced at me, and her naive face turned so red her eyes looked almost colorless. I thought for a moment she was going to burst into tears, but she gulped and found her voice, and went on. "That's not exactly what I meant. What I meant was ..."

"Yes? Go on," I teased, "keep digging that hole."

"Aw ... geez Louise," she muttered, and I burst out laughing. Her whole presence tickled me. She flared her slim fingers out and shook them just a bit, and then took a deep breath and went on. "I say the dumbest things when I'm nervous. Please, Mr. Aarons ..."

"Bud, or Peter," I corrected gently.

"Peter, I haven't done any acting of any kind in years. This is getting way out of hand ...." She set her mouth and shook her head slightly.

Tommy nodded emphatically and glared at me some more.

"Your dust jacket says you did a lot of acting and directing during your university days."

"That was years ago, and it was legitimate theater, not television or movies! I'm not trained for that. On top of which … I'm afraid I'd lose my perspective among other things."

"Like what?"

"You … were a lot easier to manage as a fantasy," she sighed, and there was just a hint of a smile. "Please, I haven't known you an hour and I already feel like I'm strapped to a rocket. When I walked in here, I was in charge of my existence, pretty much. All of a sudden, being around you, I feel like I'm losing it. I'm not what I look like I am. This is an act. I'm not confident, I'm not sophisticated, and I'm most certainly not Jean Whiteside."

"Part of you must be," I smiled, "or you wouldn't be here. And as for Jean, she sprang from your mind, like Athena from the head of Zeus.

She's in there. She was just a sweet, small town school teacher who married a film maker. What's so different?"

"For one thing he didn't try to make an actress out of her the first time they met," Philippa snorted. Good for her! She was feisty. "All of this, every bit of this, is very new to me. I just am not in a position to make a decision like that. This project means too much to me. I won't grab at some glamorous tidbit and ruin everything, much as I'd love to do it." She looked startled by her own admission, then nodded slightly and a smile tugged at her lips, "I'd love to think I could. Right now, I'm still avoiding the talk shows because I'm afraid I'll forget my name, or throw up, or do something generally disgusting. Peter, I'm a farmer, not an actress. I ride horses, I make quilts, I write. Please ..."

"I know all about you," I smiled, "because I took another look at Jean Whiteside this morning. Jean, is short on self-confidence, and Philippa Tyler is, too. We're only a week into January, and I, personally think launching your show biz career would make a great new year's resolution, don't you? In any case, whether you want to be or not, kiddo, you're in this with us, and I'm not letting you go."

There was an awkward silence in the room then that I can't quite describe - almost as if I were the one who had admitted something intensely personal. I looked at Philippa and realized she was trembling, and that this wasn't someone just looking for more encouragement to do what she'd already decided she wanted to do. This was someone who was trying to be honest about not being secure - someone sleeping in a strange bed in a strange place, among strangers.

I pushed my chair back and went quickly around the table to crouch at eye level beside her. "I'm sorry if I've bowled you over," I whispered, and when my hand touched hers, it covered it completely. Admittedly I have huge hands, but she was the size of a child, and all of a sudden I felt like I'd been abusing her. "I don't have a clue how to deal with people who aren't playing games with me. Hollywood is like a rigged auction where everybody goes loudly through the motions, but the outcome is pretty much decided in advance. Mrs. Tyler, you have honored me with your talent. I will try to honor you with mine. We have a screen play to write together, and arrangements to make that will take many, many weeks. Hopefully, in that length of time you will grow comfortable with playing Jean. I will ask only that we write the part with you in mind, but I won't make you play it if you don't want to, agreed?"

She looked up at me from where our hands were still touching on the table, and as she slowly pulled her hand from under mine, she gave me a motherly little pat and said, "I agree. However, anything I do, I have to ask Frank first, and he can be a hard man to find."

I thought about that. I put my reading glasses on top of my head, Philippa's book in my lap, and tilted back in my recliner to rest my eyes. Frank, like the Robert in the book, was a trucker, only Frank was alive. In the novel, he, or someone like him, was dead when the story started.

I'd spent the afternoon with Philippa, and she'd seemed excited about things. Uneasy, but excited. I knew she wanted to talk to Frank, just to hear his voice, just to reassure herself that she was still on track with him, and I thought it was a nice thing to do. She really hadn't talked much about where she was from these days, except to tell me that she lived in Washington. The state – like Jean Whiteside – and I could sense an almost perpetual tightness around her mouth that could have become tears of homesickness and loneliness had we dwelled on the subject. As it was, we had spoken of the novel and its characters, and had begun, without saying so, to extricate ourselves from each other's fantasies, which was not going to be easy, at least for me.

During a break I'd shown her around the studio, and she'd been as bright eyed and curious as a child. My best friend and our third partner, Kit Miller had come over to Tommy's office, and with the rest of the production board we'd begun hammering out details and signing papers. The fourth major partner was my dad, who had kindly bought in twenty-three years ago when we were a trio of struggling kids, but he never made decisions for us, or with us, and he never dabbled in the mundane. I carried his proxy in perpetuity, and as we sat around laughing and joking and eating pizza, I was just as glad he wasn't there to see the casual manner in which we did business.

He wouldn't have approved in the least.

The novel and the choice to make it into a six hour mini-series – that, would have gotten one of his slow, sage nods. He might even have liked this small, spirited woman who sat, slowly rubbing one hand against the other, watching the proceedings and smiling introspectively. She had refused both lunch and dinner and eyed the pizza as though it were alive and snarling, which was a portent of things to come. She'd asked for one thing only – a diet peach Snapple, which she sipped while we ate. She was quiet, and polite, and unswerving. She understood give and take, she was willing to learn, and she knew where she stood with the integrity of her novel.

A couple hours after dark we were largely finished, and largely satisfied, and Philippa was considerably wealthier than when she'd breezed through Tommy's door that morning. She had smiled her thanks, excused herself from the conference table and left us to further talks.

The rest of the evening, to my discomfort, included a rather intimate discussion concerning the size, shape and overall quality of P.K. Tyler, with Tommy insisting that she was not a pretty woman and that I had made a critical mistake right off the bat. And then Kit Miller, my Kit, who always plays such a nice guy on the screen, had sighed, and licked his lips and summed it up. "Great tits. I'd love to take her to bed." At that point, I got up and left.

An hour after she'd gone I'd called her, just to be sure she'd found her way back to Howard Johnson's, and that no more ladies in pink Cadillacs had chased her into parts unknown. She had a wonderful, slightly crazy laugh, and a very gracious way of saying thank you for the kind thought. A different woman, from a different planet. A rather frightened, admirable, firm-minded stranger, unspoiled by accolades, unimpressed by glamour, unnerved by the roar and the dirt and the indifference of the city.

When I hung up with her I dialed my florist and asked him to send a bouquet over to Philippa. Something that looked like it should be growing in an alpine meadow in Washington. The state.

CHAPTER TWO

Philippa was at the studio offices on time the next morning. She was dressed in a very nicely tailored grey suit and high heels that made her legs look long despite her height of, maybe five foot three. She had her hair pulled severely up into a Gibson, and she looked every inch the competent businesswoman. But her eyes were bloodshot, and we weren't far into the day before she was sitting with her chin propped in one hand, looking dazed and bemused.

"P.K.," I said, "If you're going to take an active part in this, which of course you have to, you can figure on being here in Los Angeles for several months ..." Her chin didn't move from her palm, but suddenly two big tears rolled out of her blue eyes and over her high cheekbones.

It startled her as much as it did me. "Geez, how stupid!" she said with an angry sniff.

"Aw, I'm sorry," I said, coming around the desk. I put my hands on her shoulders and she flinched. "Forgive me," I said, and stepped back. "I didn't mean to invade your space, and I didn't mean to make you cry before lunch. I try to save that for the afternoons. Is it just me who has this effect on you? Would you like me to get Tommy in here so we're not alone?"

"It's not you," she said from behind her hands, "Tommy prepared me for you." She tried for a grin and I admired her for being able to tease, even through her tears. "And you didn't invade my space. I just … haven't been touched for a while." She glanced up like she'd given me too much information, and quickly glanced away. "Too much day yesterday, I guess.

I went back to my hotel and just about had a seizure when I realized what I'd gotten myself into. Peter, I don't have any dirt to dig in. I can't go for months with no dirt to dig in." She fished a tissue out of her purse, tongue busily scrubbing one canine in an attempt to get a grip on herself. "I'm really sorry. I don't want you to think I'm like this as a general rule, because I'm not. I'm just being a baby. Right now I just want to go home to my comfortable house and my horses and my snow. Today is my wedding anniversary, and I haven't talked to Frank in nearly a month." There was no pause. "You know why your nose runs when you cry? All those ducts are connected together, and those are tears running out your nose. My vet put bright green drops in my horse's eyes once, and in a few minutes, they came running out her nostrils. Isn't that neat? Aren't you glad I shared?"

By then we were both laughing. "Truly enlightening," I said, and carefully put my hands back on her shoulders. They were in knots. "Now, don't cry. I'm going to say, months, again. There'll be trips home, of course, and location filming up there, but you need a place to call your own down here. You need to have some familiar things around you, and a comfortable bed of your own choosing, and a kitchen where you can cook anything you want. Agreed?"

She shrugged against my hands. "I could stay with Frank's sister and her husband, but I can't stand their kids."

"No, Philippa, hear me. You're going to be up to your armpits in acting lessons and screenwriting. You need a place of your own, where you can work at any hour you choose, with anyone you choose, and sleep whenever you need to. You need just a little, easy to care for place ..."

"With my own Jane Fonda workout tape, and my own exercise bike? I can't remember the last time I got any exercise except walking, and then my lungs burn. How do people survive here?" She looked up at me with six-year-old eyes as big as saucers, and I realized the grey business suit was a prop.

Matter of fact, I loved this city that had been my home from earliest memory. I wondered whether I should try to bring her around to my way of thinking, or pretend to hate the place. Best be honest. Best of all, wait until she wasn't so tired.

"Poor kid," I said, "You are a long, long way from Washington, aren't you? Well, you're now on the payroll of a production company in which I am a major shareholder. That means I have money tied up in you. Let me help you find an apartment. Bellwether will pay for it."

"Bellwether will not pay for it," She said. "Besides which, I actually looked in the paper last night, being excited about living here for a bit. There isn't an apartment for a hundred miles."

"You, are a celebrity. That opens doors."

"Don't say that," she said with an exaggerated groan, and dropped her forehead with a comic thud onto the desk. "I've got to do that talk show Tommy scheduled me for, and I'm petrified. I'm utterly, ungracefully, unintellectually, petrified sick, Bud. What the hell am I doing here? I want to go home!"

"Okay, let's go find you one," I laughed.

"What about our work here?"

"Actually we're not scheduled to start for a bit yet. I just wanted to meet you here instead of at your motel." I didn't bother to tell her why. It would just upset her. "You need some fresh air, Kiddo, and a little more pastoral setting than this affords. Let's take my car, and go up to my house, and make some coffee, and then make some phone calls." She looked dubious. "My housekeeper will be home so it wouldn't be just us out there." She was still considering. "I have dirt." I made digging motions with my fingers, and she laughed.

She put her hand over mine where it came to rest on her shoulder and said, "Thank you. Just for turning out to be who you are." There was a pause and a chuckle. "Whom you are."

"I'm not Mark Kincaid," I said wistfully, and my tone of voice surprised me. "I kind of wish I was, but I'm not."

"Well, I'm not Jean Whiteside, either," Philippa grinned, looking up at me, "but I'd like to go back to the motel and change into some of her clothes, if that's okay?"

"You're going to do away with the power suit?"

"It's my bitch suit," she intoned solemnly. "When I came yesterday I wore a skirt and sweater because Tommy said you didn't relate well to women in suits. But you tormented me yesterday. So, today, I wore my bitch suit so I could torment you back. I haven't been able to do that with any kind of success, but it was a thought."

"Tommy says I don't relate well to women in suits? Well, I never! What else did Tommy tell you about me?"

"I'll tell you when you're older," she said with an impish, nose wrinkling grin. "And you're still tormenting me. Maybe I should try something I'm really comfortable in, like jeans and cowboy boots."

"Done," I smiled. "We'll take your car back and leave it at the motel."

It definitely was not a car. It was a monster of a Ford pickup. Baby blue and white, one ton crew cab, visor, fairing, chrome running boards, lift kit, fender flares, and six tires, four in back, two in front, all with metal studs. Phil saw the look on my face and grinned at me. "I don't suppose you'd like to drive her, would you?" she teased. "You get some very interesting looks, especially with the sound the studs make."

"Tell you what," I smiled, "you bring the Benz, and I'll take the Ford."

"Are you serious?"

"Sure, aren't you?"

She laughed, shook her bright head in disbelief, and vaulted up into the cab. "See you at the motel," she called over the roar of the big diesel engine, and with Chris Ledoux audible through the partially opened window, she eased out of the parking lot. Now the suit and high heels were really funny, and I laughed aloud.

I followed her, and those tires made me nervous. Her Washington plates entitled her to have them, but they were dangerous down here on these bare, greasy highways. I could see by the way she drove, that she knew it, too. I hated to butt in, I really did, but I knew I was going to, first chance I got.

Truth was, I'd lost a very young – admittedly too young – ex-girlfriend to the traffic not all that long ago. I'd been three cars back when she went through the windshield onto the pavement, and to my grave I'll carry the image of what was left of her.

When we reached the place where Philippa was staying I pulled into a spot beside her and rolled down my window. "I'll wait here for you," I smiled. "If you have a swimsuit bring it. I have a spa, and the pool's heated."

"Winter in California," she laughed. "No, I didn't bring a swimsuit. I don't think I even own a swimsuit anymore." She turned back on the third step and said, "You're welcome to come up, Bud."

I decided to be honest. "I hate to tell you this, but every rag in this town would have us in bed together in two seconds flat if they caught us," I said.

"That'd be great to see in a truck stop," she muttered, thanked me, and went inside.

She loved the drive up into the Santa Monica Mountains, and her face radiated relief as we left the traffic behind. When we got to the end of Sweet Sage Trail and through the wrought iron gates, she was instantly out of the car and into my grandmother's wonderful, wild gardens with her face to the sun, touching the plants and smelling the fragrances. "This is beautiful," she sighed. "Very different than what I'd expected, and thank you again for the flowers. They really make a difference in that hotel room."

"You're most welcome," I smiled, watching the sky in her irises as she looked up at me. "What were you expecting?"

"Oh, I don't know exactly," she shrugged, and I nudged her.

"Yes you do. Speak out, Woman."

"Lots of redwood and weird angles on a steep hill with a concrete lot," she said very quickly, and then laughed. "In a phrase, new money. I don't mean that to be insulting to anyone…exactly. I suppose those homes are lovely inside if you like the thought of hanging off a cliff. But an old adobe on a mountaintop?" She spread her arms to encompass her surroundings, and her eyes twinkled with good humor. "This, is not long fingernails and mink coats. This, is a superbly tanned leather jacket and a Mercedes Benz, and a little grey at the temples. This, feels like home." She blushed and pulled back in on herself. “Please, pardon me for teasing you. I’m delirious. This is the first time I’ve smelled trees in forever.”

“You’re welcome to tease,” I smiled, “and you’re astute. This is old money. Pre talkies and Vaudeville, and back further than that to the pioneering days of LA, though the house doesn’t go back quite that far. My grandfather had it built as a wedding gift for my grandmother. Her getaway spot, away from Bel Air and her new in-laws and the rules that went with being under their roof. My grandfather called it her country villa, but she always called it, ‘My bird house’. She belonged to the Sierra Club, and to the Audubon Society, and my earliest memories of this place are of the wings, and the songs. I’ve tried to maintain the tradition, and Rafael, whom you met as we pulled in, is the world’s best gardener. He was devoted to my gram and her projects, and he’s one of my dearest friends. Gram had tons of huge parties here, as you’ll be able to tell by the size of the rooms downstairs. Would you like to see the inside?”

“I’d like to dig in the humus under those oak trees,” she replied, but she took the hand I extended, and let me lead her up to the front door.

“Come on in,” I smiled, and bowed her through.

She enjoyed the house, and I enjoyed showing it to her. She knew architecture and building technique, and carried on an intelligent conversation as we walked. She loved the big arched windows and the old wood, smoothed by the oil from many hands. She laughed with me at the size of the rooms, which were cavernous, but noted that it would be a wonderful place to dance. Indeed it was, I nodded. I had danced here many times. “I have lived in this house for nearly fifty years,” I said. “Since the day we came to this country. I love every nook and cranny of this mess.”

“You do … have a formality of speech which is, or almost is, an accent.”

“Much like yours,” I teased.

She blushed a little. “Where did you come from?”

I was born south and east of Saint Petersburg, Russia,” I said as we walked. “My mother and I … escaped … during the closing days of the Second World War, and came here to join my father, and my father’s mother.

This is the only home I can remember having."

"It's a wonderful space," Philippa said. "I feel like I'm in an old California mission, or some elegant hacienda, redolent with history. I love it."

Why was I breathing a sigh of relief? I tried not to look puzzled and gestured toward the east corner of the house. "Come on, let's go get some coffee. When my ex insisted on that godawful remodel in the back part of the house, Glory and I decided to re-do the kitchen, as well, and it's a great space, very soothing."

"Thanks," she smiled. "I could use some coffee about now."

I realized I'd been talking more than usual, and apologized as we walked. "I don't even know what set me off. You, I guess," I said, looking at the cowboy boots and jeans and open throated pink shirt. "My grandmother would have liked you."

"I like her," Philippa smiled back, "I like her reflection."

She paused and pointed to a picture. "Who are these adorable little dudes?"

"Royal and Titus Ruiz. Glory and Rafael's boys. That was taken shortly after they moved in with us twenty-six years ago."

Philippa gave me a more studied look. "That must have been interesting."

"Oh, you bet," I muttered. I could still remember just how traumatic it has been. "I found Glory and Rafael, and I liked them a lot. Unfortunately," I said, letting my eyes widen, and lowering my voice, "they were, as my grandmother so delicately pointed out, 'not a matched set.' In the sixties, that was a big deal. Furthermore, they had an almost four-year-old, and an almost two-year-old, and the things I did, the stunts I had to pull, just to get my grandmother to interview them ... it was awful," I laughed, "but I won, and believe me, I spray painted it on a wall for posterity. I convinced Gram that Rafael and I could tear down Grandfather's old conservatory and make that space into a cottage, wrap a chain link fence around it, and she'd never know there were kids on the place."

"And did Gram know there were little boys on the estate?"

"Oh, yes," I grinned.

"How rotten were they when she got through with them?"

"Very," I laughed. "They were the joy of her old age. They did absolutely outrageous things together. People used to be horrified, which delighted my grandmother. Ultimately, she sent Royal, the older one, to MIT to be an Engineer, Titus to Harvard Law School. Wouldn't let Rafael or Glory pay a dime of it. It was her gift to them. God, she was a neat lady. I miss her every day."

"You lucky duck!" Philippa exclaimed, "You had your grandma a long time, didn't you?"

"Eighty-eight feisty, healthy years before she dropped dead." I shook my head and laughed again. "Those boys meant a great deal to her, which was good, because I found out I couldn't give her grandchildren."

I actually remember jumping a little at my own words. Why on earth had something that personal just come out of my mouth? I hardly knew this woman and here I was, spilling my guts. I took my time getting the coffee out of the cupboard, just to buy myself a breath. "That diagnosis pretty much ended my fairytale marriage to Meg." I looked down at Philippa and whispered, "Some fairytales are pretty damned scary."

Why had I brought this up, I wondered. To see how she'd react? To see how I'd react? My gram had died, and Megan had left me inside a single month. Not one of my favorite memories. Thank God my grandmother hadn't been around to hear those last, horrific fights. I cocked one eyebrow and waited to see what this seemingly gentle person would say about such things.

"Some people handle not having children very well," Philippa mused quietly. "Some of us, never quite get over it."

"You do have children though, don't you?" I asked, remembering she'd mentioned them on our way up the hill.

"Um hm, I do. I have two daughters by my first marriage. Frank and I, have no children. And Frank, God bless him, never quite forgave me for that, so I guess we have something in common."

"You tried to have children with him?"

"Of course."

"And he assumed it was you that had failed?"

"I'm the one that ended up having to have a hysterectomy. The evidence points in my direction," she said.

"Sure it does," I said, switching on the coffee maker and wiping the stray grounds off the counter, "and the doctors never check the man until everything else is said and done - sometimes they never check him at all. Megan and I had been married close to three years when we decided to start a family. We both had careers, and we were busy. She just quit taking the pill and we figured sooner or later she'd turn up pregnant. Well, she didn't."

I reached into the cupboard and took down two coffee mugs, got spoons, sweetener, and set them down in front of Philippa. "To make a long story short, she went through nearly two years of misery, being tested and retested, having her sex life pried into, until, as a last resort, they tested me. Guess what? I had no sperm count. Absolutely none. Upon closer examination, no vas deferens, either. Poor Meg. She went through all that for nothing. In jig time she was married to someone else - nine months later, maybe a little less - beautiful baby boy."

"You've practiced that story a lot, I can tell," Philippa grinned, "and I'll bet you still feel like crap."

I looked at her, and knew I could be completely, totally honest and not be condemned for it. "Yes, I do, and you know why? I didn't care. I didn't care whether we had kids or not. I didn't marry until late. We started trying to have a family when I was well into my forties, and by the time I found out I had parts missing, Meg and I were already having a lot of trouble. I had no desire for a very iffy major surgery. Too many nice kids in the world need a home, so I told Megan it was adoption or nothing, and she told me to go straight to hell."

"Nothing like knowing where you stand," Philippa chuckled. She moved pointedly away from my cigarette smoke, and started reading the paper, which I figured was a waste of time anyway. I was wondering who I could call who might know of a place.

"Address book," I muttered, and stood up. "And since I let myself run out of contacts, I do need my stronger glasses. You'll have to excuse me a minute, Madam. I think they're upstairs in my bedroom ... on your novel."

Philippa gave me a look that was almost, not quite, come hither, and went back to the classifieds. When I came downstairs, she was just opening the kitchen door for Glory.

"Grocery store's a damn zoo! Thank you, Child. Buddy, you smokin' in my kitchen again, I can smell it," she said, all as she was setting the groceries on the counter. She turned around, said, "Whoosh!" and smiled at Philippa.

"Philippa, you already met Rafael, and this is his wife, and one of my dearest friends, Gloriosa Daisy Ruiz. Mrs. Ruiz, P.K., short for Philippa Kate Tyler."

"The lady who wrote Petroglyphs in Sunlight!" Glory exclaimed. "I loved it. I cried!"

Phipps nodded, smiled, said thank you – something passed between them like a spiritual embrace – and they'd been friends forever. She was so comfortable here, and I was so comfortable with her. I watched her with Glory and wondered if she was that comfortable with me.

"Oh, will you look at this? Decent vegetables!" Philippa gasped, and she and Glory began unloading the bags and berating everybody from the grower who used too much chemical fertilizer, to the shipper who played politics, to the distributor who sat on the produce too long, to the grocer, to the bag boy.

"You're damned well going to like what I find for you to live in," I said pettishly. I half read, half listened.

Philippa was more at ease with Glory than with me, far more at ease with fresh produce than fresh people, probably including me again. Where, I wondered, did Jean Whiteside leave off and Philippa Kate Tyler begin? Phil's insistence that Jean was much glamorized, didn't hold water. I thought Philippa Tyler was a beautiful woman. More so as she really relaxed and laughed with Glory and the little lines smoothed out in her face.

She caught me studying her, and looked self-consciously away as she went back to the groceries. "I honestly will be with you in a minute,

Bud. It just feels so good to do something normal. I mean, something familiar, you know."

"You do what makes you comfortable," I said. "You'll feel better for a couple days' rest."

"Where do you live?" Glory asked, rummaging through another bag and tossing me a box of contact lenses.

Phil smiled, "Eastern Washington, just a bit up into the Cascade Mountains, overlooking a beautiful green valley."

"You homesick, Sweetheart?"

"Sure I am," Philippa said with a soft laugh. "I miss my house and my pets and my friends and my church."

"And her husband," I added, looking over my glasses and the paper.

"Neh, Frank's gone all the time," she grinned. "One learns to live without a man. But friends and pets and church, I miss."

"What church you go to, Honey?" Glory asked.

The question interested me, but when she said she was a nondenominational … charismatic … something or other, I got this immediate image of those smarmy bastards on television, huge churches, expensive clothes – waving their arms, pounding their pianos and thumping their Bibles, praising God at the top of their lungs, pretending to channel Jesus and telling folks to send them money because it was needed for "the work." It must have registered on my face because Glory snorted, "Don't mind him. He's a heathen. A born again heathen, that one."

"I am not a heathen," I sniffed, swallowing my disgust. "My grandmother was Jewish, more or less, but mostly she was a world citizen with a world view. My Mother was a Russian Jew, or so I gather from her stories of the old days. My father is Jewish in a nonchalant sort of way. So I'm sort of Jewish." I didn't add that I was pretty much put off by the whole idea of religion. I gave the paper a little snap and buried my nose therein.

"Not a man of faith?" Philippa asked, and when I looked up, she had turned from the smaller sink looking no less disappointed than I was. Good. It was over. I was free.

"Faith, yes. Maybe. Religion, definitely not," I said defensively.

"The things you people do to each other in the name of someone who's supposed to be the Prince of Peace, never cease to appall me."

"That's kind of sad," Phil shrugged. "You seem like such a spiritual old soul."

"Amen!" Glory laughed, and they went back to the produce.

I sat with my chin in my hand, looking at Phil and deciding I didn't like her. Actually, I was relieved ... and disappointed, but the last thing I needed in my life was a rigid, narrow minded religious nut. Another rigid, narrow minded nut. Glory was quite enough. I went back to the paper, and a few moments later Phil's hands squeezed my shoulders.

"My observation was uncalled for, forgive me," she said. "I can be kind of heavy handed when I'm in a new situation and I'm not sure what to say."

I recanted my dislike, and reached up and patted her hand. It was cold. She'd been happily washing celery under the tap. "You're forgiven. After all, I started it. I think. Anyway, this is one of those weird households where we tease about race and religion, and love each other dearly. We survived the sixties, and the seventies, and we flaunt it. You'll get used to us ... if you live long enough." It was time to work those tires into the conversation. "They're going to be burying you big blue Ford and all if you don't stop running those studded tires. I wish you'd get them off of there. Like, now." I thought I sounded pretty casual as I said it, pretty laid back, but Glory shot me a look that said otherwise.

Philippa gave her hands a little slap on the rim of the sink, then turned and took the hand towel Glory was holding out to her. "And what am I supposed to do with them?" she smiled stiffly, "put them in the safe at Howard Johnson's, or just leave them in the back of the pickup, here in your fair city?"

"Put them out there in the garage," I snapped, stabbing with a pencil, "you could put them under the bed in your apartment if you'd sit down here and apply yourself."

I heard her gasp with shock. She plopped down beside me, and she'd said "I'm sorry!" half a dozen times before I could get turned in the bar chair to look at her. There were tears in her eyes. I'd cut her to the quick.

"Dammit, don't turn out to be a bawl bag," I muttered. "I can't stand women who cry all the time." That chin came up, bless her, and it was tight, but it didn't tremble. Her eyes brimmed, but they didn't spill. "That's better," I said, crimping a grin. "Now, I'll apologize for being an ass. I'm used to hard, brassy, self-assured, big city women. I keep trying to relate to something that isn't there."

"Sorry I'm a disappointment," she snapped, looking past me into the dining room. "I told you yesterday, I'm a hick."

"And a damned stubborn one, I might add!" I retorted with an angry gesture. Glory pinned my left wrist to the counter, took my glasses out of my hand, set them aside and went back to work, all in one second's motion. "Did I say I was disappointed? No, I did not ..." there was a pause. "Philippa, what are you laughing at?"

"You. I think you're pretty neat."

"I'm pretty confused, that's for sure," I sighed, folding the paper. I got up and walked it to the recycling center just inside the pantry doors. "You know we haven't accomplished anything toward finding you a place?"

"Peter," she smiled, and it was a little too cheerful. "Maybe that's for the best. Maybe I should turn this over to you folks who know what you're doing, and just go home. I can watch the miniseries on TV next winter and see my name go by in the credits, and we'll all be better off. You're right. I'm not brassy enough. I'm not self-assured enough. Even a degree in Theater won't convince these people different. I'm in over my head. I'm scared. I want to go home. I'm sorry."

I just stood there by the door, leaning against the jamb, out of words, out of ideas. I was ready to let her go home, but Glory came around the breakfast bar, reached down, gathered Philippa up in her arms and guided her gently into one of the bar chairs. Brushing some of the stray wisps of Philippa's hair back into their braid with her fingertips, she spoke gently, as one does to a frightened child.

"Sweetheart," Glory said, "We do not want to lose you here. You just tired of being alone and missin' the man you love. Mister Aarons, there, is the finest, kindest man who ever drew breath, and he die before he steer you wrong. He told me last night, he said you had more beauty and brains and talent in your little finger than most of the women do who are runnin' this town. You come on along to choir practice with me tonight, and cackle with the hens a bit, and let him be your seein' eye dog, and you be okay. My Buddy won't let you fall."

I glanced at Phipps out of the corner of my left eye and gave her an embarrassed bit of a smile. "In case you wonder why I put up with her, that's why. People who truly care are very hard to find. But … you have worked very hard for what you've accomplished. You have earned the right to do what you think is best for you."

She reached out and hugged Glory, who backed off and let her out of the chair. "You are a lovely, lovely woman, you are, and I obviously don't have a clue what's best," she said finally. "I do know it's not fair of me to expect Frank, or you, or anybody else to make my decisions for me. I'm just going to have to jump in and grab for it, I guess. Yes. Yes. I would love to go to choir practice tonight, thank you for asking." She turned in my direction then, and realized I'd dropped the paper into the recycling bin. "Find anything at all?"

"Yes, I smiled, "I have made quite a find, I think," but I didn't try to tell her what it was.

She sat beside the pool late that evening, still flushed from choir practice, back lighted, as we would say in the theater, with her long mass of brown waves freed from their braid and glowing like dying embers, and her skin like roses and gold - and I truly desired her, as one does in a relationship of long standing, where the voice and the hands and the caring and what is said after are more important than the pressure under which one's semen is delivered.

And yet she was a stranger and I knew nothing, less than nothing, about her. She was lounging in a lawn chair, skin tight jeans, incredibly tiny metal toed cowboy boots propped up on a planter, looking for all the world like an eater of men. Then she spoke, and her voice was so gentle I cannot describe it, and her eyes were shy, and her thoughts were so clear and unaffected that I had not the vaguest idea what to think, or to feel, that would be in all aspects appropriate.

I tried to convey that to my father - that first word picture of Philippa on the patio - how she had looked and sounded and made me feel, and he responded by shaking his white mane of hair and telling me not to let a stiff dick do my thinking for me.

"I can't believe you just said that," I chuckled. I accepted half a glass of wine from a liveried servant, and tried again. "A stiff dick I could handle, so to speak," I said. "At least I could understand it. This is different. This is like standing in a tunnel looking one way into one world, and another way into a different world. This is a thing of the soul and the intellect and that's all it can be. She's married."

"A fact that makes you sad, from your tone of voice."

"Not really," I said, putting my glass to my lips. I took a sip of wine, set the glass on the table beside me, and stared at a sixteenth century tapestry on the wall of the huge Moorish palace my parents called home. It was a hunting scene, and a cruel one. It had always disturbed me, and it was disturbing me now.

"Have I ever mentioned that I ..."

"Hate that tapestry? Yes, Bud. About once a month for the last forty or fifty years, which guarantees you'll inherit it. This little country girl is getting to you, isn't she? If she weren't married, you'd be ... interested."

"I don't know. Not really," I said, and at the time I thought maybe I meant it. "Because she's married we can work together without becoming entangled physically and sexually."

"A piece of paper and a ring will do all that for you, Aloysha? I'm impressed. Unconvinced, mind you, but impressed."

"Do you really think I'd...?"

"No, I don't," he said. "I'm your father. I've known you most of your life. I know you to be a man of compassion, and of honor. I know the battle will be long and hard before you finally give in to your feelings."

I sat there a minute, half nodding, before I realized exactly what he'd said, and when I turned to look at him, he was smiling rather tenderly at me. It was an odd sensation, because my father never smiled except at my mother, who was the love his life and had access to facets of him the rest of us could only imagine.

"You've been a long time without a woman in your life," he said, lighting a cigarette and offering me one. "Not necessarily in your bed, like Mi Ling, but in your life. In your heart. Someone you can work with and laugh with and relate to, like Megan. She's pregnant again, but of course you knew that."

It was a challenge, and I hedged with a nod. Oddly enough, Meg hadn't told Dad I was sterile, and I wasn't about to, either. What kind of an issue it might become I didn't know, and I didn't want to find out. I was uncomfortable with the whole topic of Megan and her expectations of me. My father had doted on the woman. Still did, as a matter of fact. Whether it was entirely her, or in some part her son, Alexander, I wasn't sure, but it wasn't something I wanted to pursue, nor did I want to discuss her second pregnancy. She wasn't a good mother to Alex, who was a wonderful, lovable little kid, and the next one probably wouldn't be any better off, though I didn't say so to my father, who would have taken it as sour grapes.

"Kit would be offended to hear you say that I have no one to relate to," I grinned, trying to steer the subject off in another direction. "He and I work together, and laugh."

"And have sex? Aloysha, this is not the kind of news a father wants to hear. I should never have let you play the piano."

"No," I said, and laughed quietly to myself, knowing I was in control of the situation, "no sex with Kit, and neither, dear boy, despite your insinuations, will I have sex with Philippa Tyler. She's another man's wife. Period."

"See that it stays that way," my father said, and his black DiPirelli eyes bored into me. "Isn't Thursday the night you and Mi Ling usually, as you euphemistically put it, play Bridge?"

I nodded and reached for the last of my wine. "It is," I said. "And we do play cards ... every once in a while."

"But you're not playing cards tonight," he persisted, "why is that?"

I shrugged uncomfortably. He was asking me questions I didn't have an answer for. "I cancelled. I had other things on my mind, and I wanted to see you and Mother."

"You have Philippa Tyler on your mind, Bud. And you need to get her out of there before she does you some serious damage."

"Dad, you're imagining things," I scoffed, stubbing out my cigarette. "She's a very sweet woman, very ... simple in a really complicated sort of a way. She's serene. She's enjoyable to be around. She is a wordsmith of the highest order. You should thank me for cultivating a friendship with her. You never know, she could write you an award winning screenplay at some point down the road."

"She could also write you a whole new chapter in your life," he said quietly. "You're already thinking of her in other than appropriate terms, I can feel it. Go ahead and take her to bed when you can't resist the urge any longer, but for Godssake don't let yourself fall in love with her. She's not your type, and she's not my type. You don't need the complications and the family doesn't need the unfavorable publicity."

"You're hardly in a position to give me this lecture," I said shortly, wondering why he was goading me. I stopped myself and turned to look at him full on in the soft light of the living room. He was wearing his usual inscrutable face. "Are you telling me Philippa Tyler isn't good enough for me, or for our family?"

"Why should you care if that's what I'm telling you?" he said. "If you're not interested in her, it shouldn't matter."

"But it does. She's a lovely human being. She's kind, she's loving, she's intelligent, and I think she's beautiful. I'd consider myself a lucky man to have a woman like Philippa."

"I rest my case," Dad said, and he almost smiled. "You're in love with Philippa Tyler, whether you'll admit it or not."

"Think what you will," I replied. "She's my business associate, my writing partner, and Frank Tyler's wife."

My father opened his mouth, and just as he did, Max called us to dinner. "Just you be careful," Dad said, nodding his acknowledgement, "I know what it's like to have a woman steal your soul. Once it happens, really happens, you never get it back. You don't want it back, and it changes your life forever."

"I was married to Megan," I said, "and I'm over her."

"Megan never even had your heart, much less your soul," Dad said, gesturing me toward the dining room. "Be careful, or you're going to lose both of them." He just shook his head, and went to kiss my mother, who was holding out her hands to him.

I watched the two of them during dinner. I never tired of watching my parents together. They were so in love - there was such a galvanizing passion between them - even as weak as my mother was, when she was with Dad her cider brown eyes sparkled like a young girl's. And Dad, power broker, inscrutable business tycoon, the White Lion of Hollywood, and all the other things the press and his competitors chose to call him, was as gentle with my mother as any lover could ever be.

I sat enjoying the fresh tuna my father had recently speared off their private island in Tahiti, wondering a little voyeuristically what all went on there when I wasn't in residence, and pondering, too, what it would be like to be so deeply in love. How bad could it be, I wondered, to give yourself heart and soul – to lose yourself heart and soul, to another human being?

CHAPTER THREE

"Well, what do you think?" Philippa asked. I looked again around the living room and tried not to groan.

"It's certainly efficient. And small, like you," I grinned, tacitly despairing of the place. "It's not the best neighborhood, but it can't be a bad complex, half Glory's church choir lives here. And it's not too far from my house, so we can work easily between them. I like the security gate between the quad and the garages. There's a grocery store around the corner, so what's missing, except furniture and, I assume, Frank?"

She turned from where she was pacing off the length of a wall and asked, "Why, when you say, 'Frank', does it come out through your teeth like somebody ripping a bed sheet?"

"It's just the slow formal bass and the ominous accent," I teased, walking into the miniscule kitchen. "When I met Kit Miller my first day of Kindergarten, I didn't speak ten words of English. That was long, long ago."

She walked down the short hall and disappeared into the bedroom. "You've decided for some reason that you don't like Frank?"

"Not true," I said, watching her pace off the room, "I'm sure I'll like him just fine. Well, M' Lady, what do you think? Too small? I'd be happy to help you look a little further, maybe for something a little more upscale?" I crossed my fingers as I said it.

"Not a chance. What's not to like? I especially like the fact that we didn't have to hunt for it. Glory's friend just handed it to us on a silver platter. Two hours at choir practice and I get an apartment that isn't even listed yet. I don't want to shop if I don't have to, and now I don't have to. That, Peter, proves that God loves me best."

"You're such a funny person," I said. "I've never met a woman who didn't like to shop. Apparently, not for anything."

"You have now. Oh, I have my passions, but I'll spare you for the moment." She wrote some figures down on a small tablet which she'd set on the breakfast bar. "Thanks again for putting tires on the pickup this morning."

"Thank you for letting me. I feel much better."

"I didn't realize," Philippa said, sitting cross-legged on the soft grey carpet, "that you'd lost someone special in a car accident recently. Glory told me last night. And then she told me to get the tires off that truck, because it was scaring you. I am sorry, Peter."

"Lora had ceased to be that special," I said, joining her on the carpet. I put my back against the wall and stretched my legs out in front of me. This place really was small. My legs seemed to span half the living room. "She was into drugs and alcohol and having her own way. Nevertheless, nobody ... should die like that."

I stared at the opposite wall and closed my eyes and took a deep breath. "Well, kid, let's get it paid for and stocked and go find you some furniture and buy you a decent bed to sleep in, and then tomorrow we can go play for a day before we start working in earnest. You can choose. I'll take you to meet Tiger Lily if the weather holds, or we can go to the zoo and see real tigers."

"Zoo!" she exclaimed, giddy as a kid. "Oh, the zoo!"

"Okay, I said. "Let's get started with the shopping. We're burning daylight."

"Nehhh," she squirmed, "let's just pay for the apartment now and get everything else later."

"No shopping, no zoo. That's the deal. You need a rest, and you cannot do it on the floor with your purse for a pillow."

"That's not fair," she pouted.

"I didn't say it would be fair, I said it would be often. Besides, you get your phone turned on, you'll hear from Frank."

"That's true," she smiled, then faked dismay. "Gee, we can't go shopping. I only have out of town checks. Nobody'll take one."

"I will," I said firmly, "Philippa Kate Tyler, we can do this one of two ways. I told you I have a service that will do all the shopping for you. All you'd have to do is open the door and put your coat in the closet. You do not want to do that. Which means we have to go out and find everything. Now get those little legs moving."

"Oh, all right!" she retorted, and stalked out the front door.

She was hysterically funny to shop with. She hated it. Every minute of it. She wasn't rude, I couldn't imagine Philippa ever being rude, but she was matter of fact to a fault. In ten words and as many minutes she had a queen sized bed, pad, sheets, pillows, comforter - all by walking full speed through the store going, "That, please. That, and that, please ..."

The salesman finally panted, "Is your wife always like this?"

"Oh, she's not my wife, I just pay the bills," I laughed, and she spun around and punched me in the gut with her tough little fist, which made me laugh harder yet.

The bed was the only furniture she bought. The other pieces she leased, which worried me. I was beginning to hope she'd stay for the rest of her life. Apparently she felt otherwise. We hauled the bed to the apartment, set it against the bedroom wall, swapped the Ford for the Benz and went back out. The woman is like following a steam engine. Short as she is, she can run my legs off, and I'm well over six feet tall.

The first place I took her was a sporting goods store where I knew she could look for a pretty bathing suit. Ha! Pale blue. Tank. First rack. Two minutes. She protested that it was an unscheduled and therefore unlawful stop, and proceeded to pay me back in spades. I finally called a halt after the furniture rental place, the computer store, and someplace else I can't remember now.

"I will be no good to you dead!" I snapped, and dragged her into a restaurant for a late lunch. She ordered a cup of coffee, nothing more.

I looked at her and clucked disapproval. “Coffee for breakfast, and coffee for lunch, and last night at dinner, part of a steak, but, horrors, not rice. No starch for you. Some zucchini, maybe, or some Swiss chard, and then you went crazy and had a second slice of cucumber. And no sugar at all, even if it’s natural. You look at fresh fruit like it’s an alien substance. No wonder you’re so frail and nervous.”

She sighed, looking ceilingward. “This town, would make any sane person nervous, Peter, and I’ll have you know I am not frail. As a matter of fact I weigh one pound more than I should. I thought women in this town were stylish if they were anorexic, which I most assuredly am not, by the way.”

“You’re right. It’s true, and I really resent the message they’re sending to the healthy young women of this nation. And as for you, why are you buying in to this? I thought you had more good sense. That sturdy little frame of yours was made to carry some meat. Philippa, you can’t weigh more than a hundred pounds.”

“I can, and I do. Substantially more. Why? Do I really strike you as frail, or are you just making annoying conversation?”

“You strike me as a superb physical specimen, P.K.,” I said, and realized … I really didn’t like calling her P.K. It was harsh compared to Philippa. I wondered if I said P.K. the same way I said, Frank. Like somebody ripping a bed sheet. I decided to reserve P.K. for reprimands and arguments. She was looking at me curiously, and I cut off the internal dialog and went on. “You’re under a lot of stress here, and that makes demands on your body. I’m worried that you don’t have much energy in reserve, and that you’re going to be sick if you don’t start eating. It is the height of flu season, you know.”

“Forgive him, Lord, he has a Jewish mother.”

“And if you don’t start eating, I’m going to turn her loose on you, my dear. ‘Have another cookie’, will take on new dimensions. That lady will give you no rest until you weigh a hundred and fifty pounds.” It was a bluff, of course. My mother wasn’t at all Jewish in her demeanor, and as tall and slender as the rest of my family. It would never occur to her to feed somebody up like a prize hog.

Philippa sighed, "I can see that I'm going to have to nip this in the bud, if you'll forgive the expression." She reached in the zipper compartment of her purse, dug around, and came up with a snapshot in a worn plastic bag. She took it out of the plastic, handed it to me and said, "I look at this every day of my life. Every time I want ice cream. Every time I think something to eat that I don't need might make me feel better. Look, and learn, and for Godssake, let it go, will you? I never want to have this conversation with you again."

Yellowstone, I recognized. The blond haired, hazel eyed, handsome young man, no. The obese, sad-faced woman, barely. "My God," I whispered, not to my credit, and she took the photograph back.

"That's me at a hundred and eighty pounds. Frank is smiling because he was having an affair with the high school girl who used to come feed our horses while we were gone. Please, Bud, please don't feed me. I'm very weak in that area, and without help, without concentrating every minute, I'll never make it. Please don't feed me. You don't know what it's like to be that overweight and have people tell you one cookie won't hurt you. Cookies can kill. Please, don't feed me. If you care for my sanity - don't feed me."

And I never have. The terror, the pain I saw in her eyes branded itself on my brain. I have learned her eating habits, and when I have felt she should eat, I have provided her with what she can eat. I have plied her with raw silk and fuzzy kittens, diamonds, sports cars, sailing trips, new homes, new jeans, horseback rides along the great wall of China and quiet walks on the beach, but I have never, ever tempted Philippa with inappropriate food, and I never will.

"I'll bet Frank is really proud of you," I said simply, and returned to my lunch. To say what was going through my brain about Frank would have been entirely inappropriate, even for me. The amazing thing was that his affair with jail bait was incidental to the point. Her tone of voice sounded apologetic, as though it was she who had failed. I didn't know at that juncture if that was good or bad, but I found out soon enough.

I asked her then if she thought she'd be eating better when she was doing her own cooking and not trying to order off a menu, and she said she was sure she would. I asked her what sorts of food worked well for her, and as she began to discuss all the things she could and would eat, and her eyes lit up at the mention of fresh strawberries, sautéed greens and rare steak, I became more comfortable.

We went to the health food store, the grocery store, the phone company. She shopped for linens, for dishes and cookware. Then, to top it all off, the little mule insisted she had to have a sewing machine. For that damned thing we shopped forever, even after I managed, quite by a miracle, to find the store, which was a hole in the wall.

"I've always wanted this machine," she said at last with a lover's croon, and I asked her why in hell we'd looked at a dozen others.

"Principal of the thing," she'd said placidly, and I'd asked them to deliver it day after tomorrow, along with a nice work table and plenty of extra ... whatever. I didn't know what was worse, shopping with Philippa when she didn't want to shop, or shopping with her when she did.

At ten o'clock, with the bed still against the wall, we put the groceries on the counter, a case of diet Snapple on the floor, fifteen bags of stuff on the living room carpet, and collapsed in the midst of them.

"Mercy," I groaned, "all your clothes are still at Ho Jo's, aren't they?"

"Um hm. They can darn well stay, too," she yawned. She reached into a bag, threw me one of the new pillows, and when my bladder woke me up it was two in the morning.

How I got my aging joints up off that hard floor I'll never know, but it wasn't a pleasant experience. It wasn't very pleasant realizing my indiscretion, either. I went to the bathroom, and when I came back Philippa was sitting up.

"How come your mother was in Russia and your father was in America?" she asked without preamble, "How did you ... get started?"

I smiled, gave her a hand up off the floor, and pulled her toward the bedroom. "We'd better put this thing together for you before the night is completely over. I do apologize for still being here." As we laid out the frame and fastened it to the headboard, I said, "My dad was a university student who came to Russia visiting in the early spring of the year, and met my beautiful, aristocratic mother – turn that the other way. Now it should snap in place – and they fell head over heels in love, and head over heels into the wildflowers, or maybe the snowbanks, I dunno, and then the government kicked him out."

"Too late, of course," she mumbled, and we both laughed.

"Hush. This looks bad enough as it is without giggling in the middle of the night."

"Of course flinging a mattress repeatedly against the wall sends no message."

"Hush," I said again, and again we laughed. There was a final soft thud as the mattress landed in place, and thirty seconds later I was slipping out of her apartment as quietly as I could. I had to laugh inside. I'd been so careful about not going into her motel room for ten minutes, but I'd spent most of the night in her apartment. I could only hope her neighbors were discreet, or, better yet, very sound sleepers.

The last thing I wanted to do was cause problems between Philippa and Frank. Actually it was what I'd have liked most in the world, but it was the last thing I'd ever do. She must really love him to put up with his shenanigans. Well, he was her problem, not mine, or so I thought at that blissful moment in time.

I slept well, took a tongue lashing from Glory regarding my whereabouts, and reported back to Phil's by ten O'clock the next morning. The furniture had already arrived, creams and greys and mauves on a scale to fit the room. The accessories were oak. She had nice taste, on top of the other things that were nice about her. She'd already checked out of the motel, straightened the apartment, put the new dishes away, hung a couple of pictures, and was drying off from her bath. She was wrapped in a huge pink towel when she let me in. She pointed to the coffee pot, excused herself and disappeared to return in a terry cloth robe and fuzzy pink slippers with bunnies on them.

"You know," I said, rummaging the cupboards to discover where she'd put the mugs, "this is a very wicked old city. You're going to open that door dressed only in a towel someday, and it won't be someone who loves you standing there." I poured her a cup of coffee and passed it over the bar to her.

"Was it this morning?"

"Was it what?" I choked. That first sip of Philippa's coffee had pretty well jolted the sense out of me. I resisted the urge to look at my tongue in the mirror to see what color it was.

"Somebody who loves me," she teased.

"Phipps," I sighed, "everybody who meets you loves you, including me. You know what I meant. This isn't eastern Washington. Here, you can be raped and murdered and never even make the papers. If I have to scare you to keep you safe, I will."

"I appreciate that," she said quietly. "I'll try to be more suspicious, but it goes against my nature. Oh, here, take the spare key ... that way you won't have to be buzzed through the security gate next time." I could hear the smile in her voice. She didn't believe a word I was saying. That security gate was bogey man repellent. "What's up for today?"

"The San Diego zoo," I grinned, and she scurried off to dress. She came out in black Levis and a navy and maroon plaid blouse, carrying her sneakers and socks and a navy blue cable knit sweater, which she tossed near the door before plopping down in a chair across from where I was anchoring the couch.

"Philippa Tyler, you have the most outrageously small feet I've ever seen on an adult, you know that?"

"Yeah, they're small, and they're world class ugly, too," she said, wiggling her toes in contemplation. "Terrible. Look at those toes. They look like a gang of tiny critters trying to boost each other over a fence."

"If you feel that way about them," I chuckled, "why are the nails so carefully polished? You don't polish your fingernails."

"Buddy," she said with a sad look and a devious twinkle, "look at the poor things. Now they have to know they're ugly. They look around at other toes and they say, 'guys, we're ugly.' But they work hard. They serve me well, and I want them to know I appreciate that, so I paint their little nails. I think it makes them feel better about themselves."

She grinned at me, and wrinkled her nose, and in an instant, like a plummeting elevator and with the same sensation, I was hopelessly, eternally in love with Philippa Kate Tyler.

"Peter?" she exclaimed, springing to the couch. I knew why. I could feel the blood draining right out of my face, even as I laughed. "Peter, are you all right?"

I nodded, still laughing, finally able to put a word with that sensation I'd had that first day in Tommy's office. Love. I was in love. Love at first sight. Something I didn't believe in. Didn't believe would ever happen for me or to me. Real, honest to God love, for the first time in my life. My father had been right, and now it was too late. It was way too late. "I'm … fine. I am."

"You don't look it."

"Looks can be deceiving," I said, dropping my hands away from my face. "It's just low blood pressure. Had it all my life." I leaned back on the couch, and stretched, and got my heart started again.

"And still you got into the military?"

"I was probably nervous that day," I chuckled. I clamped my mouth shut and resisted the urge to blurt out something catastrophic about being in love with someone I couldn't have.

She gave me a long sideways look as she excused herself to go braid her hair and I said, "Please, if it won't get in your way, leave it down. It's so beautiful."

She turned to me in absolute amazement, and Frank had strike two against him. "Why, thank you," she smiled, "thank you so much for saying that. Sometimes I wonder. Frank isn't a hair person, so he never says much."

I bit my tongue and smiled, and said those five little words that were to become a litany with me. "If you were my wife ... I would let you borrow your hair to wear places, but most of the time it would be mine to play with."

"You can play with it any time you'd like," she said matter of factly, taking her leather jacket off the back of the couch. "Someone might as well enjoy it. Darn, I need to find a good hairdresser."

"But not today," I said, picking up her sweater from beside the door and showing her out. "Today is a day for nothing but pleasure."

"Being with you is a pleasure," she blushed, and turned quickly away as I locked the apartment door.

What a day. Philippa was funnier than the monkeys, more sleek and beautiful than the big cats, more curious than any of the birds – and she was bright – God, she was bright. She knew the animals, their diet, their habits, their range. When I commented on her expertise she said that she was an avid watcher of National Geographic, and Nature, and other such PBS programs, and I said I'd been narrating them for years and hadn't learned that much. Well, she said, she had nothing better to occupy her mind, yet she quoted Shakespeare, and admitted shyly that yes, she had played Mother Courage, and Clytemnestra the Queen, in college, but really, lighting was her specialty.

We had a common interest in photography. She admired my equipment, and I ... admired hers. The conversation turned to music, which is my passion, and that, too, she knew quite well. She had been a singer in high school and college, and played at an instrument or two, but Frank had been uncomfortable with her music, and by the time he'd grown into it, she'd grown away. She did sing to her Arabian mare – and we had arrived at the subject which remains one of Philippa's deepest passions – fine horseflesh. That woman knows horses, and she rides with such elegance and control. In those earliest days before I had even seen her ride, I sensed it in the way she moved.

With talk of horses came talk of home, and she assured me, and probably herself, that this was the best time to be away. Everything was at a standstill under the snows of winter. There was little to do but see that the animals were warm and fed and that their stock tank heaters were working so they had water. Old friends were staying at the house and doing all that, and making sure the pipes didn't freeze. Feeding the sheep, the chickens and Frank's cats ... and Phil's fat cat, Saffron. She hoped they were all getting enough love.

I knew she wasn't. I could sense it, somehow. When she spoke of the animals I could feel it. I could feel all that love being channeled into them instead of the people in her life. She loved her girls dearly, but they'd started college just up the coast here, as a matter of fact, one would be eighteen in the spring, one would be twenty come late summer. They were testing their wings and needing to be prayed for and left to make their own decisions. She smiled and gave herself a little hug when she thought about being able to see them more often. Her parents were both dead. Had been for a long time. Now, with Frank on the road for his business and the girls living away from home for the moment, she was free to devote herself to writing.

"Impressive start," I smiled, squeezing her close as we walked between the habitats, and she blushed, fresh and lovely in the crisp sea air.

I offered her fish for dinner and a walk on the beach, and when I said I was surprised a country girl would eat squid, she laughed and said that even though she'd been born and raised on the Cherokee strip, she'd moved to California at eighteen with her first husband, and lived a couple hundred miles up the coast for most of her adult life. She'd only been in Washington a few years, and now she'd never, ever leave. She loved Washington, but maybe, sometimes, especially in the winter when she was shoveling snow for the umpteenth time in a week, coastal California sounded pretty good. Too many people though, and I had to agree.

We bundled up and walked on the nearly deserted beach in the moonlight, and she slipped her arm through mine to steady herself as she kicked along through the sand, and I wondered if she was as happy as I was. "What are you thinking about?" I asked.

"Wondering how Frank's getting along," she sighed, and I laughed softly, glad that it was dark so she couldn't see my face.

"Why, what are you thinking? I have a penny here somewhere."

"I was thinking, you should never ask a question you don't want an answer for. If that makes any sense."

"Um hm," she said. She stuck a hair clip in her teeth, and she was pulling her windblown hair back away from her face as we walked. She looked up at me as she fastened the clip, but she didn't say anything. She bent to pick up a piece of driftwood that caught her eye, and as we walked she swung it in her left hand, her right still holding my arm. There was a long silence that was not comfortable.

I took a deep breath. "Phipps, tell me honestly, do you love Frank Tyler?"

"Which would be easier for you to hear, Bud, yes or no?"

"Why ask me that?"

"Why ask me if I love Frank?"

"Because when his name comes up it is in sadness, or frustration, or with a sense of having failed him in some way. I just can't help wondering if he's good for you, that's all."

She laughed, and it was the harshest sound I'd heard her make. It was more a bark of derision than humor. "Marriage is for a lifetime, Peter. Remember your marriage vows? I sure do." The emphasis told me she was definitely not happy. "The world is very quick to condemn us and we are quick to condemn ourselves when we stay with someone who isn't..." she raised fingers in gesture and sand blew from the little piece of wood. "... 'Good for us'. Well, those vows don't say anything about, as long as love sings constantly in your heart, the cooking is good, the sex is good, the career goes as planned, nobody more attractive comes along. We promise to commit to our mate, and to do the best we can. And that's the way it has to be, Peter. We take a stand against the odds. Sometimes there are things that desperately need changing. Sometimes we can affect that and sometimes we can't, and there's a terrible feeling of failure and guilt when things don't go right. But luckily God doesn't say we've failed if we fail to change the people we live with, only if we fail to pray for them. He also doesn't say we have to love them, but it is our duty to try."

"If God wants His children to suffer like that, I'll take my chances as a heathen," I muttered, but it was more frustration than conviction. This beautiful, sensitive, talented woman - whom I ached to hold in my arms and make love to and make a home for - was caught in a loveless marriage. The thought of it made me physically ill. Philippa walked beside me, her arm still through mine, and even with the waves and the crunch of the sand under our feet, I could sense her crying softly, but then, so was I, deep inside, because I knew, I was lost before I began. She was Frank Tyler's wife. She would never be mine.

CHAPTER FOUR

Somehow, it was easier after those first terrible words on the beach. That first crush, that first infatuation, passed and we settled down to being friends and business associates. She could tell me Frank had called, and it didn't hurt as much. I could go out with other women and not feel cheated because I wasn't out with Phipps. I could have. I didn't. We were too busy, or so I told myself. Philippa could write as fast as she could walk. She could concentrate indefinitely, and after three weeks the screen play was beginning to take shape.

Again I felt compelled to ask the question, "Will you play Jean Wh-iteside?" and again I got no real answer. I knew her well enough by now to know she wanted the part, and there was no doubt in my mind she could do it, but she was hanging back, waiting for Frank's approval, so I didn't push her. She could be miserable and cranky when she felt herself being pushed into a corner. I asked her once in a fit of annoyance, how anyone who'd had a hysterectomy could be so damned raggy and bitchy, and she'd stabbed me with those electric blue eyes and said they were doing wonders with hormone therapy. Sometimes, she even felt like a real woman. Sometimes, days like this, she forgot she was a second class citizen – and then someone reminded her, thank you very much, Peter.

I told her she got not one stinking bit of sympathy from this second class citizen. She had two beautiful daughters. Just because she and old Frank hadn't had a baby together, didn't make her less of a woman. If Frank thought it did, that was his problem. It wasn't hers, and it sure as hell wasn't mine, thank you very much, P.K.

She reached across her little table, the one that was an extended work station rather than a viable place to eat, and squeezed my hand in that way she had, and said she was sorry, she'd forgotten that I was....

"Sterile," I grinned. "Infertile. Shooting blanks. Remember me? I'm the one who genuinely does not care, and neither should you."

But she did. In her own eyes, possibly a reflection of someone else's, she felt diminished by any physical inadequacy, any emotional weakness, anything that made her vulnerable. There was little I could do to convince her she was suffering needlessly. She'd been sat on for a long time - all her life, maybe. I wasn't going to mend her self-esteem overnight. I was doing what I could to extend her safety net, to make her laugh, to make her happy and comfortable while I modeled all the character flaws she seemed to be afraid of. Oddly enough, in me she found them endearing. I didn't know what to think about this one dark corner in Philippa Tyler, and I didn't dwell on it. I just gave her lots of hugs and flowers and encouragement, and let her dig in my yard when the mood hit.

I was formulating a plan to bring her mare down to her, and maybe her fat cat. To do that, I needed to talk to Frank, and I dreaded it. I had his phone number, I knew where to leave a message. But I was really afraid he'd misunderstand, or worse, that he'd understand all too well, and Philippa was always so desperate to please him, and I had so very much to lose. Frank, and the vibrations I got from Phipps regarding him, continued to disturb me. I knew in my gut something was very wrong. I knew it wasn't any of my business, but it just wasn't that simple.

During those weeks I spent a lot of time ... a lot of time ... trying to talk myself out of being in love with Philippa Kate Tyler. I'd have to let myself in some mornings and start writing without her. The joy of that was that I got to make the coffee. She made the worst coffee I'd ever tasted, and I'd been in the Army. I'd finally go and pounce up and down on her shoulder until she woke up, hair all in a snarl and her face still scrunched up with sleep and she'd tell me to scram because she was "nekked," and then she'd stumble off to the shower for thirty minutes or so. A morning person, she was not. I'd had time to jump rope, lift weights, practice my diving, maybe go for a jog around the nature trails on the property or on the dirt roads behind my house, have coffee and my cherished morning chat with Glory, eat breakfast, shower, shave, and drive down out of the Santa Monica foothills, and she wasn't even up.

She had a temper that would blister paint - quick and hot. Not a lot of powder behind it, but a very short fuse. She lost it and threw pencils against the ceiling, which looked silly as hell, but I didn't dare laugh. She'd decide the script wasn't going the direction she wanted it to, and she'd erase an hour's work without even hitting copy so we could retrieve it if we wanted to. It was just ... gone. Hers, mine, didn't matter. Pissed me off and I said so. She'd just smile and say, "You'll thank me later," as if I actually would.

She had a million little quirks. She talked to herself an amazing amount of the time – talked and answered – because she said what was the point of talking to yourself if you weren't going to get any answers? You could do that with anybody. At least my internal dialog stayed internal. This woman talked to couch cushions and coffee cups and people I couldn't see who later turned out to be characters in books. She talked to God like he was the man next door; a good neighbor, but occasionally annoying. She'd say things like, "Dear God, what were you thinking here?" and at first I thought she was criticizing my writing, but no; she was asking the God of the universe what He was thought He was doing. I didn't know whether to laugh, or run, and neither of those was an option for me. She'd get up in the middle of a sentence that she was writing and go sit down at the sewing machine and sew for an hour. She'd walk away from the stove and leave something to smoke up the apartment while she wrote down what had occurred to her. She was absent minded to a fault about real-world details, and had no sense of money. She hated coins, and had a coffee can full of them inside a month because she wouldn't use them when she shopped. She said it held other people up when you counted out coins to a cashier, and then other people stared at you and thought bad things. She only had the coffee can because I'd brought it to contain the coins that were spilling off one end of the kitchen counter.

When I didn't have to get her out of bed I'd find her at the computer in some sort of maniacal writing frenzy that wouldn't abide interruption. I'd find her exercising to her Jane Fonda tape, which drove me nuts for a very different reason. Nevertheless, I was pleased that she was comfortable enough to do that sort of thing around me, because she was not, in general, comfortable around or crazy about people. She was enochlophobic, and if she got too many people close to her she got this half-wild and hunted look about her that made me wonder if she didn't have some major screws loose. Part of it, I knew, was the fact that she was so short. When she was surrounded by people, she was really surrounded. She said once she never went to the state fair anymore because to her it was all boobs and belt buckles, and I could believe it.

She couldn't stand to see or hear about sad things - it made her weep. She was obviously claustrophobic, and had a terror of lizards that defied description. She had days when she was mellow and calm, and days when the slightest sound made her jump and gasp. When I asked her why that was, she said with some annoyance that she didn't know. She certainly wasn't jumpy because she wanted to be.

She was weird around food. It was like a living entity with her. She literally did battle with it on a daily basis. She picked at her food, played with her food, occasionally tossed something in the direction of the sink - ate beef that was raw, and I do mean raw. It was heated through, maybe, but when she stuck a fork in it, it did everything but moo. I told her she was going to get some kind of godawful disease from eating raw meat, and she placidly said it wasn't raw, it was rare.

She would eat chicken when it was hot, but show her a chicken bone when it was cold, when the meat was eaten off it, and she'd literally gag, or run shivering in disgust. Glory never fixed whole poultry when Phipps was coming to dinner, always boneless, skinless chicken breasts. Couldn't stand the sight of chicken bones, yet she freely discussed the techniques used to hunt, kill, skin, gut and cut up elk.

She drank diet peach Snapple by the case. She consumed enough caffeine in the course of a day to wire a small city and then complained that it was Los Angeles that made her nervous. She learned her way around the grocery store nearest her apartment, and would have none of shopping anyplace else unless she was with Glory. She would have none of shopping, period, and I despaired of getting her into a decent wardrobe for doing the talk-show circuit. The clothes she did have, admittedly, were exquisite, and fit her to perfection, but that was because she made them, and I figured sooner or later the time for that would run out and then where would we be ... would she be?

She was married, and not for the first time, which was no small obstacle. She'd married Hobert Sam when she was seventeen. He'd been a big Cherokee Irish kid who adored her and spent his spare time riding bulls and roping steers on the rodeo circuit. From this union there had come two children, Wenonah, and Kelly. Hobert had been killed when Kelly was about two weeks old. When Phipps spoke of him at all, it was with affection, and when she spoke of the girls, it was with that complete devotion some mothers have for their young. She knew they had their rough spots, but by and large they were keepers.

My experience with children other than my ex-wife's little boy, Alexander, was limited to the extreme ends of the spectrum. Glory's boys, Royal and Titus, were two of the nicest kids I'd ever met in my life. They called me Uncle Angel in true southern fashion, and my grandmother hadn't been the only one devoted to them. I adored Glory's boys, had wonderful memories of them as children, and my share of dreams for them as adults.

At the other end of the spectrum were my sister Racheal's boys, Judah and Matthias. Judah was a teenager by now. Matthias was close. I didn't see them often, but when I did, it was always a nightmare. They were rude, they were disrespectful. They were avaricious, sullen, unimaginative and altogether distasteful children. When my sister brought them to my house Glory and I both ran ourselves ragged trying to keep them out of mischief on the grand scale – rifling through china cupboards, throwing dirt in the swimming pool, pounding on my Steinway, bringing their skateboards onto my beautiful teakwood floors – and then calling Glory a nigger behind her back. When I spoke sharply to them my sister told me I was damaging their delicate psyches, and when I told her I was going to damage a hell of a lot more than that, she left in hysterics. It was a ritual with us.

What my father thought of his grandsons, he never said, but I assumed, like grandparents were supposed to be, he was blind to their shortcomings. My mother avoided them as much as possible. She had a weak heart that wasn't getting any better despite the best efforts of the specialists, and the boys were simply too much for her. The thought of having those boys in my house, gave me chills. When I wanted to write about something frightening and needed to conjure up the right mood, I thought about my nephews.

Philippa, had girls. I'd never been around girls. If they were anything like their high-tempered, beautiful mother, I wouldn't be able to cope with them, and I wouldn't be able to resist them, and I'd be ruined just as surely by them as their mother was ruining me.

I hadn't seen ... that was my euphemism for it ... Mi Ling Chang, who was an investment banker, since the day I'd met Phipps, and it wasn't that I didn't want to. Philippa Tyler made me crazy, and I needed to have my fire put out in the worst way, but I just couldn't. I had always liked Mi Ling, enjoyed her conversation as well as her training in the oriental art of lovemaking. There was absolutely nothing romantic between us. We saw one another because the sex was fantastic, and a good, safe sex partner is hard to find this day and age. We did, by the way, play bridge on occasion. Mostly, we played Kama Sutra. And yet I hadn't seen her for over a month. I'd called her and told her I was tied up with writing a script that was taking all my energy, and she'd said that was fine. A month was a record for me, and all I had to do to change that was pick up the phone and call Mi Ling.

But I didn't. Because, despite everything I told myself, all the internal dialog, all the rationalization, all the times I told myself Phipps was the quirkiest woman I'd ever been around, bar none – I was in love with her. God help me, I was so in love with her. It felt like my soul was wrapped around hers, and the thought of getting naked with Mi Ling was ... cheating on Philippa. She had stolen my heart, quite probably my soul, and the rational part of my libido, if there is such a thing. I spent my days in awe of

Philippa's intellect, and my nights in pain. And yet I wasn't worried about my sex life, I was worried about hers.

This particular evening, Glory's day off, we'd gone to Philippa's place to make supper and read to each other – started writing, and written most of the night – excellent material. Phipps had flopped across the bed to ease her back while I put on a fresh pot of coffee. I took my contacts out, put drops in my eyes and sprawled across the small couch for a minute. "Looking good," I'd managed, and she'd said something, I think, and when I woke up it was light out, and the phone was ringing.

I could hear the shower, so I reached for the phone and said, "Hello. Philippa Tyler's residence," still only half awake and expecting it to be Glory.

"Ah ... where is my wife?" asked a very cool male voice, and I realized we had problems. Damn, I would have to be yawning. I glanced at my watch. It was six-thirty.

"Frank, this is Peter Aarons," I said, vaulting up from the couch and dragging one hand through my hair as if he could see me. "Phipps, I guess, is in the shower. We've been writing all night. I must have dozed off. Let me go find her."

"I can call back," he said, not angrily. "I'm here in LA."

"Really?" I said as brightly as I could, "you're going to have one happy lady on your hands. You're all she ever talks about."

"Funny," he replied with no inflection whatsoever, "I was about to tell you the same thing."

"Altogether different, Frank. With me, the poor girl has no choice. I'm the only human she ever sees except for an occasional book store owner or talk show host, and my housekeeper has taken her under her wing. Did you catch Philippa on TV the other day?"

"Are you kidding? I live in a diving bell," he snorted, and for a minute he sounded like maybe he regretted missing so much of her life.

I realized I'd come up off that couch way too fast for as stiff as my back was. I tried to adjust myself a bit, and there was a warning twinge from my knee. "I have it on tape for you. Hey, hold on. I don't hear any water running. I'll get her."

"Don't. I'd like to surprise her," Frank said," but I'm afraid I'm the one who'd be surprised. She's never home down here."

"I can arrange it. Give me a time frame."

"And a parking spot," he said hopefully. "I have my trailer."

"Let's see," I said. I thought a moment, gave him an address, said I'd pick him up, and he gave me a time. "Thanks, Frank, I'll be there," I said, and hung up as Philippa walked in from the bedroom, toweling the ends of her hair.

"Buddy, want a shower?"

"No, thanks Sweet Face," I said, turning to greet her, and a familiar pain twisted up my leg and into my back. I eased myself back onto the couch, grinding my teeth in frustration. "I need to be gone a couple of hours. You sleep. Don't go anywhere. Just be up and ready to work when I get back. If things go well we'll take a day off tomorrow and go riding or something." I gave her a kiss on the forehead, excused myself rather abruptly, and tried not to hobble until I was out of sight.

I had a couple hours before I needed to meet Frank and I was miserable, so I drove home, hoping a soak would ease the pain. I took some medication on top of my regular dose and crawled off to the spa to be greeted by Glory's smiling face.

"You decent?" I asked.

"Decent enough for you," she said, and her smile faded just a little as she stood up to offer me her hand. "Come on in here, Boy. That knee finally went on you again, didn't it?"

I nodded and eased myself down next to one of the jets, willing myself not to burst into tears of pain and frustration.

"What'd you do to it?"

"Nothing," I grated. "Not a damned thing. I swear."

She came and sat next to me. Taking my right leg slowly, carefully across her lap she began to work it, the knee, then the ankle, then the calf and thigh muscles, and back to the knee. I sat there, saying nothing, trying to focus on the soft splash of the water as it cascaded over the boulders into the swimming pool below.

"Dammit!" I cried at last, "Dammit, Glory, I'm old. I didn't think I was, but I am."

"Go on," she smiled, still working my knee. "Look at you daddy, goin' like a fire horse. You got good genes. Aloysha, this here is startin' to swell pretty bad and turn color. It bleedin' inside the joint. You go get dressed and I take you in."

I shook my head. "Can't. I have things I have to do this morning."

"Like what, work with Phipps? She drag you to the doctor faster'n I would. That girl's no fool. She know somethin's wrong."

"No. I promised Frank Tyler I'd pick him up and take him to surprise his wife. Pain's starting to ease up. I think it's okay. Thanks, Glory."

She gave me that voodoo woman's eyeball of hers and said, "Liar. You could just call Phipps and tell her where to meet Frank, now, couldn't you? That'd be a nice surprise. But no. You gonna take a needle in the knee joint just to get a look at the competition."

"There is no competition," I sniffed loftily.

"You right there," she said in a different tone of voice than I was used to. "There is no competition. Missy Phipps, she love you, Boy. Only you."

"She's married to Frank Tyler."

"But she love you, Aloysha. She love you. I see her look at you. She married to Frank Tyler because she scared to death of him."

"Ha! She's married to Frank Tyler – ouch – because she's a Christian. According to this whole New Testament deal, a wife can divorce her husband if he is a non-believer, but not of he is a fellow Christian. That's why she's married to Frank... ouch! I did my research. I know."

"Uh huh. Hold still. That's not research, that's bullshit," Glory muttered, and I laughed in spite of myself. "You go on, you laugh. You just watch out for little Philippa, 'cause you all she got. Once, long time ago, when I was just a girl, before I met my amigo out there, I got hooked up with a big, ugly nigger used to beat me good. I warn you, Buddy. You watch him. I see the signs. You watch him."

"That, is nuts," I sighed. "Philippa is an intelligent, educated woman. If she felt like she was in danger, she would say so. Women who get beaten are generally women who are too weak or too ignorant ..." I stopped suddenly, realizing that I was categorizing two women I loved. "Glory, that's just plain nuts."

"'Bout like you prancin' off to meet himself, when you ought to be in bed."

"Now that, is typical female logic. I'm supposed to watch this guy like a hawk from the vantage point of my bed. Glory, he sounded very nice on the phone, and I think Phipps genuinely cares for him. I'm going to make every attempt to be gracious, I'm going to bow out gracefully, and then I'm going to come home and beat my head against the wall until I pass out. Then you can take me to the doctor. Sound like a plan?"

"Figures," she said. "Stubborn, so stubborn." She patted my knee gently for all her hard words. "How's that feel by now? Can you move it at all?"

I nodded and thanked her, and she eased my leg back down, then gave me a hug, and kissed my temple, and laid her head against mine for a minute. "Don't you give up," she said softly, firmly. "Don't you give up, Boy." Then she gave me another squeeze and got out. "You put that heavy brace on the second you dry off, you hear me?"

"Yes, Ma'am," I answered. I waited, but she didn't leave.

"You can't get out of there."

"Only if I want to crawl, I'm afraid. If I'm going to walk like a man, we're going to have to do it."

"You that determined to go?"

"Um hm. I have to, Glory. I really have to. I'm sorry. I know you hate this."

"You got that right," she said. She put on her robe, fished me out and eased me onto a chaise lounge beside the pool, then went into the house. When she came out she had a horse syringe in one hand and a mop bucket in the other.

"This time, hit the bucket," she said, dropping it beside me. She swabbed the knee with alcohol, and quickly stabbed the needle in under the knee cap.

I grabbed the edges of the chaise and ground my teeth and tried not to scream, and by the time she was finished I was wretchedly ill. When my head stopped spinning, and I stopped gagging, I drank what Glory handed me, showered, shaved, put my heaviest knee brace on under my 501's and went to meet Frank Tyler.

He swung into one side of the parking lot as I came in the other. I pulled the Benz across in front of him, indicated that he was fine where he was, and got out. They were a contrast, the shining red Mercedes sedan and the mud spattered red Peterbilt. We were a contrast. Me in handmade cowboy boots, tailored jeans and a cashmere pullover - Frank in tennis shoes, baggy jeans and a tee shirt with grease spots on it.

He was smaller than I'd expected – a good fit for Philippa – wiry and well built; not overly tall, with sloped shoulders and powerful arms and legs. He was sporting a mustache and goatee that made him look just a bit like a devil to me, and his fine blond hair was oily and too long in front. Still, I had to admit, he was handsome in a cocky, recently-been-a-teenager sort of way. Suddenly I felt ancient. I took a deep breath and smiled.

Frank bled the air out of the system, stood up and smiled back at me with straight, small teeth that were meticulously cared for. "I'd shake hands," he said, wiping them on a rag, "but I'd get you dirty."

He reached for a can of hand cleaner, massaged it in, and wiped them again as he spoke. "It's been a long trip. I usually run to the Bay and then back to Washington, but I thought I'd better get down to see my sister and my wife."

"She misses you very much," I said. "Need anything out of your truck?"

"Just my suitcase for now," he said, pulling his dirty tee shirt over his head and tossing it into the cab. He had long, flexible muscles, and I asked him if he was a runner. He just shook his head and said, when he had the time, he surfed. He took a clean shirt off the seat and put it on. "I suppose my wife would appreciate it if I took a shower and changed clothes," he said, looking into the side mirror on the Peterbilt and carefully stroking his mustache and goatee back into place.

"She's funny that way," I agreed, then cringed inside, wondering what sort of image I might have conjured up for Frank. Did he think I showered with her? I turned my back to the wind, lit a cigarette, inhaled through my nose, and opened the trunk of the Benz.

"My wife used to do that," Frank said. "What do they call it, French inhaling?" He tossed a gym bag in the trunk and smiled, "What, no golf clubs?"

"They're in my locker," I replied. "Do you play?"

"Used to. I don't have time, now. The truck needs too much attention."

"So, sell the sucker and give that attention to your wife," I said, half afraid he'd take me up on it. "She can well afford to keep you, and, truth be told, she'd welcome the opportunity." I looked at him out of the corner of my eye, but he just snorted soundlessly and got in the car.

"Didn't mean to offend you," I said, shifting down and lining out into traffic, "I just know how lonely she gets."

"She has friends at home," he said, and his pale eyes looked away in annoyance.

"How was the trip?" I asked, and then he talked to me. He was intelligent. His vocabulary was good. He knew what he was doing. But there was no spark. There was no emotion, no life in the man. He was a little dull, a little shallow, perhaps because he was tired. Philippa had laughed once, and described him as someone who could start a sentence with, "But on the other hand ..."

I could believe it. By the time we got to Philippa's apartment I knew why he drove a truck. Next to my sister, he was the most self-absorbed person I'd ever met. He hadn't asked one question about Philippa, how she was, what she was doing, anything at all. He wasn't an egomaniac, he was just a hopelessly introverted man with an extrovert's mouth. He was locked firmly away inside his own lack of emotions.

I'd seen eyes like his somewhere, but I was having trouble thinking over the pain, which had spread from my knee up my leg, through my groin into my back. My hands were starting to shake, and it wasn't something I was anxious for Frank to see.

I parked the car, opened the trunk, then walked Frank to Philippa's apartment, stuck my key in the lock and knocked as I opened the door. "Drat that girl," I said, then raised my voice. "Dammit, P.K., again this door was not locked."

"Sorry," she called from the bedroom.

"Come here, Phipps, I've got something for you," I said. This I wanted to see.

She came around the corner - fresh makeup, powder blue sweater, clouds of shining hair - and stopped in amazement. "Frank!" she laughed and ran to him with open arms.

"No!" he said sharply, and she wilted. "I might get you dirty, and that's an expensive sweater," he added, and bent from the waist to peck her lips.

"Are you hungry? Can I get you something? Please, sit down," she said, and I could see that while he was a very important guest – he was a guest.

"Peter, thank you," she whispered, and gave me the hug Frank hadn't taken, the fool. She sensed my annoyance, dropped her eyes with a small, secret smile and returned to her husband.

"I'm going to use your phone and then leave," I said. "By the way, I'm standing you up tonight. Can you find something else to do?"

"Probably," she winked, and I went into the bedroom.

I called my doctor's office, said I needed my knee worked on, waited while they set up an appointment, called Glory and asked her to go with me. In the spaces I could hear Frank telling Philippa about his trip, how big the apples were, how long he'd been kept waiting to unload, who all had screwed him over and inconvenienced him this time. The horses seemed to be all right. He hadn't been out there. How were the studs holding up on the pickup?

They were in Bud's garage. She was running street tires here.

New ones?

Timidly - she assumed so.

Damn, she had six new tires at home. She could at least have bought recaps.

She was sorry. She'd spent her own money. Actually, Peter had put the tires on. Maybe she still owed him. "Bud, do I owe you for the tires?" she asked, raising her voice without much need to do so.

"No," I smiled, walking into the living room. "You paid me for those tires the day we got the stuff for the apartment, remember? I see you're wearing my favorite sweater for another man."

"You didn't tell me you were bringing another man over," she grinned. "You just said you'd be back."

"That's right, I did," I said, pointing a finger at her. I smiled at the silent, sullen Frank and shook my head. "We really are, just dear friends."

"I'm sure you are," he said flatly.

I felt an odd twinge and said, "The way you say that, disturbs me. Do I need to convince you?"

"No," he replied. The original cold fish.

"Peter," Philippa laughed, "Frank knows there isn't another man alive who would touch me with a ten foot pole. He's told me so. Come on, I'll walk you to the car. I need my jacket." She gave Frank a kiss which he didn't return, said she'd be right back, and when she stepped outside to join me I was lighting a cigarette and glaring at her.

"That ..."

"... Is a very dangerous man to get sideways with when he's tired'" she finished. "He's entirely different when he's rested, and so are you. How's the knee? You look like you're walking on eggs."

"Fine."

"I don't get that impression. Keep me posted, and don't growl at me. I can't take it."

"I'm sorry," I said, and put my arm around her shoulder as we walked. I figured it might be her last hug for the weekend. "Your jacket, of course, is not in the Benz."

"I know, but there's one in the Ford. Can you unlock it for me?"

I did so. "Do you suppose, I shouldn't have used my key in the apartment door? If I were Frank ..."

"You're not," she said, climbing onto the running board to get her jacket from the back seat, "You can't begin to fathom the way he thinks. You'd be far safer to steal his wife than his money."

"I can relate to that," I laughed, and she punched me.

Maybe, probably, it was my imagination, but I thought she lingered a bit with me before she went back inside.

I ate lunch, and I shouldn't have bothered. I lost it in the course of a very unpleasant afternoon with my doctor. By the time he was through my whole leg was numb, my head was swimming, and they had to put me in a wheelchair because I was too groggy and sick for crutches.

Glory and Rafael put me to bed in the big master bedroom downstairs next to my study, and Glory sat with me and petted me and iced my knee while Rafael took over in the kitchen. God, I was jealous. I was so jealous. They, the odd couple, this mixed and not wealthy marriage, they were a team. I felt more alone than I'd ever felt in my life.

"Boy?" Glory said, "Buddy?" and her hand was warm on my cheek. "Boy, you got tears in your eyes. You hurt that bad?"

"No," I managed, feeling ashamed, "I don't hurt. My head's just messed up. I need some sleep."

Sometime in the middle of that night – whether the drugs had worn off or not I don't know – but I sat bolt upright in a cold sweat. I remembered where I'd seen those eyes.

"I was just a tiny boy, but I remember them vividly," I said, pushing my food around on my plate, "those lifeless, heartless, calculating eyes sorting us like garbage. God, Glory, I could be dead instead of sitting here having breakfast. I still don't know, really know, what saved us from that terrible time."

"The Good Lord had plans for you, Boy," Glory smiled, taking the plate. I didn't give her the satisfaction of looking irked. "What else you like to eat? You need to make up for yesterday."

"Not a thing," I said, unfolding the paper and pulling out the entertainment section, "Thanks. You know, you missed your calling. You should have been a Jewish mother. You have all the qualifications."

"I am a Jewish mother. This is a disguise," she said, pushing down the top of the paper with the spatula she was drying. "Aside from the fact that he looked like a Nazi, what'd you think 'bout Mr. Tyler?"

I let the paper settle in front of me and thought a minute. "Glory, I'll be perfectly honest with you. I don't have any idea what to think. Probably, he was just tired, and I know I was. The only thing he did that really pissed me off, was fail to return his wife's hug when he came in the door. She was embarrassed and hurt. It's hard to have someone refuse your affection, especially hard in front of someone else. She also said Frank knew she wouldn't cheat on him because no other man alive would touch her with a ten foot pole. I wanted to tell him – in front of her – that I was right at the head of a long line of men who'd like nothing better than to touch her with something considerably shorter."

"I hope to Jesus you had better sense."

"Barely, but I kept my yap shut. Do you really, really suppose he doesn't know what he's got? Can he be that far gone?"

"Maybe he tryin' to bluff everybody into thinkin' he got nothin' worth takin' 'cause he knows he can't handle what he got. Maybe that's why he sets on her so hard 'bout her singin' and her actin'. Maybe that's why he so strict with her 'bout finances and math things. That's where he strong and she weak. Maybe that's why he ain't never read her book, or says he ain't. Maybe he don't believe in settin' free what he love. Well," Glory snorted, turning to put away the ladle she'd been shaking for emphasis, "He got her caged, and he got her scared, but he ain't got her tamed, I know that for sure."

A hummingbird appeared at the feeder just outside the kitchen window, then moved on to the fuchsias, and I watched him for a minute or two, thinking about what Glory had just told me. I knew she and Phipps undoubtedly talked about things Phipps and I didn't.

I knew that, even though this conversation was supposed to be about

Frank, it was about Philippa, and how we saw Frank through her. The hummingbird darted upward past the leaded glass at the top of the casements, and it made me wonder how distorted a glass I was trying to peer through. “Are you telling me,” I said slowly, “in your inimitable Gullah speaking way, that Frank Tyler has never read his wife’s book? That’s not possible.”

“I’m tellin’ you he says to her he never read it. Where you headed with those gloves, boy? You supposed to be restin’ that knee and drinkin’ lots of water.”

“I will. I’m headed out in the bushes with your old man. Don’t change the subject. I didn’t know any of this stuff about the book, how do you?”

“Hens cackle. A hen’s a hen, any color, any coop. Hens cackle.”

I dropped my gloves back on the breakfast bar and sat down again, resting my chin on the heel of my right hand. “So, you think Frank has her hobbled because free, he couldn’t handle her, hm? I can see it. I can see where he’d be tempted to do that. I’m emotional and high strung, just like she is, and I think a lot like she does. I have the advantage, and if I was into handling, I’d have a helluva time handling her, I know that.”

I took a cigarette out of my pocket and lit it without thinking. “Damn,” I said under my breath, exhaling a stream of blue smoke, “Why do we marry people with whom we’re unequally yoked? Why do we put ourselves in this position of inequality among equals, apologies to Mr. Spinoza.”

“And you’re windin’ up to philosophize ‘bout what, exactly?” Glory said, wiping the counter around me with a cloth that smelled like lemons. “Move your arm like a good boy, and stop smokin’ in my kitchen.” She took the cigarette, not ungently, and held it under the tap before chucking it with a grimace into the wet garbage.

“Sorry. So …why would any man choose to throw water on the fire that warms him, or cover the light that illuminates him? It’s like taking the one book you own, the one thing you have to stimulate with yourself with, and tearing the pages out to wipe your ass.”

“Well, that analogy degenerated real nice, didn’t it, rich boy? See, y’all have never been out of toilet paper. That can make a real difference in you philosophy."

"Dammit, Glory, I need help here!" I exclaimed, piqued that she saw so easily through pretense. "I just ... I'd love to take her away from him. I'm sorry. I know that's lecherous and dishonorable, I know it is. But the more I work with her, and play with her, and spend time with her, and see her raggy and bitchy, and see her with no makeup and her hair wild ... the more I touch that mind, and intellect, and great, compassionate heart of hers ... the more I want her. The more I see what she doesn't have, and the more I see what she needs, the more I want to be the man who gives it to her. The more we fight, the more I know it doesn't matter.

"She just ... melts with love and compassion. Stray animals, hungry little kids on TV, guys panhandling in parking lots, she hurts for all of them. She's shy, and people intimidate her, they really do, but she grits those big white teeth and goes right in there. Aw, damn! Damn!" I cried, angry and frustrated. "Damn, Glory, I'm in love with somebody else's wife!"

"You just now figurin' that out?" she asked, completely unperturbed, and I wanted to vault the breakfast bar and strangle her. "You love her, she love you. Not the end of the world."

"Oh, but it is the end of something fine ... inside me," I said, and it came out as an agonized whisper. "I swore to God that I would never, ever become involved with a married woman. When I lost Megan I swore I would never subject anybody else to that kind of pain and humiliation. I thought, when I lost her to another man that I was going to die. Not because I loved her, I didn't, but because I was humiliated. Part of me did die. The part that knew, I had failed her. I had failed to give her what she needed and wanted. I couldn't give her a child. I thought, somehow, that I should be enough. Maybe Frank feels the same way. Maybe Philippa's love, and her goodness are all the love and goodness he has. I do know they don't belong to me. I do know, I'm trying desperately to find something wrong with Frank so I can feel justified in making a pass at his wife. That makes me feel ... like such a louse."

Glory finished loading the dishwasher, set two capsules and a glass of water in front of me, and started cleaning the stove. "Do you suppose," she said, "That Philippa knew there was a risk in usin' you in her book? Suppose she knew you could've sued her, maybe not won, but sued? That would'a hurt. What do you suppose it was like for her to put her heart on a blank page and sell it for the world to see just for the chance – the bare chance of meetin' one man?"

"I hardly think that's motivation enough to write a best seller. A fan letter, maybe, not a book." I said. But it did give me pause to think about which might be cause, and which might be effect. What did Glory know that I didn't?

"That man," Glory went on, her voice rising to something like real anger, "might'a pushed her away, or laughed at her, or ignored her, but she took the risk, didn't she? Shy little thing like that, riskin' a city like this, just to see you, just to hear you voice, to maybe touch you even once. She give up a place she love, her animals, a lot of her pride, the approval of her husband. And you set there thinkin' this is about you and the honor of men. Boy, I always knew you was a fool, but you are a big, fat fool, and I'm ashamed of you!"

She turned her back on me and it was like a slap in the face. "Thank you for your insight, Mrs. Ruiz!" I spat, grabbed my jacket and stormed out of the kitchen, slamming the door so hard the windows rattled.

"Ah, good morning," Rafael called. He watched me stalk across the cabana and the small wilderness of trees and boulders which separated the pool from the rose garden, and he was crimping a grin. "Having a nice chat with Mamacita, yes?"

"Sure. I'd love to rip off her head and spit down her neck. I hate her. I think I've always hated her."

"She has a way of inflicting truth like a flogging, doesn't she?"

"Rafael, she did not flog me. She devoured me, like a wolf devours chickens, and then she shit me off a cliff onto all four lanes of the San Diego freeway."

He tried manfully not to laugh as he handed me the pruners. "The subject, I assume, was Mrs. Tyler?"

"How did you guess?" I laughed, and exhaled sharply as the knot in my gut came untied.

"Aside from the fact that the kitchen door was, until recently open, and the discussion was quite heated? Glory's worried about her, and about you, and, risking your anger, Aloysha, she's right. The truth may have hurt, but it was the truth. Philippa is much more in control of things than you are letting yourself believe."

"You're both quite probably right," I sighed. "Hey, thanks for the help yesterday. I was a mess. Guess I still am."

"I'm your friend," he said, and touched my arm, "You have helped me many times, and I was happy to return the favor. How is the pain in your knee?"

"There is none," I smiled, beginning to prune the Chicago Peace, "I'm tempted to say something trite about the pain in muh hawrt, but I think it's more a pain in the brain, so I'll skip it. I think I'll just dismiss the whole subject from my mind."

"Good luck!" Rafael laughed, going back to his own pruning chores. "You'll need it if you're going to dismiss Philippa Tyler to anywhere – except your bed – which is where she belongs, and where both of you want her to be. She is hopelessly in love with you, you know, just as you are hopelessly in love with her. She shines in your eyes with your every word.

"When are you going to marry her, anyway? She is going to be so lovely in your grandmother's wedding dress. Her father is dead, so I claim the right to give away the beautiful and blushing bride. I think maybe you should get married right here in the rose garden. It's so fragrant this time of year, like Philippa's hair. Have you noticed that? Will you have her carry roses, since that is your favorite flower? I hope you're not planning to have a huge church wedding like that monstrosity you went through with Megan. It looked good on the society pages, but you were not so happy, I think. You will be far happier when you marry your little country girl right here in this beautiful garden. Of course if it rains, we'll have to move it in under the cabana, or even into the house. She could come down that wide, floating staircase ... so romantic ...." he heaved one of his long, Latin sighs, and I believe he was chuckling a little under his breath.

I dropped the pruners and turned slowly in his direction. His look was one of studied nonchalance, but his black eyes were dancing with mischief as he studied the rose bush. "I think I need to cool those hot Mexican jets of yours," I growled.

Rafael smiled and bowed. "Senor Ox, You are welcome to try," he said, which is how we both ended up in the freshly cleaned pool with all our clothes on, and I got my second tongue lashing of the day from Glory. Of course, in that one, I had company.

Gloriosa Daisy Ruiz was not in evidence for most of the rest of the day but she left lunch for the two of us – peanut butter sandwiches – no jelly, and two cups of cold, stale coffee. We laughed like loons.

I got the feeling it might be a long, lonely weekend for me. Glory was angry and Phipps was with another man. Truth be told, it wasn't so bad. Rafael and I got all the roses pruned and did some grafting. After dinner with my parents I spent Saturday evening at their house, at the piano - playing Lecuona, and Rachmaninoff, and Aarons - watching them dance slowly, elegantly together around their huge living room.

Sunday, Kit, Rafael and I went and got Megan's little soon-to-be-six year-old, Alexander, and took him fishing, as men will do. He was so happy to see us, so happy to have anyone give him some attention. I'd been there to see him born. Richard had been busy as he always was, and Meg had asked me, begged me, which wasn't at all like her, to be her Lamaze coach.

It hadn't done a thing to ease the suspicions in the press that Alexander was mine and not Richard's, but Megan had been so new to Richard's family, and didn't know anybody else to ask who would take part in something as messy as the birthing of a child, and so I had agreed to do it, partly because I felt guilty, I guess, and partly because I knew I'd probably never be part of anything like that again.

It had been by far our most intimate time together. I had enjoyed it. Megan hadn't. I was amazed that she was pregnant a second time. She said she'd never go through pain like that again, even for something as precious as a baby.

Megan had wanted Alex, loved him, and coddled him, until the first time he'd said, "No!" then, she'd gone back to work along with Richard, and Alex had been turned over to a series of indifferent nannies who had apparently been chosen because they photographed well.

Alexander Richardson Stein decided to get rambunctious and willful while the boat was under way, and when he told me, "No!" I pulled him away from the railing he was leaning over and gave him a swat on his little britches.

"I'll tell Mother and Father!" he shrieked.

"You do that, Alex. Maybe they'll give you to me permanently as damaged goods."

He glared at me and sniffled and calmed himself down, and came and put his arms around me and said, "Do you think they would, really? Maybe?" and it broke my heart. All these people in my life I wanted, and couldn't have. All these people who wanted to be with me, and yet because of some stupid rule or another, I was alone. Then Rafael turned from the wheel of the cabin cruiser to give me a smile and a wink, and I knew I had more than many people can ever hope to have in the way of lasting relationships.

Thinking about Philippa while I fished was soothing and pleasant and stimulating as long as I avoided the image of her lying naked under Frank Tyler, then my stomach did funny things clear up to my throat and Kit asked me if I was getting seasick. I shook my head no, and he didn't pursue it.

As much as possible, I avoided discussing Philippa with Kit. I certainly didn't discuss my personal feelings for her. I told him we were doing well with our writing, and chose to discuss the content of that writing rather than Phipps herself. When Kit thought of Philippa it was strictly in terms of being a 32D with nipples like silver dollars. A fair writer, perhaps, but mostly, a 32D with nipples like silver dollars. It offended me, and the more I loved her, the more it offended me to have him think of her as an object without a soul. I couldn't very well tell him this without spilling my whole, gut-wrenching mindset, so I headed the conversation off in other directions more suited to five-year-old ears.

I wasn't spending much time with Kit these days, but that would change. He was a shoo-in for Mark Kincaid's best friend. It was an easy scenario to work with. A small cast of really rich characters. Mostly it was Mark, and Jean. I closed my eyes and smiled as I changed places with Frank Tyler. What in God's name would I do if she didn't take the part?

CHAPTER FIVE

Ohhhh, well, gee ... yes! I'll do it!" Philippa laughed, throwing herself into my arms. "Frank says to get out there and give 'em hell. You sure you want me? Remember, I'm a novice."

"Aw, Phipps, you know I do," I said, holding her tight and kissing her hair and praising God. "You know I do. All the time you've been writing just for me, I've been writing just for you. Come in, sit down. I take it, from the look and the sound of you, that you had a super duper weekend."

"Mmm, I sure did," she said dreamily, kicking off her Birkenstocks to curl gracefully in one of the big chairs by the fire.

I settled myself across from her. "Frank must have gotten a load, or you wouldn't be at my house."

"He left about an hour ago. He's going to pick up in El Centro and haul into Portland and points north."

"You could have ridden along for the day if you'd wanted to. I could have picked you up somewhere."

She stared into the fire and said, "Thank you, Bud, but I don't ride in Frank's truck. It hurts my back." There was a tone in her voice that I had come to recognize as dismissal of a subject. "Can I be forward?"

"I'd be thrilled," I smiled, lighting a cigarette. I gestured with it. "Only my second of the day, I swear."

"Frank told me my hair smelled like cigarette smoke. He was surprised I'd let you smoke in the apartment, considering I won't let his parents smoke in my house."

"Sorry," I grimaced, looking ceilingward after the smoke. "I should try again to quit, and I'll go outside the apartment to smoke from now on. That sounds a tad defeatist, doesn't it? Frank says you used to smoke, how'd you get stopped?"

"Believe it or not, God delivered me from cigarettes. One day I just had no desire for them anymore. I'd never have been able to quit on my own."

"Wonderful. That helps me a lot. Back to the subject of being forward," I grinned, "what would please you?"

"If we could go sit in the spa. My back and my shoulders are killing me."

"I can imagine several parts of you might be a little sore," I snickered, rising from my chair. "Sorry. Couldn't resist."

"Frank can," she replied, holding out her hand to me for a lift out of the deep leather chair, "I'm not nearly as sore as I'd like to be."

I literally bit my tongue trying not to volunteer. I hurried upstairs and got out another pair of trunks, just to move around a bit and get things settled back in place. As I was coming down, Philippa came out of the guest bath with a hairbrush and some clips and asked me if I'd like to play with her hair.

"What a question," I laughed, and took the brush. What beautiful, silky hair she had. She never put spray in it, rarely used a curling iron on it - no mousse, no blow dryer - just frequent trims, and fastidious brushing. It flowed through my hands and down over her shoulder blades nearly to her waist with hardly a sensation of touch, it was so soft. I just brushed it for a few minutes, enjoying its fragrance and movement through the bristles.

"Phipps," I said at last, "you will never convince me Frank doesn't make love to this mane of hair. Please tell me this isn't wasted on someone who doesn't appreciate it."

"It isn't," she replied. "Someone especially special, likes it a lot. I wish ..." she paused, thought carefully, and then sighed, "... I wish he'd braid it, or pin it up, or something. I'm getting cold."

I quickly braided it, kissed the back of her neck and gave her a gentle push through the French doors toward the spa.

"So – ah, that's hot – so, how did you and Frank spend the week-end?"

"Is it true these things will make you sterile if they're too hot?" Another dismissal.

"Phil," I snickered, "I'm in this thing every day, and I average two paternity suits a month. I think it's a myth."

"A myth?" she echoed, putting her tongue between her teeth like Sylvester. "Thay, how was your day on Tiger Lily with little what's his face?"

"Alex. It was great, and he caught his first fish. How did you know we went?"

I called to check on your knee, and Glory told me. How is it?"

I pulled it up out of the water and let her see for herself.

She looked at it askance for a few moments, then said, "Peter Aloysha Aarons, you are, without a doubt, the most handsome man I have ever known in my life, and your body, is on a par with your face, but ... but, I would shoot a horse, even a beautiful horse, with knees like that."

"Horses do it standing up. They need their knees," I laughed, and clapped my hand over my mouth. "Gracious," I mumbled into my palm, "that just popped out."

"Gleaned from narrating all those horse programs on National Geographic, no doubt."

"Probably," I agreed, and turned against the jet to look full at her. "Can I tell you again how happy I am that you're going to play Jean? I was so afraid you wouldn't. Was it just Frank's approval holding you back?"

She shrugged and sank lower into the water. "At the end, yes. Even so, I think I'd have risked his anger and gone ahead. It's something I really want to do."

"Why?"

"Because it's the only way I can make love to you and have it look legitimate," she smiled sweetly, and I damn near drowned. "Touché" she laughed, "now we're even for the thing about horse's knees."

"You weren't serious. I'm crushed."

"Don't be naive," she said, and reached for the mug of herb tea she'd left on the deck. "I find you ... very special, on a very personal level. Can we change the subject? I'm uncomfortable."

"You ought to be," I winked, and we went on to other things.

I gave her neck a good massage after our soak, enough to get her shoulders back down where they belonged, and she returned the favor. For someone so small, she was strong. Her hands were used to hard work.

We took a brief cat nap, and had some lunch, and worked on the script. It was different, knowing for sure we'd be saying these things to one another – doing these things with one another. I could see where Philippa had been concerned about losing her perspective. It was terribly difficult to extricate ourselves from our characters, and after that day's work we were both glad she'd not decided sooner to play Jean.

We went out that evening to celebrate her decision. Just a quiet dinner at the beach, but she wore an outfit she'd been working on – wide legged camel tan wool slacks that fit superbly, and a creamy white silk poet's blouse with tiny buttons and long, full sleeves with wide cuffs – and it was raining gently, and the air was fresh, and I was so in love my hands were shaking.

I sat looking through the candlelight at Philippa and daring to hope for the first time that she cared for me as much as I did for her, daring to hope she would, or could express that.

I put my hand over hers, and she laced her fingers through mine and smiled at me, and dropped her eyes in that shy, characteristic manner which so enchants me, and I told her she was beautiful, and she replied that I made her feel beautiful. And then ... they brought dinner. Thank God! Another minute and I don't know what might have been said or done, but I knew I was in real danger of doing something lewd that would get my ass chucked out of The Dolphin forever, or get my face slapped into the middle of next week. It was one of the nights I went home, and shut the bathroom door and thought only of myself for a while. Still, I did not call Mi Ling. I just couldn't.

Two mornings later I traded my heavy brace for a lighter one, got my jump rope, cranked up Georges Cziffra, and put my knee back to work.

Forward, backward – side to side – easy, rhythmic. Painful for the body, but effortless for the mind. More than once I've been called onto a movie set and asked to do just one thing – skip rope. It is my version of dancing before Jehovah. It keeps me lean and hard and agile and at peace with the more physical aspects of myself. I shook my head and the sweat flew. I squeezed my eyes shut and upped the tempo – sweat and, ultimately, tears, running down my face until I finally missed a beat and collapsed onto the floor sobbing and laughing and clutching my knee against my chest. Good workout.

I wondered vaguely where Glory was. She usually brought me an early cup of coffee and chatted while I cooled down, but then she spoiled me, too. I could certainly get it myself, but I missed our time together. I hauled my bones up off the floor, made myself straighten all the way up, and walked slowly into the kitchen.

There was coffee, all right, but I could see why I hadn't gotten any. Philippa was there, in Glory's arms, weeping as though her heart would break. I'd never seen Phipps really cry, and it frightened me.

"I just don't understand," she was sobbing, "how can I please him if I don't understand what he wants? I just want him to love me and be proud of me, and I always do the wrong thing. I'm so stupid!"

Glory squeezed her and rocked her and soothed her and told me with a look that my presence was not welcome. Philippa, hadn't seen me. I walked through the dining room, through the living room, up the stairs – resisting the urge to put my fist into the wall, throw bric-a-brac, rip the banister off its foundation, and praying she was talking about Frank and not about me.

I jerked off my sweatshirt and threw it across the bedroom, a gesture so ineffective against the odds that it made me laugh, however humorlessly, and regain my perspective. Surely she must know I was there for her, and I could not be more than that. Surely she knew all she had to do, was ask, anything.

I stood in the big glass shower in the master bath and let my temper cool. Then I shaved, and combed my wiry, rapidly silvering black hair, put on some jeans and a button-up shirt and went back downstairs to pound my

Steinway. I wondered, glancing idly in the hall mirror, how long it would be before I looked in the mirror one morning and found my hair was white as snow. It wasn't my age, it was Frank Tyler, damn him. Damn me, for wanting his wife.

Maybe I was a catalyst. Maybe I was part of the problem Philippa was having with Frank. He couldn't possibly be a big enough fool to think I was no threat, or at least a temptation. The possibility that he considered his wife someone I wouldn't want, was so ludicrous I dismissed it out of hand. I knew one thing, if he ever read that book – really read it, there would be war. Hell, he'd read it. He must have. He must have! This was war! I could feel Philippa's agonized cry, I don't understand! Nor did I. But, somehow, I knew I had to.

I tried forcing myself to focus on the music Tommy wanted me to write for our production, but it was largely a bust, and I went on to other pieces. A coffee cup came gently down onto a coaster, and I slid over a little on the bench, allowing Philippa to join me.

"Morning Sweets," I smiled, watching my fingers, "been here long?"

"Long enough to get your coffee," she said, and her voice was exhausted. "Please ... don't stop. Please play for me."

I did. Joplin to Jelly Roll Morton to Fats Waller, Gershwin to James P. Johnson and back again, raggy and rhythmic and raunchy and sad; not saying anything. Enjoying her arm across my back and her chin on my shoulder.

"Peter?" she said at last, very softly, very close to my ear.

"Hmm?"

"Can I ask you a very personal, very embarrassing favor?"

"Sure. Is it something I can do and play the piano at the same time?"

"No," she sighed, and got up.

I stopped playing, picked up my coffee, swung around on the ebony bench, and waited. I felt a little cold inside, a little afraid she was going to say she couldn't handle Jean Whiteside. If Frank had browbeaten her about that I was going to kill the sonofabitch. Instead she looked at the floor and said, very painfully, "Can you ... please ... help me figure out what I'm worth? I guess I don't know."

I stood up, weak with relief, set the coffee cup aside and scooped her into my arms as one picks up a child. "You're heavier than I thought," I teased, hefting her gently, "You're probably worth a couple hundred bucks if we part you out carefully enough."

She laughed then, hugging my neck, and I put her back down and lit a cigarette. "Pretty Philly," I said. "Tell Uncle Bud what's wrong."

"I'm not sure I can," she scowled. "Frank called last night and read me the riot act. Somewhere along the line it clicked with him that I have more than just a set of tires here and one at home. I also have a sewing machine in both places. That didn't go over very well. Then, he thought to ask me what I'd paid for that sewing machine."

I resisted the urge to scream at the pettiness of the man. After all, it wasn't Frank who would hear me, it was Philippa. I decided to try talking her through this on a level that wouldn't upset her again. "Did you tell him what kind it is?"

"Wouldn't matter. He's not into sewing machines."

"Neither am I," I said, guiding her into my study, "but I'm a reasonably astute consumer. I know that when you pay for quality rather than gadgetry you're better off in the long run. That's why I drive a Mercedes Benz. Expensive, yes, but I got my first Benz thirty-six years ago on my sixteenth birthday, and my third, my third car in nearly forty years, five months ago. You can go through a lot of Chevys, and a few Fords in that length of time, Phipps."

"I know," she said.

"Good. Then you also know that even though twenty-five hundred dollars sounds like a lot of money for a sewing machine, you got a good one. When my mother came to this country, she felt really alone, and she didn't speak any English, and my dad wanted to give her something to make her feel better, so he bought her a really good, simple sewing machine to play with. Fifty years later, that machine is still chugging along. We'll pry it out of my mother's cold, dead fingers and give it to the next person who needs a good machine."

"I agree, of course, but then I agreed in the first place. I did my homework."

"Then I'm reinforcing your good sense. As for the tires, those, I take responsibility for. I put on the best tires money can buy, because your life is not replaceable at any price. Glory has the same tires on her car. I don't take chances with the women I love," I said, and looked away to stub out my cigarette. "They always seem to belong to somebody else, but it doesn't change the way I feel." I lit another cigarette and cracked open the window to let the smoke escape, then I forced myself to look at her, and she was shaking her head and smiling a little.

"Amazing," she said quietly, and her voice was a deep, roughened rumble, probably from all the crying, but it was infinitely sexy. "I hear your words, but how anyone like me could make a man like you ... even look twice, is beyond me. This has to be a dream."

"I resent that," I said, "along with all its implications. Basically you're telling me, again, as you did the first day I met you, that I am not a discerning enough man. I don't think you're in a position to do that. After all, I was right, and you were wrong."

"That, remains to be seen," she said, but her smile broke like sunshine, and she glanced shyly away to repeat her initial request. "Can you, will you, help me figure out what I'm worth? Frank's really angry, and I don't even know why. He wants to sell the house up there because it's a waste of money. And ... that's my home. I love it. I wouldn't have any place to go." Her voice wavered and she choked back a little sob. The possibility really frightened her. She was so insecure. "Now, I know," she said, correcting to her best businesswoman's tone, "I could just pay it off and be done with it. I'm sure I could."

"Philippa," I smiled, pushing her into a chair next to my desk, "Yes. You could pay it off and still have a little left over. You would still have a lot left over. You're fine financially."

"See, that's what my figures tell me, too. That's why I bought that sewing machine. I mean, I'm doing okay, aren't I?"

"That right there is part of your problem," I said, turning on my computer, "You shouldn't need anybody to tell you you're doing all right. You should know that in your own mind and your own heart, and be able to see it on paper in terms you can understand. It's your money from your effort. Remember that."

"I'm married to Frank. It's Frank's money, too."

"I agree one hundred percent. What input are you getting from him that is not negative? How does he want you to spend it? How does he want you to invest it? What does he tell you? Does he want a new Peter ... bilt?"

"I offered him one."

"And?"

She just shrugged.

"New house, new car, stocks, blooded horses, apartment buildings, surf shop on Maui, what?"

Again, she just shrugged.

"Have you figured out what you're sitting on?"

She looked down to either side and opened her mouth, but I pointed a finger to stop her. "None of your glib, dismissive, shallow shit this morning. And don't cloud up and rain on me, either, girl. I hadn't meant to tell you from the other side of a desk, on a Wednesday morning, with a cigarette in my mouth, that I'm in love with you. But I am. Hopelessly and eternally. You are my soul mate, and I truly believe that I am yours, and I don't want you to open your yap and say even one word until I'm finished. I think Frank Tyler is in love with his truck and the five women on his own right hand, that's what I think. I think Frank's in love with himself. He's wasting your time, don't let him waste your money. You can make money, or lose money, one or the other, but you cannot sit on money, Philippa. You simply cannot. To sit, is to lose.

"I didn't get where I am by acting, or by playing the piano. I never had to go through rising star, falling star syndrome, but I never made a lot of money, either. I'm respected for my acting, and I work a lot, but I don't have a name that pays particularly well. And musicians, even world class musicians, don't make a lot of money. I got where I am by carefully investing my gram's money, and my money. I stay where I am in the same manner."

I stopped abruptly, put my forehead against my palms, shook my head and sighed, trying my best to look contrite. "That wasn't the most romantic thing to do, was it? I just told you I love you, in conjunction with a lecture on money. I'm so sorry, Sweet Face. Sometimes I really do worry myself."

"You worry me, too," Philippa said, and when I looked over, she wasn't smiling. "Remember when I told you I wasn't sure I could play Jean Whiteside because I was afraid of losing my perspective, among other things, and you laughed at me? Well, now you see how easy it is to lose your perspective. And now you know what else I was afraid of losing; my heart, and my husband. I've lost one, and if I'm not careful, I'm going to lose the other, and that could cost me dearly in more ways than one."

She got up, opened the window a little wider and stood looking out at the bougainvillea climbing around the sill. "You're right, of course. Frank loves himself and his truck. She crosses him, he hits her with a tire iron, and she never talks back. With me it's not that simple. I've never lied to you. I've never told you that Frank loved me, only that I loved Frank. I have to. He's so wounded and so alone in there somewhere."

She turned from the cool air of the window and pointed a finger back at me, "And as for you, I lusted after you in my heart, had sex with you in my mind, loved you in my dreams – divorced myself from my own sense of right and wrong, my own ability to cope with real life, just to be with you in fantasy before I ever met you. You, and your touch and your smile and the smell of you, have given me enough memories to get me through all the dark days that will come with Frank. I love you more than life, Peter, but Frank is my assignment for life, and I'm scared to death to try to change that. Having said so, and having nothing more to say, I'll sit back down here and feel like a fool. You're going to say something sensible about money or divorce or liberated women or something ..."

"No," I whispered, willing myself not to cry. Then I cleared my throat and said, "What could I possibly say after that? Except perhaps to tell you that you honor me with your presence in my life. That doesn't mean I think you're right. I don't, and to tell you the truth, just so you know, if I thought I could talk you into divorcing Frank and marrying me, I'd do it.

It does mean that I feel you are worthy of honor, even in wrong thinking. Whatever else you may choose to do, Philippa, choose to believe in yourself, for you are most worthy.

"I will teach you what I know, but don't let it stop there. Don't be afraid to be better, smarter, richer, more famous, more talented than me, or anybody else. But mostly me, because I am and always will be your sounding board. The cleaner and more true the sound you throw to me, the better the quality of that which I can return to you. Don't be afraid to love me, to be in love with me, even though you can't give yourself to me. You need to love someone who loves you back. And don't ever be afraid to trust me. Let's start with your finances. Give me your checkbook, and your savings statements."

Odd. Amazing. Confusing. A little awe inspiring. Frustrating as hell. Her checkbook wasn't balanced, which gave me hives, but she knew what was in there, almost to the penny. Her savings were in good order and growing daily. She did know what she was worth. Still, Frank could rattle her into thinking she didn't. Why? We talked investments, and she wasn't knowledgeable, but she certainly wasn't stupid. She said she was more comfortable with real estate than stocks and bonds. She could see real estate, and she had a discerning eye. She enjoyed painting and landscaping and fixing up and remodeling. It was the pedestrian level, considering her finances, but it was a place to start. I'd ease her into stocks and bonds after a bit. My dad was a whiz. One of the best in the business. I'd get some advice from him on her behalf.

I talked to her about putting some more money back into her own work, publicity and production. She was going into her fourth month at the top of the New York Times Best Seller list, and the book was going into its second foreign language printing. When people recognized her on the street it embarrassed her to death. I wanted to let her cling, but I didn't. I nudged instead, and stayed close, and prayed that something would happen to change things.

CHAPTER SIX

Over the next couple of weeks, in addition to handing the screenplay on up for its initial critique, we shot some publicity stills. That was fun for both of us. They were playful and romantic, and we got a chance to hold each other close and pose cheek to cheek or forehead to forehead. I don't know what she thought about while we were doing that, and I was too much of a coward, or too sensitive to her feelings to ask her. I, personally, thought about wedding photos, and a nice, quiet ceremony amid the roses at my house, and Philippa Kate Tyler in my grandmother's wedding dress, becoming Philippa Kate Aarons for the rest of her life.

We put together a modest investment portfolio, and took it over to my father to polish. He'd never met Philippa, and he studied her at some length while seeming to study the portfolio we'd handed him. "What do you know about investing?" he asked her.

"Absolutely nothing yet, except that Bud tells me it's something I should do," she said, and gave him a shy smile. "I am making an effort to learn, but numbers and statistics are hard for me to see. I'm more the right brained type."

"Better than I expected though," my father said, and looked up at me as he said it. "The portfolio. It's really quite diversified for the amount of money you've chosen to invest. I approve. I'll keep this for a bit and it get back to you."

"Thanks," I smiled, and we took our leave. I told her to pack some play clothes, and then Glory, Rafael, Kit, Phipps and I got Dad's big sailing yacht out of its berth in San Diego, stocked it and spent three days sailing and fishing in Mexico. It was a time to relax a little before we started the hectic days of filming, and it was also our present to Philippa. It was her Jack Benny birthday, the big three-nine, and Frank was a thousand miles away. No card. No flowers. No present. I was there when he called the following week. Tight schedule. Phipps said not to feel bad. Peter, good friend that he was, had filled in. Hearing her say that made me cringe and fear for her safety, and then feel silly for having such a thought.

When those stills hit the trade magazines and the supermarket fish wrap, the general public really saw who P.K. Tyler was. P.K. Tyler who had written a best seller, was Philippa Tyler, who was about to co-star in the film version of same. Heads began to turn on the street, and she took to grocery shopping in the middle of the night.

One morning while I was sprawled in the living room, half on one of the big mission style leather sofas, half on the carpet, with lines to learn and revisions to cope with and music to write spread all over the floor and the coffee table, Glory walked in and dropped a newspaper on top of what I was doing. There we were, on the cover of some unspeakable rag, as the hottest, cutest sexiest duo of the decade. It wasn't the words that bothered me. Actually, I thought we were kind of a cute couple. What startled me was the picture. It wasn't one of the publicity shots, it was one on the Deep Song. We were casting off to take her out of the marina. Philippa was standing up on the cabin roof, and I had my arm around her thighs to steady her, and she had her hand on my shoulder, and we were both laughing and I was pointing at something ... I remembered, Kit was goofing off in the bow of the boat ... but the shot was clear, and nearly head on. We were on the watchable list.

Glory looked at me, and I looked at her, and shook my head. "This is not good. Did you read the article?"

She nodded. "It ain't good either. Phipps is gonna have a hissin' fit."

"Well, I hope old Frank considers the source, should he come across this in the course of his travels."

"He will come acrost this," Glory muttered, "Guaranteed."

"Let us fervently hope this is an isolated incident," I sighed, and just then we heard the Ford coming up the driveway. "Do you want to show this to her, or shall I?"

"Let me," Glory said, turning to leave. She stopped in one of the arches between the living room and the dining room and turned back to me. "This ain't your fault, Boy. You done everythin' you can to shelter her. Maybe too much. Her life gonna change, what with her doin' book signin's, and Tommy pushin' you two to do talk shows together now. She gotta get used to this, and so does Frank. Somethin' gotta give, here, and I think you've give about all you can. Now, it's up to Philippa."

I nodded silently. We heard the kitchen door, and Glory hurried off in that direction.

For as shy as Philippa was one on one, it really didn't handicap her in the public arena. She fussed about having to make public appearances, but once she got there, she was stunningly self-assured; still soft spoken, but very confident. I knew it was an act, but it was a good one, and I was always there to catch her when she collapsed in exhausted laughter afterward. I was always ... I was always there.

I knew I had to be more careful. This shot was harmless, and really quite beautiful. The next one might not be. Philippa and I were constantly arm in arm, holding hands, using one another for warm blooded leaning posts. We were two physical people who enjoyed touching and being touched. People were so willing to make so much out of so little. And, I had to admit it, when I saw pictures of me looking at Philippa, I saw a man in love. I knew her life had to change, I just didn't want it to change for the worse because of me.

As time progressed, at least from my perspective, her life changed very little. Authors, even best-selling, beautiful authors, aren't that hot in a town like this unless they're scandalous, and Philippa and I judiciously avoided that. We took to working mostly at my house or at the studio, and trying to keep our hands off each other in public.

We probably had a few blessed months of privacy left. Then, I had a feeling, when this miniseries was released things would go up like a big sky rocket, at least for a while. I was starting to hear things at the studio about Philippa as a commodity. I had sat with Tommy and Kit and viewed her screen tests – more than one of them – and she was a mesmerizing actress. She was going to be hot property. Little did I know just how hot she was going to be, and that was just as well. It would have scared me to death at that juncture to see how much both our lives were going to change.

I had time to prepare her for a higher level of visibility, to ease her into a more private living situation, to get her used to the idea that the Central Washington Guild of Quilters had probably lost a member for now. All of it was, 'for now'. As quickly as it deified, this town forgot. I could pretty well promise her she would quilt again, and write again in private if she really wanted to, or she could have a career in the flickers. Her choices were definitely taking on new dimensions.

But our lives were not all hard work and big decisions. There were things we needed to brush up on, even to have a little fun with, if we were to successfully play Mark and Jean. They both rode horseback, and so we took some time to do a little of that, though neither of us really needed the practice. Then there was the dancing we'd have to do. Line dancing, Western dancing to be more specific. Megan and I had danced often, but dancing with Phipps, whose cheek touched the bottom of my sternum when she laid her head on my chest, was going to be a challenge. I knew Philippa was terribly self-conscious, and that the acting lessons she was taking were probably enough of an added burden, so I cornered Rafael, who was a dancing fool, and asked him what he thought.

He looked up, chocolate brown eyes twinkling in his handsome face, and patted the rock next to where he was working on a water line. "Sit. What concerns you?"

"Well, I don't know whether she dances or not, so I don't know where to start. I just know what the end result has to be. I'd like it to be fun for her. For us."

"Always, you treat this woman like glass," he smiled. "Why don't you just ask her if she likes to dance?"

"What if she says no?"

"She won't," he smiled, reaching for the pipe goop. "She moves like a dancer. Whether or not she knows how to dance, is not important. That she has it in her soul, that is muy importante. Comprende?"

"Si. So I get one of her Chris Ledoux C.D.'s out of the truck and take her for a spin around the exercise room, just for fun. That way nobody sees her in case she's a little self-conscious. Of course the fact that I don't know how to do this line dancing stuff, could be a problem."

"Oy, Aloysha!" Rafael laughed, standing up and dusting the knees of his jeans. "You will see her! It is you she cares most about! Dancing is a thing of romance. You need atmosphere, some loud music, a little sweat, some cerveza. And lots and lots of people."

This was obviously outside my cultural definition of romance, and I said so, but Rafael's eyes winked slowly and he said, "Leave this to me."

That's how we happened to be parking Philippa's Ford – the Benz just wouldn't work for this – out in front of a low, dimly lit tavern halfway to Bakersfield. Rafael insisted we weren't that far from home, but it felt like a whole other world to this city boy. Phil certainly looked the part in black 501's and black boots with silver toes, and a beautiful electric blue and white shirt that made her eyes sparkle more than ever. I just dressed the part, and wiped the sweat off my palms. Rafael was the part, and Glory, as always, was Glory, though even she was wearing jeans and a western shirt and boots. I couldn't remember the last time I'd seen Glory wear anything but a dress, so this was indeed a momentous occasion.

As we opened the truck doors the music came rolling out to meet us and we allowed ourselves to be sucked in. The place was huge inside, and smelled of smoke, beer, sawdust and horses. Rafael nodded ever so slightly and winked. The real McCoy. The band broke into a rousing, nasal two step, and about six hundred people got up to dance, and I could see Phil breathe a sigh of relief. Anonymity.

The girls found a table and Rafael and I went off to get beer, because you had to have beer, whether you drank it or not. The beer signs flickered red and orange and blue, and I looked up from the bar to see Philippa smile sideways at a tall cowboy who tipped his hat and retreated as Phil sat down next to Glory. There was enough material here to write the dance scenes and have them come out looking really authentic. I took a few mental snapshots to discuss later with my writing partner, and gave Rafael a pat on the back.

I had time to wonder what our lives would be like if this were our reality. I knew it could easily be hers. I, personally, felt like I had a neon sign on my back that said, Wandering Jew. Please Stare.

"Relax," Rafael smiled, pushing a beer and a diet root beer my way. "Let the music have its way with you. Let it ... heat your blood."

"I don't think I can do this," I laughed. Actually, I think I was giggling. It felt like it, anyway. I felt like a complete freak. My acting ability wasn't doing me a damned bit of good.

"Leave it to me," he said again, putting the beers on the table. He winked at his wife, then bowed to Philippa and extended his hand. "Dance with me, lovely one."

She smiled, gave him her hand, put her chin handily over his shoulder, and they whirled away.

I looked at Glory, and she was uncoiling out of her chair. Her hand closed over my shoulder, she pulled me in to her, and I knew I was about to learn how to do the two step whether I wanted to or not.

It was easy, and fun – with Glory – who is nearly six feet tall and weighs more than I do. When it came time to dance with Philippa it was another story. I was nervous. She was nervous. We weren't really sure what we were doing. She was like dancing around a fence post. Then, suddenly, I was back in Glory's arms, and the short folks were dancing gracefully away.

After about five repetitions of this scenario, I began to come out of myself and realize it was going on all over the room. We weren't the only rookies on the floor. Soon Philippa was laughing and dancing with someone I didn't even know, and when I cut in, I didn't let go of her until the dance was over.

The line dancing was great. Everybody danced with everybody, and I vowed I was going to do this again, soon. I did discover that Phil didn't know her left from her right, but she was graceful and light on her feet, beautiful to look at, and the fact that she didn't know which way to turn about half the time didn't seem to make any difference in the grand scheme of things. I suggested later that it might be fun to have her do that in the film. Tommy agreed, and from then on Philippa couldn't pick up a wrong lead to save her soul.

I sat smoking and sipping my beer while Philippa danced close by with a white haired gentleman old enough to be her grandfather, and even with all that noise I could recognize her laughter. I heard myself say aloud, "God, please let us have a future." and looked quickly around to see if anyone had heard me.

Everyone was too busy having a good time, and I couldn't help thinking about some of the parties Megan had thrown. No, not thrown. Megan never threw anything together. Some of the parties Megan had orchestrated - how carefully the guest list had been planned, so that the 'thems' didn't inadvertently get mixed in with the 'us's'.

The laughter at those parties had had a cruel edge to it, usually directed toward someone. The topic at breakfast the next morning was inevitably what everyone had worn; the horrible sin of wearing the same gown twice. Who had failed at what. How glad Megan was that she was Megan rather than any of ... them. How beautiful the dancing had been, so carefully choreographed for best effect, the orchestra so carefully arranged near the staircase in the spot my grandmother had designed for such a purpose. Everything, so carefully arranged. Occasionally I'd caught Megan rehearsing what she was going to say to whom, which in retrospect was far more alarming than the delightful and perspicacious conversations Phil had with mythical people. Glory had worn her maid's livery, and Rafael had helped serve, and I had been uncomfortable in my own home. I had told Philippa the truth. Megan and I had danced in the dining room, but we had never laughed. Not really.

I had figured out how to wiggle out of the thick of those parties by playing piano for them. The guests raved about me, which made Megan happy, and aside from making them keep their damned champagne glasses off my Steinway, I had little to do besides what I did best. But you know, after every single one of those parties, I felt like I had to apologize to Glory, and to Rafael. Thank God they love me as they do, or I'd have lost them in those years. What would I have done without them in that sea of trouble? Them. What a concept.

Philippa would definitely have been a 'them', and the thought of Megan and me going dancing with those whom she had referred to as, the hired help? Well, that was just unacceptable. I could even hear her tone of voice. Had I loved her? I don't really think so. After a couple years, I know so. I was fond of her in certain ways, and she was certainly desirable. A trophy wife. Influential family, conspicuously absent though they were for the most part, career, fabulous good looks, social standing. All the things I came to realize didn't matter to me any more than they'd mattered to my grandmother, scamp that she was. How she would have loved my little pal, Phipps.

I heard Philippa's laughter again, and an ebony hand with a well-worn wedding ring gleaming on one finger closed over my shoulder. "You tired, Aloysha? That knee ain't botherin' you, is it?"

"Glory, old girl," I grinned, "Nothing is bothering me. Let's dance!"

We faced that day, after thirteen weeks of work and three visits from Frank, when we were going to start filming. Just over three months from initiation to rehearsal, and we owed much of it to Philippa and her boundless talents. We were not in full production yet, by any means, but the interiors between Jean and Mark were to get underway in the morning. Quite an accomplishment for a newcomer.

I'd told that to Frank, at least half a dozen times over the phone and in person. I'd asked him, too, about bringing Phil's mare down. Phil was tighter than a drumhead. She needed a toy, something to get her out in the open air and take her mind off work for an hour or two once in a while. Frank had said he had no idea how to ship a horse, that he only shipped dead meat. Why didn't she just get a new one and be done with it? She had two of every other damned thing. Surlier by the minute, that man. I'd decided to quit asking him anything, conveying anything to him that I thought he might find amusing, trying to communicate with him in any way, shape or form. He really was a scary bastard, and the way he looked at me gave me the willies.

I had proceeded to engage Phil in a rambling discussion about horses, and neighbors, and horsy neighbors until I had a name. Then I swiped a number out of her ancient, scribbled in address book, had a couple of long chats with a perfectly delightful old gentleman who loved Philippa almost as much as I did, and in six days I'd been standing at a stable in the foothills with a beautiful, bug eyed Arabian mare spraddle-legged on a very short rope in front of me.

"A little too small for you," the stable manager had said, and I was profoundly grateful.

But to see Philippa's face – to have her whoop with joy and run to that mare – to see that chocolate brown horse explode sideways through a gate, white mane and tail flying, four white socks blurring as she picked up speed, to see Philippa lean serenely out of her saddle at a pounding gallop to check her stirrup leather, my heart rate still goes up. God, how that woman can ride. Some of our happiest times, some of our most cherished memories, have come from the time we've spent together with our horses.

This particular evening, when we'd been over our lines a last time and I was getting ready to say goodnight, Phipps said, "Don't go," and her hands were like ice when she touched me. "Bud, I'm scared. I'm going to be in bed with you tomorrow, and I've never even kissed you – not really. We always just say 'kiss kiss' and go on to the next line because we're scared to death of each other. But tomorrow, I don't think Tommy's going to settle for 'kiss, kiss'. Why do we have to start in the bedroom? The book doesn't start in the bedroom." She spun in a tight circle in front of me, flapping her arms like a frustrated first grader.

I didn't laugh and tell her we were not scared to death of each other. I was being a gentleman and trying not to scare her to death, that's all. I caught her shoulders and she looked up at me from what seemed like a long way down. "Remember, Philippa, film is a thing of the moment," I said calmly, "The logic and the passion and the motion of that moment is all you have. There is no continuity as there is in legitimate theater. In a film you start where your production schedule dictates you start, in this case, the bedroom. Minimum of set, costuming and characters. It's too early for the location summer scenes and no scouting's been done for the location winter scenes. You've been brushing up on your acting for lo, these many weeks. Tommy says you're great. He says you're a natural." It wasn't helping.

"Hey," I said, and kissed her hand, "you're pretty spooked. Why don't you come out to the house for the night?"

"I'd better not. I have to be on the set really early, and Frank might call, but thanks, I'd love to. I love waking up to the smell of the oak trees when I stay out there."

"Is there anything that would make you feel better?"

"Yes," she said, and blushed. "I hate to ask ... but ..." my, how she could worry her cuticles when she was embarrassed, "Would you ... aw ... see ... if I knew maybe ... what to expect ... see ... Frank isn't a kisser, so I don't know how to ... I'm just so out of practice," she squeaked.

She looked up, red as a beet, and my lips were already coming down on hers. I kissed her. Not long, not hard, with only my lips, seeking not to possess her, but rather to be allowed to approach. It was untrained, but sweet, and passionate, and not at all naive. I rubbed my nose against her forehead, and my thumbs against her high cheekbones, then tilted her chin with my trembling fingers and kissed her again – longer, deeper. "Something ... like that," I whispered, bathing my face in her hair and kissing her up the side of her neck, "only tomorrow there will be bright lights, and microphones taped to our armpits, and people watching. But what is between us, will be, between us, because what we have in the next few days, in front of all those people, a minute or two at a time, may be all we ever have."

"I hope not," she said softly, and I kissed her goodnight.

When I arrived at the studio at the crack of dawn, Phipps was nowhere to be seen, though her truck was in its assigned spot just down from mine. I poured myself a cup of boiling hot coffee and went to start my make-up, accompanied by our esteemed director, who watched me for some time in silence. When I finally got to a stop spot and took a sip of coffee, I nearly choked. "Holy Toledo!" I said, looking with dismay into my cup, "Did you guys let Phipps make the coffee this morning?"

Tommy just laughed. "P.K.'s so nervous she couldn't have made coffee to save her soul. I made that myself." He took a make-up sponge and started working across my shoulder blades and down my back.

"You guys share a recipe, then," I grimaced, setting the cup back on my dressing table. "Boil a pound of coffee with a gallon of water until a horseshoe floats, and it's ready."

"I skip the horseshoe. I just set the next morning's coffee to boiling before I go home at night. Same effect. You seem nervous, Bud. Are you nervous?"

"Of course I am and you know it, having talked me into it in the first place," I groused, dabbing at my makeup. "I'm not used to having that camera see Peter Aarons. I need that character to hide behind. And … and, I am used to considerably more clothing. There, how do I look?"

"Handsome. I like your hair without any white in it. Why you hide behind war paint and whiskers and characters from Shakespeare, I'll never know," he said, making a couple of swipes just behind my right ear. "This, is going to make you very hot, Bud. It's going to change your image."

"Only if I let it," I said. He handed me back the sponge he'd been using, and I stood up. "Phipps ready?"

"Well, she was here early so they could dye her hair," Tommy said, and I gasped with dismay. "Put temporary color in her hair," he corrected, "and do the final fit with her contacts, and she's getting makeup from the waist. You're lucky. You're mostly fur." Tommy held my robe up for me and I shrugged into it. "Bud," he said, "Down to the speedos, now. Get rid of the boots and jeans. I don't want the belt mark around your middle."

"Now?" I managed, and my voice sounded like something from the Vienna Boys' Choir.

"Bud Aarons, you are blushing!" Tommy laughed. "You're blushing! I don't believe it. You've kissed girls on the screen before. This time you're just doing it lying down. Hey, pretend like it's any other night in the sack with old P.K."

"Should be a neat trick," I muttered, over-handing my boots into a corner, "considering I've never touched her."

"You're not going to sit there and tell me you're not screwing her, are you?"

I winced. "We are talking about Mrs. Tyler, are we not? Frank Tyler's wife? She who is loyal to a fault despite my lecherous intent? I've kissed her like she was my sister and held her like she was my child. Period."

"Well, I'll be damned. What are you doing then? I mean, you guys are together every single minute of every single day, almost. You've got to be doing something besides writing."

"You got your screen play in jig time, didn't you?" I snapped. "As for our extra time, I don't know about her, I guess she sews and rides horses. I personally skip rope and dive into a cold swimming pool."

Tommy laughed again. I tossed my pants over a chair, reached for a cigarette, glanced at Tommy, put it back, and followed him out to the set for my final touch-up.

Ten minutes later Philippa, or, to my shock, someone who could have been Philippa, joined us. She hugged her robe around her square little frame and stood as close to me as she could get, teeth chattering so hard I could hear them.

"I like your hair," I said helpfully, even though I didn't, and she made a little squeaking sound.

"Remember now," I said softly, just to her, "this is being made for prime time television, not a plain brown wrapper. We're not going to do anything you can't handle, I promise. Also, we are not going to do anything I can't handle," I added a trifle louder for Tommy's benefit. "You just relax and begin trying to fit your mind into the story, hm? The hair color does make you look very Jean-like. I doubt anyone would recognize you as Philippa." Hell, I was having trouble recognizing her as Philippa with all that makeup, but then she had looked at me a little strangely, too.

"Peter," she murmured, leaning her head against my breast, "I just want you to know ... I have scars. I have terrible scars, and you're going to be shocked. Please don't say anything out loud."

"You have me confused with someone else," I said, kissing her coppery hair. "Do you need to talk about this to be comfortable? We have a couple minutes."

I was vaguely alarmed. When she said, scars, I immediately thought, horses, but then I'd seen most of the parts of her a horse could damage, and knowing Philippa, if it was a horse scar, she'd be okay with it. Now, I was thinking ... Frank. "Phipps, is this something they couldn't fix with make-up?" I asked, leading her a little further to one side.

How different she was when she glanced up at me in the dim light and shook her head. How unlike my simple country girl. I felt like I was talking to some glamorous, green eyed stranger. She looked slightly harder, and surer of herself, and that made it difficult to treat her as I always did. I resented whichever makeup artist had stolen my dear friend at a time like this.

I cupped her chin to make her look up at me again and said, "Just spit it out."

"I ..." she sighed, and pulled her head away from my hand to stare at the floor. "I did a very stupid thing. These," she said with a slight gesture across her chest, "aren't real. That girl that Frank loved and probably still does love, had really big breasts, and Frank just went crazy. I thought, if I lost the weight I'd gained, and had this done, I could show him how much I wanted him to love me, too. So I did it. I sold my favorite horse and just did it. But they scarred."

"Enough said," I whispered, hugging her close. "Phipps, a lifted face is still your face. A lifted breast is still your breast. Pardon me for saying so, but I think they're gorgeous. Please don't feel like you have to be perfect for me, it makes me feel inadequate and self-conscious. I mean, I have scars, too. Lots. Look at this nasty little number on the back of my left hand. I got that in a sailing accident with my grandfather when I was just a baby."

"At least you didn't get yours being stupid."

"You haven't seen those … yet, but believe me, I've got 'em," I muttered, kissed her forehead and steered her close to the action. "The bigger the risk you take for someone you love, the bigger the chances of failure. Frank should love you for the risk, not the result."

"It doesn't bother you?"

"Not in the least, my dear," I said. It did make me curious, but I didn't say that. I knew Philippa tended to exaggerate her flaws. As nonchalantly as I could I added, "Why, does it bother Frank?" I could have shoved bamboo under her fingernails and not gotten an answer to that one. I forced a smile and gave her a one armed hug. "Just don't ever tell me that's a wig, and we'll be okay."

"But it is," she grinned, and I told her to shut up.

I asked her if the set looked like the bedroom in her house, because that was the house she'd used in the book, and she said, yes, pretty much, it did, only her bedroom had more substantial walls. And I asked her if she was looking forward to sleeping in her own bedroom after all those months away, and she said yes – with me – and laughed a little.

It helped us ignore the part where we were props to be dusted and lighted properly and put in place and inspected. Then Tommy said, "Okay, kids, you ready? Bud, are you wearing your contacts?"

"Of course I am. I'm legally blind without them. You know this."

"Are we seeing them?"

"No," someone said, off in the darkness.

"Proceed. Kids, we're going to film what we can as we go along. If we flub, we'll call it rehearsal, okay? Bud, I want you to put your left arm under P.K.'s neck, your hand against her back, right hand on her butt outside the sheet. My God, I'd forgotten what huge hands you have. I'd really hoped to see a little more of her curve than that. No, leave it where it is. It looks ... protective somehow. Now, with both hands, pull her toward you until her breasts flatten out against your chest. Good."

It was. It was great. Matter of fact, I cringe to admit, I came up and I stayed up, and from where Phil's knee had been positioned, I knew she couldn't miss it. I wanted to tell her I was sorry, but I was afraid she'd think I meant she wasn't worthy of such a … gesture, so I just pretended it wasn't happening and hoped she could do the same.

"Phipps, cock your bottom hip toward Buddy and your top hip away from him just a tad. Good. Roll that left shoulder back into his palm. There. Good girl. Ray, let's have just a little more voluptuousness to Jean's hair. A bit more blush to the lips."

In the five seconds Ray had her hair out of my sight line, and in hers, I looked down and pulled away ever so slightly, then pulled her close again with a small sigh of relief. Terrible scars indeed. The girl had no self-perspective at all.

"Bud," Tommy said, and I jumped, "heel of your right hand ... your other right ... just below that girl's left breast on her ribcage. And there you are, Mark and Jean, in bed for the first time together. Not something you've taken lightly. Mark, this woman is the most precious thing in your life. Someone to ease the hurt and emptiness. She is vulnerable and she looks a little frightened, just a little, like maybe she isn't quite sure yet ..."

It was all I could do to keep from bursting into hysterical laughter. I felt like chubby, sweet, carrot-topped Tommy had been a fly on my wall the last few months. "Peter," his voice said gently, "You're not concentrating. Focus. Focus. Deep breath. Good. You want her, almost, not quite to the point where you can't control it. Force yourself to slow down for her sake. Give her time to say no. I want to see that tension in your jaw and across your shoulders. Jean, stay with him, trust him. You know, you really know, he's not going to hurt you. This man adores you, and you adore him. Let him have you, slowly, like sipping fine wine... three, two, one, line."

"I love you, Jean," I breathed, and it was easy.

Tommy Sinclair is an excellent director. His voice never intruded sharply. He never yelled 'cut!' He would simply say, very quietly, "Again from your line, Mark," or "Beautiful, Jean. Your voice is beautiful. Now, again, with that left elbow down ... back ... so I can see Mark's collar bones. Beautiful, Jean. You're doing fine. Deep breath, smile - tilt your chin up. Kiss the man. He loves you, so much. Just like that."

Her concentration was flawless. Those college years on stage were serving her well. She was real – absolutely real – and the passion that made her tremble was just as real. She was helping me, and I'd never felt better in a part. We were rolling smoothly, half hearing Tom's soft voice, half doing what felt right, lost in the blessed anonymity of two people we couldn't quite bring ourselves to be.

The lights were hot. We were sweating with the effort of balancing ourselves for best effect. I could feel Philippa sliding against me as we shifted positions under the sheets. "Jean, drop that left shoulder, and Mark, you let her down … easy … strong arm ... right hand coming across her left breast so we don't see a nipple ... good. Slide your hand back, bring your mouth down where your fingers were ... just a momentary gesture ...."

I'd read the scene a dozen times. I did what I was told, and I was shaking all over. I could hardly breathe. I brought my mouth down to kiss her breast, and, because I was thinking more of Peter Aarons than Mark Kincaid, I lifted just a little with my lips, and ran my tongue across her nipple. Stupid man. Stupid man. The old safety valve just ... popped. My back jerked up, my pelvis thrust forward, and with one, utterly horrified, wide eyed gasp – I lost it. I buried my face beside Philippa's neck to hide my breathing from the microphones, Phil's left knee came up, bringing the sheet with it, and Tommy said, "What in hell's going on, Bud?" all in the same second of time.

"What in hell do you think's going on?" Philippa snapped. "You take some poor guy with a screwed up back, and put him in bed with someone a foot shorter than he is, and tell him to make love to her for hours, and make it look easy. What do you expect? He probably ruined something."

Like my chances with you, I groaned inside.

"You'd better let him out of this bed for a break, and me too, for that matter. I have to pee like a racehorse and these contact lenses are driving me nuts. Buddy, are you all right?"

She knew I was. She'd felt me stop shuddering and relax back into myself. She'd heard me say, "Shit, shit, shit," very, very quietly through my teeth.

"I'm okay," I said, shifting my weight a little and grinning the cheesiest grin of my life. "Thanks, Phil. Tommy, she's right. I've got to get out of here for a few minutes and take something for my back. May we have our robes, please?"

"You may have noticed that I am the only female on this set," Philippa growled, sitting up with the sheet under her armpits. "In light of that I will be along after you gentlemen have left for your break."

"Now, Phipps, we won't look, will we?" Ray teased, and she flared in his face.

"Damned right you won't!"

"Phipps," I said with a placating smile, "Sweet face ..." and she punched me in the shoulder. "You, too. Get out, Aarons. All of you guys, get out! Leave me alone!"

We fled, avoiding the laser beam of her angry eyes. Tommy turned to wait for me and said, "I'd never have guessed she was a bitch."

"That's my girl," I smiled, wanting to smack him, and wondering at the same time how much of the tantrum was real, and how much of it was a ruse to be alone with that bed for a minute. "She's nervous. This is just a pop and cool. She'll be good as new in a few minutes."

"Fine actress, though. I'm impressed."

"Excellent actress," I muttered, "you have no idea how good, really." I almost missed the look he shot me. I went into my dressing room, shut the door, and began to snicker. I was so disgusted, and so in love, and so damned mortified. I just went into the bathroom and shut the door as quietly as I could, hoping my indiscretion would diminish with silence.

Five minutes later there was a gentle tapping, and I opened the door for Philippa. I just cringed, and put my face in my hands, and stood there like the idiot I was, not even able to look at her. "I am so sorry," I said, mostly to my palms, "I feel like the biggest fool who ever lived."

She took my wrists and pulled my hands down. "You okay?"

I nodded and made myself look at her. "I had a … wore a … because I thought … anyway … taken precautions and …you were … thank you very much," I mumbled, and kissed her forehead. "Phipps, don't think for one second that I meant to do that. I would never use you in such a manner." I turned away from her eyes and reached for a cigarette.

"Don't feel bad, Bud, and please don't keep apologizing. It makes me feel ugly. Women are lucky, of course. We can do things like that, maybe even more than once, and nobody is the wiser." She opened the door, stepped outside, then looked back around the door and winked at me. "Well, come

come, Peter. We have work to do, and please grab a breath mint. I don't like licking an ashtray."

CHAPTER SEVEN

How I got up the courage to face those people again, I'll never know. How I managed not to do it again, I'll never know. She had shaken her head and smiled that tender, funny, dancing eyed smile of hers, told me I'd been very smart to come prepared, and very lucky to have had clothing on, such as it was, and walked arm in arm with me back to work.

Later, when I'd asked her what I could do to make up for my idiocy, where I could take her, how I could please her, even to half my kingdom, she'd asked me if I would play the piano for her. I did, of course. I also told her she'd have to let me do more than that, because I couldn't play the piano nonstop for twenty years. She'd leaned against me on the piano bench and asked me if – when we got a break – I'd like to go up the coast with her and meet, 'the girls.'

At last, I was invited into Philippa's world, as I had invited her into mine, and I was delighted. When we shut down for set revisions, I booked rooms in a beautiful place right on the beach and went prepared to spend money on this woman. She went to have fun. We got checked in and had lunch, then Philippa put on her usual play clothes – cowboy boots, black levis, a pretty, tailored blouse – made a phone call, and we were on our way again, just a few miles, to where a small town nestled between hills and ocean. The air was full of sunshine, the hills a bright, spring green, and Philippa Tyler, behind the wheel of that sleek new Mercedes, was a sight to behold.

We pulled up in front of a slightly ramshackle two story house with outrageously purple shutters and enough ivy clinging to it to make me think that was largely what was supporting the place. The windows had college banners in them, and science experiments on the sills, and mismatched curtains that suited the overall effect. Then the door flew open, and two young women came running into my heretofore well ordered, childless life yelling, "Hi, Mom! Hi, Peter!"

There was a lithe, serene pit bull who checked me out but passed no judgment for the moment, and these two girls who were hugging and kissing Phil, and turning to greet me, as well. Beautiful eyes, grey as storm clouds on the younger, green with hazel flecks, Jean Whiteside's eyes, on the older. I was introduced, as always, as Bud Aarons, period. No qualifications. We'd decided early on to let people think what they wanted. What we said wouldn't change things anyway.

Kelly, with light olive skin, grey eyes and sun-streaked ash blonde hair, was tall, slender and pretty much solid muscle. She was pragmatic, and, as I would soon discover, temperamental. The science experiments turned out to be hers. She was a freshman, planning to feed the hungry of the world by teaching them to feed themselves. Her first few words told me she had a wacky sense of humor, and her nose wrinkled when she laughed.

Wenonah was obviously and beautifully Native American. She was slightly shorter than her sister and not as angular, but taller than her mother by some inches; softer of body, with glowing olive skin and long, jet black hair to go with her big green eyes. She had the warmth, and the bubbling laughter, and an almost Mediterranean effervescence that made me fall for her instantly. She was quieter than her sister, and her speech was deep and thoughtful, full of kindness and a smooth, unpracticed intelligence that reminded me a lot of her mom.

They dragged me in the house, sat me down, and we laughed for three days straight. We went to the beach and looked for 'dead stuff'. We went to Hearst Castle and decided money can't buy taste. They took me to a little hole in the wall fish place for the best squid I've ever eaten. We played Trivial Pursuit and Diminishing Whist. We toured the wineries and walked in the hills, and ran into Frank's parents when we were out for Sunday dinner.

Now that, was an interesting, eerie experience. They were nice enough. They spoke mostly to the girls and not to Phipps or me, and I was introduced by Kelly as Philippa's business partner, but that was fine. It was the feeling, I guess, of standing there with Frank's family – the three beautiful, talented, loving, crazy women he could have every day – standing there with my arms around them, and letting Frank's father know with a single look ... you betcha, I'll take them all if he's fool enough to let me. We nodded, said our good-byes, and went on to our own table.

The last day, we went to Philippa's Alma Mater, just the two of us. The girls had classes there, and then work. We visited all the animals, of course, and walked around the campus, which Phipps said had lost its charm and was full of little kids, and then stopped by the Theater Arts building. "It's been a long time," she laughed, and that laughter was remembered.

"Philippa," the old gentleman said, and there was much in their embrace. Phipps knew him only as her beloved Drama professor, but I was standing there with my mouth open. I was older. I knew who he was, and I knew now why Philippa could act. He stuck out his hand to me, eyed me up and down as we were introduced, and nodded. "You're just in time," he said, and there in the huge scene shop which he had designed long before, surrounded by eager young actors and actresses, I spent the shank of the morning teaching a class in film technique. Phipps claimed to be only a student and joined the others to listen and ask questions.

By the time we left I had been invited back, as the very elderly gentleman had been since his retirement, to teach a class for a quarter, and I had accepted. Again, my world had been enlarged. Phipps said she was proud of me. I liked that.

We drove around the town, then the surrounding area, and she pointed up a sagebrush studded hill at the house that she and Frank had built together years before. It was a charming, sprawling, old fashioned thing, with a big barn, an exercise arena, lot of white, four rail fences – an expensive layout.

"I gardened here all year around," she said. "I rode all year around, jogged all year around. I loved it here. I did some of my best writing in that house." She rubbed her hands together like she did when she'd been digging in the dirt, or handling inky paper.

"And yet you left," I said, dropping an arm around her.

"Frank left, and I went with him. You can't run an engineer's home on a truck driver's salary. We'd have lost it eventually."

"And now?"

She shrugged. "Other people live in it. They've painted it white."

"You could come back to this area."

"Why?" she asked, squinting up at me, "The work I do for my one life is in Los Angeles, and I have an apartment there, and Flyer there, and you there. My other life, is in Washington State, and I want it to stay there. Bud, let me tell you something. This may look rural, but it isn't. The attitudes are very urban. I love it where I am. It's slow and beautiful, and the people are kind and good and open and friendly. They think like I do. Here, I was a freak for wanting to raise the food my family ate. Up there, I have a garden, and alfalfa, and livestock, and sprinkler pipe to move and equipment to mend. I hunt in the autumn, just like everybody else. They let you do what you can do, not what you look like you should be able to do. I like it there." There was that final challenge in the voice that dismissed a given subject.

I acquiesced. I did get the cold feeling, though, that if farming and mending fence was the norm, Philippa might go back to Washington and find herself as much a freak as she'd been here, for different reasons. Needless to say, having grown considerably in wisdom, I didn't mention it. As usual I was working on, 'In the autumn I hunt.' I looked at her again and tried picturing her tramping through the woods with a Coors in her hand and Old Betsy under one arm, seeking the elusive elk.

The girls rattled in after school, each in her beat up old car, and on the spur of the moment, her eyes dancing like a child's, this woman who hesitated to buy a sewing machine for herself, took the kids to town and bought them each a new automobile. It was like her, bless her heart.

It was an experience akin to a Christmas sale at Macy's. As we drove to town, Phil said absolutely no looking at the two or three cars she knew had bad crash test ratings. I did the same with half a dozen or so more for various reasons which did not endear me to Kelly, who was six feet tall in her cowboy boots, and could look me pretty much straight in the eye with her storm-grey, vaguely petulant gaze.

We breezed through three dealerships before Kelly found something she liked. She kicked the tires and asked hard questions, and ended up with a two-year-old silver and blue four wheel drive Nissan pickup that had been traded in. Wenonah got the bright red Honda Accord she'd fallen in love with walking onto the lot. I, playing Shylock and devil's advocate, took care of the money end of the deal, and I was pleased. The girls were sensible, the salesman pliable, and in less than four hours, the kids drove their new cars home.

"If I wasn't scared of Frank's temper I'd buy them the world," Phipps said on the way back to the motel, and I should have heard her. God help me, I should have heard what she was telling me. But I was happy, and a little tired, and because she laughed when she said it, I didn't listen. I let it go by.

She cried saying goodbye to the girls, and I winked at them over her head, and invited them down to play in my back yard, gave them both a hug and a kiss, and told them we'd see them soon.

Los Angeles was rainy and cold and stinky and dirty and Philippa sat on her side of the car, looking out the window and saying little. I knew now what she'd meant about feeling like she was on another planet. I felt a little that way myself right now. But I loved my old bird house in the hills, and Glory's warm hug, and the feel of the spa on my back and my knee. Running in the loose sand, throwing a Frisbee for Clip, the Pit Bull, had left me feeling muscles and joints I'd thought were in pretty good shape.

Philippa perked up, and that night I sat in my recliner close to the fire reading the next day's script and listening to Phipps and Glory sing in the kitchen. Almost, sometimes, I wished I could believe as they did, just for the wonderful gospel music. Their voices changed, blended to a minor key, and they began to sing one of the Psalms of David – those two dark, clear altos – one on harmony, one on melody, and I sighed and closed my eyes, utterly at peace.

A couple afternoons later Frank came to the studio to watch us work, and Phil's concentration went out the window. She tried, and she was still better than most, but she shook every second, and even Mark Kincaid with his words and arms and gentle kisses, couldn't stop the trembling. I could feel her trying physically to push me away. At last, between takes, when they were setting the lights on us and I had a moment, I whispered, "What's wrong? Are you okay?"

"Frank has never seen me act before, and … you know he didn't like this part of my life to begin with. Anyway, I want to make him proud of me, that's all. I'm fine."

When we had a break she hugged him, and he smiled and hugged her back, but he was ill at ease and his eyes were hard, and I couldn't fault him. I wouldn't want to sit around all afternoon watching another man kissing my wife, either.

I knew Tommy would close the set for bedroom scenes, but I couldn't help being grateful that it wasn't something we needed to contend with. Even being fully clothed and kissing Philippa rather innocently, made me feel naked in front of Frank.

I watched him, incessantly stroking that devil's goatee. How good looking he would be, just with a haircut, just with a little better grooming – a smile wouldn't hurt, either. I wondered if it had really dawned on him that he was married to a celebrity. Of course Philippa didn't think of herself as one. I saw Tommy watching me watching Frank with her, and I turned away and went back to my own business.

Philippa said she'd just have to hope there wouldn't be any script changes coming down and left early. Frank had several things to discuss with her, and she was going to take him out for a nice dinner and maybe a movie or something. She left beside him. They never touched each other in public. In private, she touched him. I sat in the shadows wondering if they had any sex life at all. Any life of any kind at all. Then Tommy called me into his office for an impromptu production meeting, and once again, I realized I'd been minding other people's business rather than my own.

In the course of our meeting the script changes came down, and I took Philippa's as well as mine. I didn't want to phone her, just in case they were not anxious to be disturbed. I ran a couple of errands, and on my way home, I stopped by Phil's place. Her pickup was in its spot, and I wondered, a little amused, if they'd taken the Peterbilt out on the town.

There were no lights on, and it was after dark. I knocked, and there was no answer. I put my key in the lock, opened the door, and stepped into the chilly, darkened living room, thinking I'd drop the script on the coffee table. As I leaned forward I banged into something, and realized the coffee table was on its side. I took three steps back and flipped on the light.

Until the day I die ... every time I hear or stop a joke about men who beat their wives ... I will see Philippa huddled there. She was beside the couch, legs close under her, left arm on the couch itself, face down on that left arm. Her right arm was just ... hanging. I could see an awful, bloody welt on the right side of her face, and for about half a second I thought she'd fallen over the coffee table. She was dressed in her camel slacks and that beautiful blouse - and by then I was on one knee beside her.

"Philippa?" I said quietly, "Sweetheart? It's me, Peter. Can you hear me?"

Her head came slowly up, her eyes came open, and I groaned, "Oh, dear God," and burst into tears. Her sweet face, her kind and loving face, had been slapped bloody. Her nose was bleeding, her cheeks were bruised and there were deep, jagged scratches under her left eye, probably where she'd put her hands up to protect herself and Frank had slammed her own fingernails into her face. Her poor lips were swollen and broken. The front of her blouse, what was left of it, had a bloody hand print on it where he'd grabbed her. The rest of the blood had dripped there from Philippa's face. "Oh dear God," I groaned, "Oh, Philippa ...."

"You know," she managed, looking right through me, "this is my fault. I shouldn't argue with him. I know he can't handle it. He doesn't mean to." She laid her cheek over into the palm of my hand, closed her eyes and mumbled, "Just leave those. I'll look at them later. I don't feel very good right now."

I was shaking so hard it's a wonder I could function, but somehow I did. I said her name and touched her face, but she didn't respond. Because she had controlled the use of her neck, I didn't think about the possibility of it being broken, but her right wrist was purple and swollen and bore the print of a man's fingers. I kissed her, slid my hand out from under her head, told her I'd be right back and ran for a blanket and a bath towel and some safety pins.

I spread the blanket on the couch – her fuzzy green cuddle wrap with the wild ducks on it that she liked so much – put the towel over it at shoulder height, then, cradling her as carefully as I could, I picked her up in my arms and turned with her onto the couch. I put her arm over her breastbone, pinned the towel in place to hold it, and wrapped her in the blanket.

And all that time, when all those years of first aid training were coming out of my hands, my brain was going absolutely crazy with hatred and sorrow and confusion. I was crying, and shaking, and horrified beyond anything I can describe, to learn that these things really do happen to people we love.

I realized with terrible clarity that Glory had told me she'd been beaten, and I hadn't turned a hair or given that precious friend one moment of sympathy. Somehow, in my ignorant, self-centered mind, I must have filed that information away under such topics as, long time ago, Deep South, black man, she obviously survived, not my world.

Both phones had been ripped out of the wall, so I kissed Philippa, told her I'd be right back, and sprinted upstairs to the manager's apartment. He opened the door, took one look at my face, and took off after me back downstairs.

"What happened here?" he gasped skidding into the apartment behind me, and I cried, "What do you think happened?"

I caught my breath, got a semblance of a grip on myself and muttered, "What does it look like? I want you to notify the police. Call New American Hospital and tell them I'm coming with her. And if that sonofabitch comes back here I want him arrested. Do you understand?"

He said yes, and touched my arm, "You look pretty badly shaken, can you drive?" he asked, and I nodded. I wasn't entrusting Philippa to anyone else but me just now.

I picked her up, her head rolled against my breast, and she whimpered, half conscious with pain. "I will kill him for this," I said through my teeth, squeezed my eyes shut and willed the tears to stop flowing. I eased Philippa into the front seat of the car, tilted the seat back, buckled her in, and sped for the hospital.

They were waiting for us. They lifted her out, told me where to park the car, and when I got inside a doctor was already with her.

"We've sent for a specialist. He should be here momentarily," a nurse said, and a ward clerk sat me down at her desk and began asking questions for the admission paperwork. A specialist? Why in the name of God did she need a specialist? What was wrong? I was totally distracted, and the fact that I hadn't brought any of Philippa's personal information with me was not helping matters. The private door at the far end of the Emergency Room came open, and a man hurried over to where Philippa was lying. Two minutes later the first doctor left. In a few moments, the nurse was back at my side. Maybe it was the look on my face, more likely it was the expensive car and clothes, I don't know, but the nurse took me to be with Phipps rather than making sure I could pay the bill.

"We'll get the admit information we need later," she said.

The doctor nodded toward a stool at the head of the gurney and I sat down. It was a wobbly landing and I realized that I was shaking all over. Even my knees were knocking. "Good evening, Mister Aarons. I'm Dale Layman," he said with hardly a glance my way, and went back to his examination. He was a big, powerful man who looked more like a football player than a doctor, and he was too young for me to want to trust him.

Philippa wasn't moving, and then, suddenly, she was. Her eyes came open and she gasped for air and cried, "Where am I?" By then Layman had his arm across her chest and she could see me out of the corner of her eye.

"It's all right," I soothed, "We're going to get you some help. It's okay, Phipps. I'm right here."

"I want to go home!" she cried. Her lips began to bleed, and I could see the absolute panic in her eyes. She gagged then, and vomited from shock.

Layman guided her head to one side, and her nose began to bleed again, and I felt tears running down my face. I was going to lose my girl. She was going to choke. She was going to bleed to death, I just knew it.

Through my tears I hushed her and soothed her and kissed her hair, keeping out of her range of vision so she couldn't see my panic stricken face. Layman stuck a needle in her, and pretty soon she whimpered off to a restless sleep. He ordered X-rays of her arm, her skull, her jaw, her neck. A technician wheeled her away, a nurse beside him, and Layman turned to me. He threw me a moist towel and said, "Your hands are bloody. Did you do this?"

I guess the shocked look was answer enough for the moment. "Come into my office, please," he said, and I dropped the towel and followed him down the hall. He offered me an overstuffed chair, turned briefly to the computer on his desk and then said, "I feel like I already know you. I remember that great TV series you did a couple years back, and you were the dirty dog that owned the town, and the saloon, and you'd come in and sit down on the farthest stool at the bar, and the bartender would say, 'Well, Boss, has it been a single shot day, or a double shot day?'"

He got up and walked to a piece of furniture on the west wall that looked more like a wet bar than a medicine locker. "Today," he said, setting a small tablet and a paper cup of water in front of me, "looks like it's been a double shot day. Here, take this. It'll have about the same effect, and it won't interact with your knee medication."

I thanked him and did as I was told. "I hope you don't think you know me because of the character of Nathan Strauss," I said warily. "He's not somebody I'd care to share a reputation with."

"He always came through in a pinch, though. Underneath it all, he was one of the good guys."

"Way underneath," I muttered. Then I sat back, and allowed him to contemplate me. I wanted to shake him until he told me about Philippa.

"Let me see your hands," he said at last, and I held them out, turned them over, and brought them back. They still had traces of blood around the nails.

"I did not hit her," I said. "I've never really hit anybody in my adult life except once, and that was in self-defense."

"Of course not. I just wanted to see if you were still shaking. I see that you are, but not so badly. Would you like to wash your hands?"

"Literally or figuratively?"

"Literally," he chuckled, "though it may be hard to separate the two."

He showed me into a bathroom adjoining his office, and I gave my hands a good scrubbing. It made me think of Lady Macbeth, and of Pilate. Nothing could sweeten this feeling. Nothing in my experience could allow me to wash my hands of this good woman's blood. I returned to my chair, and Layman gave me a moment to get comfortable.

"Any idea what happened this afternoon?" he asked.

"You mean, why it happened, don't you? It's obvious what. The mud sucking sonofabitch hit her. As big as he is, he hit her."

"Size has nothing to do with it. Logic has nothing to do with it. Remember beating your fists against your dad's belt buckle when you were little? Ever kicked a lawn mower? These things are done without logic."

I just shook my head. I was exhausted, and I was scared witless. "Is she badly hurt?" That was all I wanted to know.

"I don't know yet. I would say so. If not physically, then mentally and emotionally. Her wrist is obviously broken. Her teeth seem fine, and her jaw, I think, is okay. The bruises on the temple and forehead concern me. But we'll just have to wait to get that information. Her apartment manager said her name is Philippa Tyler, that she'd been beaten, and that you were bringing her in. That's all I know. What's your connection?"

Even in my state of disrepair his line about 'that's all I know,' seemed a little innocent, but I was too rattled to challenge him. "I work with her. She's a novelist, P.K. Tyler. We've been writing a screenplay together, acting in a film together. And, then, I'm in love with her, for whatever that's worth."

"That's obvious, Mr. Aarons. It's been obvious to the media for weeks. You think you know who did this?"

"Her husband, I would assume," I snapped, wondering why he was asking me what he already seemed to know.

"So, you're in love with a married woman. Do you suppose you caused this?"

I just shook my head. God, I wanted a cigarette. "I don't know. Truly, honestly, I don't know. I haven't been sleeping with her, except on film, of course, or actively trying to steal her away, if that's what you mean."

"I'm not trying to imply anything, Peter. May I call you Peter?"

"Of course." I didn't add, you can call me any damned thing you want, if you'll tell me what I want to know. "I'm having a hell of a time reasoning right now. I'm ... numb inside."

"You're the victim of a beating," he said. "You have the right to feel numb. You also have a possible need to feel responsible, if not for what has happened, then for what is to happen. That's a heavy load, and I'm here to help you shift it around to where you can carry it."

I sat in silence and contemplated the smears of blood on my favorite grey sweater. Philippa's blood. Not happy blood, like childbirth blood, or having an accident while having fun blood. Violent blood. I realized my body was quivering deep inside, like I was chilled, and that my teeth were still chattering slightly. I wondered if I was cold, because I really couldn't tell.

I pried my jaws open and said, rather too sarcastically, "Not your average ER meat cutter, I assume?"

"Not your average Emergency Room," he said, tipping his head in acknowledgment. "But then you know that, having been admitted here yourself once upon a time."

I flinched. He ignored me. "We're very exclusive, very expensive. I do one thing, Peter. One thing only. I treat and then counsel people involved in cases just like this. You'd be horrified to know who I see come in here all beat to hell, or shot, or stabbed or whatever."

"Would I? Don't forget, I live and work out there, Doctor. I see the pressures, and the drugs, and life in the fast lane in general. But Philippa Tyler is different."

"How so?"

"No booze, no drugs, no bed hopping, no clawing her way to the top.

She writes, makes another pot of coffee, goes to choir practice, writes some more. She's so unaffected by most things. She's shy, she's simple. As far as I can tell, her biggest sin is drinking too much diet Snapple. She's ... aw, hell, I don't know how to explain her. She does not deserve this."

"Does anybody?"

"I don't know. Do they?"

"You're honest. I like that. Do you think this has happened before?"

I nodded. I really didn't want to wade into this. I wanted to see Philippa. I wanted to see her breathe.

"Why?"

"Why what?"

There was a pause. "You won an Emmy for playing Nathan Strauss, didn't you?"

I wondered why in the hell he'd ask me such a thing, veer off subject like that, and I know it crossed my face, because he smiled ever so slightly. "I did, yes. Why?"

"Because most award winning actors can focus under stress," he shrugged.

"Just ask me what you want to ask me," I growled.

"Why do you think this has happened before," he asked patiently.

"She said ... he doesn't mean to do this sort of thing. Implying, to me at least, a precedent has been set."

"When did she say this?"

"Tonight," I sighed. "If I'd known sooner, I could have done something to prevent it."

"Like what?"

"Believe me, young man, I'd have thought of something. Perhaps not honorable, but effective."

"And what will you do now?"

"Exactly the same thing."

"Who do you love more, Philippa, or her husband?"

I just looked at him and said nothing. It was a trap.

"Take my advice, concentrate on the person you love. She's the one who's messed up in the head. If she wasn't she wouldn't stay with him. Tell me, is she overly submissive?"

"I'm not around the two of them that much. She's eager to please him, I know that."

"How eager?"

"Pathetically eager. But then you're asking the wrong man. She isn't submissive with me. With me she stands on her hind legs and gives as good as she gets. We're ... a team."

"What else did she say tonight?"

"Nothing," I said. I could feel myself turning to jelly and began to wonder what the hell was in that pill. I ground my teeth and sat up straight and willed myself not to fall on the floor. "Oh, except that this was her fault. She knows he can't handle an argument." I paused and thought as best I could, knowing that Layman was trying to help someone I loved. "And ... I had a script with me that I was bringing by for tomorrow's shoot. She told me just to leave it and she'd look at it later ... as though ... she expected me to leave her like that."

"She was merely giving you the option of not becoming involved, Peter. A very decent thing to do under the circumstances, don't you think?"

"Philippa Tyler is a very decent person," I said, and the tears burned in my eyes. "Damn. Philippa Tyler is a decent, kind, loving person, and she's lying out there hurt, scared to death ...." The tears ran down my cheeks and I just gave up. I was going to weep the rest of my life. My elbows thudded onto the arms of the chair, my mouth against my folded hands, and I sagged in despair.

"I don't suppose I could convince you to go home and eat dinner and get a good night's sleep, could I?" he asked gently.

"Not a chance," I said, raising my head, "But the sweet lady who provides me with such things ... who told me ... aw, God, she did, didn't she? She told me to watch Frank Tyler. Just to have her here, even if she's chewing my ass, would do me a world of good."

"Call her," Layman said, "and then come on out. Mrs. Tyler's back from radiology."

I nodded. He left. I dialed home and Glory answered on the third ring. "Hi," I said, and it was all I had to say.

"Aloysha, honey, where are you and what's wrong?" she said in alarm. "You hurt?"

"At New American. I'm okay, but Frank Tyler ..." I choked. "Aw, Glory, why didn't I listen to you?"

"Is she bad?"

"I don't know yet."

"I be right there," she said. "You just set tight, Love." and she hung up.

Phipps looked so pretty lying there. I know that sounds crazy and I'm sure I was at that point, but they'd taken the pins out of her hair in radiology, and it was loose around her face, and her fair skin was almost transparent. Her face was distorted by her broken lips and the ugly welt that seemed to be spreading down one side of her temple across her cheek and jaw. The eye with the scratches under it was swelling, but at least I could tell it was her, and that she was alive. She rolled her head toward me, and opened her sleepy eyes and smiled just a bit. "Hi," she whispered and reached for my hand. "You look like hell."

"Hi," I whispered back. I took her left hand and held it against my lips for a long while, then against my breast and sat rubbing her forearm and watching her drift in and out of slumber.

Layman set her wrist, a simple fracture. Her skull, "Like a damned rock. Woman's got a head like a rock. Bet she's stubborn."

"You bet. No damage?"

"Oh, plenty. There's a pretty good concussion, and she has some deep bruises on her shoulders and arms and shins. Her neck is going to be stiff as hell. We'll keep her a couple days ..."

The blue eyes came open and Phipps gasped, "No! I want to go home."

"I'm not going to leave you," I said. "I'll be right here. Glory's on her way ..."

"No! I want to go home!"

"Why?" Layman asked, gesturing at me to shut up. "Why do you want to go home?"

"I just do."

"Not good enough. Why?"

"Peter?"

Again Layman's gesture, and I bit my tongue and rubbed her arm in silence.

"Why do you want to go home, Philippa?"

I could see her eyes change shape. He was making her mad. Her pulse was going like crazy in the wrist I was holding against me. "I just do," she said through her teeth. "Bud, please, I just want to go home. Please take me home."

"Phipps, Sweet Face ..."

"I'll pitch your ass outta here, Aarons," Layman warned, and I was silent.

"You answer me, Philippa. Give me one good reason why you want to go home and I'll let you go. I promise."

"I just ... don't want Frank to see a bill for this. I've made him so mad already."

What the hell was she thinking? She had insurance. She had her own money. I felt my jaw come open to say so, and then shut again with only a growl having escaped.

"I can see that. There won't be any bill for him to see. You can stay." Philippa jerked her head away from him, looking at me. Talking to me.

"He didn't ... see a bill for the cars ... but I spent the money without asking."

"This is about the cars?" I gasped, ignoring Layman. "He did this to you over those goddamned cars? I'm going to kill him."

"I don't know. I don't know why he did it. I want to go home."

I looked in those frightened eyes – weeping, pleading with me – and did something terribly, terribly hard. I told her, "No. You're hurt, and I'm really scared. Please stay here, for my sake if not your own. I'll stay right here with you, and I'll straighten the whole thing out with Frank, I promise."

I wasn't sure just how I was going to do that, since what she'd told Layman didn't make a lick of sense, but I would have said anything at that point to keep her safe. "Please, Phipps, just for tonight. I'll sit right beside you and hold your hand."

Then, drifting, she agreed. She was too tired to argue. They parked me in a waiting room with one of those terse "Sit. Stay," commands you get in hospitals, and that's where Glory found me.

"You, are such a fool," she said, and caught me close in her strong arms, murmuring, "dafa, dafa, dafa..."

"Don't call me dafa dafa ... I'm definitely a fool, but I'm not fat," I managed, and, even as tired and empty of tears as I already felt, I began to weep.

She kissed me and wept with me until the need to do so was gone. Then, finally, I felt better. Most of it, I know was Glory's sturdy presence, but I did feel more able to cope with whatever was to come. I splashed some water on my face, grabbed Glory's hand, and they let us in to see Philippa.

She was still asleep, too small, too pale in the white sheeted bed. We sat awhile, just looking at her, and then Glory said, "Go home, Buddy. You can't do nothin' here but just sog in that chair and be miserable."

"I promised I'd stay, Glory."

"You stayin', Boy. I'm here. I'm the same as bein' you. She rather wake up and see me, anyway, count on it. You go on home. You dinner's in the microwave. Just give it a coupla minutes on medium high. Relax. Go to sleep. Be back early so's I can go home. Go on."

"Glory ..."

"This discussion's over. Hi them long legs outta here, Boy. I mean it."

I went, not so much because I was intimidated as because what she said made sense. Maybe Phil would rather see Glory than me. Hopefully, it wouldn't be a permanent condition. God, I should have done something to protect her. What must she think of me? I should have done something. I was so big, and she was so little, and somehow ... maybe ... I had let this happen to her. I kissed Glory, and then I kissed Phipps, and whispered that I was sorry for not being there for her, and found my way out of the hospital and into a cab.

I choked on dinner, threw Philippa's blue tank suit across the downstairs bathroom, bloodied my left fist against the stonework on the fireplace, and collapsed on the sofa. I knew one thing for damned sure ... but I couldn't remember what it was.

Before dawn I crawled off the couch, shivering and stiff, and went into the bathroom to put on some swim trunks. When I pulled my sweater over my head I could smell Philippa's fragrance, and I could smell Philippa's blood over the smell of the cologne and the wool, and just for a moment, I thought I was going to be very sick. I left the sweater inside out in the clothes hamper, and I never saw it again. A week later, one that was nearly, not quite identical, appeared in my cedar closet. Glory and I never discussed it.

I went and sat in the spa until I warmed up and loosened up, then skipped rope until my knee dumped me, and dragged myself into the shower.

By then I was beginning to wake up for the first time since I'd found Philippa. The shock and the numbness were ebbing. Anger had set in. Not rage, luckily, but a fairly keen edge, nonetheless. I called Tommy at home and told him what had happened, asked him to shut her down or shoot around us, grabbed an apple, threw my pack of cigarettes in the garbage one last time, and got Rafael to drive me back to the hospital.

I found Dale Layman sitting in the hall outside Philippa's room. "Waiting for a bus, or what?" I asked.

"I upset Mrs. Tyler," he shook an accusing finger toward the door, "and that ... linebacker, that Rottweiler you left on guard in there .... Peter, you said she was a sweet lady. That is no lady. She threw me out," he said, and glared at me as I sucked on a smirk. "You, ah, wouldn't care to sell her, would you?"

I jumped in spite of myself. I just was not used to such terms. I could see Layman smirking in retaliation, and quickly recovered. "Sell? Not hardly. She's a free agent."

"Make a helluva clinical psychologist out of that woman, provided she could be sufficiently tamed and trained."

"Got a thing against large, assertive women, do you?"

Dale ignored me. "Is she a nurse by any chance?"

"It's the dress, isn't it? She always wears that white dress when she's on the job, or a yellow one. Has for twenty-five years. Well, not that same dress, of course, but ones like it, you know. Sometimes they're navy blue. I'm not sure why, either. I certainly don't care what she wears. Maybe it's something she worked out with my grandmother. All I know is it makes her look bigger and more formidable, and I cross her as little as possible, because she could take her fist and drive me like a nail. She has a whole bunch of aprons that go with the dresses, though. All different colors and prints. Kind of softens the look."

"I'm asking you a serious question here, Aarons."

I blinked at him. "Sorry. Which was ...?"

"Is she a nurse?"

"Yes," I nodded, "She's an LVN, why?"

"She's very good. Why is she just a housekeeper?"

"Just?" I exclaimed, "Just? The woman manages my household, oversees the offsite cleaning staff, makes most of the budgeting decisions, keeps me in food and new underwear. Without Glory I would be naked and helpless. Well, I've always been helpless, but I'd be naked, too. Anyway, I broke my back and crushed my right knee in a riding accident a few years ago, and Glory took a couple nursing courses, just so she could help out. She liked it. She finished. She uses it occasionally through her church, and occasionally on me, but basically, she's one of the dearest friends I've ever had."

"Lucky man. You look much better this morning, Peter."

"Thanks. I'll feel much better when I know how my girl is."

"Very stiff. Very, very sore. Very subdued. She really doesn't want to be here. She really does hate hospitals. She won't touch a thing we've tried to feed her," he gestured with his chin, "and what's her name ..."

"Gloriosa Daisy Ruiz."

Layman's face creased into a smile. "Mrs. Ruiz is backing her up."

"I can take both those problems off your hands. I can take them both home."

He shook his head. "I dunno. If Tyler comes back and pops her again, he'll kill her, or worse. I don't want her in a vulnerable position. Would you take her to her house, or yours?"

"I'm pretty sure Frank Tyler is long gone," I said, "but I'd definitely take Philippa to my house. Glory's there, and I guarantee you, Frank Tyler won't be." I reached for a cigarette, even though I knew I couldn't smoke in a hospital, and cursed myself for being momentarily strong when my pocket came up empty. "Anyway, Phipps spends a lot of time with us. I think she'd be fine."

"On a couple of conditions," he said. "Just, love her, cuddle her, coddle her, comfort her, spoil her rotten, but do not, do not try to push her into divorcing Frank."

"Me?" I blinked.

"Bullshit. I can see it in your coal black eyes, Aarons. He's pushed you over the edge, which is likely to make you think the rules have suddenly changed. Don't drag her with you. She's not strong enough to take the fall. I am telling you what I told you last night. She is seriously injured. She's in superb condition, or she'd likely be dead. Just love her, to whatever extent she wants you to. Promise?"

"So far," I muttered. Well, hell yes I agreed. How could I not agree when we were talking about somebody's life? The fact that he could read me like the morning paper was a little disconcerting.

"Number two, she comes in for counseling, you come in for counseling. Separately, and together."

"I could sure use it," I sighed. "I need some help working through this. Phipps, can be pretty stubborn, as you've seen."

"And you outweigh her by how much? Seventy-five, eighty pounds? Philippa can be carried. Philippa can be dragged kicking and screaming, but Philippa comes because Philippa is screwed up in the head. Philippa comes. Promise?"

"On exactly those terms, yes. But don't berate me at some future time for, as you put it, not loving and coddling her. She doesn't always need loving and coddling. She needs to be put in her place once in a while or she'll go over top of you in hobnailed boots. I've had her try it."

"Then you know something very important, don't you?" Layman said quietly. "You know she can be argued with, and made to see another's position, and persuaded to reassume her own, without being hit."

"I'm sane," I muttered. "That helps."

"Well, prepare yourself for the fact that she might not be right now. Let's go see her. I'll use you as a shield against ... what's her name again?"

"Mrs. Ruiz," I snickered, and we went on in.

Glory had pulled in her claws and Philippa was drowsing. She looked ten years old lying there, or a hundred, I'm not sure which, but she looked frighteningly frail. The bruises were worse on her arms and face. Suddenly, I didn't want to take her home. I was scared. Her eyes flickered open at the sound of my voice, and the hand she could move inched across the bed for mine as I sat beside her.

"Hi," she whispered.

"Hi. You about ready to go? We're late for work," I teased, kissing her hand, trying to picture just the right wedding ring for those slim fingers as I kissed each one in turn. I'd berate myself later, I promised; right now I desperately needed hope. "Or would you rather bag it for the day and go riding?"

"Mmmmm, tough choice," she said, and her lips would hardly move.

"Doctor Layman says if you're a very good girl I can take you home with me."

"When?" Her eyes brightened just a little.

"Today, I think. But if you'd rather, you can stay here and rest a day or two yet. It might be best."

"You, are no comedian," she muttered, and Layman chuckled from the foot of the bed.

"But he loves you, Philippa Tyler, and I want you to behave for him. You've both had a bad scare. I want you to rest and take care of each other. Promise?"

Phipps tried to smile, winced, and her hand tightened over mine.

"Um hm," she said softly.

"He's had to make some hard promises to spring you from here. Don't make him look bad by not cooperating. Take your medicine, complete bed rest, and eat what you can. Let Peter and Mrs. Ruiz, take care of you. The first day you're up for it, I want you in my office."

She nodded sleepily, "Um hm."

"Aarons, is she lying to me to get out of here?"

"She probably would," I said, "but I'm not. We've agreed on a price, and I'll honor it. When do I get the merchandise?"

"When can you be ready?"

"Right now," I said, and gave Phil's hand a gentle squeeze.

"Give me until ten O'clock," he said, and I agreed.

Phipps said she'd be fine alone for a bit and promptly went back to sleep. Glory left for home and I drove over to Philippa's apartment. It was hard for me, going in there. It frightened me, and made my blood boil, and generally gave me the creeps.

I straightened the coffee table back up and stood in the middle of the room trying to imagine, based on the various maniacs I'd played, how I would go about grabbing someone no bigger than a sixth grader by the front of her blouse, and hitting her with the flat of my hand. That's what Layman had said made contact with Philippa's face. I turned my left palm up, and contemplated the size of it. At what point would I wrap my hand around her arm, using her own body weight to snap her wrist, and fling her into the heavy oak coffee table? At what point would I leave? Before, or after I'd established that she was still alive.

The bed, hadn't been used. Not until I'd jerked the little green blanket off the end of it, had it even been disturbed. I looked around, wondering what to take that would cheer Philippa - what to take for her to wear. She slept in a terrycloth hair tie, or so she said. Couldn't abide nightgowns, barely tolerated pajamas. She wouldn't be able to manage buttons or snaps or zippers without help. Glory should be here, I decided, not me. I ended up taking the luggage out of the closet, putting everything out of the drawers into the suitcases, and declaring it a victory. I needed to get back to the hospital.

I met the manager as I was going out. He asked how Philippa was, and when she would be back. I told him that, with time enough and care enough, she would be well. I also told him she wouldn't be back, and wrote him a check for the balance of the lease. Someone would be around to deal with her things.

When they were getting her ready to go with me, and I realized that she could barely stand, couldn't walk at all, could barely move her poor arms to let them put her robe on her, I got scared again. She didn't seem really conscious, either. What kind of a mistake was I making with this most precious of friends? Who was I kidding into thinking I could take better care of her than a hospital? How fair was all of this to Glory, who already had a full schedule and then some?

Layman saw it in my face and walked with me as Philippa was being discreetly wheeled out the back door to where I'd parked the car. "Don't worry," he said, patting my shoulder, "She's not as fragile as she looks. She's sore, she's bruised, she's in shock, but she's not really breakable. I wouldn't let her go with you if she was. Just stay right with her, and don't let her fall. That's her biggest risk right now ... outside of going back to Frank Tyler," he added, sotto voce.

Those words were like a cold knife in the gut. "She can't," I said quietly. "I flat won't let her. I don't care whose wife she is."

"Remember you said that," he smiled. "Peter, she's wife, not chattel. She can't be kept, she can't be traded, by Frank, or by you. Philippa needs to belong to Philippa, and until she can break free of the fear that holds her so rigidly in place, she can't take true ownership of herself. You own yourself, free and clear. I know you've done a good job of modeling how it's done. Don't spoil that now."

I put her in the car, and as I had done just the day before, I tipped the seat back, buckled her in, and drove very carefully. I wondered if I'd done what was best for her, but as I carried her through the kitchen I could hear her sniff at the freshly baked bread, and as we started up the graceful, floating staircase, she sighed and snuggled against my shoulder like a child after a hard day.

I took her into the big, sunny bedroom that had been mine since Gram died and Megan left, eased her robe off and carefully straightened the PJ's they'd stuffed her into. She had bruises on her arms, collarbones, and ribcage, her thighs, her shins. No wonder she whimpered as she breathed, poor baby. I tucked her into Gram's huge old four poster bed with lots of pillows and her fuzzy green blanket for company, and then sat beside her, looking at her battered features, and the cast on her wrist, and wondering again if I was in some way responsible for this.

It's a terrible thing to admit, I know, but I was grateful this wasn't the first time it had happened. It had happened before she knew me, which gave me some hope that I wasn't the third side of a love triangle. Not that Frank loved her, psychotic fucker that he was. She shifted a little against the pillows, her eyes came open, and she gave me just the hint of a smile.

"Don't worry," she whispered.

"I'm just ... I feel so bad that I didn't make sure you were safe, Phipps."

"Not your job," she murmured, and drifted back to sleep.

"It is now," I said quietly, and kissed her forehead before going downstairs to find a bite to eat.

That afternoon, while I sat with Philippa, Rafael and Glory called the furniture rental place, packed everything else up, put it in Philippa's big Ford, and brought it out to the house. As far as I was concerned, Philippa Tyler was home. With us.

CHAPTER EIGHT

I don't think he'd have called at all except that I had Philippa's number forwarded to mine, and her number rings on my phone."

"What did he say?"

"He asked if Phil was there."

"And?"

"I said no. I told him she was in the hospital. She wasn't of course, but it was an easy lie. Better than I had on that last hole, by the way, and it's your shot."

"What did he say when you told him she was in the hospital? Did he ask which one?"

"No. He asked ... what had happened," I said in wonderment. "I couldn't believe it."

"Denial," Layman said, teeing up his ball. "Frightening, isn't it?" He eyed the fairway, sliced at the ball, and picked up his shattered tee. "So what did you tell him?"

I shook my head, dropped the piece of straw I was chewing, and stepped up to the tee. "I told him, very calmly, because I figured at that point he was a madman, that she'd been beaten. She had a concussion, and a broken wrist." I picked a spot in the general direction of the flag stick and swung at it. "And then I asked him if he really didn't know what he'd done. Didn't yell, didn't threaten, I just asked … firmly."

"Good shot. Awfully flat swing."

"Bad knee. No lateral flex in it."

"So what did he say?"

"Nothing. He just hung up. Not abruptly, but after a bit, and quietly. I actually felt a little sorry for him."

"Very noble."

"Dale, give it a rest," I said, shouldering my clubs and falling into step with him. "How's Philippa?"

"You live with her," he grinned, and I hiked an eyebrow in his direction.

"I answer your asinine questions, young man. You could at least answer mine. Why is she having trouble keeping anything on her stomach?"

"That whack on the head. It'll pass with time. I did some more imaging, and ran a CAT scan. I can't see any physical damage. The woman's as strong as an ox. Physically, she looks great. If you told me that a week ago she was lying in a hospital bed beaten unconscious, I wouldn't believe it. How is she at home?"

"Stronger. Better," I smiled, but it was a weak smile, and we walked awhile in silence. "She's just so quiet all the time, like she's far away. But she is stronger. Those first three or four days, when I had to sit her up, and carry her to the bathroom, and she just laid in bed and held my hand and looked through me, I was damned scared."

"You still are, aren't you, Bud?"

"Um hm. I think you're wasting your time looking for your ball on the fairway. Try the right rough just west of that oak tree. Has anybody told you that the object of this game is to keep track of the ball?"

"Yes, thanks. Does she push you away at all, or seem to resent you?"

"No."

"I'm wondering, if maybe the only tenderness she ever got from Frank was after he beat her. She put up with it just for ...aha, there you are my little beauty ... she put up with it for the attention."

"Sounds pretty immature. Besides, he hit her and left, Dale. A body'd be pretty damned stiff in four days. I think personally that she's afraid of committing a sin by divorcing Frank."

"He's her second husband. Why didn't she go through this with hubby number one? Where is he, by the way?"

"Dead. He was killed in a motorcycle accident. Anyway, Maybe Frank's the ultimate penance, visited on her by God for some sin we aren't privy to."

"Could be. Say, you're good at this. What was your major in school?"

"Screwing around."

"Bachelor's or Master's?"

"Both. Seriously, I have a double Bachelor's in Acting and Piano Composition, and a double Masters in Piano and Theater Arts, all from UCLA."

"The working man's school," Dale snickered.

"And a Doctorate in Playin' Piano Real Good, from Juilliard," I added, piqued by his comment, "The playing man's school."

Dale whistled. "I'm impressed. But not even a minor in Psychology?"

"Acting is psychology. Music is psychology. It's helped me a great deal."

"Good," Layman sighed. "We'll need it. Philippa may not resent you, but she resents hell out of me."

"I got that feeling," I grinned, sizing up Dale's next shot.

"Thanks. She's mentioned me, has she?"

"Oh yes. Bear in mind, you're just seeing her for medical reasons right now. She resents you because you frighten her, and she hates being frightened. She'll talk to you. Eventually. Maybe."

"Swell. You getting enough sleep?"

"I'm getting some right now," I growled. "If I'd known golf with you would turn into four hours on the couch, I'd have said no. Shut up and hit the ball, Layman. I promised I'd be home for lunch."

"Phil is trying to eat, isn't she? I mean, the vomiting is a once in a while thing, you said."

"Yeah. She eats, mostly with a fondue fork. Little chunks of steak and cream cheese, though Glory baked her some bread with Soya flour and no yeast. She seems to like that. No meals yet, but, oddly enough, she's eating a little fruit these days. Strawberries, kiwis, even an occasional banana."

"Mmmmm, call me," Layman sighed. "I'd love to watch." He glanced quickly my direction, cleared his throat, and applied himself to his game. "Just wanted to see how you'd react. I am her doctor, after all."

Though I resented it, Dale had merely observed the inescapable. I couldn't fault him for that. Philippa was far sexier now than she'd ever been, her voice just above a whisper, her eyes sleepy and introverted, her manner languid and her mind, very slow. She was a creature of the body – of wondrous curves and limber joints – who was content to purr in my arms and rub her head against my shoulder. She was a sleepy baby, a very, very desirable, sleepy baby. One that Frank Tyler could easily have handled. That was my theory as far as what Frank was thinking.

We got around to it on the back nine. Dale, agreed, with reservations. He did think that if Philippa was doing penance, she might well think a little physical punishment was in order, and Frank was glad to comply. That, gave me the creeps. He was trying to figure out Philippa, of course, and I was working on Frank. He did agree, absolutely, that Phil was very sexy and very pliable, and because he didn't know her when she was otherwise, he wasn't nearly as worried as I was. He did ask me if I was going to take advantage of it. I told him hell yes, I was. I'd already done so half a dozen times. When she finally came back into herself she'd never know the difference, so what was the harm? I was tired of having him tell me I was noble.

Late that afternoon Philippa drowsed in the spa, her left hand on my chest, her casted wrist on the deck behind my head, resting in my arms, drawing strength from me. Not for anything would I have betrayed that trust. That trust was my foundation. From that trust I had to build any relationship I ever hoped to have with her. It was worth the occasional pain and frustration.

Even so, even so ... as I shifted her slight weight across my lap and her head rolled back and her lips moved toward mine, I found myself kissing her, really kissing her, and she was more awake than her eyes had indicated.

I raised my head and smiled at her, lying there in the crook of my arm, and she smiled back, and her left hand caressed my cheek.

"Is this where I say I'm sorry?" I asked, turning to kiss the side of her hand as she traced my jaw line. "If it is, I am. If it isn't, I'm not."

"I'm very much in love with you," she whispered, and I kissed her again – several times – before I came up for a breath of air and cleared my head a little.

"Philippa, I cannot do this," I said, and she smiled her languid, slightly swollen smile.

"I probably look pretty awful, hm?"

"Not the reason at all," I responded, catching her hand and kissing it.

"Are you worried about Frank?"

"Piss on Frank. I'd screw Frank over in a New York minute. I can't do it to you, Sweet Face. I feel like I'm taking advantage of you."

"I'm a big girl."

"Right now you're a big, loosely wrapped girl, you are. When keen eyed, keen witted Philippa Tyler stands square in my face, convinces me she's got this all worked out, and says 'kiss me, you fool', she'd better look out. But you, are in no danger from me."

"Funny," she said softly, thoughtfully. "This is the part of my personality that I never get any complaints about. Sometimes I forget it's there, and then it just ... appears, somehow. For months, I've wanted to ask you to make love to me, and I've never quite been able to. Now, I could, and I know you won't. How do I react to that?"

"Phipps, is that you in there?" I asked, really looking at her. "You sound a little sharper all of a sudden."

"I was just enjoying the rest," she sighed. "Frank drove me so hard. Philippa, drives me so hard. You are so easy on me. I was just resting. Recharging my batteries. I'm sorry if you thought my mind was gone."

I sighed a great sigh and began to laugh. "Thank God! Oh, thank God! Philippa, don't ever do that to me again. I really thought the bastard had scrambled your brains."

"Oh, he did," she sighed, and laid her weary head back against my chest.

"I was also afraid, he'd scrambled your sense of morality – the morality that's right for you, Phipps, not for me. The only thing I want more than making love to you is having you be comfortable with our decision to do so."

"And if I said I was? That I'd let you make love to me right now?"

"Phipps, this isn't a one shot deal, here. I want you for the rest of my life, sex or no sex. I want you to be my ...uh …" I mumbled to a halt, but the damage was done. The promise was broken. "Well, hell." I muttered under my breath. "Just … forget I said anything. Phipps, we shouldn't talk about this right now. Not until you feel really well."

"Oh, sure," she chuckled, and her fingers traced the side of my face. "I thought you were acting a little funny. Layman told me he'd made you promise not to push me before he'd let me leave the hospital with you. That is what this is about, isn't it?"

"I promised I wouldn't push you into divorcing Frank. And I'm sorry, Philippa, I honest to God didn't mean to bring it up, but when I think of sex with you, I think of marriage. Layman knows I'm angry enough to go after Frank with both barrels. He was just trying to protect both you and me. Don't you worry about anything, just focus on getting better."

"Are you going to? Go after Frank, that is."

I thought about that for a few moments. "I don't know anymore. I want him out of our lives, but the thought of going after him, personally, on some level or another ...."

"It isn't easy, is it?" she asked quietly. "I told you, he's wounded, and he's alone inside himself. Once you see that, you can't help feeling pity for him."

"You're right, of course," I lied. I'd have more pity for a rattlesnake than I would for that bastard. Still, saying I didn't want to get my hands dirty didn't sound very heroic. "I guess, eventually, I'll ask what you want me to do. What we should do."

"Eventually?"

"Do you have an opinion so close to the act? I mean, a sane opinion?

I'm not sure I do."

"You've lived with it a week, I've lived with it for ten or twelve years. I think, that's when he actually started hitting me, and not just throwing things past me, or at me. But always, almost from the first, he hit me with his coldness and his indifference. At that point, I believed I could love him enough to change him, to warm him. I guess my last hope was that he'd finally fall in love with me if I was successful and brought in lots of money. Obviously, I was wrong there, too."

She sighed, and shifted, and sat up a little straighter, so she was talking to my face rather than to my chest. "You and I argue, and while we argue you're asking me what I think, and why I'm reacting in such a manner, and I'm doing the same for you, even though we're angry. Frank, hates and turns away, or hates and explodes and then turns away. I can't explain it, exactly."

"Why, Philippa? Why do you stay with such a person? Surely you can't force God to take the blame for Frank's actions, and you sure as hell can't still be thinking you'll change him. Frank is afflicted by an evil spirit. I saw it in his eyes, and it chilled me to the bone. Frank Tyler is not sane, Philippa."

She nodded and I tightened my arms around her, holding her closely, securely against me. "I know, but I had nowhere to run, until now," she admitted, and looked away in shame. "My mom and dad were drinking too much and fighting too much, and when my first husband died I was told ... there was no place for me back there with them. I'd already started college here, and I decided I was going to finish, come hell or high water.

"I made it. Got through school on loans and scholarships, had some nice boyfriends and a few laughs, before I met Frank. I had two little girls who needed financial security, and I wasn't really trained to do anything but write, or act, and I didn't have time for those particular indulgences. I was working three jobs, and Frank was shy and attractive, and had the promise of a good career, and he and Kelly loved each other almost instantly." She shrugged, and I could see that moving her shoulders was still painful for her.

"I guess I'm admitting I was lazy and spineless, and being hit and demoralized from time to time was the rate of exchange for my laziness. But, you know ... I grew up being hit and demoralized. It was a way of life, Peter, and it has taken a long time to realize that it isn't the way things are supposed to be for me ... or for anybody else. What I thought was real life, isn't real life at all. Real life is the way I raised my girls, to be strong, and self-confident and unhurt."

She looked up at me, and I nodded. There was nothing I could say, even if I'd wanted to. She swallowed hard and went on, and though I could see it was sucking the strength out of her, I let her speak. These were words I needed to hear, and she needed to voice.

"He was not, and is not, all bad. He adores the girls. And, you know ... there were times ... when he would laugh and those eyes would light up and I could bring myself to hope."

She choked, and wept then, just for a minute, and I let her. It's hard to say goodbye to someone you've loved, and, with rising, totally inappropriate elation, I realized that's what she was doing. I bent and kissed her temple, and it was fever hot against my lips. Her whole face was flushed, and I began to worry. She laid her head back against my collarbone as though it was too heavy to hold up any longer, and went on speaking softly.

"He had that affair, and things got worse. I knew he'd never cheat on me. I knew it. It was the one thing I'd stake my life on, and when that trust was gone, it was all gone. It was a lie. I prayed, I really did. I prayed that God would save my marriage. There was a terrible fear I can't describe. Maybe it was my pride. Maybe I just couldn't bear to lose my husband to a teenager."

I adjusted myself against the spa jets, and Philippa with me, and just looked at her in wonder, as one does at a baby, only I was wondering how anybody, anybody, could give up a woman like this one for a giggling, gum chewing nubile teenager. "Go on," I murmured.

"The Lord granted my prayer. Frank stayed, more or less. He bought the truck and left, but I was still married. Technically, my prayers were answered. Then, I realized, my prayers hadn't been answered on my terms. I had Frank, but I didn't have his love. I loved him so long and so hard and he never, ever loved me back. Finally, I had to let go of the love, and the hope, or go crazy. And all I had to do ... was loosen my grip, and it was gone. I resented him so much I couldn't even pray for him anymore, and then I felt guilty and I started running from God, and from myself, and hiding in books and rational, romantic characters who loved me as I loved them. Maybe I've been trying to be a good wife as an apology for not loving Frank anymore. Maybe I do love him. I don't know. I don't know much of anything right now."

"You did your best," I whispered, pulling her close against me. "Don't browbeat yourself, Phipps, just rest. Take time and sort things out. Dale Layman's a nice young man to talk to. Lousy golfer, but he's a good counselor."

"So are you," she smiled, "You haven't steered me wrong yet. I'll try talking to him. But there is one decision I have made."

"Hm?"

"Kiss me first, please?" she asked, putting her arm around my neck, and I did so, with more happiness than I can fathom, even now. Again I raised my head, and smiled, and waited for her.

"Being with you, knowing you, having the warmth of your emotion and your intellect and your love in my life, and for my life ... seeing what I can be as part of you, and how I can grow, has spoiled me for even trying anymore with Frank. It's not fair to him, or to me, or to you to take up any more of our lives with a lie." That hand, small and trembling, was tracing my cheek, my jaw line, the slope of my collar bone to my shoulder and back. Checking my reality against her decision. "I know there is no justification for my position, and there may be a very hot place waiting in hell for me ..." she paused, took a gulp of air that physically lifted her in the water and blurted, "I want a divorce! God, I said it! I said it out loud! I'm actually going to do this. I know it's not my place to divorce Frank. I want to anyway. I want to be free ... to be with someone who loves me and values me and helps me grow. I want to be with you! Please, I just want to be with you!" Then, she began to cry, really cry, as one does from relief after great pain. "I'm scared," she sobbed, "God, I'm so scared! Don't let go of me! Peter, don't let go of me, please!"

"Never," I whispered. "You'll always have me."

I hushed her, and kissed her, trying to quiet her before she made herself sick. I realized she was much too hot, got out of the spa and carried her into the house. Her whole body was wracked with sobs, and Glory looked up in alarm. I shook my head and went on upstairs and by the time we got to my room Phil had stopped sobbing. She was too tired to weep for long. I laid her on the bed and pulled her green fuzzy blanket over her, figuring her nylon tank suit wouldn't be wet enough to matter.

"I just ... want to go home," she murmured, and in a few moments she was asleep.

I went through the adjoining door into the room I was using for the moment – the one that had been mine nearly all my life – got dressed, and came back in to sit with her. The watery, afternoon sun was ebbing through the arching French doors, and beside those doors, where it had sat for as long as anyone could remember, was Gram's old rocking chair. She'd been a tall woman. Her chair fit me well. I sat rocking in it, admiring the deep purple bougainvillea which climbed beside the second story balcony, watching Philippa sleep, wondering where home was for her, would be for us. For ... us.

I leaned my head back and closed my eyes. I could feel my gram's strong arms, lifting me out of bed as she hushed my sobs. The war was far away. It couldn't reach me here in this new place. We were safe with my father now. And Gram. Then she'd carry me through that door, and sit with me in this rocker, and rock with me, and though my English was still very poor, I sensed her love for me, and the security of her arms, and I would wake up, and it would be morning in America.

"Live, Aloysha!" Gram would call to me, waving from the front door, and off I'd go. Even in college, and after, she'd call to me. Now, Glory did it sometimes in remembrance and we'd laugh, or cry, whichever seemed appropriate. We were tied together here, all of us, by old loves, old roots, anchoring us firmly, securely. This was my home.

Philippa, had none of that, and it broke my heart. Philippa, had lived with anger and frustration and blaming and hitting – with disrespect and rootlessness and fear and shame – from the time she was tiny right up until now. No wonder she was afraid to let go. Her grip was so tenuous, and she had no idea how far she'd fall. Apparently, a time or two, it had been quite a drop.

How did I know all this? Many sources. Bits from Phil herself, mostly in laughter. Bits from Kelly and Wen, whom I really needed to call. Mostly, from Jean Whiteside. The more I read of Jean, the more I studied Jean, the more I understood Philippa. When one is an actor one must have good recall, and I recalled Phil saying, "I write for therapy." I'd have to remember to give Layman a copy of the book.

I could feel myself drifting. I'd been sitting up at night with Philippa, sleeping lightly when I did sleep, and I was tired. There was a soft gold splash of sun on the side of Phil's bed closest to me. It beckoned, and I accepted. At some point, I put another cover over Philippa. Later yet, Glory's hand closed over my shoulder and she whispered, "Dinner, Buddy."

"You did it again," I laughed, joining her in the kitchen. "Caught me in bed with that woman. Glory, it smells wonderful in here!"

"What was that woman cryin' about? She scared me, sobbin' so, and her so frail yet."

"Phil has made the decision to divorce Frank."

"Then why you wearin' the loser's face?"

"It would be unkind to grin like a Cheshire cat, wouldn't it? Besides," I said, sitting at the breakfast bar, "I'm worried that she made the decision too fast."

"Boy," Glory said, putting my dinner in front of me, "When you make the decision to make a decision you have lots and lots of time to ponder. But even so, when you make the decision, you make it fast, otherwise, it's just another decision to make a decision."

I pulled my eyebrows together, and squeezed my eyes shut, and thought very hard, because Gloriosa Daisy Ruiz never said anything stupid.

"When you quit likin' my Burgoo, Boy?"

"Aw," I said, "Aw, I'm sorry! I didn't even thank you for dinner. It looks great, and I love your Burgoo, you know that. I plan to be embalmed in your Burgoo. It's your philosophy that has me going. I think I've tripped a circuit breaker."

"You tired. See it this way. You decide you need to go to the store. When does it get done, when you decide to go, or when you get off your butt and go?"

"Oh."

"You too thick even for that one? I can't get no simpler."

"I got it. I got it."

"Beer?"

"Please. You think she's been pondering, then, hm? Mmmmm, great stuff, as always," I smiled, and gestured with my fork, "I kind of figured when Frank turned up dead at the beginning of the novel ..."

"You be careful 'bout that book, Love. That book may just burn you bad." She snickered, "worse than that corn pudding. You need agua?"

"Neh," I choked, "I'm tough," but I drank the water she handed me.

"Thanks. And I hear your words, believe me. I know Jean isn't Philippa, but by damn, she's close in spots."

"It ain't the people that's in the book, necessarily. It's the people that ain't in the book. For them, you got no warnin'."

I thought about that one, too, and decided she was right. I had to be careful of assuming anything. For instance, I'd assumed Frank knew about the cars first-hand. Thinking further, I'd bet he didn't. I knew Phil didn't tell him. I knew he seldom called the girls ... damn, I needed to call them! This time I reached over and set the phone beside me.

"What you thinkin', Bud?"

"I'm thinking Frank's father told Frank about the girls' new cars, along with the fact that Phipps and I had been up there two or three days and nights. He just had that look about him. Like what a blasting cap is to dynamite. Frank, by himself, isn't volatile, I don't think. He needs something to set him off."

"If he ain't volatile, I don't know the meanin' of the word. Eat."

"Darlin', I'm doing my best here."

"That isn't no man's portion," she snapped. Jewish mother. "Men don't eat like that. Little girls who want to be skinny eat like that. Philippa eats more than that."

"Funny, when I looked in the mirror there was a man in these pants." I glanced at her out of the corner of my eye. "Ah ... speaking of being in somebody's pants, can I have a brief but meaningful discussion with you?"

"A little too late for the birds and the bees," she chuckled, sensing my discomfort. "Phipps got no plumbin', and you shootin' blanks. What's left?"

"Christmas. And you're getting rocks in your stocking," I chuckled.

"Tell me what you needin' to know," she said gently.

I put down my fork and let my elbows prop me up on the breakfast bar. I could see a distorted reflection of myself in the highly polished oak, and it made me feel like I was in some play from the Theater of the Absurd.

"Glory," I sighed, "I just had the most terrible, sinking feeling, just this second."

"Bout what?" She put down what she was doing and came to sit next to me, giving me her full attention.

"Christmas, and it's all tied in together. Christmas, and the birds and bees, and the whole Christian ethic."

"That's Judeo-Christian ethic, I believe."

"I stand corrected. Glory, I was propositioned today by a very beautiful woman. One I love like life itself, and I had to say, no. After wanting her all this time, I had to say no." Glory just nodded. "You see, I understand much of her mind and her heart, but not her faith. Not really. What if I'd said yes, like I wanted to, and we'd had sexual intercourse? Now, I've made love and she's committed adultery. I'm happy. She slits her wrists. I blow my brains out. Period."

"Even a not real serious Jew knows the answer to that one, and you know what it is. You don't want to, but you do."

"In other words, until our wedding night, which could be months or years, I don't make love to her? Glory, I'm fifty-two years old, for Godsake. Philippa's got thirteen years that I don't have!"

"You get no sympathy from me, Boy. I'm havin' hot flashes of my own. I'm tellin' you the Commandments say, no. Thou shalt not commit adultery. The loophole," she grinned, "is in the word, adultery. Adultery is sex with a body who married to somebody else. Once she's cut herself loose ..."

"You people amaze me!" I said, too sharply. "You spend half your lives trying to get around your own set of rules!"

"Why bite me? You asked. You asked for the cut and dried of it. You got it. Now I'll tell you the truth of it. When that girl says no to Frank Tyler and yes to Peter Aarons, she belong to Peter Aarons. In her heart, and forever, 'cause that's her way. She and the good Lord'll work it out, 'cause it wasn't done lightly, and it wasn't done mean. It was done desperate, and after a long time."

"I just don't want to do the wrong thing," I said softly. My head felt like somebody was inside it with a jackhammer. I did not know the rules, and I needed to. I didn't want to, because I thought religion in general was a lot of hokum, but ... I needed to know.

"Aloysha, Honey, listen to me, and try not to laugh out loud, 'cause it does annoy me somethin' fierce. The old Devil, Satan, he's layin' a super guilt trip on you, and you lettin' him. You playin' in a field he's all too familiar with, and that give him a big advantage.

"Remember this. Satan, he don't come at us with big lies. Big lies is too easy to spot. He comes at us with little hurtin' lies, and off kilter perceptions of familiar things. Instead of drivin' wedges between us and our beliefs, he just drive them splinters under the fingernails of our relationships. Bud, you gotta tell him, no, and you gotta speak against him, or that splinter's gonna turn into a wedge, and you gonna lose the woman you was always meant to have."

I resisted the impulse to roll my eyes. "Glory, I'm not a Baptist. I don't know how to do these things. I'm not saying you're wrong, because I've seen you be right too many times about spiritual things. But I'm not sure I even recognize ... Satan... as an entity apart from the evil he personifies."

"You didn't believe smart women ever got themselves beat, either, but it sure existed, didn't it?"

I just nodded. She got up out of her chair, squeezed my shoulders and kissed the top of my head as she walked behind me to the pantry. "You, Boy, are pooped. You need to remember that Rome wasn't built in a day, not by no fifty-two year old, long legged piano player, it weren't. You need sleep. More than that, you need rest. Good, bone settlin' rest somewhere's quiet. None of this in and out of the spa there I done rested malarkey. You need to quit worryin' like nobody else can do any right thinkin' 'cept you, and let things fall in place."

"She's right, you know," a dark voice smiled, and Philippa Tyler had reappeared in my life. The eyes, and the voice of Philippa Tyler had reappeared. The body, though freshly showered, was propped up in the doorway.

"You nut!" I exclaimed, vaulting from my seat to get hold of her. "You can be up to the bathroom, and to eat, and to soak. Period."

"So," she grinned, "I'm hungry."

"So call me. I don't want to find you at the bottom of those stairs with a bashed-in head. What you've got is bad enough. Sit. Is that stool okay? How about the table in the morning room instead? Did you have trouble managing a shower?"

"How's about you relax and sit down? I feel guilty enough about what I've put you through, without giving you a heart attack," she said. She leaned back in the bar chair, elbows on the arm rests, and contemplated me.

I scowled at her, and it felt so good. "And now you're going to ask me what happened this afternoon, and for the last week because you have no memory of what went on, or what was said, right?"

"Oh, you are SO close," she said, measuring with her fingers. "Couple small changes. First, I ask you if you have a good divorce lawyer, then I eat some supper, and take you upstairs to bed with me. Other than that, you are completely correct. Glory, what is that wonderful, fragrant mess in that pot?"

"That's Kentucky Burgoo," Glory smiled, vastly amused by my expression. "It's got – push up on that poor fool's bottom jaw, will you, before somethin' nasty flies in there – it's got pork, should have veal, but we don't eat it outta protest for how them poor little feller's is treated, and beef and lamb, chicken, potatoes, onions, carrots and green peppers ... cabbage, should have tomatoes, but Bud hate cooked tomatoes, corn, and some lima beans ..."

"I can't eat it," Philippa sighed.

"... should have squirrels in it, but I can't catch none. All the acres around this house, and I've never caught a one. Anyway, you cook this about three days, and then, at the exact moment, you wave a rabbit's foot on a yarn string over the open kettle."

"I can't eat it. Damn."

"It's the boy's favorite. I made it to perk him up. I see you done better with less effort. This here pot's southern corn puddin', and this is fried apples."

"I can't eat it," she sighed.

"You, are not thinking clearly," I smiled. I got up, kissed her hair, took a ladle, and, having thought a moment or two, I dished out Phil's supper and put it in front of her. "That, you can eat, Sweet Face. There's meat, and green vegetables, and broth, but no lima beans or potato, though I did slip you some carrots because you need to gain just a little weight. Am I right?"

"Absolutely," she breathed, and gave me an admiring smile. "I'm impressed."

"Good," I replied, "I intend to keep impressing you as long as possible. Eat just a little more than you can hold. I'm going to make a phone call."

I walked out of the kitchen and down the hall to my study, sat down and reached for the phone. I sat there with my hand on it for a few seconds, then got up, and went back to the kitchen.

"Line busy?" Phil asked.

"I don't know," I sighed. "I didn't call. How's the goo?

"As I was just telling Glory, it's very warm and comforting, thank you. You look troubled. Can I help?"

"Well, I don't know. I was going to call the girls and tell them you were hurt, and that suddenly didn't seem like such a hot idea. So, I thought

I'd invite them down for a couple days and just let them see you, and then that didn't sound so bright, either. And here I sit. Can you help?"

"No, I can't," she sighed, concentrating on her dinner. "I don't know if they know, and I don't know how to ask. I hinted once about it to Kelly. She was badgering me to go more in the truck with Frank, and I said something veiled about him hitting and throwing things. I'd rather wait a week or so until my face heals up and I'm back in the apartment. I don't want to run Frank down to them."

Glory and I exchanged a glance, punctuated by the sound of my elbows hitting the counter. I sat there a bit, looking at the spot where the tall, old-fashioned cupboards met the ceiling.

"Bud, are you okay?" Philippa asked.

"Oh, for the moment."

"And then?"

"Then you find out about the apartment."

"I'm still interested." There was just a bit of an edge to her voice.

I forced my eyes down from the ceiling and looked at Philippa. "Well, Phipps ..."

"The boy said he wouldn't sleep a wink with you where Tyler could get at you," Glory said quietly. "He works hard, he should buy hisself somethin' nice once in a while. This time, he bought a little peace of mind, and I think he done good."

"What she's trying to tell you, Phil, is that you no longer have an apartment, because all your things are here. I am so sorry. I should have asked."

"You did what you thought was best, and I thank you," she said. Then she looked at me with her heart in her beautiful eyes, put her hand over mine and added, "If anything has happened to my sewing machine, you're a dead man."

"You've been looking at it for the last week," I laughed. "It's against the wall in the morning room. Look."

She swiveled the chair and nodded with a sigh of relief. "Could I use it there, since I'm homeless?"

"Your home is here with us," I said, "and you can use it anywhere you'd like. One of the rooms upstairs might convert as a space for you to use. Even the morning room might work. Glory, what do you think?"

"That mornin' room don't get no use 'tall since Megan left. She usta have me serve her breakfast in there. No sittin' at a breakfast bar for that one." Glory made a wry face, then glanced apologetically at me. "And of course it was Mrs. Aaron's favorite downstairs room, too, being part of the kitchen and all." I noticed with a slight smile that Megan did not rate the Mrs. Aarons label, but, of course, Gram did. "I think it'd make a nice place to do sewing and such. You plannin' to do some sewin', Phipps?"

"If you'll help me cut out."

"Then, could I ask you a favor, "I asked, swiveling her chair back to look at me.

"Anything," she smiled, "I owe you my life and my sanity."

"Heavy debt to pay," I winked. "I guess then I'm within my rights to ask. Please, remake that white silk blouse for me. I love that blouse."

"And I love you," Philippa whispered. "Kiss me, you fool."

I was doing just that, when Glory said good night and quietly shut the kitchen door.

Philippa was still so weak, and so bruised, and I asked her more than once if she felt ready for this thing we were about to do. She assured me, as I carried her up the stairs, as I placed her on her feet beside the bed, that this was what she wanted. To give her a little more time to think, I asked her if she needed help with anything, then excused myself and went to my own room to undress and get a robe. In those minutes, while I flossed my teeth and contemplated myself in the mirror, I tried not to think about ... anything, because I wanted this to last a little longer than the first thrust.

When I returned there were no lights, just a single, modest candle and Philippa's honey colored hair spilling against the vanilla silk of the bed-clothes. "I wish I could do something about this cast. It isn't very romantic," she said, and studied it long enough for me to drop my robe and slide in beside her without embarrassment. How kind.

"At least you'll have a weapon," I whispered, and gathered her into my arms.

She replied with something akin to a growl, and when she kissed me, she meant business. I wanted her so much, and yet those bruises on her shoulders, and her shins, and her beautiful lips ... I was so afraid of hurting her and spoiling this moment.

She laughed softly and thanked me, and told me not to worry. I'd be the first to know. I kissed her, longer, deeper as we grew more comfortable with one another – caressed her – brought my body partly across hers to keep her warm.

Her touch was firm, her fingers sensual, almost languid, despite their trembling, and she gave the part of me she was holding a gentle squeeze and said, "Very impressive Peter."

"There's a comma in there," I whispered, and we both cracked up.

What passion – what electrifying passion there is between us, and strength, and yet kindness and companionship to slow us, and blend us as we couple together, even today, and then by the light of that candle, with Philippa's hair to bathe my face in, and the surge of her body around mine, there was such joy, and such fulfillment that I found tears on my face afterward, and Philippa with me, because there was nothing else to express what had been between us.

I raised myself on my elbows and studied her, and marveled, and asked quietly if she was all right, because she is very tightly put together, and I am not. She responded by smiling, and putting her arms around my neck, pulling me down – kissing me with such wondrous tenderness and telling me she thanked God for my presence in her life. And thus it began. The very good sex life of Tyler and Aarons.

When we finally wore ourselves out, which took a good long while, we laid in each other's arms and watched the moonlight as it filtered through the trees to touch Grandma's rocker. I could see her sitting there, and I smiled at her, giving her the slight nod that had always meant, I'm okay. Then Philippa said she'd love to sleep in my arms forever, but her back wouldn't let her just yet, and I managed one more groggy kiss before I fell asleep.

When I woke up the next morning, I was in bed with Philippa Kate Tyler. I pinched myself, and I was still in bed with her, and we were still naked – although at some point she'd gotten out of bed and tied back her mane of hair. I rolled over against her back, and kissed the spot where her long slender neck met her square little shoulder, and whispered, "I love you."

"Mmmmm, I love you, too," she murmured. "Have a nice day at the office, dear.

"Can I bring you anything?"

"Um um ... no. Thanks. I'm still sleeping."

"Call me when you're ready to get up?"

"Um hm."

"Philippa..."

"Out."

I laughed, and left. I'd worked my knee hard yesterday, skipped rope, played golf, made love, and it was hurting. I decided to let it rest. I showered, put a brace on it, dressed, and went whistling downstairs. We were going to be perfect together. Hadn't even argued about who got which side of the bed.

"Well, boy, you have a nice sleep?" Glory asked, pouring me a cup of coffee.

"Wonderful. Best I've ever had."

"All of it," she asked, arching her brows, "or just the sleep?"

"All of it," I sighed, and grinned like a Cheshire cat.

CHAPTER NINE

Phipps has the Benz to the doctor," Glory said. "It bein' easy for her to drive, and she say she had shoppin' to do. Silk for a blouse, I do believe. You have a nice mornin' with your daddy?"

"Um hm. Wasn't exactly an easy morning. I mean, the subject of Philippa Tyler did come up, and I dodged, and hemmed and hawed and then had to admit he'd called it pretty close. Other than that, it was great ... except for the smell of cigarettes in Dad's limo."

"The smell of smoke makin' you queasy?"

"No, it's making me crazy."

"It'll pass. Give it time. I keep tellin' you, you need to chew gum."

"Nasty habit. I already have cow eyes, I don't need to be chewing my cud. Did Phipps say when she'd be back?"

"No. You need the car?"

"Um hm, but I can take the Ford. It hasn't been driven since it got here. If Phipps gets back before I do, tell her I've gone shopping for Kit's birthday."

Glory said she would, and I took the keys to the Ford off the kitchen peg and went back outside. It was a beautiful, clear day after another beautiful night with Philippa, and I felt really good. I was a little worried that Phipps was driving so soon, but I hadn't said anything. Glory might feel responsible. The Benz handled well and Phipps was a superb driver. She'd be fine. What did surprise me was that she'd choose to go shopping with her poor face looking the way it did. But she had gone, and good for her.

The pickup was a formidable beast, but I was going out on the freeway, and the long wheel base and the hippo hips in back didn't matter so much out there. I buckled myself in, put a C.D. in the player, and turned my thoughts to Kit Miller's birthday present. After forty odd years, he still wasn't an easy man to shop for. Probably wouldn't do me any good to think about it. Probably just have to look.

There was the lawyer to think about. We'd been in his office day before yesterday. Philippa had come downstairs after our first night together, said "call him", and we'd gone. It was the second time I'd seen her wear her bitch suit.

She wanted her house and her furniture, and the livestock. Frank could have his truck, his cats, and his business. It was paid for. The money she'd made on the book she was willing to split with him. I'd opened my mouth and we'd had a mild set to, and Marion had said he'd come up with something equitable.

Too, there was Philippa to think about. Still weak, but gaining her health back, regaining an interest in the film, familiarizing herself a bit with my business dealings, making the sweetest love to me that I have ever known, and crying in her sleep at night.

I took my mind off Phipps, looked in the rearview mirror to change lanes for my exit, and saw the flashing lights on my tail. I glanced at the speedometer. A little over sixty. Probably not that. I knew better than to daydream in midday traffic, I could have done anything.

I pulled over as far as I could and stopped. The Highway Patrolman stopped behind me, and another one stopped in front. Now, I was alarmed. What if Phil had been in an accident? That thought passed almost instantly. This vehicle wouldn't link me to her in any way. They'd have called Glory, or some number in Washington State somewhere.

"Good morning," the officer said, cordially enough. "May I see your driver's license and your registration, please?"

"Certainly," I said, unbuckling the shoulder harness. I didn't bother to ask; they'll never tell you. I was reaching in my left hip pocket for my wallet when there was a movement on the passenger's side. Another officer, and this one had his hand on his gun.

"Oh shit," I said, about an octave too high, "Whatever I did, I'm sorry." I handed over my license and sat there with sweat running down the back of my neck.

"I thought that was you. I enjoyed your version of King Lear very much," the officer smiled.

"Thank you. Does this mean you're not going to shoot me?"

"May I see your registration, please?"

"Well, it isn't mine, but let's see if we can find it," I muttered, checking the visors. Phil was so damned disorganized, and right now it wasn't endearing her to me. I really didn't want to open the glove compartment. What if she had a pistol in there? Boom – no Aarons.

I conveyed that to the patrolman as I inched the thing open. The registration was there in a plastic bag with the service receipts, and I was in love again.

The officer took it and said, "This vehicle is registered to Frank W. Tyler."

"I'm sure it is. It should also be registered to Philippa K. Tyler."

"How do you come to have this vehicle, Mr. Aarons?" he asked, and the light began to dawn.

"Philippa has mine this morning."

"You know Mrs. Tyler?"

"I do."

"And do you know her whereabouts?"

"Not at this particular second, but she'll be home for lunch, I would assume."

"And where would that be?"

"The address on the license," I sighed. "Which are we dealing with, a stolen vehicle, or a missing person?"

"Mr. Tyler reported this vehicle stolen and his wife missing yesterday afternoon."

"My dear sir, I hate to tell you this," I said, "but you've been sent on a wild goose chase. Mrs. Tyler does have the truck, which is registered to both of them, not just to Mr. Tyler. And as Mr. Tyler well knows, I have Mrs. Tyler, which is how I came to be driving this vehicle today."

The officers were very polite, very understanding, and very sympathetic. Then they arrested me, impounded the truck, and hauled my ass downtown. "You have one phone call," they said, and I laughed. Intimidated as I was, I laughed. All my play with prop guns and tough guy lines wasn't helping me a bit right now, and I said so, because I admire the California Highway patrol as the finest in the world. That, I didn't tell them. I just dialed home.

"Hi, Glory, it's me. Is Philippa home yet?" I looked at the Sergeant and nodded. "She's there. Hi, Sweet Face, I hate to bother you, but could you do me a favor?"

She was agreeable. Obviously only half listening, half doing something else, and it set me off. "Philippa Kate, I'm in the damned slammer, thanks to dear old Frank! Do you suppose I could have your undivided attention for a minute?"

"What?" she cried, and even the officer heard her.

"Oh yes. He reported you missing and the Ford stolen, and guess who was driving the Ford when the cops found it?"

"Oh, God," she groaned, "Oh, Peter, I'm sorry," and she began to cry.

Then I was sorry. I'd been thinking of myself and I'd forgotten what she'd been through. Now I'd made her feel guilty for Frank's idiocy, and I was stricken. "Sweet Face, I'm sorry," I said, loving her as best I could with my voice. "Philippa, don't cry. It's not your fault. You, are not responsible for Frank's actions, period. I am in a tight spot, though, and I do need your help. Now you and Glory put down what you're doing, you get your identification, and have Glory bring you down here. Don't drive by yourself, promise?"

I told her the address, told her I loved her - told her again I was sorry for upsetting her, and hung up. "That man," I said, rubbing my face, "is rapidly becoming the bane of my existence."

"His concern seems justified, Mr. Aarons," the officer said.

"Does it? I find it interesting that he can have me arrested for stealing his truck, which I didn't do, but I can't have him arrested for beating his poor wife half to death, which he did do. His car carries more legal weight than his wife's life, and I think it sucks."

"If what you say is true ..."

"Look at her when she walks in here. Look at her temple and the side of her face. Part of that damage might be permanent, and ask her what she did to end up with her wrist in a cast."

"Did she file a complaint?"

"No. She filed for divorce instead. How many wives file a complaint?"

"Not many," the Sergeant replied. "Not enough. We're Highway Patrol, of course, not city, but you'd be surprised at the things people do to each other in cars on the freeway."

I reached for a cigarette that wasn't there, and knew I had to train that hand to do something else. The Sergeant recognized the gesture, and I quickly said, "I quit. I just can't seem to convince my left hand."

"You'll make it," he smiled. "Mister Aarons, I am sorry. I know who you are. I respect and enjoy your work. I live a sheltered life, and even I have seen pictures of you and P.K. Tyler together. I have every reason to think you're telling the truth, and that you are the victim of a very unfortunate set of circumstances."

"Thanks to Frank Tyler," I said, exhaling sharply. "The man's a menace. And don't feel like you have to apologize to me. Most victims are not as lucky as I am. At least, I'm alive and unhurt."

We drank coffee and talked about movie making and police work, and more time went by than I was comfortable with, and I began to worry that something had happened to my girls. I could see Frank Tyler's diesel running up their backside on the freeway somewhere and leaving them both dead. My life was so close to coming together. I had so much to gain, and so much to lose. I was hungry, and worried, and the medication for my knee and my back was in the Ford.

I was getting to the point of being really miserable when the girls walked in, and I was weak with relief. Phipps saw me, and started to cry. I could see that she'd been crying already, and I hated Frank for that. I'm not someone who hates very much, and it twisted me inside.

I caught Philippa to me, and kissed her tears away and begged her please, not to feel bad. Really, it hadn't been a wasted few hours. Every man who plays gangsters should have the experience of being arrested at least once.

Phil's ID was sufficient, her charm more so, and I was immediately released. Philippa told them under no uncertain terms to keep the damned pickup. Let Frank pay the impound fees and figure out how to get it home.

I told her, gently, that I didn't think that was a very good idea. Her eyes blazed with anger and frustration until I told her my tapes of our sound track, and my medication, were in the truck. Then the fire cooled. She loved me. They went home. I went to get the Ford.

It took me forever at the impound yard. By then my face was grey with pain and I was out for Frank Tyler's ass. I'd planned on getting the Ford, grabbing a bite to eat, and going on to shop. As it was, I had to double up on my medication just to drive the damned, unwieldy thing. By the time I got home my back was in spasm, and I slammed that behemoth into a spot under an oak tree where every bird in the neighborhood could shit on it.

I stalked into the house with the last rays of the sun, still grinding my teeth and cursing under my breath. The girls were trying, bless them. Dinner was ready early, the cover was off the spa, Rachmaninoff was on the stereo ... and Philippa was wearing her powder blue sweater. I sank into my recliner and let her pet me a while, for both our sakes.

Times like these, I wished I could have a couple of Sidecars, straight up, but I couldn't. It had been one beer, or one glass of wine a day for the last ten years. I took medication every day of my life, three or more times a day, and medicine and booze don't mix. Being stupid, I'd tried it once, early on, and awakened in an emergency room somewhere.

Now Philippa was my sedative, she soaked me, rubbed me down, and fed me. She apologized again for spoiling my shopping trip for Kit's birthday tomorrow, and then volunteered to take my place. What this problem needed was a fresh perspective, she reasoned. What did successful actor Kit Miller have? Everything. What did he like to do? Where did he like to go? Where and how and with whom did he live? Did he like animals, music, toys, games, sports? Yes. Phil insisted she could do it, Glory said she needed an evening out, and they left me to my own devices. Rafael was bowling.

I had the house all to myself, which was rare, and should have told me something about my mood, I suppose, but I wasn't feeling introspective. I wasn't up for hard questions, even my own. I devoted some time to my portfolio, talked to Kit and Tommy on the phone, and turned to the script. They needed me on camera tomorrow. It wouldn't be that much work. Most of the lines were Kit's, I was just the straight man.

I realized it had been weeks, maybe months since I'd gotten together with my friends. The time I had, I spent with Philippa. The time she had, she spent with me. That, would have to change. We both needed outside friends and outside interests to keep ourselves fresh. Phipps ... needed to go home. She was a creature of the open air and flying hooves and hard physical labor. With that gone, her perspective was shifting. Just slightly so far, but she would lose that part of her, and I loved it.

I wasn't concentrating, so I got up and stretched and went for a brisk walk to clear the cobwebs. It was a pleasant evening, nippy but fragrant, and I headed out on the network of nature trails my grandmother had so carefully designed, and Rafael so lovingly maintained in her memory.

What would it be like, I wondered, to be away from this place in the spring of the year? I thought back. Yes, there had been a spring like that, hadn't there? I'd laid in that hospital bed with my back in traction, my knee in a cast, the pain constant and exhausting, and watched the month of April inch by on the calendar. I'd been home in May, flat on my back or in a wheelchair. June, my back was strong enough for crutches, barely. That whole time, even with the knowledge that Rafael and Glory, Gram and Megan were there to keep things going, I was miserable. Those were my roses, my special roses. My citrus trees, my bougainvillea.

I knew how Philippa felt, talking quietly on the phone every few days. How were the kitties? And how was her old Arabian stallion? Was the permanent pasture coming on, and the alfalfa? The tulips and the daffodils and the flowering shrubs must be beautiful by now. Had they seen Frank? Occasionally, for a day or so. He seemed to have someplace to stay at the other end of the line. He did seem to miss the cats. She knew they were sorry about the breakup, so was she. How was Flyer's beautiful little filly? Yes, she must be growing. She'd be ready to start under saddle this summer. Irrigation well holding up? Mainline in good repair? Tractor running? Hot wire?

No, no garden this year, she guessed, unless they wanted one for themselves. She knew. Four months. She was sorry. Then she'd hang up, and smile, and go off by herself for a bit.

I went back to the house, poured myself a glass of wine, and called Tommy for the second time that evening. "I want to take my lady home for a bit. What can you do for me?" I asked.

He said he'd check the weather and the production schedule and get to me at work tomorrow. If nothing else, he could cut me loose at the end of the week to go north and scout locations with Phipps. I told him I was very grateful, and I knew Philippa would be. I'd see him in the morning.

In my peripheral vision I could see the garage door coming open to my right and Glory's station wagon gliding into its accustomed spot. So, Philippa, the world's fastest shopper, had been shopping for Kit, hm? This, I had to see. Glory called goodnight from somewhere out back near their house, and I waved to her as I opened the door for Philippa. She had two bags tucked under her left arm, and she was carrying a large box which she handed to me.

"Here," she said, "Kit will like this."

I set the box on the breakfast bar, took the lid off, and began to laugh. "Yes, he will," I said. "He will just go crazy for this one."

In that box was the cutest puppy I've ever seen in my life. "Aw, he looks like Glory!" I laughed, taking his sleepy little body out of the box and holding him up to look at him. His tongue reached for my chin, but I was too quick for him. "What a great face! He's, what, a Boxer?"

"Um hm. He'll be big enough to jog and play Frisbee with. He can be taught to hunt. He'll be a good watch dog if he's handled right, and he'll love the boat."

"Phipps, this is exactly right. It's perfect. And yet, I know I've told you, as Kit has told me for the last year ..." I did my imitation of Kit's voice. "'No more dogs. Now that Satchel is gone, no more dogs.' What made you choose a puppy?"

"The probability that he was trying to talk himself out of the heartache and not the dog. He's all urine, Bud. I'll be in the library if you need me."

"Ah, Phipps?" I prefaced, and she kept on walking.

"Food's in the bag, along with his dishes. Try the laundry room. Myself, I don't like dogs."

"Aw," I said, holding the pup under my chin, "how can she say that in front of you?"

Damn thing howled all night, and he had a set of lungs like furnace bellows. By morning, I shared Philippa's opinion.

But Kit? Kit was thrilled with that howling little monster, and HLM was thrilled with Kit. I took credit only as the delivery boy. Phipps got the accolades for intuition. We worked hard that morning, and between every take, at every break in the action, Kit was holding that puppy. I finally told him I was jealous, and he grinned, "With what you've got to hold? Jeez, you're greedy, Bud."

"You assume much," I said, looking down my nose and sniffing in exaggerated distaste. "You assume too much, Kristoffer."

"You lie through your pearly whites, too. When's P.K. coming back to work? As other than a bed warmer, that is?"

I glared at him and we dissolved in laughter like we'd been doing since kindergarten, and Tommy shook his head at us like he'd been doing for thirty-six years, and we quieted back down. I'd never been able to lie to Kit. Never really wanted to until recently. "I don't know when she'll be back. She's under a lot of pressure because she knows what it's costing us to shoot around her. But that bruise down the side of her face still looks ... I can't even describe it. They'd never be able to cover it with makeup. And her wrist is so sore she can't write. She just isn't ready. She sits up in bed and just cries at night, her head hurts so bad. The doctor says it's mostly tension. Anyway, to answer your question, I don't have an answer to your question. She was doing a radio talk show this morning, so she's out and about a little."

"Do you suppose the host will ask her how one of the most dignified and respected advocates of serious acting in this town came to be busted yesterday? It has been mentioned by the media, y'know."

"Private Citizens shouldn't be allowed to own police scanners," I sniffed. "It would solve most of the problems."

"Not yours, it won't," Kit replied, and put an arm around me. "I guess she's worth it. You seem very, very happy, Aloysha."

"I've never been happier in my life," I smiled, returning the embrace. In a scant two hours, I wouldn't be able to say that.

"Bud, we just got a phone call ... Aloysha?" Tommy said, raising his voice over the noise, and I looked up from the crowded table in the studio commissary where I was sitting with Kit and most of the crew.

"Now what?" I frowned, expecting the worst. I'd already talked to Phipps, the radio show had gone well. Couldn't be that.

"Never mind," Tommy shrugged, still shouting from the head of the table. "You probably don't want it."

"Don't want what?"

"Neh, never mind," he said, and I could see that he was ready to burst. "It's just another damned Russian speaking piano player. I'll tell David you can't be bothered."

By now I was unfolding ceilingward like a column of smoke, and my eyes were getting bigger by the second, and the whole place was getting quiet. "Rachmaninoff?" I gasped, and Tommy whooped, "Yes! Yes! Yes!" at the top of his lungs, and grabbed me in a bear hug.

"You got the part! You finally did it, Bud. You're going to portray your idol! And, and, you're not only going to do all your own piano playing, you're also going to do all your own conducting, and they've asked you, please, because you are a recognized authority on Rachmaninoff, to arrange all your own music and advise the film! Damn! Nice work!"

That moment, being applauded and slapped on the back and congratulated, was the emotional high point of my career. I, the shy little boy who'd been teased mercilessly about my big eyes, big feet, big hands. I, who had turned to the piano because the other boys couldn't understand what I was saying. I had been chosen above the others to play the part of Sergei Vassilevich Rachmaninoff. I was to portray one of the world's great pianists. These hands – my hands – would give that music to millions who had never heard it.

"Aloysha, You're gonna drown me, buddy!" Kit laughed, and I realized I was crying all over him.

I straightened up, laughing, gasping for air, and said, "Neh, tell 'em I don't want it. Thanks anyway."

The rest of the day certainly paled by comparison, but I did manage to concentrate most of the time. They got a few shots for the bloopers, but not too many. I sort of ... floated home. I came in the door and the girls looked up from Philippa's sewing, and Glory said, "If you was a woman, I'd say that was a pregnant smile."

"Ladies, I am pregnant!" I said, and shouted for joy as I scooped both of them into my arms. "I am pregnant with Sergei Rachmaninoff! I got the part!"

A hundred questions later Rafael joined us, and I went back again over the details. We would be filming in Russia, and in New York. "I'm going to play Carnegie Hall, and the Bolshoi in Moscow! I'm going to play piano in two of the most acoustically perfect places in the world! God, pinch me! I got the part! Me! What luck!"

I was still so excited I could hardly breathe. Now, my current film had to really go into high gear. I'd be working on both at the same time as it was.

"But," Philippa said, after thinking hard for quite a while, "I don't see where there was any competition for you. Did anyone else who tried out for the part play the piano even remotely as well as you do?"

I shook my head. "No, but that's not the point. A lot of very high draw names tried out for this. It's the big budget flick of the year, not just a scholarly one. In movies like this very often everything is dubbed. The actor just goes through the motions. If I hadn't been the right actor, my musical talent wouldn't have gotten me the part, I don't think. They may have asked me to play the piano, or even advise, but not act."

"They'd be crazy not to," Philippa said firmly. "You're a fine actor, you play the piano, you speak Russian. The part was written for you."

"Two in a row," I laughed, "How do I rate?"

The phone rang and Philippa was closest. "Hello?" she said, and I saw her face change. "Oh. Hello there." There was a pause, and her eyes began to narrow. "Well, now you know how it feels, don't you?" she said. "I didn't know they'd impound your load, but I figured they'd pull you over, and maybe arrest you, and humiliate you, and frighten you, just like they did to Peter ... that's right, he was, and when you hurt Peter ... yes, I do, almost as much as I loved you all those years."

She hopped onto a bar chair and swiveled away from the sudden silence. "He didn't take me, Frank. He could never have done that, even if he'd wanted to. I chose to leave because I was tired of waiting for our relationship to go somewhere. I was tired of one step forward and two steps back. I was tired of always being the one left behind, of loving someone who had ceased to exist. But that person, that lost person, I will always love, Frank. And I will always be his friend. If he ever needs a place to crash or a shoulder to cry on, or someone to be with just to talk to, I'll be right here, I promise."

There was a long pause and Phipps wiped her eyes. "I'll get you out of jail if you'll get yourself some counseling ..." there was another long pause, and I could hear Frank's anger from halfway across the room. "Too bad," she replied, "there's a very nice guy in there somewhere. When you get tired of cooling your heels, give me a call. If I'm not here, talk to Peter. He knows a sharp lawyer." She listened for a few moments, and quietly hung up the receiver.

She swiveled back around on the stool, glanced up at me, blushed, and looked away. "Sorry I was late yesterday. I knew if I didn't do it mad, I wouldn't do it, so I did it mad."

I raised her chin with my fingers. “Look at me, Sweet Face. Why?”

“Because he damaged your reputation! He shamed me in front of you, and you in front of me. He has no right to do that.”

“Pretty Philly,” I murmured as I kissed her. “My beautiful Philippa. You have been too long without self-regard. You have been dragged into doing the right thing for the wrong reason.”

I saw her defenses go up, and soothed her with my hands. “None of that, now. Don’t be mad, just listen, hm? What Frank did to me, to us, yesterday, falls into the ‘all’s fair in love and war’ category, and I thought it was pretty ingenious. For what he did to you – you, Philippa Kate Tyler, human being – for hurting you physically, he deserved to be arrested.”

“Then you don’t understand,” she sighed. “My threshold of pain is far higher than yours. Far higher than most people’s. I don’t remember physical pain much past the point of impact. But the mental anguish, the feeling of ... being unworthy before those with whom I wish to be equal ...” she flapped her one good hand in frustration. “Nuts! I’m doing a lousy job of this. Let’s just drop it.”

“Okay,” I smiled. “We’ll drop it. Hey, Kit loved the puppy, and his party is at seven tomorrow night, not eight. Glory, I want you to take off your apron, and you and your husband go get fancied up so we can all go out to dinner. Kit and his femme du jour, and Tommy and Emily, are meeting us at the beach. You, too, Philippa. Scoot.” I lifted my eyebrows and smiled at her. “By the way, I have a surprise for you. A very nice surprise.”

“Nicer than you getting that part?”

“Different kind of nice.”

“Well, tell me! You know I hate suspense!”

“Nope. Nope. I’ve thought the better of saying anything. Can’t tell you. Not sure I have just the right words. Let’s ... drop it.”

“You should have been a parent,” she sighed in disgust. “You have such a way of manipulating the juvenile mind.”

“I believe childlike would be a kinder description,” I grinned. “I just hate to see you running from yourself. I hate to see you unable to look in the mirror and say, ‘I don’t deserve to look like this. He had no right to do this to me. I have the right to chuck his ass in the clink for it,' and do it on that basis."

"But that part of it doesn't matter," she smiled. "That's what I'm trying to tell you. The physical part doesn't matter. Bud, I look in the mirror and there's nobody there. I see myself in your eyes, or in Kelly or Wenonah, or in my fruit trees or my garden or the colors I choose for my house, or in what I write. It is there that I exist. There is no face that goes with that. The arm ... pisses me off. I need my arm to work with. I am what I can do."

"You are, what you are, and what you can do is a reflection of that."

"This is goin' nowhere," Glory said. "We gonna go get dressed. We see you all after a bit. Boy, she be tryin' to tell you the truth, don't tell her different."

When they left I walked her upstairs, and as we walked I said, "Am I doing that to you? I don't mean to."

"You're not, Bud. We're both groping right now. I just wish I could explain this better. I sound so evasive and more than a little nuts, and it's because there's no tangible core to my thinking. I may be like you, preferring to hide behind a character. And you!" she said, stopping on the step above me and turning to look at me a little more straight on than usual as she wrapped her arms around my neck, "You, my dear friend and lover, you are going to be Rachmaninoff! You are going to play the Bolshoi, and Carnegie Hall! Wow! I'm so excited for you! It certainly makes Mark Kincaid look tame by comparison."

"Never compare apples and oranges," I said, scooping her up and starting up the stairs again, "Besides, Rachmaninoff won't bring me what Mark Kincaid has, will he?"

"I hope not. I hope I don't lose you."

"Phipps, some of us in this business are easily lost, and some of us just aren't," I said, dropping her with a gentle bounce on the bed and pulling off my shirt as I headed for the shower, "I'm one of those that isn't. When I'm happy in a relationship I stay there until the other person changes it. Please don't worry about giving up Frank only to lose me. We fit like a hand in a glove. One of us will hold the other in death." I could feel my eyes burn with tears, and it made me chuckle. "I really hope it isn't me, because I couldn't bear to live without you. I'm taking a shower now. I smell like a hard day's work."

I had just gotten in and started lathering up when the door opened, and Philippa stepped in with me. "Hey, you," she said, rubbing up against me and sticking that bottom lip of hers out as far as she could get it, "I want my surprise."

"I lied. There isn't one," I laughed, "but don't you feel better for having talked?"

"No."

"Well, if you're going to pout," I said, bending to kiss her, and dripping foam on her nose in the process, "I guess I'll have to tell you. We're leaving Thursday to scout locations ... somewhere in Washington State. Saturday night, you'll sleep in your own bed, Lady."

CHAPTER TEN

It was a beautiful trip, fresh and green, bursting with new life. The streams and reservoirs and lakes were full, and we stopped often for picture taking and short walks to smell the air and get away from the pounding of the Ford for a few minutes. The pickup was not my idea of a road car, even though I'd suggested we take it. Philippa did some of the driving, and she loved the thing. I did most of the driving, and I didn't. It was my devious plan to drive it up there and then fly back, leaving the thing stranded where it belonged, in a place with no traffic.

The hardest part of the trip was getting Philippa to eat anything. Two restaurants she knew on the way up, and in those two she ate something. Other than that, she chewed on beef jerky and drank diet Snapple. I told her she'd been released into my custody on good behavior, and that included eating right and getting plenty of rest, and not overdoing it. She just looked out the window and grinned like a bratty kid.

We spent our second night in a town called Weed. They said there was a town, I never saw one. It was odd, checking into a motel as Mr. and Mrs. Bud Aarons. Funnier because the clerk recognized us and knew damned good and well we weren't married. We were embarrassed, but held our poker faces – he held his – and we got to our room before we burst into laughter. That night we just bathed and slept, leaving no tracks for the curious who would follow.

We turned east, and the next morning's drive was full of mountains and wetlands, migrating waterfowl and incredibly blue skies against the pine trees. We climbed into the high desert, through rocks and brush and patches of late spring snow and tiny isolated hamlets with massive grain elevators. Then down, across the mighty, swollen Columbia, and out of the gorge on the Washington side. We passed through Sam Hill's domain, Stonehenge and Maryhill Museum, and promised ourselves we'd visit someday. We stopped to look at the snowcaps, and I could see Philippa's face starting to effuse with happiness.

We went up again, and down, and through a long, winding gash in the hills, then out to overlook the valley. "The home stretch," Philippa sighed, and in those words was absolute peace. Then, for an hour and a half she fumed quietly. What if something was wrong? What if there was a for sale sign in the front yard? What if somebody was sick? What if the place had burned down? What ... if Frank was home? That one didn't make me laugh quite so condescendingly. She'd dropped the charges and let him go, of course. I knew she would. I grudgingly called it love. She called it pity for a very old, very sick friend.

We went through a small city, which Phipps informed me was the place to shop when we needed to, and climbed along a road that was curving and narrow, through miles of apple trees. Then Phipps, who was driving, put her hand on my thigh, and I realized I'd been dozing. "We're here," she said, and it was like being awakened in heaven. You know, to this day, when the city is smoky and I am tired, I can close my eyes and remember my first glimpse of that utterly tranquil setting. There were apple trees on three sides, their buds swelling with the promise of fragrance, and brilliant fruit to come. "Welcome," she added softly, her hand still on my thigh. We shut off the engine, I covered her hand with mine, and just looked.

A huge willow clad lawn sloped toward the barns and the exercise arena and round pen, then came the pastures, glistening from the sprinklers which arched above them. A creek meandered across one end and dropped out of sight at the edge of the property. Just above us was a tall post and beam house, sturdy and simple and inviting.

An orange fluff of a cat came bounding to meet us, and other cats from various places as we walked across the grass and up onto a deck that was garlanded with roses and plum trees.

"Peter, you haven't said a word," she smiled, scooping up the cat, and I just shook my head in wonder.

"I'm afraid my voice will shatter the spell," I said quietly. "It's so beautiful here it doesn't seem real."

"It's very real when you have to take care of it," she laughed. "Think we could use it for some of the filming?"

"Definitely. Come on, show me around!"

We went in, and there was a note from the Hitchers, welcoming their dearest Philippa home and inviting her to a family dinner at their house Sunday after church. Her, and Mister Aarons, of course.

"Oh, they did a beautiful job!" Phil laughed, trying to go everywhere at once. "My horses! I have to go see my horses, and my sheep! My lambs!"

Well, your bladder's better than mine," I laughed, "I'll be along in a bit."

"Oh," she said, stopping short midway through the kitchen. "Oh, now that you mention it, yes, I do. There's one for you upstairs at the top," she said, turned back and scurried off down the hall.

I stayed upstairs for a few minutes and just relaxed. We were up high here – on a mesa or close to the edge of a rocky bluff. One view from one bedroom was pasture, the river below in the valley, the mountains beyond. From the other, endless apples. The bathroom window looked out on Philippa's own fruit trees, and a beautiful, willow draped pond beside an old bunk house.

I parked my hip on the desk in the huge west bedroom and watched Philippa as she hurried down the slope, calling her old stallion to her. He was long and lean and red as flame, and he came pacing with elegantly lifted knees and an arching neck which belied his twenty odd years. He shook his mane and stopped in front of her, dropped his head over her shoulder, and I could see him sigh with contentment. He, too, loved Philippa. I felt, somehow, that I was intruding, and went downstairs.

I had to admit it, Frank Tyler was an excellent carpenter. He'd built the house by himself from a design of Philippa's, and done a fine job. It was bright and open, turned to the slanting winter sun, and it seemed larger than its twenty-two hundred square feet. The huge old beams were weathered and grey, most likely out of an ancient barn somewhere. They had to have been lifted into place with a crane. Not even Frank, musclebound though he was, could have lifted those things. I eyed them for a minute and contemplated what he could do to me if the mood struck him. I had the reach … and the multi-million dollar hands. I snorted without humor and moved on.

To the south, and through a sliding glass door which helped light the family room, I found the spa. It was in Philippa's greenhouse, surrounded by plants which the Hitchers had obviously babied. There were zucchini, and tomato plants, chard and lettuce, chives and other herbs amongst the flowers; truly a balm in the bitter cold of these winters. I uncovered it, checked temperature and chemical levels, and set it to begin recirculating. Like mine, it was a simple passive system; a nearly guilt free luxury in this day of dwindling resources.

I looked around some more, at the frilly, old fashioned curtains and the photographs on the walls, and the old treasures, the beautiful, practical antiques. North of the family room, east of the kitchen, where it would get the morning sun and a view of the roses on the deck, I found Phil's study. Even the Hitchers hadn't touched it. Definitely a one woman place, this. It was a pleasant chaos of books – hundreds of books – floor to ceiling, and fabric, and bolts of laces and trims, and quilt squares and half-finished garments and five years' worth of ironing. Shrine like, were the diet Snapple bottles, bits of paper, a dozen dull pencils, half a dozen sharp ones, as though she'd left midway through a thought. I sat down, and leaned back, and thanked my lucky stars for admitting me into such a mind as Philippa's.

I spied a pencil sketch on a scrap of paper, and simple notations around it. It was a ring. A wedding ring. Tiny ruby hearts outlined in gold, tiny gold daisies with diamonds for eyes. The ring Mark Kincaid had given Jean Whiteside. I spent some time studying it.

"Woolgathering?" Philippa smiled, and I nearly broke both my knees on the underside of the desk. "Aw, I'm sorry, Buddy," she laughed. "I thought you heard me come in. Would you like an early dinner?"

"Sounds good. Want to go out?" I asked casually, trying not to indicate I'd nearly killed myself.

"No. I want to cook. Tomorrow after church we'll have to grocery shop. I mean, I'll have to shop. No, wait. We're going to dinner after church, in there, and you'll still be out here." her pale, slender eyebrows came together, and I could see her beginning to twist the Gordian knot. "We can do this a couple of ways. Skip church, turn down dinner ... you could drop me off at church and then come back ..."

"I could go to church with you, or am I not invited?"

It was one of the best blank looks I've ever elicited from Phipps. "I kind of assumed … that was not an option."

"Why?"

"The way you and Glory fight about religion, for one thing."

"I'm not marrying Glory. I am, whether you know it or not, marrying you." She blushed and dropped her eyes, and I wanted to gobble her up like candy. "Your faith is more important to you than mine is to me." I said gently. "If I choose not to believe, at least I can understand, and I can be with you. This is an area where I will give. There will be areas where you will have to give at some point, agreed?"

"Oh, yes," she smiled, and came to sit on the desk and kiss me.

"You know this won't be easy," I warned.

"I'm dreading it. But the longer I don't go down and face them, the longer I'll dread it."

"Astute of you, as usual."

"By ear, as usual. Oh, look. There's Wes, out in his garden."

"Garden?" I gasped, squinting slightly downhill and across the road, "Holy Toledo, I thought it was a corn field."

"Not in this neck of the woods. I think I'll walk over and say hi to Alice, just to let her know I'm home."

I'll go with you," I said, rising out of her desk chair, "That is, if you don't mind. Wes is the one who shipped Flyer to me, and I'd like to give him a proper thank you."

"You are always welcome to go with me," Philippa smiled.

I picked up my jacket and stepped out on the deck, and Phil's eyes reflected that perfect blue sky – and it was like an electric shock – she was mine! I inhaled sharply, then caught her, and kissed her, and my heart rate and a few other things went up, and I realized I was being indiscreet. There was Wes, not more than a hundred yards away, plowing his garden, and here I was, thinking very seriously about plowing another man's wife. She was, still, Frank Tyler's wife. I wondered what that meant here on the rough side of civilization. What kind of code was I violating, and who might put some buckshot in me for what I was doing? Too darned many westerns under my belt, I guess.

"Sorry," I murmured and let her go.

She just laughed and stayed close. "Do you have any idea at all how flattered I am that I have that effect on you? I hate one way streets. Come on, Sugarfoot. Ain't nobody gonna plug yuh."

Amazing. She'd read my mind. She still does it, and it still amazes me. We walked back down the driveway, across a winding two lane road, through a gate, and into Wes's garden. Garden. It must have been half an acre or more. Phipps waved to Wes as he came around, and he pulled up close and idled the engine down and leaned off the tractor for a kiss. She chatted a minute, told him we were home for a bit now, introduced us, asked if Alice was in the house, and hopped off across the furrows in that direction. I watched to make sure her feet stayed under her, then turned back to Wes.

"I won't keep you from your work," I smiled, "I just wanted to thank you for shipping that mare. Philippa was so happy, and I was very grateful for that."

I really looked at him then, adjusting my angle to the setting sun, and his eyes were going straight through me. I've never seen eyes to this day more powerful than Wes Snyder's. I had no clothing, and no defense except who I was, and I knew it that fast.

"I'm always happy to be kept from my work," he smiled, and shut the tractor down. "I didn't quite catch what Phipps said happened to her arm and the side of her head."

"She didn't answer you, that's why," I sighed, and breathed deep of the freshly turned earth. I was so tired of this story. "You sure you want to know?"

"Already I don't like it."

"About as much as I don't like him," I muttered, looking away toward Philippa's house. "Wes, I've been trying to work up a standard, two minute line of patter about how I ended up with Frank Tyler's wife, but it just isn't coming together. I don't want to make Frank out as the bogey man, mostly because Philippa's too darned decent to stand for it. To attempt to ennoble myself into a knight in shining armor is obviously ridiculous, so what do I say? We're friends who fell in love and finally gave in to it, I guess."

"You really going to try and take P.K. away from Frank?"

"Oh, you bet I am!" I said, looking him right in the eye, and he was smiling, really smiling, as one friend smiles at another when there is much between them. "Do I need to get in line?" I grinned.

"No sir. I'm too damned old and too much in love with Alice. But Philippa deserves a chance to be happy. She needs more of everything than what she gets, that's for sure. Frank worked her like a dog. The Hitchers tell me you're an actor."

"Um hm."

"And what else are you?"

"You mean as in, too old for her, city boy, former smoker, cries easily? Or, doctor, lawyer, Indian chief?"

"You're all right," Wes smiled. "I like a man who knows his limitations, and then stacks 'em up and stands on 'em and grabs what he wants."

I laughed, but I shook my head. "Believe me," I said, hoping he would, "I did not set out to take Frank's wife. It seemed like, after a while and after a fashion, he kind of pushed me into it. I am deeply in love with Philippa, and I have been since the first week I met her, but I'm not into taking things that belong to other people. So, let me off the hook here. What are you getting ready to plant?"

He told me. I leaned against the tractor wheel and learned a bit about the rhythm of the seasons. About the land as it is meant to be loved, not as a vicarious experience, but as a taskmaster. Philippa, I learned, could teach me these things, too.

Single handedly she had managed that place, up on a tractor, down on her knees in the mud. Chasing cattle at midnight. Lying on her back in the snow thawing pipes - working until she wept from exhaustion, turning to Wes only as a last resort. A strong, hard working woman. The more dirt, the more beautiful she became. Frank had built the house, yes, but Philippa had built the farm. Her light had burned late in the study as she wrote, and to hear that beautiful voice singing to greet the morning ... I was a lucky man.

I thanked Wes for the kind words, told him we'd talk again, and went back up to the house. I'd left the spa running. Mostly, I wanted time to think, not about anything in particular, just things in general. Little things, like how to make Phipps happy. Yes, I know we are supposed to make ourselves happy, not expect others to do it for us, but she made me happy. I wanted to return the favor. How was I to keep this woman I loved, this woman worthy of great respect, from becoming an object of raised eyebrows and whispers and tawdry comments? She'd stand for them rather than run Frank down, and I had no idea how to deal with that.

I'd unloaded the pickup and was soaking my poor abused back when I was joined by Saffron, a giant fluff of a cat who looked like Morris with beige toner, and I discussed the problem with him. He groomed his already immaculate white vest and spats, and rolled idly against my shoulder to tend his cotton candy tail, and he said, between licks, that anyone could be made happy by enough luxury and enough petting, as long as there was genuine love underneath. That's why he was glad to see Philippa. With her, there was none of this 'good kitty' malarkey. He was, simply, the center of the civilized universe. And, by the way, what was with the parade of strangers, including me? I wasn't bad. I had lots of fur and could possibly be a lower species of relative, but having to teach the drill to every Tom, Dick and Fuzzy who walked in the door was a drag.

I told him I was sorry. I told him he had my sympathy. I told him we had logistical problems. Umbilical problems, maybe. I knew if I asked Philippa to move she would. She'd lean her soft head against my chest and nod so I wouldn't hear the tears in her voice, and she would go. I was the one who was unwilling to pull the plug on simplicity. Saffron could groom himself as well in the Santa Monica Mountains as he could right here. I'd thought long and hard about selling Gram's house and buying someplace where we could have the horses. We were zoned for them where we were, and we had the acreage, but we also had neighbors who would most likely lose their minds at the thought of horses next door. I could sell. The place was worth a fortune. We'd be rich beyond our wildest dreams of avarice. We could retire on what we'd save in heating bills, alone.

I'd thought about building Phil a nice house on some acreage up near the kids, and each time, my mind went blank. I couldn't imagine going home to anywhere but the bird house. That's what all Gram's friends had called it, and that's what it had been – all nine thousand, three hundred and sixty square feet of it. She'd designed it herself, landscaping and all, using the bottom of a coffee cup and one of her father-in-law's business cards. It was her getaway spot, close in, but away from the hustle and bustle and the horn honking melee that was Hollywood in the roaring twenties. Then the stock market had crashed, the main house in Bel Air had gone on the block, and the country house had become home. Eventually, my home. Even when my mother and father had repurchased the family home in Bel Air and moved there to refurbish it, I had stayed with Gram.

I sometimes thought that I was a bit of an embarrassment to my parents. To Gram, who was a scandal all her own, I wasn't. I was, of course, a bastard. I believe the term now is love child, or no term at all, which is far better.

My father did everything he could, including producing some very convincing forged documents, to shake us free of the Third Reich, but the fact remained. They knew it, and after a while, so did I. So did all their friends and relatives and all the people they cared most about, and there was really no good explanation except that they'd been indiscreet and unprepared.

Suddenly, one of Hollywood society's darlings, one of its most eligible young bachelors, had a wife on paper and a son he couldn't even speak English to. Mother, noble Mother, would probably never even have told him about me had it not been for the sound of marching feet across our part of

Russia. By then, of course, it was nearly too late. God, what a mess. And I was back to Phipps and me.

Like my parents, Philippa and I had loved each other almost instantly, and been comfortable with one another just as fast. We were soulmates and we knew it. There had been no on again, off again romance, no serious drama between us. But around us, it seemed to be gathering momentum, and I wanted with all my heart to shield her from it. Had no idea how to do that, mind you, but it burned in my chest like a small, unquenchable fire.

She came hurrying in with apologies and kisses and went to start dinner. She was a fine actress, but I could see that her chat with Alice hadn't been all together upbeat. I got out and got dressed and went to help her, and as I was walking into the kitchen, the phone rang. Phipps had her hands full, so I answered it, and a very angry voice that I recognized as Kelly's said, "What the hell's going on, Bud?"

"I wear contacts, Kelly, not a hearing aid. Give me a reference."

"My grandparents," she said, and in those two words were a compendium of tears and pain and confusion. "My grandparents, just told me I wasn't welcome in their home! I stopped by to say hello, and they wouldn't even let me in the house!" By now, of course, she was crying.

Philippa's eyes were huge, and she kept saying, "What's wrong? Bud, what's wrong with Kelly?"

"Nothing is wrong with Kelly," I said. "Both of you, calm down. I'll switch the phone to the speaker, and I want this thing talked over, if not out."

I switched the phone over, put the receiver aside and told Kelly to repeat what she'd said. She did, a little more calmly, and Philippa burst into tears.

"Going well so far," I muttered, then added, louder, "Kelly, honey, I'm as sorry as I can be for what happened to you, and doubly sorry that it happened just before your birthday. I'll try to make it up to you, but the facts won't change. I don't quite know what was said, if anything, but ..."

"Daddy and I are getting a divorce. I'm sorry," Philippa said.

"That involves getting Dad arrested, put in jail, and you moving in with your boyfriend, Mother?"

Phipps clammed up, so I said, "It does when you've put your wife in the hospital, yes."

Another voice, Wenonah's, from another phone, and much more calm. "Mom, are you all right?"

"Of course I am, honey. It really wasn't ..."

At that point I figured what the hell, and said, "She's about to lie to you, and I'm not going to let her. I might as well have the whole harem mad at me at once. I found your mother unconscious, with a broken wrist, a smacked-in face and a nasty concussion. I moved her in with us because that was the only way the doctor would release her to go home."

"You just goaded Dad into hitting you so you could blame this on him!" Kelly sobbed.

I came back with "Funny, the argument was over your cars!" That was a mistake.

Wenonah started to cry with Phipps and Kelly and say she was sorry, the car could go back if it would help anything, and I laughed and told her she was a sweet kid.

"Girls, all of three of you, please calm down. The cars were just a flash point, as other things have been in the past. We have two people here who tried hard and failed. Frank's temperament is best suited for quiet, occasional, unemotional contacts with whomever he chooses to see. From now on …" I said, trying not to snarl, "that's not going to be your mother. Your mother, wants a different life, with a little more laughter and affection, a little more art and adventure, and I have come to fit in there, and I'm thrilled, because I love your mother, and I'd like the chance to love you, if you'll let me."

Phil's head came softly to rest in its accustomed place on my breast bone, and I bent to kiss her. "The whole thing with me getting arrested for stealing the pickup, and Frank getting arrested back, falls into the category of emotional idiocy on all sides, and it's between the three of us. It sure as hell shouldn't involve you two, or Frank's parents. I cannot apologize enough for that, nor can I do one thing about it. Just remember that all of us, even though we're bickering amongst ourselves right now, all of us love you, no matter how we're handling it, and all of us need you as a point of stability."

Philippa told me later, over a quiet supper by the fire, that I'd handled myself very well in the face of mob hysteria, and again, she was sorry for getting so upset. I reaffirmed my lifelong belief that people who remain calm when they should be upset, have every reason to be upset, can enjoy the emotional luxury of being upset, are not just so in the head. She said maybe that was why she loved me so much, and I said, likewise, I'm sure. I asked her about her visit with Alice, and she said it was fine. Period. I told her I'd had a nice visit with Wes, and later with Saffron, and they'd both given me some useful information. I didn't push her to confide in me. I could see she was tired, and I knew she was nervous. She called the Hitchers to let them know we'd made it safe, confirmed dinner, asked what we could bring, said we'd see them at church.

It was nice, being alone, just the two of us in a manageable little country house far from the noise of the city. It was nice to clear the dishes and bundle up to walk arm in arm in the moonlight. It was nice to be able to see the moon, and hear the crickets and the coyotes. We could do all those things at my house, but somehow this was different. This was like ... playing house for me. I'd never been without staff before. We were alone on the premises, and it made me feel really free, though I knew I'd have to learn how to do chores of different kinds and be a partner in all of this if it was going to work for us as a second home on a permanent basis.

Philippa apologized briefly for Kelly's sharp tongue. There had been a few other things said, though in a somewhat calmer vein. I needed to understand that even though Kelly wasn't Frank's by blood, she was still Frank's by inclination, much more so than Wenonah. She thought like him at times, and acted like him a little too often, and loved him dearly despite his faults, and that was as it should be. I agreed wholeheartedly. What puzzled me was that Kelly's grandparents didn't see that. I felt terrible for Kelly, but I really couldn't bring myself to feel guilty, and I wondered if someone would expect me to. Obviously, Philippa didn't. She would have spared me all of it, and I told her I had no desire to be spared. She had been married to one observer, she was not marrying another.

I didn't feel like I was harping marriage in the least. Philippa was not a woman to enjoy a dishonorable position. 'Living in sin', for instance. The term made me chuckle. What could be more sinful than marrieds who were abusive, or hateful? But then the whole Christian concept of sin was outside my realm of expertise. I was letting her know, from time to time, that it wasn't my desire, either, and it certainly wasn't permanent.

But it was ... delightful. I could turn her, so, in the moonlight, and tilt her chin with my forefingers, and stroke her cheekbones with my thumbs, and rub noses with her, and see the stars, literally see the stars reflected in her eyes, and kiss her, and pull her body against mine ... and know there was a future for us. She traced my face with her fingers and told me I took her breath away.

It made it easier to face Frank's clothes in the dresser drawers. I said I would make love to Phipps as often as she'd have me, and then some, but I would sleep ... upstairs. If I had to face Frank in the middle of some night, it would be with a semblance of dignity. Phipps said she was sure nothing would happen, but she could readily see my point. If I'd be more comfortable upstairs, that was fine with her. She asked me which room I'd prefer, and I grinned and said, "The one without the big train set in it. Is Frank a railroader?"

"No," she grinned back, "I am."

I added that to the list of things I knew I could buy and please her. I asked her if there was anything else I could do for her this evening, or if she'd prefer just to take a nice bubble bath and go to sleep. She assured me, even though she blushed, that in order to be as good as she'd need to be tomorrow, she'd need to be very bad tonight. I was agreeable, and asked her if she had anything in mind.

"Well, yes, I do," she squirmed, "but ... well, I'm not very straight laced when it comes to sex, and if I offended you, I'd be embarrassed to death, Peter."

"Does this involve whips or animals?" I teased. I know it's mean to torment someone who's flustered, but you haven't seen Phipps. Ordinarily, she's the soul of calm, even to the slightly aloof and silent side, mostly because she's shy, and to watch that dissolve into sputtering adolescence, is so endearing to me. I love watching that serenity start to simmer.

"It doesn't involve anything or anybody but you and me and the somewhat opposite ends of our anatomy, so to speak," she snapped, and I knew what she had in mind. "Now, of course, I'm too embarrassed to do it."

"Mmmmm, bet you're not," I whispered. I sat down in the big recliner and put her across my lap, cradling her in my arms as I kissed her and unbuttoned her blouse to fondle her. Apologies to Phipps, but her breasts, hairline scars notwithstanding, are truly exciting. They are large, and firm and round, and her nipples are upturned and pink and just about the right size to fit a wine glass over. They respond quickly to the touch of fingers or a tongue.

They responded to both this evening, and Philippa began to tremble under my hands. My breath quickened with my heart, and Phipps slid out of my lap onto her knees in front of the chair. She brought her elbows through between my knees, and I let my head roll back against the chair and closed my eyes. She released me from my jeans and that was fine, stroked me with her hands, and that was better, but when her mouth took over I gasped for air, broke out in a cold sweat, and slapped my hands, priest-like, over my private parts.

"Oh, shit," I groaned, realizing I'd whacked her nose. "Oh, Phipps, I'm so sorry!"

I forced my head up, forced my eyes open, and Philippa was looking at me, arms discreetly folded across my lap, waiting. I just shook my head and looked away. "You didn't hurt me," I said. "I'm okay. I didn't scratch your nose, did I?"

She moved the casted arm just a bit and I could see where she'd placed her left hand. "These aren't just little stretch marks, are they?" she said quietly, and her fingers traced an inch or so of the scars without her hand moving. "Either your Rabbi was a friend of Jack the Ripper, or you really had a kinky girlfriend at some point. Are those tooth marks, or fingernails, or both?"

I just nodded. I couldn't look at her. I was too embarrassed. "Well, now you know where my stupidity scars are," I muttered. "Should have explained those before now, though when, exactly, escapes me."

God that had hurt. Dear God, how that had hurt. I could still feel it. I could still hear myself scream. I could still feel my palm cracking into the side of Lora's face to make her stop. It bled horribly, and Lora had blood all over her teeth and her face and her fingernails, and she was smiling, and I knew, beyond any lies I'd told myself and any excuses I'd made for her, that she was not perceiving what normal people perceived. And all the time I was looking at that smiling, blank, bloody face I was fighting shock and nausea, and trying to figure out how I could stop the bleeding, how I could get help, how I could face the help I'd get.

Somehow, God's mercy, I suppose, the bleeding reduced to an ugly ooze, and in the morning I'd managed to get to my doctor's office, figuring I was a goner and knowing for sure I didn't care. Someone I genuinely cared for had done this to me. I was so blind, and so stupid I didn't even see the drugs she was using.

I could feel Doctor Hammond's arms come up to steady me ... and realized it was Philippa, snuggling her head against my chest. I drew a deep breath and began to unknot inside. "I honestly had no idea that would happen," I said. "I was ready for you."

"Good," she smiled, "because I'm still ready." She could see I was somewhat startled and gave me a moment to recover while she shut off the lights, leaving the woodstove as our only illumination. "Get back on that horse, Aarons," she grinned settling at my feet.

"Get me up in the saddle," I murmured. I kissed her and slid my hand in where her shirt was still unbuttoned from before. No tales to tell, confessions to make, therapy to go through. Best of all, no sympathy.

"This time, keep your eyes open," Phipps said as she unzipped my jeans. "Watch ..." a gentle lick, "... and tell me what you like." Then she made a little purring sound and began. My little gardener, my blusher, my quilt maker, was indeed an eater of men, and I wasn't the least bit sorry.

When I had shuddered back into myself and managed to extricate my boot heels from the carpet and begun to say rational things again, I stretched in the chair and said, "You, are a marvel, Sweet Face. Thank you. Now, are you hanging by your fingernails?"

"Anticipating, perhaps, but not hanging," she smiled. "You relax and have a cigarette. Ah, no. Sorry. Have a ... well, suck your thumb or something and I'll make some tea."

Hanging by her fingernails. Why had that term come to mind? Doctor Hammond had used it, too. Apparently the damage I'd felt from Lora's teeth wasn't the worst of the damage done. Her nails had ripped deeply into my groin and the underside of my thighs, as well.

"Bud," he'd said, "I wish you'd let me put you in the hospital. "You came damned close to being bit in two. You need a catheter, you need stitches. You may well need a transfusion and surgery."

"Do it here," I'd snarled.

He'd given me what he called a saddle block, and two seconds after I stopped hurting I was sound asleep. I'd awakened at some point and seen blood draining into my hand. Hammond had assured me that this pint was mine. The last pint, had been Kit's. I'd wept, brought my arms across the sudden, excruciating pain in my chest, and quickly found myself in the same hospital to which I'd taken Philippa. As Layman had said, very expensive, very discreet. I'd wondered, when he gave me that tranquilizer, how he'd known I took other medication. My records were right in front of him. He knew all. Damn.

I'd spent four days in the hospital having EKG's run every day, a week at home barely able to walk – a week avoiding Lora for fear of killing her with my bare hands – and two minutes telling her goodbye. A month later, while she was still trying to patch things up, and I was still trying to get things up, she went through the windshield into oncoming traffic. I'd taken up with Mi Ling Chang again, having been tested to be sure I hadn't caught anything from dear little Lora.

Mi Ling and I indulged in all sorts of activities of a sexual nature, but one thing Mi Ling and I didn't do, and never had done, was perform oral sex on one another. I loved it, but she'd hated it with something amounting to religious fervor, so I couldn't very well have known I was gun-shy.

Actually, I'd not had a partner who was really into oral sex since my twenties. Since that wild eyed redhead, Bobbi Bates. Megan certainly hadn't been much for that sort of thing. She'd thought it was germy and nasty, and had said so under no uncertain terms the first time I'd approached her with the idea. Everybody had thought she'd be good in bed because she was tall and gorgeous, and she wasn't good at all. She was unimaginative, a tad frigid, occasionally disinterested, often condescending. More into being beautiful than passionate. At least she had been with me. I chuckled softly and smiled with the foretaste of things to come. If tonight had been any indication, I was going to be both indulged and re-educated by somebody who flat out knew what she was doing.

Philippa handed me a fragrant cup of herb tea and folded gracefully onto the floor near the fire. What a beautiful woman. What a sane, sweet, intelligent woman. How had I managed, with all the men there are in the world, to attract this person who dovetailed so perfectly with me?"

"Penny for your thoughts," she said softly.

"You, Philippa Kate. Always," I said, and my heart was so full of love for her I could hardly speak. I finished my tea, set the cup aside, and took her to bed.

There is something to be said for sex at any age. Sex at sixteen is novel, at twenty-one it is strong. At thirty it becomes more mature, more passionate. At forty it truly fills the senses when it is present, and leaves you pretty much alone when it isn't. At fifty, or thereabouts, if you are healthy, and alert, and keep yourself physically fit, you have the maturity and experience to call all those things into play – novelty, strength, passion, sensual fulfillment – all those and more. To discover at that age that you are truly in love, for the first time in your life, really, truly in love, is electrifying. To know that the person whom you love, loves you, and honors and respects you for yourself alone and has dreams for you and about you, and wants to live with you always, that knowledge, can bring you such peace, and such fulfillment that you will know for sure no part of life is meant to be wasted. I learned that in the arms of Philippa Kate Tyler ... my sweet Phipps.

I awoke to the crowing of roosters, and to a gilt edged gossamer morning such as this old world hasn't seen since the fall of Adam. Even now I can close my eyes and bring back the colors, the fragrances, the beauty of that perfect morning. Had I been told at that point that it was rather a usual morning here, I'd have shaken my head in disbelief. As it was, I had only to push the sheets down under my arm and gaze in wonder.

There were brown Mallard ducks and huge white geese splashing in a pond which mirrored the rose gold east horizon. There were cattle and horses and fluffy white lambs almost close enough to touch, it seemed, and purple topped alfalfa, and crystal jets of water circling above the green of the permanent pasture, and Philippa's fruit trees just outside the frame of white chintz curtains. And beyond, on the hills that rolled to the north – apples, endless apples. All this, and I had done nothing but move my eyes in my head, or so it seemed.

I yawned, and stretched, and eased myself onto my back, adjusting the covers against the cool fragrance of a breeze through the partially opened window. I began to hear the animals. The colors became less pink, more gold as the sun came up. A pump stopped, and to the left of my vision the sprinklers stopped also. I closed my eyes. Somewhere down below in the pasture I heard Phil's raised, slightly irate voice say, "Grandpa, move your fat butt. Now!"

I figured it wouldn't hurt me to do likewise ... in a minute. I'd had a bad night. My knee had forced me out of bed every couple of hours, demanding to be massaged and walked, thoroughly waking me up each time. Usually, I could sleep at least three hours at a stretch without problems, and right now, I needed my sleep. I just was not ready to get up.

What a pretty, soothing room. Blue with a white ceiling and white stenciling at the tops of the walls. Massive old mahogany dressers, intricately carved, polished until I could see myself in them, and the huge, comfortable bed that held me so lovingly, so possessively, refusing to let me go. I'd decided I'd have to take my chances with Frank. Just this once.

I heard sprinkler pipes bang together and realized with a guilty start that Phipps wasn't out visiting the animals, she was out moving sprinklers and I was lying on my indolent ass in bed. I was up and dressed and down beside her in five minutes flat.

I kissed her good morning, handed her a cup of coffee and said, "You know, Sweet Face, this is not doing your wrist any good."

Instantly, a dozen words into the morning, she had her defenses up. "There's work to be done, Peter." she said edgily. She realized she was snapping, nestled the coffee cup down in the young grass of the pasture, and gave me a much nicer kiss than my whiskers warranted. "Do you have any suggestions?"

"I do," I smiled, returning the kiss. "We need to set about finding a permanent couple, like Glory and Rafael. I was looking at the house, and it would be easy to go off the living room with an addition. Or we could tuck a modular or build a cottage like Glory and Rafael's behind those willows over there," I gestured with my chin, "and both of us would have more privacy, which I would prefer. I do think the bunk house is a goner for all intents and purposes."

"The geese love it," she grinned. "Besides, you have the cart before the horse. Frank may want the place sold."

She picked up the coffee cups, and I picked up a length of aluminum pipe. "So," I said, "we buy it. He can't prevent that."

"No, but he can put a higher price on his half if there's more square footage, or improvements to the property."

"True," I smiled. Good businesswoman.

"Maybe, we should just sell it, Bud," she sighed. "Why have it if somebody else is going to work it? Your home is in Los Angeles, and you love it there."

"I thought you loved it here," I said, and her eyes filled up with stress. "Philippa, let go of some of your money worries. Money, you have. Me, you have. Money, I have. Don't feel that you have to be painfully practical to stay on my good side. How do I do this?"

"Bend at the waist, line up the pipe in your hand with the pipe you're joining, reduce the angle, and give it a gentle push 'til it clicks. Very good! I'm gonna make a farmer out of you. Now, give it a little tug to be sure it catches, and straighten the riser. That's the part with the head on it. Look behind you and line it up with that white marker on the back fence. There you go, you got it. Just be sure you don't catch any weeds or grass in your couplings or they'll leak."

"I hear," I said, starting back across for the next thirty foot section, and stopping for a minute to pet the old stallion who was supervising, "You're a beauty, yes you are. Now, move over there. I hear, that you work on this place until you cry, sometimes."

"It happens. One gets tired and frustrated, and there's no one to turn to, even for a hug."

"But it looks like you made it, Kiddo."

"So far. You see, the secret to success, as Jean told Mark, is in not stopping to cry. You cry while you work."

"What if you get tired of crying while you work?"

"You choose to give up, or not to give up," she said, puzzled.

"P.K., you can choose at this point not to cry and work. Many, many people own farms who neither work them nor live there full time. These people are called, gentry. Say it after me."

She laughed, and her face brightened. I still found it odd that when it came to money Phipps needed to be told the obvious. I have since learned it's easier just to accept that little quirk and explain things. "The house in LA is paid for. This could be our getaway place. I think, I really do, that here, with all this peace and all this beauty, I could write the very best music I'm capable of. Obviously you write incredible books here. Phipps, I love it already. I don't want to sell this place."

"I don't either," she sighed, and I scooped her up in my arms. She let out a startled little squeak, then laughed her deep laugh and put her arms around my neck.

"Say you'll teach me to be a farmer!"

"I'll teach you to be a farmer," she laughed. "Say you'll teach me to be a city slicker."

"Never!" I laughed in return, "but I will give you your very own patch of dirt to dig in. Oops, that's soil, isn't it?"

"Um hm," she murmured, nuzzling my neck where it joined my shoulder. "We'd better find a couple fast. We'll never get anything done at this rate."

We did get done. We got everybody fed and watered and I managed to get the shock of my life on the hot wire. Phipps had told me it would knock a horse down. How I forgot it was there I'll never know, but I sure as hell never forgot again.

We went in the house to have breakfast and dress for church, and I could feel Philippa getting tighter, quieter …tighter and quieter … then something set her off and her hairbrush bounced off the wall along with a couple words I'd never heard her use, followed by a quick, "Sorry Lord, sorry Bud."

I rubbed her shoulders and kissed her hair as I brushed and braided it, and felt like I was trying to hold a wildcat in a sack; one false move and she'd go spitting and scratching up the front of me. It gave me an inkling how Frank must have felt, and why he may have reacted as he did.

Poor Phipps wanted to go to this church she loved so much, and missed, so much about like I wanted a root canal. She was in her place of refuge, and there was none. She wasn't comfortable with anything – the house, the workload, the people – who might come driving up the driveway. She was better off in Los Angeles, at least for now, going to services with Glory and coming home to hide herself securely behind our wrought iron gates.

It was hard for me to think about, because there were things that were sacred to me, too. I had not the vaguest idea how to convey to her that I understood what she was feeling. I knew if I mentioned it to her, she'd feel guilty. She'd think it was a weakness in her own personality. She'd wonder what she'd done to deserve it. She'd wonder what evil thing she'd done that her God was punishing her. That, would be immediately obvious. She was living in a dishonorable situation with a non-Christian.

Now there was an idea, I thought as I crouched slightly to rake a comb through my hair – I needed to raise the bathroom mirrors in this place – I could just give in to Glory's years of gentle persuasion and my Russian Orthodox heritage on my mother's side. Throw in the towel, go from Shylock to Antonio for Philippa's sake. I could turn Christian. But Shylock has such great speeches.

What a mess. All I had to do was mention religion or morality, and Philippa was an instant basket case. I just cannot believe God meant for us to love Him amid all these unjust and immoral rules of our own making. God was meant to be loved as God. People were meant to be loved as people. When we try tying the two relationships together, we have problems. We have problems like my precious, kind, long suffering Philippa, fighting her tears all the way to church, afraid of what her fellow believers would think because at last she was happy and in love.

I wasn't thrilled either, but I've played the provinces before. Too, my eyes are so dark my pupils don't show. I can look just a tad above people's eyes if they bother me. Besides, dammit, I'd won an Emmy for best supporting actor in a dramatic series. I was supporting Philippa. If it took an act, so be it, but she wasn't going in there alone.

As we got out of the Ford I said quietly, "Do I touch you? Do I not touch you?"

"Frank never touched me, ever," she responded, looking embarrassed and a little ashamed.

"Frank, was a fool," I said, pulled her to me, kissed her temple, and started across the parking lot. "Now remember, this is being made for prime time television, not the Plain Brown Wrapper of the Month Club ..."

"We're not going to do anything you can't handle, and we're not going to do anything I can't handle," she grinned, and her chin came up.

"Ovid said, 'We two form a multitude,'" I whispered to her as the first pairs of curious eyes turned our way, and with those words in mind, I took the pastor's outstretched hand, and went on in to my first Christian church service.

CHAPTER ELEVEN

My father would have been disappointed. They didn't sacrifice a virgin. They didn't sway or chant or read chicken entrails, or do anything even vaguely bizarre. Little strange, maybe, but not frightening. They sang songs and clapped their hands to the accompaniment of a nice piano and a skillfully played guitar, and at prayer time they prayed aloud, each his own prayer, and some of them sang before God, softly. They did, many of them, raise their hands in prayer. Phil raised only her left hand, bent at the elbow. Her casted arm, she kept around my waist. Her voice was strong and beautiful, and blended with the others as they sang, and the whole church sounded like a choir.

While it wasn't my cup of tea, I honestly was not uncomfortable. Of course I had Phipps on my left and Oscar Hitcher on my right. Phipps sensed what I needed to know, and Oscar was asleep most of the time, so I was well insulated. Pastor Knox welcomed all the guests, including me, preached a moderately interesting and somewhat condescending sermon about perseverance and released us with a prayer. Ruth gently jostled Oscar back to life, and we were ready to go.

It wasn't until we got to the Hitcher's house that I met the whole clan. I'd met Oscar and Ruth, now I met their daughter, Adelle, plump, petite and dark haired – her native blood obvious in her features and the timbre of her voice. There was Adelle's husband Dennis, who had helped lead the service, their son, Kenny who looked to be about Alexander's age, and baby Sarah, who was seven months and utterly charming.

To Philippa's delight the elder daughter was there, visiting from Spokane. Jan, was her name, and she was a taller, heavier copy of her sister. Her husband, Steve was with her, and their teenage sons, Matthew, and Mark, and daughter, Mary.

"Mary was supposed to be a Luke," Oscar said, "but Lucretia seemed a mite cruel, even for her. Bud, sit," he said, pointing to a chair. The men sat down in the living room, the teens went outside, and the women disappeared into the kitchen.

Before I had time to dread the silence, little tousle topped Kenny sidled up to me, gave me a long look – the street shoes, the tan slacks, the pink shirt and tan sweater, the silvering sideburns – which he puzzled over for some moments. Then, slowly, he smiled and lisped through the gaps in his teeth, "I thtill know who you are, even wearing old hair."

"You think so, do you?" I grinned, winking at Dennis, who had his mouth open to apologize. I arched one eyebrow in mock disbelief. "You mean this disguise won't do?"

"No!" he laughed, wiggling like a puppy, "You're Nathan Sthrauss."

"Foiled again. You got me," I smiled. "What did you say your name was, stranger?"

"Kenny John."

"Kenny John what?"

"Kenneth Othcar John," he laughed. Cute. Rumpled, but cute.

"Tell me, Ken, what grade are you in?"

"Firsth," he sighed. Obviously not a favorite subject. "But thcool's almotht out."

"You ready, hm?"

"Oh, man, yeth!" he exclaimed.

"Bad year, first grade?"

I felt Phil's hands on my shoulders as Kenny said, "English, wath pretty awful."

"Boy, I hear that!" I laughed.

Philippa asked, "Did your grandmother really, truly send you to school without knowing any English at all?"

"Well," I shrugged, "I'd been in the States a couple months. I knew please, thank you, and bathroom. I guess she considered me adequately prepared."

"Seems awfully cruel," Dennis said.

"Oh, it was. I cried for a solid month. Max, Gram's Chauffeur, was black and blue from trying to drag me out of the car every morning. But, at the end of that month, my English wasn't all that bad. If she'd babied me it would have taken much longer. I really don't hold it against her."

"You're amazing," Phil said, and kissed the top of my head. "Who wants coffee, who wants tea, who wants iced tea?"

She counted hands and left, and Kenny went with her, figuring where there was coffee there must be cookies. Here, there was silence.

"So, how about those Mariners!" Steve said helpfully.

"No, let's just get this over with," I sighed, "while Philippa's out of the room. I don't know who feels more awkward, you or me, but I am very much in love with Philippa, and Phipps loves you guys. You're her family. And I know you love Frank. I'd like to think I can give you some decent explanation of what I'm doing with his wife ... if I can. Especially you, Dennis, because I know you and Frank are very close."

"I also know Frank and Philippa weren't happy together a lot of the time," Dennis said kindly. "They just have so little in common. I'm not surprised she left him. She hated being left behind, she hated what he did for a living ..."

"She's not that petty ..." I snapped, and immediately caught myself. "Sorry, go on, Dennis."

But he didn't. He just looked at me. They all did.

"I'm really trying to get over being so defensive. My emotions get the better of my common sense and I shoot my mouth off."

"Me, too!" Steve Kirk said. "At least now I'll have some company at family gatherings. Phipps tried really hard with Frank, at least around us. I've often envied him his solicitous and caring wife. But you know, she'd be cutting up with the girls," there was a shriek of laughter from the kitchen and Steve grinned, "...like that. She's so crazy anyway, and so much more intellectual and sophisticated than the rest of us, and Frank would walk in on them, and instantly, she was on her best behavior. She'd stop laughing if she was laughing, stop saying whatever it was she was saying, even if it was some really beautiful idea. Instant silence when he walked in, even though I never heard him raise his voice to her."

"You're imagining things," Oscar said. "I wouldn't want my husband to see me act the way those girls do when they're alone."

"You're there and they don't shut up," Dennis said. "I'm there and they don't shut up. But Frank would walk into a room and they all shut up. There was just something about him."

Something menacing as hell, I thought, but my lips didn't move.

"Bud," Steve smiled, "how came you to have Frank Tyler's wife? Tell us, get it off your chest, and forgive yourself."

"All right, for good or ill. I came to have her because I treat her like a human being," I sighed, still wishing for that cigarette. "I met her, one smoggy Los Angeles morning, and she was bright and windblown and beautiful, and her voice was as mellow as a Stradivarius, and in five minutes, maybe less, from the first time she laughed, I cared deeply for Philippa Tyler. She's everything I've ever wanted in a friend, in a business partner ... in a wife. And Frank ignored her long enough, and browbeat her enough, that she took her eyes off him, just for a second, and there I was. And here I will stay, between her and that ..." Damn, I couldn't say it. I couldn't tell them how I had felt ... the grief and outrage ... seeing that big bloody hand print, like a brand. I pressed my thumb to my mouth, and willed myself not to mist up.

Steve asked quietly, "Frank work her over like that?"

I nodded, and caught my breath, and the tears receded. "I found her afterward. Funny, she was wearing that blouse ... only that's a remake. The other one was bloody and torn. Blood won't come out of silk."

"It won't come out of that cashmere you're wearing, either," Phipps warned beside my left shoulder. "Don't pick on Frank."

"And which of these gentlemen has a sister we can introduce to Frank in your place?" I said testily.

"Phipps?" Jan said beside her, and the war was put on hold. "Did you sugar Dad's coffee?"

"Yes, I did," Phil said, handing me a dainty cup and saucer. She smiled at me, and kissed my temple, and the fire cooled in her eyes. I hoped, someday, she would be so loyal in defense of my idiocy.

I shouldn't even have thought such a thing. It was like throwing up a red flag in the face of the gods. Jan perched on an ottoman close to me and said, "I know this is a terrible question to ask a perfect stranger out of the blue, but you are a movie person, and this is important for me as a Christian."

I just smiled and gestured for her to speak.

"Is it true that ... well, I've heard that in some of those movies, people really ... make love. Do they? I mean, I'd hate to think we're supporting that."

I resisted the urge to snicker and shook my head. "If you're talking mainstream and not porn, and if you are using make love as a euphemism for have sex, I wouldn't know, but I'd seriously doubt it. A movie set is a very unromantic place, actually. Usually." Good. I wasn't turning any particular color. I'd have felt it if I was.

"I've heard that girls have gotten ... pregnant ... I mean, that they've actually been ..."

She turned really red and I hastened to say, "I know what you mean. Again, I doubt it. I'm sure they make movies I'm not invited to, but the ones I've been in on, have been relatively clean. No intercourse on camera." Not quite a lie on my part. I was fighting to keep a straight face.

"No need to change sheets between scenes," Dennis teased, just to make Jan blush, but it was Philippa who clapped her hand over her mouth, and headed for the kitchen.

My mind went right out the window. "You're comparing apples and oranges," I said stiffly. "Sexual intercourse is, please God, always voluntary. The rest of it, as you gentlemen well know, can be strictly an involuntary, physiological phenomenon."

Oscar, who was dead serious, asked, "How do you know that?"

And Steve, who is a rascal, said, "Yes, Bud, how do you know that?"

Then I came up out of my chair a little too fast and said, "Excuse me while I go kill that little hyena in the kitchen."

Nice day. Nice people. I got my hands on Sarah and kissed her, and played with her tiny fingers and toes and wondered when Kelly and Wen would bless us with grandchildren. Grandchildren. Granddad. "Go tell your grandfather he wants you." Grandpa Aarons. I could handle that. Like the chance, as a matter of fact. Actually, when I looked at Phipps, the thought of a baby of our own sounded wonderful, but not very likely, given the mutual dearth of equipment. I wondered, just for a second or two ... or three ... what she'd say if I said, adoption. I looked at Phipps, looked at Sarah ... back at Phipps ... and sighed. Better marry the girl, first. Beautiful baby, Sarah. Kenny, was great. Normal. Slightly unhinged. I vowed to myself to get Kenny and Alexander together. Poor little Alex needed someone normal in his life. Maybe this summer.

Kenny climbed in my lap and I explained to him that Nathan Strauss was a character, like somebody in a book. The town he owned, and the mill, and the people, were like a game, played on film. Like when Kenny was He Man, he went back to being Kenny in time for dinner.

One of Grandma Ruth's dinners, definitely. There was an excellent roast from beef Philippa had raised for them, and six kinds of vegetables and four salads, and three different kinds of pie, including wild huckleberry, and I got regaled with the story of how all of them had gone to get the huckleberries, and Phipps had been so worried about bears she'd hardly picked any berries. There was quite a row over that. She'd picked as many as anybody else. Frank had come sneaking, growling, shaking the bushes, and Phipps had screamed, and nearly bashed his head in with a tree branch. Another row ensued. She'd known all along it was Frank. She just wanted to humor him. She had. Everyone agreed she'd been most convincing.

Fascinating interplay of family. Oscar, half Lakota Sioux himself, had married a beautiful, half Nez Perce woman while they were both still in college, and their first pastorship had been in Muskogee, Oklahoma, Philippa's hometown. These girls had been born in the same hospital, raised in the same church, been babes and best friends together in Oklahoma for many years before Oscar's denomination had sent him to pastor a newly built church in Washington State. He'd built it up, nourished it, and two years ago, he'd turned it over to Pastor Knox. Philippa, his beloved foster daughter, had moved there in the not too distant past, supported his efforts, sung in the choir with Adell and Dennis, and celebrated his retirement.

As they reminisced, I realized was a window through which I could look into Philippa's past, and I listened very carefully to what was being said. She was, as I suspected, a rowdy, impetuous, impertinent, precocious, fiery tempered brat. They loved her, were proud of what she had become, had faith in what she would later be, and trusted her good sense. I knew that in there someplace, was an acceptance speech. I was welcome to make myself part of the family.

Frank's name came up more directly, and Phipps asked them all please, please to be supportive of Frank. He didn't have the emotions to yell and cry and be angry and blow off some of the hurt. He would hold it inside and let it fester, and even though he couldn't say so, he would be in a lot of pain. His pride must be hurt if nothing else. Everyone said they liked Frank because he was Frank, not because he was Philippa's husband. He was no less loved and no less welcome than he'd ever been. They would pray for him.

Oscar, who was a no-nonsense sort of a guy, asked me what my plans were for Phipps, and I said I planned to marry her as soon as legally I could. Other than that, I was sure the lady had plans of her own. She was still on the Best Seller list, she'd written a screenplay, she was starring opposite this lucky man in a six hour TV miniseries....

The gasps were audible, and the whole family started talking at once. Phipps hadn't said one word, not a word to them about the fact that she was acting. From the look on her face, she hadn't planned to, either.

They watched mostly Christian Broadcasting, never even looked at the supermarket rags. Somehow, they'd missed it all. Amazing, isn't it, that once you know something, you begin to assume its common knowledge? I cringed and bit my tongue. Even though these people loved Philippa, they were straight laced, fundamentalist folk. What would they think when they saw some of the hotter scenes in that miniseries? If they didn't support the film industry, how wholeheartedly could they support someone who was in it? Too late, I realized the damage I may well have done. But if Philippa hadn't wanted anything said, why didn't she tell me? Another puzzle. New game. New rules, and I didn't know them.

I took a chance, and I bragged about Philippa Kate Tyler. I told them she was not only very talented, she had the guts and integrity to give that talent meaning. Our production company, which was an associate satellite, was honored by her work, and by her presence, and when we were through with the miniseries, we were hoping to have her develop another of her manuscripts into a regular network series for us. We also had plans – several – to utilize her acting talents, and I needed her to help me research a part I had coming up.

This, of course, would leave us pretty much in Los Angeles for the foreseeable future. I thanked Ruth and Oscar again for the job they'd done and the peace of mind they'd brought Phipps and me, and told them we were going to need a permanent couple for the farm. Perhaps there was someone in the church or community they could recommend? Everyone said they'd ask around.

What a day. How good it was to hear Philippa laughing. How special to take her in my arms and kiss her – actually I'd kind of forgotten where we were momentarily and we got caught – and have her blush, and have them know I treasured their friend. As the afternoon waned we said goodbye, invited them all out to the house, and said we'd see them soon. Phipps seemed relaxed and happy and back on firm footing emotionally.

I'd learned a truth I'd suspected. Philippa could handle most things that came her way as long as she worked with a net. She needed people. Not many, but a few, who truly loved and supported her and questioned her only sparingly.

We declined the invitation to evening services; farm chores had spoken for us already. And what an evening. What a different evening than those I'd always thought women considered romantic. No theater tickets, no smoky lounges, no clinking crystal, nothing that glittered but the silver lengths of sprinkler pipe, nothing intrusive but the horse's soft muzzles, checking for more apples. It wasn't easy work, but it was pleasant, with all Frank's cats bounding like tigers through the jungle of alfalfa and grass and walking the lengths of pipe as I linked them up.

Philippa pointed, and there was a lone heron, black against the deep orange sky as he skimmed over us headed down river, like a painting on a butterfly's wing. The fragrances were crisp and separate, then blended by a very soft, cool breeze. It was heavenly, and Philippa advised me to enjoy it. Tomorrow evening at this time the humidity might be hellish. Then again, the pipes might be frozen together. One never knew this time of year.

Supper was simple. A thick chicken soup, full of vegetables and superbly seasoned, and corn bread made from freshly ground field corn, and sliced tomatoes still sun warm from the greenhouse. I was amazed – I was awed – and I'm not even sure why, anymore. I think maybe it was the dichotomy between beautiful, educated, witty woman and old fashioned, hard muscled farm woman that dazzled me. A Renaissance female of the first order. She could, and can, change so quickly. Now, I'm used to it. Then, I wasn't. Now, I'm used to seeing her in a variety of settings. Then, the setting itself was novel.

I felt, perhaps incorrectly, that I was really beginning to know Philippa by then. I was beginning to see not only her great depth and variety of emotions and mentality, but her flaws and shallow spots as well. I think, because of her vast range, her ability to change almost from one person to another, Phipps is a bit unstable. I don't think it's anything Frank did to her. I think it's something she'd been all along, and he couldn't handle it. It didn't, and doesn't bother me. I'm high strung myself. I saw it only as an area where she needed extra support from time to time. I saw no need to run, or hit, or even be concerned. People had certainly compensated enough for my foibles over the years. I was trained to return the favor.

She went into her study to work on an idea for a new novel, and I sort of wandered around at loose ends. I turned the TV on, and turned it off. I found Philippa's twelve string guitar and tuned it and played it for a while, and fiddled with the stereo, and turned on the spa.

At last Philippa came out of the study and said, patiently, through her teeth, "Babe, please go in the living room, and push all the furniture around. Throw away anything you need to, until you have room enough for a piano. Then, first thing tomorrow morning go into town to the Steinway dealer. He's been there since 1910 – he carries splendid pianos. Try them all, and buy yourself one. As a matter of fact, I'll buy you one as an engagement present if you'll just light!"

I laughed, and lit. I'd already figured out where the piano needed to go. It involved losing a very nice Duncan Phyfe dining room table. I mentioned it a little later. "You know," I said tentatively, "maybe we should put an addition on the house, but not for whomever comes to help us ..."

"You mean like a music room," Phil said, coming to sit on the arm of my chair.

"It's either that, or chop up that table for kindling."

"Or, let me think," she put her finger to her temple and looked terribly studious, "we could slide the buffet in next to the table and put the piano where the buffet is."

"See, you're smart. I don't know why people say the things they do about you," I teased, not bothering to tell her that the piano I had in mind was going to need a lot more floor space than moving that buffet was going to provide. I tugged her belt loop just a little, just enough to topple her into my arms, and we vowed we'd get to work ... tomorrow.

Monday morning there was no need to move sprinkler pipe. It was pouring raining and freezing cold. I unplugged the diesel, and armed with Philippa's directions, I gingerly skidded back into town. The store wasn't big, but it wasn't hard to find, either. It was right on the main street in an older section of town where the trees were well established, and so were the businesses.

I was greeted by an elderly gentleman who reminded me a little of my father in a white-maned sort of a way, and I told him I needed a good piano to practice on. He showed me several; a Yamaha, a Wurlitzer, some Steinways. Then I said, "I don't mean any offense, but I need a good piano. May I play one of these for you rather than you playing it for me?"

He nodded, looking a little annoyed, so I sat down at one of the baby grands, and played it for him.

"You should have mentioned you'd had lessons," he said when I was finished. "I thought you meant you needed an indestructible piano. How important are looks to you?"

"What do you mean?"

"You said a piano to practice on. Does it have to be new?"

"I ... no, I guess not," I said, feeling that I might be let in on some marvelous secret. "What do you have?"

"Come with me," he said, and as he led me down a narrow hall into a back room he explained. "There is an old theater in this town. Originally, it was used for Vaudeville, and many fine artists played here. It has been restored now. Have you seen it?"

I said I had not. I'd only been here a couple of days.

"You must see it." He said. "It has good acoustics. The man who owned the theater wanted to attract not only the popular artists, but the fine ones – great pianists and singers who would need the best accompaniment. In his quest to do this, he sent for a piano." We had stopped in a room where a piano sat under a dust cover. "This, is the piano," he said, and removed the sheet.

It was a forty-six inch professional Steinway. It was scratched, and there was green paint splashed on its brown stained legs. Its finish was marred with rings from wine glasses and vases. Two of the keys were whiter than the rest, indicating they'd been replaced. He pushed a bench up to the keyboard, said, "It's tuned," and gestured for me to sit down.

My first music on that piano, was like love with an older woman – mellow and responsive and deep. It had a nice crisp bite and the superb action you get only from that magnum opus of pianos. When I finally turned on the bench to look up at him, it was to ask, not how much he wanted for it, but rather if he would part with it.

"The great pianists were few and far between, and this fine instrument has spent years being pushed into corners of a stage, being whacked by giraffe doors, and used for a cocktail table. Finally, she was dug out of the storage room to which she had been relegated, and sent to me for disposal. I think it's high time she went on to more dignified things," he said, and reluctantly gave me a price.

I choked a little, but I didn't sputter, and I didn't haggle, I just handed him a credit card. I'd come to town to spend money, after all, and this certainly qualified. I made arrangements to have the piano delivered that afternoon, which was no small accomplishment, and asked about a good jeweler.

Caldicott sent me three doors down to a business as old as his, a man as old as he, and I went home with a pair of very simple diamond earrings for Philippa. I figured I'd have trouble getting her to wear even a wedding ring, and an engagement ring seemed somehow inappropriate. Earrings, she wore. I'd put them aside for a romantic moment.

That sweet person was not at home. She'd left a note. She was checking on some of our elderly neighbors, and she'd be home when she saw the truck. She'd see two. I could hear the air brake set on the tractor over the sound of me moving furniture. "Well," I said to Saffron, "at least I've got my pants on."

I went out the door into the ragged, watery sunshine to greet ... or something ... Frank, but he was holding the old black cat, and didn't seem to notice me. His voice was gentle, his hands were gentle, his eyes were soft, and I had no defense for that. He looked up, his eyes hardened, and I knew how Philippa had felt. She'd told me once when I first met her that her big desire in life was to be treated as well as her husband's cats. As usual, she'd laughed when she said it, and as usual, I hadn't understood. Until now.

Frank released the cat and just looked at me – not kindly. I had time to wonder whether it would be better to let him break my jaw, or risk breaking my hands on his face and losing the part of Rachmaninoff.

"My tools are in the shop," he said, looking toward the highest door on the barn. "It'll take me some time to get everything out."

"There's ... no need for that," I managed, much against my better judgment. "Phipps wants you to have the use of the shop, and I'm not going to fight her on it."

He just looked at me, but his stance was not aggressive, and I realized I was in no danger of a fist fight. I was too damned big. He knew it, and so did I. I was not consoled, but I was considerably enlightened. I resisted the urge to become more aggressive myself and show him what a man I was. Philippa had chosen, that was comment enough, and Frank was standing on his own property, after all. My telling him what I'd personally do to him if he ever lifted a finger toward Philippa again, was moot. He had lost to civility, and I needed to maintain it to keep my own trust. I cleared my throat and picked up my train of thought.

"Neither Philippa nor I have any use for that part of the building. We won't even be here that much. You might as well use it for now. Besides, it's still half yours, anyway."

"That'll change," he said, and bent to pick up another of the cats as I walked away.

I could see the bright blue of Phil's jacket in the distance, and I walked to meet her. Surprisingly, she hadn't noticed the big rig. "We have company," I said softly as I got in step with her, and her whole body went rigid when she spotted the Peterbilt.

"What'll I do?" she whispered. "What will I say? I'm cheating on my husband in his own home."

"Your soon to be ex-husband in your home," I corrected gently, but it made me feel really ... cheap. If a man can feel cheap. Anyway, I did. Personally, I was so upset I couldn't think straight. That man affected me like fingernails on a blackboard. Having to share the same space with him was almost more than I could tolerate.

I heard Phipps suck in for air, then she put on her own award winning face and walked into the shop just ahead of me. "Hi," she smiled. "I see the kitties have found you. How was your trip?"

He turned around, looked at her face and the cast on her arm, and turned back around in silence.

"Frank, please ..." she quavered. She was shaking all over, and I was afraid her legs were going to come right out from under her.

"Phone's ringing," I said. "be a good girl and run answer it. It might be the piano movers. They're coming today." She studied my face for a moment, then sighed and left, and I stayed where I was. "Frank, have you talked to Kelly in the last couple days?" I asked.

He glanced over his shoulder past me and mumbled something, probably, no.

"I wish you would," I said. "I guess your folks wouldn't let her in their house the other night, and she's pretty hurt and confused."

Frank put down what he was doing and turned to face me. "They what?"

"Told her she couldn't come in, so she said. She was still upset when I talked to her."

"Kelly is closer to me than she is to that ..." He gave me a look that mingled hatred with confusion, and his jaw jutted out at an ugly angle. "Her mother."

"Then call her, Frank. She needs you and she loves you, just like Philippa did. Don't turn your back on her. You have a lot you can salvage from this if you just don't turn your back." I got as far as the open garage door and turned around. "You know," I said, "Phipps still loves you, probably always will, and that's hard for me, because for the life of me I can't ..." I made myself stop. "Anyway, I have to get to work. They'll be here with that piano soon."

"Yeah," he said, and went back to whatever he was doing.

It was the beginning of an uneasy alliance. I stayed out of Frank's way, and he stayed out of mine. Whether or not he thought I was afraid of him, I don't know. He was welcome to think what he wanted. My concern was for Philippa and her feelings. I was not about to make her home, her sanctuary, a battleground. If I did, it would tarnish this place forever. The issues I had with Frank, I kept to myself for the time being.

Philippa walked out there one more time and told him to hook up power and water to the fifth wheel and stay in it, if he wished, but he just made a soft sound of contempt and turned away from her. He left the big rig, and took his Camry back in the direction of town, telling Philippa over his shoulder just to put his clothes and personal stuff in the shop.

She was shaking, frustrated, and close to tears. I could see her poor heart pounding in her throat, so I called and asked Ruth and Adelle please to come pack up Frank's things, and then I put Philippa to work in other directions. We got in the pickup and went to scout locations. That took every daylight hour of two days, and the third day, Frank was gone.

By now the camera crews and the necessary cast were making preparations to head north, bringing Flyer with them. She, too, was going to be in the movies. There was plenty of snow at the higher elevations to do the winter scenes. Disturbing amount of snow, as far as I was concerned. Phipps, had missed the stuff, or so she said.

She laughed and reminded me that I'd been skiing in San Moritz not so long ago, and I explained to her that there is a distinct difference between riding a ski lift, shushing to the bottom and then going back in the lodge for hot cocoa, and slogging around in ungroomed snow, especially with no lodge in sight. She laughed harder.

I took her to see her local doctor, and he X-rayed her arm and backed the cast off to a heavy plastic guard and an ace bandage, and no stress. No stress, he'd said again, shaking a pudgy finger in her face. Seems he knew her pretty well, too. I said I'd do what I could to keep her quiet. He just shook his grizzled head and chuckled.

The Hitchers called. They had a couple interested in working for us. What were the terms? Well, if they knew farming, beef raising, gardening, had good references, twenty-five thousand a year, plus housing, plus a steady meat supply and whatever else they wanted to raise. Two weeks paid vacation a year. Sounded wonderful. What was the housing?

Philippa and I had debated between a mobile home and an attached apartment. Because of the weather, the apartment definitely had its advantages, but I wanted more privacy than that, plus these days all the living room furniture was pushed into one corner of the room to accommodate my piano. We had decided to attach a space for music and exercise downstairs, and a new master bedroom, bath and a deck upstairs. We were adding over a thousand square feet to a two thousand square foot house, and I had some real concerns about it losing its country shape and cozy feel. Adding an apartment to all of that, was out of the question. I told them the housing would be a smallish modular, which would fit nicely behind the willows to the west of the house.

Domestic duties? Not many when we were in residence. This would be pretty much what the Hitchers had done when Philippa was gone. They asked if they could send the couple over to chat. Of course. Phipps wasn't here, but this was just preliminary.

Loved 'em. Hired 'em on the spot, Philippa or no Philippa. When she came home I simply told her the deed was done. I was half-hoping she'd stand on her hind legs and tell me I shouldn't have made that choice by myself – that this was her home and her decision. She didn't. She sputtered a little, but there were no sparks.

"Are they a nice couple?"

"Delightful," I smiled, making changes on the score in front of me. I played it again just with the right hand, and nodded. "Very nice people."

"What color? Not that it matters."

I waggled one hand, "Eh ... to the reddish-olive side, I guess. Do you have any more leads for this pencil?"

"Peter Aloysha Aarons, do you hear that faint cracking sound?"

"Should I?"

"Um hm. It's the thin ice you're skating on. Are these people going to be able to take care of my horses? Our horses? What about the cattle and the sheep?"

"I really do need a sharp pencil, Sweet Face. I'm trying to concentrate, if you don't mind."

She disappeared long enough for me to get control of my smirk, and returned with a little tube of leads, which she handed me. I thanked her.

"Film crew should be here with Flyer in an hour or so," I added. "How's the arm feel? Don't you love the sound of this piano? God, I'm so lucky!"

"How old are they?"

"Mid-sixties or so. How's that arm feel?"

"That's pretty old, isn't it? Do they know anything about gardening and orcharding?"

"He's a hobbyist, and the son of an orchardist. She's been a country girl all her life. How's the arm feel?"

"It's fine!" she snapped.

"What's fine?" Still no smirk. I was proud of myself.

"My arm," she said through her teeth. "Are you deliberately trying to goad me, Bud?"

"Hm?" I said absently, making notes. "What, Love?" I stuck my pencil behind my ear, and shook the ceiling with about eighteen bars of Rachmaninoff. "There, I like that, don't you?"

"Um hm. Except that's not what's written down there, you stinker! Are you playing head games with me?"

"Apparently not," I laughed. "You will like the couple, I guarantee it."

"Do they have a name?"

"Glad you asked. Their names are Oscar and Ruth Hitcher."

Philippa was so happy, and so surprised. I had been, too, but their reasons for wanting the job had been very well thought out. Their house was not paid for. Oscar had always been a pastor and had only a tiny pension and Social Security. Ruth had worked very briefly for the Cherokee Nation, then married and spent most of her life tending home and garden as a wife and mother. If they took this job, they could live simply while enjoying the country, save their money, rent their house out and let it pay for itself. In a few years, they'd have a nice nest egg and a home they owned. I gave them an A in the logic department. The only drawback I could see, at least at that point, was that we wouldn't have them very many years. That, we'd face later. Philippa was happy, and so was I. Having Oscar and Ruth here would really smooth out the transition period while Frank was still in our lives.

The Hitchers were happy, but they'd be a lot happier when Philippa and I were married. Oscar had brought that up in his usual forthright manner in the course of our discussion. They were uncomfortable enough with divorce. This arrangement was a real compromise for them, and for Philippa even if we weren't ... well, you know ... and they didn't want to know whether we were or not. I felt bad, and I told them so, and asked them please not to mention it to Phipps.

They wanted to know if there would be wild parties, and people they didn't know using the house, and inquired in general about the strange goings on that could be expected from Hollywood people. I hadn't laughed, I hadn't snapped, didn't roll my eyes and snort derisively. I'd been as honest as I could. The house would hear a lot more laughter than it was used to, and there might be an occasional friend in to stay, but nothing too decadent.

The whole conversation had made me worry about the moral vice that might close around Philippa with her foster family right on top of us every minute. But the pros far outweighed the cons, so we called Frank, made him a too-generous offer for his half, forced the thing into escrow and began scurrying around calling contractors and excavators and getting ready for yet another transition. The camera crew arrived, and behind them, Tommy and Kit and the other actors we'd need up here, and the place began to fill up with sound trucks and gear trucks, and passenger cars, and people – everywhere.

I rather expected Philippa to try to do all and be all, but to my vast relief, she called a caterer, a temp service, made dinner reservations for a couple dozen, and devoted herself entirely to the production.

This was the part of the story where I felt strangely like we were chasing our own tail. In the miniseries we were making, as a side plot, they were making a miniseries – a Historical Docu-drama about Jim Bridger, whom I got to play – pardon, who Mark Kinkead got to play. I let my beard grow for two or three days, roughed myself up, rode the kinks out of Flyer, who was, I admit it, a dream under saddle, and we picked up the rented stock from a friend of Philippa's, and headed for the mountains.

Spring in the valley was still winter in the Cascades, and we found plenty of hip deep snow to slog through, and lunge the horses through. Tommy was thrilled. This would put us back on schedule. Maybe I wouldn't have to work on two films at the same time after all, which was precious little consolation at that point.

By turns, we sweated and froze. Even with heavy leg warmers under my buckskins, and a knee brace to steady me, I was ready to scream with the pain in my knee. Of course when my knee hurt, my back hurt, and I was a pretty grouchy guy.

The horses were young and spirited and used to maneuvering in the snow. We, were none of the above. We got knocked down, lunged over, jerked around, mainly because the horses knew more than we did. Tommy was still just thrilled to death, bundled up behind the wind machines.

After three days he shut off the machines and we did some tranquil, sunny day shooting. We had set up a Sioux village, using extras from the Yakama nation, and I enjoyed watching James Horse, the young man playing Black Kettle, ply his trade. He'd come up in poverty on a Sioux reservation in the Dakotas, gone to USC on a scholarship, and impressed hell out of us during his interview and screen test. He rode well, acted well, and responded well. He was a pleasure to work with, and I was pleased to see Native playing Native.

The man playing Custer, wouldn't you know, was a pain in the ass. He complained bitterly and incessantly about everything. It was amusing, really. In Phil's book the man had been exactly the same way off camera. Kit and I buttonholed Tommy and gave him hell for type casting. He just smiled. His feet were warm.

Astin Martin – I kid you not – had just enough parts under his belt to make him cocky. He knew it all, spouted it all. The perfect Custer. Acting on camera as though you're off camera between takes, can be tricky. It took a while, and Martin whined about the delay. He whined about the mare he'd been assigned to ride. Custer had a beautiful horse. He wanted a beautiful horse. The one I was riding would do nicely.

I told him there was no way he'd get near Flyer, and he walked off the set. We all stood there, frozen to mid-thigh, shaking our heads in disbelief. The man had been in one print. One print the whole film, while the rest of us had slaved, and he'd brought us to a standstill.

"Bud, let him ride her ... if he can," Phipps said, and I could see the annoyance in her eyes. That mare, had a mouth like spun silk. Phil had sat on the arena fence and told me to ride only with my fingers. Not my hands, not my wrists. Just my fingers. I had listened. Martin, we feared, wouldn't. But time was of the essence. The warm sun was causing the trees to drop their snow and it was starting to get slushy and treacherous around the trucks. We needed to hurry.

One of the wranglers made Flyer's blaze into a star so she'd look like a different horse, braided up her light mane and wrapped it with dark yarn, tacked her out as a Cavalry mount, and we cajoled Martin back onto the set.

"I still can't believe we're doing this," I growled, trying to get my legs to move. "Where in God's name would a bunch of mountain men get two horses that looked like she does? You do know she looks EXACTLY the same," I said, raising my voice so Tommy could hear me.

Philippa handed me a cup of coffee and half a handful of pills, and I tossed them down as Martin was climbing aboard Flyer. "Martin, That mare is in foal," I said. "Do not do anything stupid."

"... or I will personally cut your balls off," Philippa added.

Martin, I give him credit, did a fairly good job. He tried, but he was no rider, and Flyer knew it. He was working several hundred feet out, listening to Tommy, and doing what he was told, when Flyer decided the hell with it. She was going back with the other horses. She spun around, jarred Martin loose, and took off at a dead gallop back toward us.

Phipps, who had seen her getting ready to run, hollered, "Easy! Sit back hard in the saddle and tell her whoa! Don't jerk!"

Too late. Martin hauled back on the reins, Flyer's feet went in four directions at once, and she slid into the whole crew of us before I could move a step. All I could think about was the fact that this was a fraction, a fraction of a six hour film, and we were all going to die over it. I'd never play Sergei Rachmaninoff.

There was a lot of flying mud and snow, and I'm not sure what part of the mare hit me, but my shoulders and the back of my head hit the side of the sound truck. No sharp edges, just a nice, even splat.

"Bud? Buddy?" I knew it was Phil and I could hear that she was scared. "Peter? Sweetheart?"

I gasped for air and forced my eyes open – sans contacts, of course

– dammit. "I'm okay," I whispered, still trying to regain my residual air supply. "Phipps?"

"I'm okay."

"Buddy, are you okay?" Kit asked, kneeling to my left. "Damn, you've got to be quicker than that or you're going to be dead one of these days."

"In other words, I'm still alive?" I realized my bad knee was bent under me and rather gingerly began trying to get it back where it belonged. "Kidding," I managed.

"You scared me bad, Boy," he snapped, Glory-like, and I had to laugh.

I sat up, rotated my neck a little to see if it worked, and looked around for Philippa's horse. "Is Flyer okay?"

"She tried to kill me!" Martin exclaimed. Actually, it was more of a shriek. "She tried to kill me! You knew she'd do that, didn't you, Aarons? You arrogant asshole!"

I looked at him, and he was plastered with mud, and Flyer was leering at him with contempt, and I laughed. We all laughed.

He quit, and we gladly let him. We flew in a replacement that evening, and the next day we tried it again. This time Custer rode the horse assigned to him, and things went fine.

They brought several grade school classes up to watch that last day in the snow, and since we were filming the part about making the film we got to use them as extras. It was fun, aching joints and all. During one break I spotted a familiar face in the crowd, walked over, and snatched him up from among his awestruck classmates.

"Well, Kenny, How's this disguise, any better?"

"I thtill know who you are!" he laughed.

"Who am I?"

"You're Bud," he giggled, and hid his face against my jacket.

"Philippa," I called, walking her way, "look who I caught."

She tickled him and he wiggled, kissed him and he squirmed. Then I gave him a big hug and made him promise to come see us soon, and he scurried back to his class.

How nice, to be part of the home crowd. How nice, to put my arm across Philippa's sturdy shoulders and lean on her just a little, and feel her arm come around my waist, strong and comforting. How nice, to know it was spring an hour away.

That afternoon I shaved off my whiskers, took off my buckskins, went from Jim Bridger to Mark Kincaid, fighter to lover, older man to younger, and it took the last of my energy. My body lost its ability to fight the pain and the cold, and I faked it until dark. I was shaking miserably, and doing my level best to hide the fact.

Tommy said he was taking us all out to dinner, but Philippa and I begged off and went home. I collapsed in a chair, too exhausted even to be hungry. Phipps turned on the spa to recirculate, but she also went and ran a hot bath in the huge footed tub in the master bathroom.

"In there, first," she said. "Let your muscles soak up that cider vinegar. There's Epsom Salts in there, so don't drink it."

I felt like a head of lettuce, being dipped in vinegar and oil, but Phipps said my body had taken enough of a beating. It needed relief from the ravages of cold, overwork and being pinned by a flying horse to the side of a truck. So I laid in the tub for a while, and Saffron came and sat on his special stool and visited with me and fished idly over my shoulder.

Phipps offered me supper, or a soak in the spa, or both. I said no, thanks. I crawled out of the tub and collapsed into bed. The last thing I felt was her hands on the small of my back.

I don't believe I twitched for six hours. When I did wake up, the pain was excruciating. My back wouldn't move, my legs wouldn't move. My neck felt like a block of concrete. I ground my teeth and willed myself to roll over without screaming like a banshee. My hardworking partner needed her sleep, too. I made it onto my left side then onto my back, and sat up.

God, my knee hurt. God ... my knee hurt. It felt like it was being sawn slowly in half. Too much stress on it. I'd probably popped it out in my sleep. It moved, though, which surprised me. It flexed enough that I could pull it up toward my chest and get my arms around it. Sitting there like that

– exhausted and hurting almost beyond bearing – I thought seriously about just having my leg taken off above the knee and learning to use a prosthesis. I straightened up a little, turned at the waist and got my medication and a glass of water off the old cherrywood night stand. I doubled the dose, laid back, and waited.

The pills didn't touch it. I crawled out of bed, showered, shaved, dressed, wrapped a heating pad around my knee, and sat by the banked fire in the family room. It was four O'clock in the morning. I chewed on my lips, and the sides of my index fingers, and wished for a cigarette, and let my mind wander back over parts I'd played, people I'd cared for ... and Philippa's hands came down on my shoulders.

"Dear Heart," she said quietly, "You've got to do something about your knee. You cannot go the rest of your life in this kind of pain."

"I know," I said without unclenching my teeth, "I'm willing to listen."

"I'm taking you to my doctor."

"The man has eyes like a mouse, and his name is Doctor Denton," I scowled. "Come on, P.K., give me a break."

"He's a place to start," she said firmly. "Merrick Denton is an Osteopathic Surgeon, and a good one. He has a fine reputation in eastern Washington. I've already called him."

He had Phipps take me to the Emergency Room, which was as depressingly unlike New American as night and day. He still looked like a mouse. He listened to what I told him I usually had done, gave me a rather mad little smile, and said, "Humor me, Aarons. Just let me poke around a little."

I nodded, gasping with the effort of fighting the pain, and he said something my doctor never had. "There's no need for you to hurt like that while we're setting up. Here. This will sting. Try not to jerk away from it."

He stuck a needle in my thigh, not under my knee cap, mind you, but into the fleshy part of my inner thigh, emptied one syringe and then another into it.

"Something for the pain, and to make your muscles let up on you," he said, gently slapping the spot he'd just injected. "Great thigh tone. What do you do for exercise?"

"Skip rope," I replied.

His head came very slowly around, then his body, and he peered down into my face in utter amazement. "Are you out of your fucking mind?" he asked in a conversational tone.

I didn't say a word, but I felt like an activity I treasured was about to meet an untimely end at the hands of an eccentric country doctor.

"Phil, stay with him while I order X-rays, will you?" he said, and scurried away. He moved like a mouse, too. A little grey, scurrying mouse with shoe button eyes. I couldn't help liking him any more than I can help liking mice.

I was there an hour, maybe longer, and Philippa went to call Tommy. Again, one of the two of us was screwing up our shooting schedule. He said not to worry, they'd go shoot backgrounds and filler.

I was in and out of X-ray, subjected to gentle probings and tappings and flexings. He drew some fluid from my knee. Put some in. Back to X-ray. He didn't say much until he was finished, then he sat down beside me with a handful of film and said, "Well, you cracked your knee cap the other day, but that's not what's wrong. Aarons, I'm sorry, but you have absolutely no knee left at all. It's gone."

CHAPTER TWELVE

I skipped rope, and when I went to take a shower as I always did, there was no hot water. Odd, we never ran out of hot water. I went to the laundry room and checked the heater. It was working like mad. There had to be water running somewhere in the house.

Meg was still asleep. Glory wasn't in the house yet. Surely my grandmother wasn't going through all that hot water. "Gram?" I called softly, knocking as I opened her bedroom door. Her bed hadn't been slept in.

"Gram?" I called again, panic rising in my throat.

I could hear water running in her bathroom. I opened the door, and I could see her – crumpled in the shower – cold water beating her in the final indignity of death. She was old. I knew sooner or later, I would lose her. Even as I sprang, sobbing, to shut off the water and gather her into my arms, I couldn't fault the way she'd died. Quick, painless, probably no foreknowledge at all. I'd known it would happen. I'd known this was the only possible, ultimate outcome, and yet, Dear God, what a shock!

"Aarons, are you going to pass out on me?" Denton said.

I shook my head against the pillow, and opened my eyes. "No, I'm fine. I'm just thinking. This is quite a shock so far from home."

"Could be a break for you," Denton muttered. "I don't claim to be more than I am, Aarons. I'm a horse and buggy doctor in a horse and buggy town. Lucky to have the buggy. But I'll tell you something. I do a lot of knees, and I've never seen one screwed up this bad."

"Sounds like an accusation," I said, reaching to pat Philippa's hand on my shoulder.

"Suffice it to say I wouldn't let the sonofabitch trim my toenails. He's neglected the knee, which was repaired for style and not service in the first damned place. He's allowed you to abuse all hell out of it, and you've got nothing left but a little jelly and some nerve endings. And you're wrecking your back in the process, by the way. I have no idea how you've stood the pain this long, even with all those drugs he's letting you pour into your system, which is probably making you into an addict."

"What are we looking at?"

"About the first week in July."

"That's not what I meant," I snapped.

"That's what I'm telling you, though," he retorted. "Right now, you're as big an idiot as your doctor. If you're into pain have Mrs. Tyler hang you up naked and beat you with a riding quirt, but for the love of God don't skip rope. You fool! Don't you know you're bringing nine hundred pounds of pressure down on that knee, every lick, every jump? That's crazy. I don't care how vain you are about having a flat gut. I go to the effort of putting a new knee in there, along with all the extra repair work that's going to have to go into this, and by George, you're going to do as I say with it, or you can walk out of here right now."

That made me laugh, luckily, because the rest of it stung. I resented being thought of as vain. I may be vain, of course, but I resented having it noticed.

"I do a lot of hard working knees, Aarons. I do farmers, truckers, orchardists, cattlemen, people who have to get back to work, strenuous work, and fast. I work on people who don't have the money to spend twice. Your knee, has been shot so full of shit to make it feel like you have a knee ..." he paused and smiled at me. "We can make it work, but it'll take some time, and you're going to have some serious scarring this time around. Plus I'm going to have to immobilize your whole leg, which ordinarily I wouldn't do, but there's a lot of damage to your long bones and muscles, not to mention your back." He paused again, longer this time, and those little mouse eyes of his glittered. "You're teetering on the brink of being a cripple for life, my friend. Your choices are limited."

"I am in the middle of a shoot up here, Doctor. Phipps begged us off for today, but I am supposed to be on the set at five A.M. tomorrow morning."

"At five A.M. tomorrow morning, you'll be recovering from surgery," he said, and I was. I didn't even bother with a second opinion. I just told him to cut me before I lost my nerve, and he did.

I bobbed at the end of some ethereal tether for a long time, and any noise was too loud, any voice intrusive and startling. I felt, a lot of the time, like I was dreaming of suffocating, and if I could get a breath, one breath, and get myself to speak out loud, I could wake myself up. People kept touching me and deciding I was alive, I guess. I heard Denton telling ... someone, to keep me ... something. My tolerance for pain was ... something, and I wasn't a prime candidate for ... something. I didn't need to be alert, just responsive.

I woke up, really woke up for a minute or two, and Phipps kissed my forehead and said I'd done fine, and she says I asked her something bizarre about Jim Bridger, but I don't remember.

I went back to floating on my tether ... bob, bob ... nothing. Bob, bob, bob ... nothing.

A hand on my face that was female, but not Philippa's. Someone taking my pulse and saying, "Is that catheter tube kinked somewhere?"

Rustle, rustle. "Um hm, right here. My goodness, wouldn't you like to get that up and play with it? Too bad he's so old."

"Vickie, that's both inappropriate and unprofessional." The more mature voice, reproving, "Plus he's not asleep. He's not awake, but he's not asleep."

Squeak of dismay.

"Did you check his toes? I really think they're of more concern than the square footage of erectile tissue."

Just wait, girls. I'm good with voices, even in this condition.

Pat, pat. "Sorry about that. She's just a kid. Sleep now." Bob, bob...

Lights. Tinker, tinker, pat, pat ... bob, bob ... Philippa's fragrance. Philippa's lips.

"Don't try to wake up, Babe, just rest."

"I want to go home," I managed, because I just flat couldn't resist it, and the little mule punched me. In my fragile state, she punched me. And kissed me, and stayed close. I was aware of her presence.

I dreamed about children. Little chocolate-eyed boys in blue sweaters, baby girls in sunbonnets with their bare toes curling in the soft green grass – about what it would be like to give birth to such miracles as these – the pain.

I felt Kit's hand resting over mine, heard his voice, felt him kiss my temple just at the hairline as he said he loved me. I'd always be his buddy.

"Don't worry about what the other kids say, Aloysha. I'll always be your buddy, and you'll be mine. You're my buddy. Go ahead and laugh, Keiger. At least they don't call him Junior, like you. Joonie, Joonie! Sounds like a girl. If my Dad's name was Herbert and I got stuck with it, I'd throw myself under a bus. Joonie, Joonie, pus belly girl. Come on Buddy. Let's go home."

"Kristoffer ... what was he ... ah ... talking?"

"Saying. What was he saying. He's being stupid. Nonsense? Dumb? Stupid?" He added a face and a stance and I nodded and laughed. "Stupid. His name is like your name. Your dad's name is Peter, and your name is Peter. You with me so far?" I nodded. "His dad's name is Herbert. His name is Herbert. Your folks call you by your middle name, Aloysha. His folks call him, Junior."

"Why?"

He made the face and the gesture again. Max pulled up with the limo and we got in, laughing.

Lights. Tinker, tinker, pat, pat. "Mr. Aarons?"

I managed to move my head about a quarter of an inch.

"Peter, come on, wake up for me, just for a minute."

I squeezed down on my eyelids, then forced them up, much as you have to tease a window shade into opening.

"Hello, how are you feeling?" the nurse asked.

I swallowed to speak, and my eyes closed again. "I am ... all right."

I wasn't. I was thinking in Russian, having to translate everything going both ways.

"Are you in any pain? Peter?"

"Nyet," I whispered, and she left me alone.

I heard Denton's voice a time or two, and may or may not have responded. I hurt like hell from time to time, but they seemed to know that, because they kept giving me shots, and those hurt, because I was getting bruised. I finally woke up ... not just thought I woke up ... finally woke up, a couple days after surgery, to the touch of warm, familiar hands, and a kiss on the forehead. "You in there, Boy?"

I woke up smiling. "Glory!"

"There he is. How you feel?"

"Actually, not bad," I managed. I swallowed hard, trying to lubricate my throat enough to speak. "Are you here ... or am I there?"

"I'm here."

"Aw, thanks, Love. It wasn't necessary. I know you're busy."

"Always take the opportunity to travel, Darlin'. Philippa, she filmin', and you girls don't want you layin' here alone."

Again, I told her thanks, and we visited as best my throat would let me. Glory gave me some ice chips to suck on, and things got better. She told me what was going on at home, how the roses were doing. Another spring without my roses. I drifted back to sleep. Awakened again to the click of Glory's knitting needles and a terrible, twisting pain from my groin to the arch of my foot.

Glory moved the covers aside, put one hand under my arch, her other palm down over my toes, and pushed, very, very gently.

"Excellent technique," Denton said as he walked in. "Helping the pain any?"

"Um ... some."

"You always carry an LVN around with you?"

"This one is an old and dear friend. Doctor Merrick Denton, Glory Ruiz."

Glory didn't laugh. Quite. "Doctor Denton," she managed, and walked to the window, seemingly to get out of his way. Then I winked, and she broke up.

"Your bill just doubled," Denton muttered. "How would you like to go through med school being called Jammies?"

I laughed and it hurt like hell and he said it served me right. "Well, you're a modest man, Mr. Aarons," he went on. "I had no idea who you were. I wouldn't know yet, but I recognized Kristoffer Miller and he filled me in. Turns out I have a couple of your Rachmaninoff C.D.'s, and a Lecuona. Somehow I just didn't connect you with the name on those cases, or with Nathan Strauss."

"I'm just as happy you didn't," I smiled.

"Nevertheless, I'm impressed. You have a wonderful gift. And a pretty high powered friend in Miller. I guess he's been a terror around here seeing that you were properly taken care of."

"High profile," I corrected, wincing away from his touch. "Kit and I have always taken care of each other. I hope he and the rest of the cast are making headway without me. I feel very guilty."

Kit assured me they were doing fine. Philippa assured me they were doing fine. Tommy said they were filling in with a double for me to voice over as much as possible.

I told him I was sorry, and he said the hard part – the part in the snow – had been finished. We had no need to come back for any winter filming at all. We could bump up our release date if we could get a slot. We'd get all the summer footage we possibly could up here. Lots of stuff of me from the waist up, lots of blank location filler. Hell, we'd fake it. I needed to worry about me, not them.

Three days after surgery they started clamping off the catheter and giving me liquids. A day after that, Denton took the catheter out. At five days I began eating. The sixth day, I insisted on going home. There was work that absolutely had to be done before the film crew could leave for LA.

When you watch a movie, appreciate it. What you are seeing is not what was there. A good movie is an illusion, created by technicians, sound mixers, camera people, and film editors. A good crew can take a groggy, greying guy in a wheelchair, put dye in his hair, makeup on his face, drops in his eyes – alter lighting and angles – and come up with the kind of man women swoon over. A movie, remember, is a thing of the moment. Those moments can be interchanged, just in flashes, interspersed, to give the illusion of a whole which exists only on film.

"Too bad we did the bedroom scenes first," I laughed, but of course I'd have looked a little strange flat on my back all the time. I lay in the meadow grass amid the flowers, smiling, one arm behind my head, the other around my beautiful co-star. Her knight in shining armor, that was me. Put a knight on his back in full armor, he can't get up, either.

I laugh about it now, but it was not funny at the moment. I looked like warmed over death, which is hard on the ego. I was weak, I was helpless in that brace and bandaging. I felt like such a burden on these good and talented people. They'd used a stand-in all week, doing those romantic scenes with Philippa. No face shots, of course. If they hadn't been so loyal they'd have written me out of some scenes, made them friendly rather than romantic, and gone at twice the pace using Kit. At the time, I wished they had.

But they never let go of me. Kit on one side, Philippa or James or Glory on the other, someone leaning against my back if I had to stand and speak. Glory kept me as comfortable as she could without knocking me out, and somehow, I made it. There was once scene, one, where we could see that my hands were shaking, but in the context it could have been passion, and was passed off as such. They pulled me out of the chair one more painful, exhausting time and eased me down into that big, cool bed. Glory and Phipps helped me out of my jeans and my shirt. It was unseasonably warm, I was overheated, and I said my boxer shorts were plenty to have on. Damn, I hate boxer shorts, but briefs will not go on over a brace that size. I could hear myself inside, cranky, sour, self-pitying. Philippa helped me remove my makeup, stuck around for a few kisses, and petted me off to sleep before returning to the shoot.

I woke up for a late dinner, but I didn't try to get out of bed. Another day, a little rest, a little more strength, and I'd be much more able to help myself. I noticed my evening meal was different than what Phipps had been feeding me. This was Glory's cooking and that involved grocery shopping. I wondered if there had been any kind of set-to over who got control of that little kitchen. That would be all any of us needed at this juncture. I ate what I could, which wasn't much, and told Philippa I was satisfied.

I was even more satisfied later on, when Philippa asked if she could sleep with me. "This is your bed," I smiled.

"Yes," she smiled in return, "and in it is the man I love. I want him to be comfortable."

"Phipps, I never feel you moving around at night," I said, reaching for her hand. "Thank you for the concern, but please stay. I really need you." I saw the look that crossed her face and knew I'd said enough. She remembered what it was like to be hurt and need someone, just their closeness, just the warmth of their body to snuggle against.

She said she didn't have to be asked twice, inquired about any needs I might have before she came to bed, shrugged out of her robe, and turned off the lamp. She slid up close to my left side, filling my mind with the firmness of her, and the fragrance of her, and I realized why I felt so irritable. I was horny as hell.

I made up my mind I wasn't going to say anything. I was going to suffer. If I'd wanted to be on the bottom, or given a blow job, it would have been different. Since I had no choice, my ego said it wouldn't stand for it. I had no desire to feel like a buggered turtle.

Phil sighed, nestled her head against my shoulder, dropped her arm around my waist and said, "I have seen people act with great courage in the face of a handicap, and I admire that. But, to me, someone who isn't used to a handicap and acts with great courage is pretty special. I was very proud of you today."

"Being slung around like a sack of barley is worthy of honor, all right," I muttered. "Holding everything up while I get enough of a grip on myself to say my next line, is certainly worthy of honor. Saying, 'I don't remember,' ten thousand times, is most worthy." I paused to listen to myself, then sighed and gave Philippa a hug. "Thank you for the compliment, Sweet Face. I just ... I felt like a real idiot out there today."

"I know you did," she laughed. "You said that almost as many times as you said, 'I don't remember.' That's my point. You're a big, powerful, graceful man. You're the one who always adds his shoulder if something won't move, stands on his tiptoes and reaches what nobody else can reach. You dominate the set and the production, just with your professionalism. Your shirt's still dry when everybody else is sweat soaked and dragging. You're the one who always knows everybody else's lines. You're the one who never works with idiot cards. Today you gave all that up. Not part of it, all of it. You had nothing to fall back on out there ..." Her gently massaging hand came to rest. "Mmmmm, speaking of things to fall back on, do you have plans for this?"

"No," I chuckled, touched in more ways than one, "I briefly considered using it as a spear to martyr myself with, but that idea passed. You can have it if you want it."

"Ah ha, the ultimate challenge." She brought her hand up to brush my cheek. "Dear Heart, I know this is hard on you ..." pause, "... so to speak...."

We both cracked up, and I quit taking my manhood in chains quite so seriously.

"I heard about you and Vicki, by the way."

I searched my memory banks for a long moment. "Ah yes, the young lady who made me feel like Gulliver."

"You know who she is, don't you?"

"No. Should I?"

"Vicki Denton," Phil chuckled. "I don't know where her head was that night, but she comes out of your room, back to the nurse's station, and she puts her hands out like a fisherman, and her eyes get big, and she says in this stage whisper, 'that dude, the one who played Nathan Strauss, has got a dick' ... and her hands start toward opposite walls. Somebody gives her the elbow and she turns around, and I'm standing there."

"Good so far," I snickered. "And what did you say?"

"I told her what you've always said, not to judge the depth of the well by the length of the handle on the pump. I also told her that discretion is the better part of valor, especially if she wanted to keep her job. Just to be sure she understood my displeasure, I reported her to the head nurse, no pun intended, whatever they're called, anyway. And I reiterated my position on indiscreet student nurses."

"Well, the poor little girl paid her dues. She came in yesterday morning, so embarrassed, and stammered her way through an apology. 'If I said anything to offend you,' and so on, so I asked her what she'd said. Poor kid damn near died."

"And did she repeat it?"

"Are you kidding? Hey, why are we discussing her opinion of me when we could be discussing yours?"

Phil made that special sound she reserved for such occasions - sort of a cross between a growl and a sigh, and came up to kiss me. We padded underneath my knees and just a little behind my shoulders. Not exactly spontaneous sex, but workable. I could hold her weight.

I hadn't realized ... what a pleasure it would be to lie there and let her do all the work. With the way she rides a horse, I don't know why I was surprised. She handled me the same way she handles the other old stud she owns, and it was truly wonderful. I hope to come back as one of my wife's horses.

She told me all I had to do was respond convincingly at the appropriate moment, which I did, releasing frustration, fear, bitterness and tension. When I finally gave out, I gave out all over at once, sagging damply into the pillows. I asked Phil if she was satisfied, and she said definitely. I asked if she was hurt, and she said definitely not. Of course I've known her to lie to make me feel good, and it usually works.

I could feel myself going to sleep. The motion had done wonders to loosen my back. It flickered momentarily in my brain that there was a flaw in our otherwise well executed plan. I couldn't move to help myself. "Are we a mess?" I ventured, realizing it would have taken me about half a second to slide on a condom, which would have been the considerate thing to do.

"We? No. You, yes," Phil laughed, and it's really the last thing I remember. Terrible thing to admit, I know. Didn't even have time for that mental cigarette I still envisioned at times like these. She could have given me a shower and I don't think I'd have noticed.

My knee woke me up three or four hours later, but Phipps helped me shift around a little. It responded well to medication, and we were able to let Glory sleep all night. Early, when I was sitting up with a cup of coffee, and Phil was sleepy eyed in her robe beside me, I asked how she and Glory were getting along.

"Oh, as well as can be expected," she replied, blowing on her coffee. "She's used to running your house and your kitchen. She expects me to have better things to do. Like Megan and your Gramma did."

"This, isn't my house," I said gently.

"You are here. Glory is here. It's yours by default."

"Philippa, Love, is something wrong, or are you just needing a rest?" I asked. I knew she did. The last two weeks had been a madhouse of activity, and I was beginning to notice a pattern of depression following over-stimulation in her.

"I'm fine."

"Did you get a chance to go to church this week?"

"We were shooting," she said, and her voice was infinitely, frighteningly sad.

"Sweet Face, what's wrong? Please tell me."

"It isn't fair," she began, and thought a long time. I could see her tongue, busily scrubbing the canine tooth on the right side of her mouth. That was her distress signal. If rubbing that tooth couldn't control her tears nothing could. "It isn't fair that when you marry somebody before God, and all you want is to love that person, and have him love you back, it isn't fair that God shouldn't honor that. It isn't fair that I had to give up my love, and my prayers, and my faith to save my sanity. I miss that place in my life."

I set my coffee cup aside and put my hand on her thigh, mentally bracing myself for the worst. "Having second thoughts about Frank?" I asked. He'd been here while I was in the hospital. Luckily for my peace of mind, so had Kit and Glory.

Her chin came up, and she drew a long, shuddering sigh. "Having second thoughts about God," she said, and her eyes didn't quite spill, even then.

"Religion, any religion, has always been a dark glass through which to view God. But if we are to believe the philosophers, God doesn't change. Only our perspective changes," I said.

"Piss on philosophy!" she cried. "God is God! He could do anything he wanted to, religion or no religion. I'm tired of lying. I'm tired of going to church and paying lip service to a Being I can't even see anymore, when what I really want to ask is, 'Why in hell are you doing this to me?' What have I done except use the gifts God gave me to escape an intolerable situation? I should be so happy, and so contented, and I'm not. Part of me is ecstatic about being with a loving, romantic, talented and wealthy man, and part of me is scared to death of the wrath of God. I feel like I'm being torn in half."

"It isn't what God has done to you," I sighed. "I don't think God works that way. It's what you have done to you by seeking me out, and it's what I have done by falling in love with you. I let you into my life without ever really asking myself if it was what was best for you. I invaded your life, changed all the rules on you, inflicted my profession, my friends, my pressures, on you and deliberately drove every wedge I could between you and Frank. It's no wonder you're confused and unhappy. You're fighting with Kelly because of me, you're fighting for kitchen space because of me. I created all these problems for you, thinking I was helping you create a new life for yourself. I can't even sweep you up in my arms and tell you I'm sorry."

I shifted my shoulders against the pillows and thought a moment. "As a matter of fact, I don't think I am sorry. I love you too much. Frankly, I don't think your religion is all that good for you, and I'm not sure this place is, either. You talk about either one, try to deal with either one, and you're an instant basket case. If it were in my power to take you home to LA right this minute, I believe I would do that, for both our sakes."

I picked up my coffee cup, and we just sat there – mute – looking at the beautiful handmade quilt, with not one thought, or at least one word to express our thoughts, between us. "I'd love to have this quilt on our bed at home," I said at last. Nothing more. Phipps just nodded obediently.

"How's your knee?" Phipps asked after a couple minutes.

"About like your heart," I replied.

"That bad?"

"At least I have something to take for the pain. Philippa, I love you, and I had no intention of using you. I brought you up here to rest and recover from your own injuries. Into the enemy camp, as it turns out. Then the production crew arrives, that's restful. Then my knee decides it's time to retire permanently, and here you are, stuck with a man so bandaged up he looks like Mount Rainier. If I stay, I'm a burden. If I go home, I'm running away in my own mind. I will do whatever you think is best for you, Love, short of leaving you here by yourself for Frank to prey on. That, I won't do."

"You," she said finally, smiling a little, "are a charming liar, and I adore you. But trying to shoulder the blame for how I feel about my faith, and how that is making me feel about my life choices, is not the answer to my problem. It only makes me love you more, when who I need to love, is God."

"Who you need to love, is you," I corrected, taking her hand and kissing it. "If you're going to pray for something, pray for that ability, and I'll agree with you for it. You can pray for Frank without loving him, and I think you should, but you need to love yourself to save yourself, to salvage yourself before God."

Philippa's expression had lightened a little. I could see the wheels turning. It showed in the shape of her eyes. "Praying a prayer of agreement, is a New Testament concept."

"Oscar slept through the sermon, I didn't," I chuckled. "I feel my belief in the one true God, whomever that may be in the grand order of the universe, gives me the right to stand with you in prayer."

"Peter, I don't think I could face God in prayer right now. Maybe someday. For now, He knows I believe, and that will never change. He knows I'm grateful for His creations, and He knows I'd love to be right with Him and love His church and all the things it teaches. With as far as I've dared to reach inside, and with what analytical powers I have in my own behalf, that's as honest as I can be with Him, and lying to God is the ultimate ego trip. Anyway, enough of this. Are you ready for some breakfast?"

I nodded. Enough of this was right. While my first inclination was to tell her that giving up the whole idea that God was tied to religion in any way, shape or form would probably cure her ills, I couldn't do that. I decided what Phipps needed was a good shrink. Not Layman, he couldn't address her religious concerns, and what was at the heart of this woman, was her faith. She needed somebody different; maybe a Baha'i. Or a Unitarian. They had such a clear, loving, accepting view of God as a universal concept. I'd ask Glory what she thought. I knew I was tired of patching the same problem day after day, week after week. Things had to change somewhere on a molecular level. A good Baha'i psychologist, like Gram's old friend, Steven Effendi, who used to come to our house and bring his basketball to play with me while we visited.

Phipps kissed me and left, and when she was gone, I prayed for her. I felt downright silly, talking to the God of the universe, but I was getting used to feeling silly. I found myself telling Jesus that if he loved that good woman ... and I stopped ... and I wondered if I could believe in him on Philippa's behalf and not on my own. I mean, even if you're talking to a rock you're acknowledging its existence. I realized I still had way too much medication in my system, and wondered if a clear mind would make this any easier. Probably not. The phone rang, and I was profoundly grateful.

"It's for you," Phipps announced, coming into the room, "Big, powerful voice. Used to being in control. Could be your father? I don't remember his voice being that commanding."

"You haven't heard him when he's upset," I grinned, and picked up the phone. "Hi, how are you? How was your trip?"

"The trip was fine, but I am disturbed. I come home from the Orient to discover that my only son has had major surgery in some God forsaken whistle stop somewhere and that the doctor who did the original surgery knows nothing about this. Damn, Bud, are you all right?"

"I thought maybe you weren't going to ask," I chuckled. "I feel fine. Another few days and I'll be on crutches. Prognosis is excellent. I'll dance at the wedding."

"Wedding? What wedding?"

That was a jolt. It was the first time I realized I had the whole thing planned out in my drug-addled mind and the date all set and I hadn't even discussed it with Philippa. Now, thanks to that damned pain medication, I'd opened my mouth, any hope of a romantic moment was gone, and I was stuck. I looked up, and she was standing in the doorway with a breakfast tray in her hands. "Dad, hold on a minute, will you?" I asked, and put the phone against my chest. "This has got to be quick. He has a very short attention span about most things. Philippa Kate Tyler, I love you, and I want you to be my wife. Will you marry me August ninth at the Bird House?"

"Sure. More coffee?" she grinned, and I blew her a kiss.

"Um hm. Hi, Dad. I'm back. Well, August ninth was Gram and Grandpa's anniversary, and Phipps and I thought we'd like to honor that day with our own marriage – just a small wedding at Gram's house – a few close friends and family."

There was silence. "Dad, are you there?"

"Yes, Aloysha, I'm here."

"I notice you're not wildly happy at this point. Why is that?"

"Let me get out the list," he sighed. She is not of your social standing, you haven't known her nearly long enough, she's married to someone else …"

"She's not. She and Frank are divorced. Divorcing."

"On top of everything else, she is not of our faith, and rather outspoken about her own."

"She's not of your faith," I responded. "I have none."

"Aloysha, you lack of religious morality in this matter shocks me!"

"What? What? I don't remember this coming up when Esther wanted to marry Aengus. Why is it coming up now?"

There was a considered pause. "Esther was my daughter," he said quietly. "You … are my son."

"Well, that certainly makes sense," I snapped. "Why is everything in my life suddenly revolving around religion, anyway? What does my marriage have to do with religious morality? Phipps is okay with getting a divorce, and she's the religious one. I've never done a religious thing, much less a Jewish thing in my life, and as far as I know, neither have you. When your father died and that was a long, long time ago, like forty-four years if my math is good, the last real Jew exited the family, except for Racheal, and she's Jewish because her husband is Jewish. You're talking to the son you gave to your worldly, largely agnostic mother to raise while you made a new life with your wife and daughters back down in Bel Air."

That sounded harsh, even in to my heavily medicated ears, and I took a quick breath and tried again. "Sorry. That came out wrong. What I meant was, if you were concerned about my beliefs you should have seen to them yourself, or at least said something about the way Gram was raising me. Your mother, you know, was a scandalous old rascal. She let all manner of people into her circle of friends - Buddhists, Taoists, Baha'i's, Muslims, Catholics, Protestants, Hindus, and heathens. I've sat at table with the religions of the world. This has to be about something besides religion. It has to be. What is it you're really thinking? What's upsetting you?"

He ignored the question. "So now, with twelve hundred miles between us, this comes out," he said in a wounded tone.

"Twelve hundred miles and about half a century," I said quietly. "Dad, I'm not bitter. I never was. By the time I got over being grateful just to be alive and in America, I was so attached to Gram I'd never have left. I sure didn't want to travel with you and Mother, and by the time you guys settled down and started having babies again, I was almost a teenager. I'm happy with the way things went." There was silence.

"Dad, you're my hero. I wouldn't hurt you for the world. Please believe me when I say I know what I'm doing. I've been around Kit and his family since I was five. They were Christians and no harm done. Glory's a Christian. I'm reasonably comfortable around most doctrines and most people of faith. I'm going to marry a woman who takes her Christianity very seriously. I have to respect that if my marriage is going to work. As a matter of fact, to simplify things, just as a gesture, I might ..." I stopped short, realizing what I'd been about to say. Another jolt! "Ah ... forget that last part.

The meds are making me punchy."

"You wouldn't!" my father exclaimed. "For the love of God, Bud, are you insane?"

Why did people keep asking me that lately? "Dad, please," I squeaked. "You're overreacting completely ... oh, ouch!"

Phipps sat quickly beside me and reached for the medication on the night stand. I asked Dad please to hold on, tossed down a pill, and held Philippa in place against my ribcage. "I'm okay," I said to both of them. "Dad, don't get upset over what you haven't heard, please. I care for you. I would like your blessing, but its absence won't ... damn ... make a difference." I handed Phipps the phone, squeezed my eyes shut, and gritted my teeth as Philippa said hello to my father.

"Peter is having a little trouble with his knee right now," she said, and listened for a few moments. "I couldn't change his mind if I wanted to. He's too stubborn. You know that. We're both trying to feel our way through this situation, and honor others and ourselves in the process. Please don't be concerned, and don't be too hard on him right now. He's so drugged up he has no idea what he's saying half the time. I do have to go. He needs a hand ... yes, Sir. One of us will call you every day or so. Yes, Sir. Goodbye."

Philippa hung up, ran to get Glory, and for the next few minutes we were concerned with getting the pain in my knee under control. When I'd finally collapsed in a sweat soaked heap and Phipps was blotting my face with a cool washcloth she said, "Your Father's afraid you're going to become a Christian."

"Yes, I know."

"Where would he get an idea like that?" she asked, though she'd been standing right there.

"Because I almost told him so," I muttered. "I just almost told him so. Why did I do that? I have not the slightest intention of embracing religion. I think religion is the root of all evil."

Philippa told me not to worry, things would be clearer when the drugs wore off. She also told me that, while I was not, as I had put it, an observer, this was an excellent time to enjoy pretending to be one.

I agreed. I laid in bed and let my mind wander for a bit until I had a little strength back, then the girls helped me into the wheelchair and into the bathroom for a sponge bath. I felt better after a good scrubbing, and Glory wheeled me out on the deck to bake in the morning sun. It eased my mind not to have any more filming to do for awhile, and I was content to let the heat soak into my bare chest and fantasize about life without a knee brace.

I slept, ate lunch, stared at my piano for a bit ... talked to Oscar about getting the music room started, and the foundation poured for the modular. I also told him Phipps and I had decided to convert the ten by twenty foot storage room in the shop into a small place for Frank to use until he could find a place of his own. Phil had the sketches, would Oscar please see that they got to the architect and on to the contractor who was doing the rest of the add-on?

Glory and Philippa went to the store, and I called Rafael. I asked him who the last person was to use the tennis courts, and he said – maybe Megan and her buddies? Long enough. I told him to have it jackhammered up and hauled away. I wanted a garden for Philippa. The woman needed a garden of her own at the birdhouse. Maybe a nice little greenhouse at one end.

He was quiet for a few seconds and I knew he had something on his mind. "Are you going to tell me this is a bad idea?" I groused. "Is this a bad idea?"

"Absolutely not," he said quickly. "But consider this. Gophers do not generally gnaw through concrete. If we put raised beds on top of the court rather than having it jackhammered up and hauled away, there will never be gophers in the vegetable garden. Plus it's already fenced. I think this could be the ultimate in recycling, my friend."

"Of course," I murmured. "Why didn't I think of that?"

I could hear him laughing quietly to himself. "Should I start without you, or do you think it would be better to let Philippa design her own garden?"

I told him I wanted to surprise her, and asked him to do something in a standard configuration. We could always change it around a little if she so desired. I told him to get things started, make some drawings and take some bids. I was going to head south as soon as Denton would let me.

I also asked him to come up with a good excuse to lure Glory home at the end of the week. She and Phil were getting on each other's nerves in this tiny house. She'd stated early on that she'd either fly back or go back with us – that she'd brought the Benz so I didn't have to crawl in and out of the Ford. We could put her on a plane and have her home in a jiffy. Other than that, things were fine. I was fine. Crew was shooting a last day of city streets and they'd be leaving. Oh, beware of Peter the elder. I told Rafael why. Rafael said not to worry. Things would be clearer when the drugs wore off.

I tried, I really did, to make my mind relax, to let go of that which I had to work my way through, and go to things I could kind of ease my way through. It was largely a lost cause at that point. The drugs which blocked the pain signals to my brain were blocking most of the other signals, too. I wasn't hungry, or thirsty. My bladder didn't want to function. Everything ... was an effort. I finally gave up trying to think at all, gave up fighting sleep. Saffron curled in my lap, or on my chest if I was lying down, and I relaxed into the fur and the purr of him – practicing his philosophy of nap and let nap for a couple of days.

Then I went back to the doctor, and Merrick said he'd need to scope the knee every three days for a month. I was horrified. I told him I had the most important role of my life coming up. I had work to do. He didn't yell at me. He didn't change his mind, of course, but he didn't yell. He reminded me that I'd agreed to this on his terms, and said I wasn't thinking thoroughly enough yet. He'd cut back on my medication. Change it a little so I could use my head for something besides a hat rack.

I asked him why the huge brace, and he said he didn't trust me, or what my fellow professionals might demand of me. And just what was it I'd done my first day home from the hospital? See? He'd cut it back in a week or two, but I had to swear I wouldn't use the knee, or any part of that leg. I dutifully crossed my heart and hoped to die.

We discussed the part of Rachmaninoff, and I told him what was expected of me. He said great music could be arranged in this neck of the woods. Mercy sakes, look at that group from Union Gap. I had to laugh and agree with him. His reasoning was so clearly nonsensical that I just couldn't resist him. There were resources here in the valley itself. There were fine music libraries at the Universities in Ellensburg and Pullman, and Seattle would soon be a reasonable trip. Not to worry. Things would be clearer when the drugs wore off.

He even said I could try crutches in three or four days – as soon as some of the medication got out of my system. My blood pressure looked good. Must be eating like Philippa. Exceptionally healthy woman. Seemed very happy these days, too.

So, this was Phipps at her happiest. Why did I think she was depressed? Maybe that was just Philippa, good days and bad, like a roller coaster with a nice view from the top. Knee looked good so far. He gave me permission to lower it so I could sit normally. Half an hour down, half an hour up. Set a timer so I didn't get carried away at the keyboard.

Definite turn for the better. I began thinking in complete sentences again. I was able to sit down with Philippa and Glory, and really have a talk with them. I came away much relieved. If I'd had to choose between the two of them, it would have killed me. They were figuring it out. What they couldn't figure out, they'd fight out, make no mistake, but they were a team. They'd make it work. Thank God. Thank God they love Him – and me – as they do, or it would have been war between two of the strongest women I've ever known.

Rafael called right on time. Indeed, no excuses needed. He sure could use his wife back home. The contractors had been there to give him bids. He had chosen one, and now everything had to be moved so they could get their equipment in. He needed help. The offsite staff was in disarray, the phone rang constantly, and Glory knew all the answers. He was starving, and dammit, he was horny, too.

Oh, scuttlebutt had it that Megan and Richard were in real trouble marriage-wise. He wasn't sure whether it was being blamed on Alexander's behavior, or Megan's near term second pregnancy, or Richard's long absences, or what, but they'd made more than one scene in public the last week or so. Apparently they were back to that kind of nonsense again. Alexander had called for me yesterday. I said I'd call him from here. Ah, problems with the children. Whoever said if they aren't your blood it isn't the same, had his head up his ass.

I assured Glory – reassured Glory – ten dozen times at least, that I would be fine. The pain had subsided to a dull ache. My head was clear. My strength was coming back. I could get to the bathroom and back on crutches. Soon I'd be discarding the wheelchair altogether. Please, Rafael sounded like an orphan over the phone, and if anything went really wrong between Meg and Richard, I wanted someone close to catch Alex. Glory hugged us both until our bones cracked, and caught a plane for home.

The time which followed, brief though it was, was one of great peace and contentment for me – for us. Music flowed from my mind, my pen, my fingers – the best I'd ever written of my own, or arranged by another. I sat and watched Philippa as she trained horses, or worked in her orchard or her flower beds or at her desk, and rejoiced quietly as the last of the marks Frank had left faded to leave her physically untouched. I marveled at the power in her, physical as well as mental, and I sought its source ... by observation. What a delightful pastime. There is no one on earth who looks better in a filthy, sweat soaked, open throated shirt than Philippa Kate. She'd stand before me with her face glowing – teeth flashing in laughter, and stir such desire in me that I cannot to this day fathom it.

On one such occasion, I gave Philippa the diamonds I'd bought for her, and the tears welled up to sparkle in her eyes as the gems reflected the midday sunshine. No one had ever given her diamonds. They go amazingly well with horsehair and baseball caps with a ponytail pulled through the back. At least they do on Philippa.

The air in that place was so clear, the activities by and large so time honored and wholesome, the people so honest and so fine, that no activity was without some beauty of purpose. I don't say that in meaning to diminish their efforts. I've never seen people work so hard for so long, but I was a city boy, and most of the pioneer activities I'd seen were make believe. Some of them stirred very old memories of Russia, and my grandparents, but I had been little more than a baby, and they were feelings rather than remembrances. Even the elderly strode forth with enthusiasm to their gardens or on their daily walks, and I ached to join them.

Phipps had her quilting group at the house one day, and a lady who had practically vaulted onto the porch told another lady, that she'd never even heard of machine quilting until she was in her eighties. That had been a dozen years ago, of course. She was used to the idea, now. Amazing people in that neighborhood. Many of them are still with us to this day.

The addition was going up like wildfire, and making nearly as big a mess. We put a lot of the furniture in storage and I had my piano moved into the family room to save it from the dust and the occasional flying nail. Because I couldn't very well compose over the noise of the tools, I took to playing at odd hours of the night. Phipps just rolled her eyes and retreated to her study.

I spoke almost daily with David Swift and the other producers of Rachmaninoff. They were extremely pleased with the music I was transmitting to them via Ma Bell and the Internet. Of course I was channeling Sergei Rachmaninoff, so I was working with some pretty good stuff.

Kit checked in every day. HLM, Hell for short, was growing like a weed. The editing staff was doing a superb job with the film we already had. Petroglyphs was a shoo-in for an Emmy nomination. Every second morning I called my father at his office and chatted uncomfortably for a few moments, mostly about the weather.

I couldn't get out to church, for good or ill, but Tom Knox came to see me. Yes, he knew I was Jewish. He also knew, being a skier, how knee surgery could feel, and mine had been a doozie. He just wanted to check in on me.

Phipps fixed coffee, then went outside, and I picked Tom's brains about Christianity, and his particular denomination, until it's a wonder he didn't kill me. Looking back on it, it's a wonder I didn't kill him, or, more exactly, tell him what I thought of his rigidity and intolerance, and that odd, condescending tone that surfaced in him from time to time. I refrained from saying anything in the hopes of figuring out whether it was a reflection of his faith, or his personality.

I did tell him what Philippa had said, and he replied that facing the sin in our lives can be very difficult. Acknowledging it is the relatively easy part of that difficult process. Eliminating that sin, and changing our attitude so that particular sin does not occur again, can be terribly painful. When we are living in sin, the adjustment becomes impossible to make, and drives a wedge between us and God. "Once you've had God," he said, "nothing, no one can fill that emptiness, and that's what she's feeling."

I asked him if he thought Phipps and I were really that lost in sin. It didn't feel like it. Our relationship was mature, and stable. We loved and honored one another, had forsaken all others, as the Bible commanded. I asked if he thought my leaving Philippa alone, as she had been even in marriage, was the lesser of two evils. He thought about that, and smiled, and said, rightly so I suppose, that evil is evil and sin is sin. It is only in the mind of man that they become greater or lesser. It seemed a very human, very honest reaction to deny God love, in return for being denied human love. It wasn't right, of course, but it was honest. Phipps, by nature, didn't have a religious bone in her body. She was a born heathen. For her to fight those odds and win to any degree was something for which Christ would honor her. What she had to do, was love and respect herself.

At last he hit something we agreed on. I said I'd be in church with her when I wasn't packing quite so much weight around, and he said he was a patient man.

The drywallers came and the floors downstairs disappeared under layers of white speckled plastic. The carpet people arrived to measure and show us some samples, then the painting contractor visited, and we arranged to have the whole house redone outside.

Denton eased my brace back, ran some tests, made some X-rays and gave me a standard knee to toes wrapped walking brace with a metal stabilizer at the knee and the arch of my foot, and told me I could go back to being on top. By now, of course, I was spoiled and didn't want to.

The morning came when, just at dawn, Philippa touched me and said, "Come see what we have." I dressed, and went out to the barn, and Flyer was nursing a beautiful little colt. A flame red chestnut with a blaze and four white socks. He wobbled over to see me, nuzzling under my chin with velvet nose and milky breath. I kissed the cowlick between his soft, dark eyes, and Phil said she was glad I liked him – he was mine.

Then Glory called. Megan had given birth to a baby daughter. Alexander had been insanely jealous. He'd said he was running away to live with me, and Megan had said, fine! Alex had gone down their driveway on his little bicycle and right out in front of a car. He was in critical condition, his father was out of the country, and his mother was totally incapable of coping with what was happening. Could I please fly home?

CHAPTER THIRTEEN

Where is this child's father?" I said through my teeth, and for the hundredth time, but no one answered me. I was alone in a room with a battery of machines and poor, broken little Alexander, lying there with his head in some evil looking contraption that bored into his skull.

I kissed him, held his hand, told him all about life on the far side of civilization. I told him about the farm animals, about the beautiful rivers full of fish, about the trees and mountains, and about Mount Saint Helens, and how she had all but buried the town in the valley below Philippa's house under tons of ash. In Philippa's yard you could still pick up the stuff in handfuls. I'd met a nice little boy just about his age, and I wanted them to get together. But Alex couldn't hear me, because Alex was in a coma. His skull was fractured, his little body had been dragged down the pavement and nearly skinned alive. His bones were broken. He ... was going to die. The doctors all said ... he was going to die.

Then – I decided in a moment of total exhaustion and absolute clarity – he wasn't. Not without one hell of a fight. There was a merciful God for such things, and a man who had said, "Take up thy bed and walk." And I knew people who knew where to reach him. I spent a few indecisive minutes feeling like a hypocrite, and wishing at the same time that the part of my brain I'd given over to scoffing under my breath, had been paying more attention to what was actually being said. I realized I was in a foxhole, and that my rational self was still scoffing and feeling utterly ridiculous, but the emotional side of me was in panic mode, and that part of me was willing to believe in anything that would save this child. Anything.

I folded my hands on the bed beside Alex, and really turned my weeping eyes heavenward for the first time in as long as I could remember. "Dear Jesus, friend of my friend," I said quietly, "If you will save this child ...thereby proving your reality to me ... I will worship you the rest of my life. I will trade Judaism for Christianity … of some kind. I promise." Even in my state the thought made me want to chuckle. When it came to being Jewish, I had nothing to trade, since I didn't put any stock in Judaism, either.

I knew, of course that it was absurd to ask God for proof of anything, but I've always been brash, and since I was basically neither Jew nor Christian, I had absolutely nothing to lose. Then I remembered what Phipps had said about praying for God to save her marriage – and being sorry when he did. If Alex lived, I was committed. I'd have to become a Christian, even though I thought all religion was man's manipulation of faith – Christianity especially so. I would lose my father. I sagged against the side of Alex's bed and closed my eyes. There was something to lose, after all. Maybe I didn't want to do this. But … I'd promised. The words had been uttered. Maybe I'd get lucky and Alex would … die. That thought was a knife in my heart.

I wished desperately for Philippa's loving presence. She was so wonderful with small, wounded things. But she wasn't here. I'd told her to stay up north, that there wasn't anything she could do. I must have been crazy to think that. Here I was, alone with a dying child, ready to commit my soul to something I'd disapproved of all my life to save him, and I didn't have a clue how to begin. Worse – more pathetic yet – I'd never paid enough attention to my own beautiful and ancient faith to know how to access it, either. I felt like there had to be some formula, something one said or did to activate the system, and the only people I'd seen do that, were Glory, who was now caring for both Megan and a newborn, and Phipps, who was not here.

But Flyer's foal was still so tiny, and the addition to the house needed supervising. She had so much to do. That had been – I looked at my watch – nearly thirty-six hours ago. Many of those hours I'd been here in this room. Soon, Glory or my dad or Kit would take my place for a bit and

I'd go home to bathe and shave and have a bite to eat and a nap. Then, I'd be back, because visits from Megan were few and far between in this eerily quiet and sterile smelling room, and I was the closest thing to a father this little boy had. Megan had an excuse of course. Megan had a week old baby. Megan could not take the strain, probably not even without the baby.

Those two were currently staying at our house. You see, Megan believed in servants who stayed in their place, and friends who led independent, carefree lives. When she desperately needed someone who cared deeply about her, she had no one. They were still searching the wilds of Mexico City for Richard. He was making a movie. Had been for some weeks. Hadn't been home to help his daughter come into the world any more than he'd been there for Alex. Apparently, he and Megan had fought, and he'd left.

I hadn't seen Meg yet, and didn't particularly want to. She was given to yelling and screaming hysterically, and it was the last thing any of us needed, especially Alexander. I stood up, got my crutches under me and went over to look out the window. Late afternoon. Dirty air. Aching knee. Aching heart.

"Buddy?" I smiled at the sound of that voice, and as I turned, Kit was already reaching to hug me. "How's our fishing partner?"

"Still with us, I said. "I see you brought his fishing pole."

"It's like chicken soup," he winked, "It never hurts. I thought I'd sit and visit with him for a while if you want to go home."

"Thanks," I sighed. "I hate to leave him but I've got to take a break. Have they found Richard?"

"Who knows? I quit asking. Go on, I've got a cab waiting downstairs for you. Can you manage that far?"

I told him of course I could, but getting to that cab, was a major undertaking. In Washington I'd had very little need to go anywhere on crutches, a few yards in any direction, but here, and before that at the airport, I'd been on them forever. My shoulders, and my armpits, ached to the point of cramping.

Glory got an arm around me as I got out of the cab, and I staggered into the living room and dropped into my favorite recliner.

"Alexander?"

"Kit's with him," I groaned, leaning back. "God, it's hot out there. Could I trouble you for something to drink?"

"What'd you like, Love?"

"How about a nice glass of iced tea?" I said, and almost, I could smell the apple tree that we'd so recently been sitting under to enjoy a tea break. God, how I missed my loving Philippa. And what had I to offer her half as beautiful as the spot she was right now? Maybe she'd call, and I could at least hear her voice.

I thanked Glory for the tea, and took a few sips, remembering the laughter of the days before, as Flyer's new foal had run in stiff-legged circles around his mother. Philippa's crazy, delighted laugh. When I opened my eyes it was getting dark outside, and Glory was touching my whisker roughened face, telling me supper was ready. It was another of my favorites, Jambalaya with shrimp and chopped ham and lots of vegetables and rice. I realized I was starved.

It was at that point, before I'd really started dinner or my first cup of coffee, that Megan came downstairs. "Hi," I said in surprise. "I guess I forgot you were here."

Looking back on it, it was a very stupid way for me to greet her. Here was this poor, distraught woman to whom I'd once been married. I could at least have gotten up and given her a hug and told her I was sorry for what had happened. Actually, it did occur to me ... just a little too late.

I swung around on the bar stool to get up, and she cried, "You sonofabitch!" and slammed into me so hard with both her fists that the bar stool came off its base, and I went flying. I was startled, and stunned, and it's God's mercy that I didn't break something, because I had no time to catch myself.

I did whack my cheekbone and bloody my nose against the kitchen floor. Luckily we have teak and not tile or I'd have killed myself. I lay there for a long minute and watched the kitchen cruise by. Meg was still screaming and sobbing, wriggling in Glory's iron grasp, and I could hear

Glory yelling into the intercom. I shook my head and got one elbow under me, and by that time Rafael had whipped through the kitchen door and had his arms around me.

"I'm fine," I said, mopping under my nose with the back of my hand. "Really, I'm wonderful. Perfect. Just help me up."

I got to my feet with Rafael's help, and stood, leaning against him and glaring balefully at Megan. "What the hell was that for," I growled, "Old times sake?"

"You sonofabitch!" she cried again, "this is your fault! You take Alexander, you spoil him, you lure him to his death wanting to be with you! You killed my son!"

I just walked out. I had not one rational thing to say in reply. I washed up, and shaved, changed my clothes, and Rafael drove me back to the hospital.

I took Kit's place beside Alex, talking to him about nearly anything as the darkness outside stretched forever toward morning. Then I smelled coffee, and a small, work-worn hand that I knew very, very well came across my left shoulder as someone kissed the back of my neck.

"Philippa," I said with a deep sigh, and gratefully took the cup she extended.

I stood up and folded her in my arms, literally gasping with relief. How desperately I had needed her. What joy there was in her presence. I set the coffee on the bedside table and kissed her, really kissed her, until I began to unknot inside. Then I offered her the chair I'd had my leg propped up in, and realized she hadn't said a word.

"You must be awfully tired," I said. "Did you drive straight through?"

"Yup," she grinned, reaching to take my hand, "Trucker's wife. How's your little fella?"

"Holding his own, I guess, but I'm glad you're here," I said, then shook my head slowly and muttered, "He's just barely alive, Philippa. They say he won't make it, and I need prayer power. That's the only thing that's going to work."

To her vast credit she didn't arch her brows and comment on the sudden turnaround. She just smiled and hugged me close. "The church has been praying. So has the Bible study prayer chain. So have I. You haven't been alone, Peter." She reached then with her fingertips in the dimmed light and touched my right cheek. "How did that happen?"

"Leave a mark?"

"Just a reddened spot about the size of a half dollar," she said. "As tough as your hide is, you must have hit something pretty hard. Did you run into a cupboard door?"

"Ah ... yeah, more or less, but I'm fine. Have you had supper?" I glanced at my watch, "or breakfast?"

"I grabbed some elk jerky out of the freezer on my way out the door, and a six pack of Snapple," Phil smiled. "I'm fine for now. Are you hungry?"

I was starving, but I shook my head. "The coffee'll hold me for a while. Right now I need a favor."

"Here?" she teased, wide eyed, and I laughed softly.

"Not that kind of a favor. Philippa, Sweet Face ... I understand how you feel about your relationship with God. Right now I know you two are kind of on the outs. But this little guy is so precious to me, and the only thing that's going to save him is prayer. I do not have the relationship with God that you do. I do not have the prayer vocabulary that you do. Could you please, put your differences aside and lean your shoulder into this with me? Please?"

She hugged me again and kissed me, sat me down beside Alex, and pulled her chair up next to mine. "You don't need a certain vocabulary to talk to God," she said. "He honors us at the entry level. The Bible tells us the prayer of a good man availeth much, and you're a good man. Maybe not a religious man, but a good, moral man. It also tells us that the man who thinks his prayer will be heard because of his many words, deceives himself. God looks on the heart. Don't despair, Sweetheart, your prayers for Alex have been heard, and honored." That was it. I was sunk. I was on the express track from Shylock to Antonio. Luckily I wasn't capable of running away screaming, or I might have done just that.

"The Bible tells us that when we pray a prayer of agreement, what we agree to on earth will be agreed to in heaven. What we allow on earth, will be allowed in heaven. The Bible tells us that when we pray God's Word, we pray His perfect will. Are you with me so far?"

"Um hm," I nodded. Actually, I was a little annoyed, as I always was when religion came up. I felt like I was listening to a somewhat patronizing stranger. I'd told her I didn't have the vocabulary, and she had just turned it on, so I shouldn't have been irked. But when religious Philippa came to the fore, my Philippa vanished, and that was scary, because I always wondered if she'd come back. I sensed that she was trying to keep this simple for me, so I gritted my teeth, plastered on a studious look and bore the irritation that was creeping like spiders up the back of my neck.

"I know I'm annoying you with this religious mumbo jumbo," she said quietly, "but you can't fully agree if you don't know what you're agreeing to, and while we might be able to fool our fellow humans into thinking we agree with something when we don't, fooling God is not an option."

I nodded. My body was so heavy I felt like I'd been eating rocks, or sand. My head felt like a melon on a twig. I'd asked her to throw her prayer power in with mine, and I had none. I wasn't sure I had the energy to look for any. I glanced over at Alex. "Keep going," I said.

"I have been given the gift of intercession. In layman's terms, I seem to be good at praying for other people and getting results. That gift will not function and does not exist outside my belief in Jesus Christ. Can you accept that?"

"Um hm." I didn't actually believe that, either, maybe because I didn't yet understand it, but I nodded and hoped God would be understanding on behalf of this child.

"You sure? You cannot agree to what you cannot accept."

"I ... am open to a miracle," I said quietly. Phil put my hand on Alex's, hers beside mine on his arm, then took my other hand ... and praised God for his presence, and his hope in this humanly hopeless situation. She prayed God's word, as she said she would, called upon the name of Christ, as was her right as a Christian, and called upon me to agree with her for the healing of this child, which I did.

She prayed for the forgiveness of her own sins, then she just ... the word escapes me. She ... entered another dimension all together. There was an intensity there, and a power that I will never be able to adequately convey as long as I live. On a typical, sunny, cynical day I'd have called it self-induced hypnosis, or even a sort of quiet hysteria ... but that, it was not. I guarantee it. That power was, and is, real.

She told me later that if my mind had resisted it, I'd not have felt it the way I did. She said the Holy Spirit is a gentleman. He never goes where he is not welcome. Apparently, I was tired enough to be open minded, because whatever electrified that hospital room that night – those hours – still makes my skin tingle. I have tried to explain it to a few people, and either I come across as nuts, and no amount of explaining will help me, or they understand and accept it with no explanation at all. It certainly negated everything I'd been telling myself for my entire adult life.

I was drifting in the grey light of morning – my arm on the bed, head on my arm – when Alex started to cry. My eyes flew open, I caught his hand, Phipps kicked her chair back and stepped out of the way.

"Aw Alex. Don't cry. I'm here," I said, laughing and weeping and trying to keep my voice low and calm.

"Please ... help me," he managed. "My head's caught."

"It's supposed to be," I soothed. "You bumped it really hard, and that's to protect it. Try not to wiggle around and hurt yourself."

"You cry? You're too big."

"I'm crying because I'm happy to see you, and that's a good thing. Don't let anybody tell you different."

Two nurses came in, and a doctor, and they were laughing and saying it was a miracle. I got up, but I stayed where Alex could see me, and I muttered, "Well, God ... that was a personal phone call if ever there was one."

One of the nurses turned and smiled at me. "What did you say, Mister Aarons?"

"Nothing," I grinned. "Just saying thanks."

She looked into me, and I realized there is something that passes between those who truly love God. It is universal, but at the time, I thought it was a code for Christians only – something with the eyes. I'd seen it pass between Glory and Philippa that first day. Philippa? I looked around, and she was gone.

"Her prayers are the reason that child is alive," I said aloud, and that same nurse shook her head.

"No. She would be dismayed to hear you say that. Here, come hold Alexander's hand for a bit. I'll go check on your wife."

I didn't bother to correct her. I was too tired. When Phipps came back in, I was shocked. Her face was grey with exhaustion, her eyes red and swollen from weeping, and I realized what had transpired had been hard, hard work – rebirthing a life to life again. I realized then that all of it was going to be hard work, and was relieved. Work, I understood.

We just clung to each other – too weary to laugh or cry, and in one of Alexander's waking moments I introduced her to him. He said we both looked awful and drifted back to sleep.

An hour later Megan came in, tears in her eyes, beautiful face glowing with happiness, and as I stood up, the tears spilled down her face and she sobbed daintily against my chest and told me a dozen times she was sorry for last night.

I rubbed her back and kissed her hair and asked her if they'd found Richard. They had. He'd called and was on his way. I noted that she was freshly bathed, coifed, and impeccably made up. First things first, I guess. I did not, by the way, murmur the usual garbage about, "Oh, I understand perfectly. No apology needed." I understood only too well. She was an unspeakable bitch.

Meg looked Philippa up and down – travel creased shirt, faded jeans, worn cowboy boots, no makeup, swollen, bloodshot eyes, knotted back hair that needed washing – no contest. She gave me a smile that was ever so slightly pitying, ever so slightly seductive, and I felt sorry for her.

"Will you be here for a while?" I asked, and she nodded.

"Two hours. Then I have to nurse the baby. Take a peek at her when you get home. She's really cute."

"Bet she's not as cute as the baby Philippa gave me," I grinned, put an arm around that dear, greasy little person, and hobbled out, exhausted and exhilarated. I stopped at the nurse's station and told the nurse not to leave Meg alone with Alex. If he woke up, the first thing she'd do was rag his ass for riding out in the street. I'd send somebody back to make it a trio when we got home.

Glory was out the door before we went in. She didn't trust Megan either. There was a fresh pot of coffee – strawberries, kiwis, bananas all sliced in the bowl by the stove, pancakes and bacon in the microwave, chunks of rare steak and cream cheese in that blue plastic thing in the fridge for Phipps – oh, there was a baby upstairs. Her name was Octavia. Diapers on the dresser. Megan's mother had called from Bermuda, or Japan, or some damn where. She'd be here sometime tomorrow. Sleep! The Benz shot down the driveway. No point digging out another car. No time.

"What would we do without her?" I sighed, and Phil shook her head.

"Not as much, Dear Heart. Not as much. Can you get the rest of the way to the kitchen, or are you rooted?"

"I only know that wherever I light, it may be for a long time. Let's get where we're going."

We settled ourselves in two of those wonderful, plushly padded Captain's chairs that pass for bar stools in our kitchen, I poured coffee, Philippa got two bowls and a couple of fondue forks, and we propped our elbows on the counter and fed each other.

"Hear the one about the big carrot and the little carrot?" Philippa asked, and it was the sanest part of the ensuing fifteen minutes or so.

I told Phipps I absolutely could not sleep as filthy as I was, so she helped me wrap my brace in its waterproof cover, and we took a long, hot shower together. Just a shower – It was all we could do to keep each other awake. I got dried off, took the plastic off my leg, and keeled over into the bed in the downstairs master. I'd never have made it upstairs at that point.

I was vaguely aware that someone came in and went upstairs – came down, went out again. I was really too tired to sleep soundly. I drifted out again, and awoke to the sound of a baby crying. The stairs creaked and I knew either Phipps or Glory was up there, but I did want to check, so I got dressed, picked up my crutches, and made my way upstairs.

In the filtered afternoon sunshine, scrubbed face, shining hair, Philippa sat in Grandma's rocker with Megan's baby. Beautiful picture. A memory I cherished, because I knew I would never see Philippa rocking a baby of our own. She looked up and smiled, and I came to stand beside her.

"Octavia, hm? A name usually reserved for the eighth daughter in a Roman household. Quite a handle for such a tiny being."

"Not any worse than Philippa," she grinned. "Maybe not even as bad."

"I love the name Philippa," I teased, nudging at her with my thigh. I moved the corner of the blanket for a closer look. "So, is she cute?" I asked, "In your opinion."

"If you're into babies I suppose she is," Phipps sighed. "God ... I am so jealous."

I jumped a little. "What you are, is crazy," I replied.

"It is in the heart of every woman to want to give her husband a child. It is the height of femininity, and the reason for which God created us."

I resisted the urge to say anything clever and urbane about ZPG, or how our lifestyle would be impacted, or how old fashioned and uneducated she sounded. I thought a moment instead.

"You ... gave me a child today," I said quietly, "and I have no more idea how to express that to you, than I can express what I felt in there. But I am very much in awe."

"Me too," she smiled, touching the baby's face. "God does wonderful work in spite of us, doesn't he?" She glanced up at me and then away, and her tone of voice changed. "So, did you keep your promise?"

"What promise?" I gasped, feeling suddenly naked. I hadn't said a word to her. Not to anybody but ... Him. I was sure of it.

"As it is in the heart of every woman to bear a child for the man she loves, so it is in the heart of every Jew to strike a bargain, Aarons."

"Yet another sweeping generalization," I sniffed.

"Remember what the New Testament says about tempting God with a foolish test. Did you tempt him with one life for another, by any chance?"

"Ah ... can I hold her?" I asked, partly to change the subject, partly because Octavia was irresistibly precious.

"I mean, it is a sweet deal," Phipps said, relinquishing the chair and the baby, "being able to save a life, and gain a soul, maybe two. You will, because of the kind of person you are, tell Alex at some point how he came to be alive. He might just come to believe that stuff."

"True. Of course his mother will put a bullet between my eyes, and my father will never forgive me. But, I assure you, that if there was a bargain struck, there will be a bargain kept."

"Peter, look," Philippa said softly, blessedly changing the subject, "she very nearly fits in the palm of your hand. I need a picture of this." She got the camera from the big, walk-in closet, and took a picture that I still have in my wallet.

The moment was short lived, as moments with babies often are. As she was putting the camera away I gasped, "Aw, Jeez Phipps, this baby just peed right down my arm, and now she's smiling."

Phil burst into laughter at the look on my face, and dropped the subject of who and what had been promised to whom.

It dogged me, of course. I felt guilty about hanging back – about not saying something. I wasn't sure where to begin, or with whom. After all, I'd made the bargain with God, not anybody who needed to know, right? I was profoundly grateful for the saving of Alex's life, and I told God that a hundred times that afternoon. I also told him I was terrified of losing my father, and Alexander, and my own identity and that I could never, ever be part of a denomination as closed minded and intolerant as Philippa's and asked Him please, please to be patient with me.

I knew, self-indulgent as it sounded, that I absolutely had to get some rest. Mentally, physically, emotionally, I was shot. Philippa is one of those people who can carry on a lucid, well thought out conversation and be sound asleep. I've watched her do it, and then have no memory of it whatsoever. I go blank when I'm tired. Everything is intimidating. My nerves get raw, my tongue gets sharp. I can't even bear myself. I noticed Phipps was leaving me pretty much alone.

The house itself seemed to be on edge. The baby cried. Megan was in and out. Glory was out, period. Doors opened and closed louder than usual. The air was dirtier than usual. My knee and my back ached more than usual.

I gave up trying to sleep and eased myself downstairs to see how things were coming with the tennis court. Dismal mess. The pool was tarped, the boulders, the waterfall. The trees and plants were dusty and forlorn. How I longed for simpler days, when this transition would be over, and things would be normal again.

Rafael gave me a smile and a one armed hug and assured me things weren't as bad as they looked. A good hosing down would cure ninety percent of our ills. I resisted an off-color comeback.

"What are you doing?" a voice asked behind me. Damn. Megan.

Rafael beat a hasty and unceremonious retreat, whispering, "You're on your own, Cochise."

"Converting the tennis courts to a vegetable garden," I replied, pulling back the dust cover on one of the chaise lounges. "No one plays tennis, why keep them?"

I sat down sideways on the chaise and braced myself for whatever mood Megan might be in. I had married this woman. Six interminable years I had spent with this woman. I had made love to this woman. We had seen each other naked. Amazing. I felt nothing but irritation, and a slight jolt of shock.

"I assume, from the look of her, that Mrs. Tyler does not play tennis?" Megan smiled.

"That is correct. Mrs. Tyler has not played tennis since high school. I am no longer a tennis player. Nor are the elder Ruiz's, and both Royal and Titus are off on their own. We have no use for a tennis court in this family group."

"There's no need to snap," Megan said, still smiling, "and there's certainly no need to keep something you don't use. I am sorry to hear you need to grow your own food." She brushed the dust cover aside on the chaise next to mine, and perched on the edge of it, facing me. She looked pretty, and somewhat pensive, and I knew she was getting ready to spring something on me. "So ... you're really going to marry her?"

"Philippa? Of course I am."

"What will you do, the two of you?"

"Well, we're not really sure. In the short run we have this miniseries to finish up, and Rachmaninoff to do, and Phipps has promised the production company she'll adapt another of her manuscripts into a series. That book is in a set of three that she wrote several years ago and never published. The first one is coming out December twelfth, in honor of my birthday, or so Philippa says. I've read it – read the set – prize winning material, I think."

Megan smiled sweetly. "It sounds like you're going to become her husband rather than her becoming your wife. She looks like the domineering type. The little ones always are."

"You had a career, Megan. I didn't feel intimidated by advertising. I don't feel intimidated by writing. Philippa is brilliant. I'm honored to share her life ..." I crimped a grin, "... regardless of who's on top at the moment."

"And in the long run?"

"In the long run," I said with some enthusiasm, "we have plans to develop a really good, mainstream film or two about the men who helped shape the National Park system, starting with Yellowstone – Nathaniel P. Langford, Thomas Moran, William Henry Jackson, Ferdinand Hayden. We would very much like to see William Tecumseh Sherman vilified properly once and for all as the mad, murdering bastard he was. The Civil War, the plains Indians. Those are Philippa's pet projects. For myself, I'd like to write music for the flickers, you know? And try my hand at cinematography. If we invest carefully, we can afford to try our own film making. We'd like to do an in-depth study of the Anasazi, just for our own edification, and I'd like to do a lot more with my music than I have been, more concerts, more composing ... a bit less acting, I think."

"My God, listen to yourself," Megan said softly. "Sweetheart, listen to yourself. The drive is gone. The fire has gone out. You sound like some stuffy old Ph.D. in a college somewhere."

I could feel it coming. "I am a stuffy old Ph.D. Meg. Well, D.M.A., actually, since my doctorate is in Musical Arts, not Philosophy, but ..."

"Stop it! I don't care! You're an actor, Bud! You're sexy and talented and dynamic. She's making an old man out of you!"

"She's stimulating me to think in areas other than those I'm used to," I said, listening to my stomach growl and realizing I hadn't had more than snacks in two days. "Phipps is, above all else, a scholar. She loves knowledge. She admires people who accomplish things. She loves the outdoors and hard physical work. She's different from you, Megan. I can just be myself and please her. I can have dirty hands and please her. I don't have to strive every day of my life to be bigger than life."

"You had to do that for me?" she asked quietly. "I wasn't aware of it."

"Perhaps," I sighed, "it was my reaction to you, rather than a direct result of your demands. But I do seem to remember you telling me, even after we were divorced, that I was boring. I didn't like to party enough. Didn't have important people over enough. Didn't go out enough. Didn't play hard enough on my Emmy. Didn't push my own talent enough. Didn't take roles I should have. Phipps, cares about how I feel and what I think. About who I am inside and what I really want to do. I am comfortable with Philippa."

"She seems the comfortable sort," Megan drawled, sounding disturbingly like my sister Racheal. I wondered if those two had been chatting, and if the third weird sister, Amber Kestrel Tirino, had been part of the witches' brew. "Old shoe, TV watcher, mall crawler ..."

"Thin ice, Megan."

"Well," the condescending little laugh, "She's not exactly a sophisticate."

"She doesn't put on airs, but there's not a place in this town I couldn't take her. She has manners. She's well liked. She's brilliant. She's dazzling when she's all dressed up."

"She's sure as hell homely when she's not, Bud. She's got the ugliest hands I've ever seen on a woman, and awful crow's feet, and those jowls, oh, my God. She's dumpy, and she's middle aged!"

"She's younger than you are," I said, and Megan's eyes glittered unpleasantly.

"Well, then, I hope she likes being childless more than I did. Peter, she's not going to do one thing for your standing in this community. Not socially. She's a redneck hausfrau who writes books, and I hope to God you've got a prenup at least as good as the one we had, or she's going to take you to the cleaners! She's acting only because you swing a lot of weight with Tommy and Kit. I warn you, she'll be an embarrassment."

"She hasn't thrown a glass of wine in my face at a thousand dollar a plate fund-raiser, like you did to Richard a while back," I replied. I refrained from telling Meg that the thought of a prenuptial agreement with Philippa had never entered my mind, and that the bulk of my estate had long since been willed to Titus and Royal – the sons of the hired help. I'd have to make some changes in that, wouldn't I? Again, my stomach growled, and I was trying not to growl with it. Best let Megan play this thing out, or it would come up and up forever, and Alex would have to listen to it.

"You really don't understand, do you?"

At last, the preface. "Give me a hint, Meg, but make it brief. I want to go sit with Alex."

"I don't love Richard. I never did. I ... I love you."

I managed not to burst out laughing. This woman was no actress. "Ah ha. You just wanted to get us some children and then you were coming back."

"Yes!" she cried, "I was! Bud, I love you. I want you. Why would I have let Alexander get so close to you if I hadn't wanted you to be his father?"

"Richard is never home, you wanted Alex out of your hair, and I like kids, that's why, Megan. You don't want me, you want out. You want the man who's starring in the biggest film of the year. You want to play both ends off against the middle and come up on the society pages looking desirable, just like you did when you left me for Richard. Maybe six years is your limit, you know? Maybe you have an accelerated case of the seven year itch or something. Look, Meg, I just want to be one of a pair of comfortable old shoes. I want to enjoy my wife, and the two beautiful daughters I'm marrying into, and all the new things that are opening up to me. I'm happy. Please don't begrudge me that. I tried with you, I really did. I didn't leave you, you left me. I want to let it go at that, and you should, too."

"Your father's right," Megan hissed through her teeth, "the woman is a witch! She's put a spell on you!"

"Do not," I said sharply, "drag Dad into this. As for Philippa being a witch, you may have noticed your son has taken a definite turn for the better thanks to Phil's intercession on his behalf. I'd hardly call that witchcraft." I knew it was a mistake as it was coming out of my overtired, unguarded mouth. I'd sealed my fate and I knew it.

"Tell me, please tell me you don't believe that Christian garbage of hers!" Megan gasped, and I stood up abruptly rather than yell at her.

"I don't pretend to understand it yet," I replied. "But … I think maybe I do, or at least I will someday. I've seen it work. Don't worry that I'll inflict my beliefs on Alex. I won't."

"Damn right you won't!" Megan said, her voice rising to a shriek, "You won't have the chance! I'll get a restraining order if I have to, but you stay away from him – forever – I mean it! And stay away from me, you devil!"

Her receding footsteps clicked like snapping fingers. The man in the bright red military uniform. Snap, "You, over there." Snap, "You, with him." Snap, "You, boy, over there."

I sat back down, buried my face in my hands and wept in utter frustration. "What has been accomplished?" I cried. "God help me! What has been accomplished?"

Kit found me at some point after Meg's departure. I remember the feel and the fragrance of him – the rusty hair and hazel eyes that blurred through my tears as he crouched in front of me, gripping my upper arms – his voice telling me, sharply, to breathe. "Again, deep breath." I remember leaning on him – cursing every painful, miserable step it took me to get to the house.

I could hear Megan, and ... Richard, maybe ... and Philippa, talking. Not angrily. Just discussing. I didn't want to see them, or have them see me, so Kit steered me through the kitchen and down the long L shaped hall into the bedroom I'd been in that morning. He pushed me none too gently into the bathroom, stuck my head in the shampoo bowl, and turned on the cold water full blast.

"Oh ... shit!" I gasped, then yelled, "Miller, you bastard!" and after a minute he let me up. I stood there, leaning on the sink, shaking my head like a wet dog and cursing in three or four languages.

"Better?"

Damn! I could hear him grinning, even before I looked in the mirror and saw him handing me a towel.

"I've seen you a lot of things, Buddy, but never hysterical," he said. "What's wrong?"

"Eh, not much," I muttered, scrubbing at my head. "Megan just told me I could never see Alexander again, that's all. And I'm sure her next stop is my dad's doorstep." I dropped the towel and grabbed a comb.

"Why?"

"Because I've made the decision to leave Judaism, not that I was ever in it, and join some kind of Christian … whatever. Or thought I had. Now, I don't know."

"Come," he said, leading me back out of the bedroom and down the hall to my study. "Sit. Talk to me. Have a cigarette ... no, sorry, don't have a cigarette. I'll have a cigarette. What's going on?"

"I really don't know, Kit. I've watched Philippa. I've seen what she has to hold onto with her faith, and I've watched Glory, and I watched Philippa pray for Alexander, and I saw him come back to life, Kit. I was there. I saw it! And I told God, that if this Great Physician could make that boy live, I would worship him. I promised. Now I lose Alex anyway. I lose my Dad. I lose God only knows what else, and all of a sudden I'm asking myself if the God of Abraham is punishing me for crediting his miracle to a false prophet."

"It's a valid question, and I'm amazed to hear you asking it," Kit said, knocking the ash off his cigarette and cracking open the study window, "but I'm not sure this is a good time for you to tackle it. You're so tired and hungry you're shaking."

"I'm not ..."

"You are. I've known you since you were six, for cryin' out loud. I know what you look like when your blood sugar's in the toilet."

"I'm beginning to think my nerves are shot to hell."

"They're next, Buddy. You can't ignore your body right now. It's trying to heal itself, and you're fueling it with coffee and adrenaline."

"Glory's not here."

"Poor Aloysha! Six foot three, hands like tennis racquets, and he can't open a refrigerator door. Maybe the world's better off without you, hm?"

"Don't know that, either."

"Hysteria, and now self-pity. Bud, you're a man of surprises. Is this something Philippa's encouraging in you, or what?"

"I'm used to being able to be honest with her. You said talk, I'm talking. If you don't want to hear what I have to say, don't ask."

"Hitting that stone wall pretty hard right now, aren't you, Bud?"

I rubbed my forehead and sighed, "God, Kit, I'm sorry if I sound like an ass. I just ... can't do any of the things I usually do to blow off stress. I can't skip rope, can't swim, can't take a walk. I'm shaking so bad I can't play the piano, plus there are people in my living room who might object to the noise. I'm trapped in this body with a madman who's doing everything short of strangling me to get out. It's every bit of all I can do just to keep a grip on him."

I stopped, caught my breath, and tried shifting to get more comfortable. My knee bit me again, twisting up into my back, and I tried not to look pained. I didn't want my best friend to think I was a complete baby.

"When's the last time you took something for that knee?" he asked, and I knew I wasn't hiding anything.

"I don't know. Yesterday, I think. It hasn't really bothered me that much until now. I'm just tired and hungry ..."

"Score!" he yelled, throwing his arms in the air. "I win again. Where's your medication?"

"You drive me nuts," I chuckled, closing my eyes, "I took some just before supper last night. Probably, in the kitchen?"

"I'll get it," Kit said. He put out his cigarette and left, and almost immediately there was a knock on the study door.

"Come," I said, and in walked Richard Stein.

He looked worried, and tired, and he gratefully took the chair I gestured toward. "Glad you could make it," I said, and he laughed humorlessly.

"Glad I was invited. Do you know that until an hour ago I didn't know I had a daughter?"

"You had no idea when that baby was due, hm?"

"She was early," he said defensively. "Look, Aarons, you don't like me because I stole your wife. Well, guess what? I don't particularly like you, either. We do have a lot in common. We've both had to cope with Meg, and we both love Alex. I came in here to thank you for all you've done. You, and Glory, and Philippa. You're a lucky man. She's lovely."

"Megan's not exactly a mud fence."

"She's not exactly deep, either. Philippa most definitely is. I'd love the chance to direct her in a movie sometime."

"Stein, if you look at Philippa cross-eyed, I'll cut your damned heart out."

"Never entered my mind. I swear," he said quickly.

He stretched his blue jeaned legs to ease his back, folded his arms, and contemplated a spot on the desk just beneath where my chin rested on my right fist. "I had, by the way, been sleeping with Megan for almost a month – already had her knocked up – before she bothered to tell me she was still married. Then, she told me her full name, and who she was married to. I suppose I should have told you I was sorry, but damned if I knew how. Anyway, thank you," he said, bringing his eyes up to mine. "You put your own concerns aside to help my family when I didn't even know they needed help, and I'm grateful."

"You are welcome," I said slowly, and resisted the urge to give him a piece of my mind.

"Philippa had the most amazing talk with Megan," he said, looking disturbingly besotted. "Never retaliated once for the nasty things Meg said. Won me over ...." He paused, smiled, shook his head in wonder. "She thanked Megan for letting her take care of the baby, thanked her for seeing that you were called to come be with Alexander. All the things Meg is far too selfish to do, she'll go out of here thinking she did. Oh," he chuckled, "She also volunteered the two of you for baby-sitting duty from time to time."

He stood up, walked to the door, and turned again to face me. "You are free to visit my son any time, Aarons. I told Meg, and she agrees with me. Grudgingly, but she agrees, and she knows better than to cross me beyond a certain point. I told Philippa. I'm telling you. Now, I'll take my wife and my daughter and get out of your hair so you can rest. You're just a little too old for this kind of strain."

The door closed, and in a moment or two Kit walked in, placed a glass of water in front of me, read the label on the bottle, shook a capsule into my hand, and said, "Insolent young pup, isn't he?"

"Shame on you for eavesdropping, Kristoffer, and Stein is, exactly, the same age as Frank Tyler," I muttered.

"And Peter Aloysha Aarons is a better man than the two of them put together," Kit soothed, patting my shoulder. "Put that in your mouth like a good boy. At least he's going to let you see Alex, and I think that's good. Probably for Alex more than you."

"You see now why I give credence to Philippa's beliefs," I said quietly, reaching for the glass.

"I saw it before, Bud, but then being raised the son of a Methodist minister helps. Stein's right. You look terrible. Come on, let's get you fed before you faint on me." He draped me over one shoulder rather like a woman carries a full length fur coat, and eased me down the hall.

The kitchen smelled wonderful. I leaned out of Kit's arms into Philippa's embrace, kissed her, and let them help me into one of the bar chairs. I got to finish the dinner I'd started the night before. Jambalaya's great reheated. Phipps fixed green vegetables while Kit made a salad and regaled her with stories about what a terrible kid I'd been.

I don't think I quite fell in my plate, but I came close a couple of times. Kit helped me into the bedroom and out of my clothes and then left. Phipps came in to kiss me and rub my back, and I managed to keep myself awake long enough to tell her how very, very precious she was to me. Then I kissed her, and slept with her beside me.

CHAPTER FOURTEEN

I dropped my crutches on the undulating aggregate edge of the pool, stripped off my sweat-soaked shirt, and flopped down in the shade of the cabana beside Glory and Rafael, who were lounging in their bathing suits.

"That pool looks so inviting," I sighed.

"'Nuther long day," Glory said. She poured me a glass of iced tea, squeezed a lemon wedge into it, and handed it to me. "Did you film today, or just rehearse?"

"Thank you. Neither. We recorded, which was nice. No costuming, no makeup. I got to work in jeans and my shirtsleeves for a change."

"You been playin' the piano since five O'clock this mornin', Boy?"

"Afraid so," I laughed, blowing graphically on my fingers.

"When are they going to finish casting this thing and take some of the pressure off you?" Rafael asked, and I shook my head.

"I dunno. There's so much to do just with my character in isolation ... this could go on for weeks yet. Where's Missy Phipps?"

"She left this mornin' to go somewhere with a young man name of James Horse. He called, oh, 'round eight, I guess."

"Hm, I wonder if they're with Tommy."

Glory shook her head. "Nope."

"Well then, I wonder what the young and handsome Mr. Horse wants with my lady." I said quietly. Saffron rubbed his silken presence against my pant leg, and I leaned from my chair to pet him. "Where's your mother?" I asked him.

"Behind you," Phipps said in her darkest, creepiest voice, and ran her fingernails up the back of my neck. She dropped her towel on the deck and bent at the waist to kiss me, roses and gold in the late afternoon sunshine.

"How was your day, my love?" she asked in that ever soft, ever slow voice, and any jealous thoughts dissolved like the sugar in my tea.

"I had a wonderful day," I smiled, kissing her fingers. "How was your day?"

"Lots of fun," she laughed. "I didn't get any of the work done I'd planned to do. I got a call from James this morning. He was trying out for a part, and he wanted someone to go along and read with him. So, we went over to his place and read through a few times, went to the old stampede, and I think he did really well, at least I hope so."

"I hope so, too. He's a very talented man. What kind of a part was it?"

"An Indian lawyer," Phil said, and dove into the pool with hardly a ripple behind her.

I loved to watch her swim almost as much as I loved watching her ride. She did it so easily. She never fought the water; she became one with it, as she did on horseback.

"You know, she said, surfacing back at my side of the pool, "I was thinking that if we develop those books of mine into a TV series, and you play Duncan March like you promised, James would be a good choice to play your sons."

I just smiled and didn't say anything. Was I really old enough to have a son his age? Yes, I was. I was twenty-five years – a quarter of a century – older than that gentleman. I felt momentarily hoary.

"Peter, are you thinking about Friday? You're not worried, are you?"

"No," I smiled. "I was thinking about James as the twins. I think you're right. He's a little young to play the part, but he looks older than he is, and the boys supposedly have that ageless quality about them, like their father."

"And you're too young for that part," Philippa grinned, reading my mind as usual, "but I won't trust him to anybody else."

She got that look on her face that said she might be overstepping her bounds and added mockingly, "Now that I'm a partner in Bellwether, and all. Bud, you look so tired. Are you sure you're not worried about Friday?"

"Really, I'm not worried," I said, fishing her out of the pool. "I've got nowhere to go but up with this knee. I am ready, believe me."

"What if he doesn't take the brace off?" Phil asked. She leaned against me, and her wet, cool skin felt good.

"I will wring his little neck," I laughed. "Glory, can we help you get dinner on the table?"

I lied, of course. I was worried. Twelve hour days in the sweltering heat, in a brace that heavy, was hell. My thigh was perpetually bloody where the support rubbed. My opposing knee was scraped and bruised from bumping it in my sleep. My foot was raw from the constant stream of sweat draining onto it. If Merrick Denton didn't take this sucker off, he was dead.

But I was busy. I didn't have time to dwell on the possibilities. I was up at four to be at work by five – worked until four with an hour for lunch – stopped by the hospital every day on my way home to see Alexander.

Praise God, he looked so good. The doctors said, amazingly, miraculously, there was no permanent damage. There would be some scars where he'd lost flesh to pavement, but they'd be on his back, where he'd been least protected. They wouldn't show under ordinary circumstances.

I'd showed him a couple of scars I'd picked up as a kid, including my favorite – the one on my left hand – and told him he'd need that sort of thing. It added pizzazz to the stories he'd tell his grandchildren someday. He'd laughed and agreed with me. So wise for only six. I'd told him I was getting married pretty soon and I wanted him to be there.

"I hope you're not getting married with that ugly brace on your leg!" he'd grimaced, and I heartily agreed.

Phipps and I flew into Seattle as we had been doing on Thursday afternoons – took a commuter flight over the Cascades and had the Hitchers pick us up and take us home to the farm. They were now in residence, had been for two weeks or so, and they were getting really settled.

All the animals looked fine. My baby, Aleko, was long legged and ornery as sin. I loved him, and chanted over him weekly, hoping to cast a spell that would give him his mother's looks, but his father's mellow personality and long legs.

The air was fragrant, heavy with moisture and the lingering hum of late afternoon bees. We sat on the deck until ten o'clock in the evening, and it still wasn't dark. Quietly, happily, we welcomed in the longest days of summer.

"Didn't sleep last night, did you?" Denton smiled, and I shook my head and smiled back. "Well, I can't say I blame you. Try to relax. How's the boy? How's the movie going? I see they've stuck you with Rachmaninoff's buzz cut, or almost, anyway. How are the wedding plans coming?" He pulled the brace and the bandages off, warned me that the leg looked like hell, sprayed something soothing on the raw spots, and told me to hang onto what I had, this might hurt.

"Damn good looking knee if I do say so myself," he mumbled, poking and prodding and bending it gently between his hands. "That hurt, or are you sweating because it looks sexy? You are, y' know."

I just made a sound through my nose. My jaws were locked too tightly to speak. "How about this way?" he asked with a gentle turn, and I groaned, but I didn't unclench my teeth. "I like to see a man enjoy himself. See if you can bend it. Scream if it'll help."

One bend, one lousy bend, and I was soaked in sweat and gasping for air like I'd run a marathon.

"Good," he said. "Do it again. Make a man out of you."

I tried. My back twisted and I very nearly did scream.

"That's to be expected," he said, holding my hand and forearm tightly against his own. "Your back is used to the weight of the brace. Try to relax a minute. We'll do it again. Relax. Drop that right hip back on the table. That's it. Deep breath. That's the secret of a long life, you know. Remember to keep breathing."

An eternity we worked that knee, until I gagged from straining the muscles in my gut, and the sweat ran down my face, and I thought I'd faint from the pain. In the end he patted my cheek and told me to put my britches and my regular knee brace on – I was a free man. I'd have to use a cane for a bit, and I'd still need crutches once in a while, and a good physical therapist was a must, but I could stay in LA next weekend; he didn't need to see me for two weeks. He knew I had a swimming pool because all of us Hollywood types did. I was to use it every day at least twice a day, as much as I could tolerate without drowning myself. Oh, and did he need to warn me at this point not to jump rope or ride horses? No, he didn't think so.

"You're still pretty green around the gills," he said. "Get dressed, lie down, try to sleep a few minutes. When you're cooled off I'll check your vital signs and let you go home with your little gal."

"I'll have to call her," I said, and he cocked a bushy grey eyebrow and grinned at me.

"You don't really think she left, do you? You lucky stiff. I'd send her in to sit with you, but I'd like a normal reading on your blood pressure."

"She didn't go home, or shopping, or something?"

"No, Aarons, of course she didn't, any more than you'd leave her. The two of you are sickening. Put your damned slacks on."

To be without the weight of that brace – just to be able to flex my ankle, to lie on my left side, to take a cool bath – was such a pleasure. Best of all, it did not hurt, not deeply. For the first time in a decade, my knee did not really hurt. I promised God something else. The first time I could kneel, it would be to thank Him properly for the people He'd placed in my life.

I was awakened from my after lunch snooze by a kiss, and Philippa's soft chuckle. "Come on!" she said, eyes dancing. "It's the longest day of summer. It's a holiday for farmers, hicks and hillbillies. Come on!"

It did me no good to ask. By the time I was up and dressed in what Phipps told me would be appropriate garb, the aluminum boat was atop the fifth wheel, the Hitchers were heading out of the driveway with their travel trailer, and the Johns had honked and pulled away with theirs.

"I love a parade," Phil laughed, and fell into line behind them.

I was content to stretch my legs, plural, and watch the scenery go by. And what scenery it was. From doorstep to destination, it was heavenly. We had been in such a hurry in previous weeks, with little time to do more than supervise the building, see the doctor, fuss with the animals, and hop a plane back to the city. Certainly there had been no time to explore. Aside from our trips to the mountains to film, when I'd been more focused on the icy road in front of me and the six horse trailer behind me than on the scenery around me, this was my first trip out.

It opened up a whole new world for me – the world of Washington State – where even to this day we can camp, hike, backpack and horsepack, and not see another human the whole day. This was the short trip that made me an avid, if not particularly rugged outdoorsman. It was my introduction to freshwater fishing in the alpine lakes of the Pacific Northwest, and I loved it. I still do.

The hunting thing ... stalking those beautiful elk with blood in my eye and murder in my heart ... that, I don't do, though Phipps has tried to convert me. Yes, it's true, though in those earliest days I was still shaking my head in disbelief. My dainty darling is a Bambi stalker. That sport, she shares with Steve and Dennis, even Kit, and now that they're getting older, those inseparable buddies, Kenny and Alex. Myself, I pretty much stick to fishing with Viktor. What an amazing story that is; Viktor, and where I met him and who he turned out to be. But it is not a story that belongs here, because this story is about my beloved Phipps, and how she came to be mine and I hers.

We wound out of the valley's heat into the Cascades, following yet another fast flowing river. Higher, cooler, through the pines, to stop beside a small, placid lake, deep in the shaded forest. Uncrowded, unhurried, quiet. As unlike camping in California as anything could possibly be.

"Don't you girls plan on insulting us with steak," Oscar laughed, reaching up to take the boat from Dennis. "We're celebrating Bud's parole with fresh trout!"

I could go out fishing again! If I fell overboard, I wouldn't sink like a stone. Wonderful! I felt ten years younger. Oscar, and Dennis and I just sat and fished and looked at the scenery. Didn't talk. Didn't have to. We were comfortable with our mutual passion. We could hear Kenny whooping up and down the beach, and an occasional burst of laughter from the girls as they set up camp.

When we got back to shore around seven o'clock, supper was laid out, and a fire was crackling in the pit. We stirred it down and set the fish to cook over the coals. Then Oscar called us together around the fire, and we joined hands and thanked God for the beautiful world He had given us. We thanked Him for the fragrance of pines and water, the sound of the wind in the trees and the crackling fire, the love and fellowship we shared one with another. What a miracle, to be able to see, and hear, and smell, and taste, and touch, and comprehend what we are doing. What a miracle ... not to hurt. I thanked God for that, myself. We prayed for Alexander, and for Frank.

Then we ate too much, and set up the camp chairs around the fire, and leaned back with coffee, and popcorn, and S'mores, for the adventurous – Phipps and I not among them. We talked about things besides family activities. The economy and the apple crop, and how the asparagus had done on the market. We discussed the news, the collapse of the Soviet Union, the terrorism, the frightening things that were happening to children everywhere, and that led into the discussion of what the Bible told us we could expect to see yet come.

It was during those latter discussions that I listened far more than I talked, because so much of what they said were things I couldn't agree with - a view of God and His workings that I just couldn't accept. It was enough for Phipps to know how I felt, I wasn't going to go to war with the Pentecostals of the earth. It wouldn't solve a thing. They were so convinced that they were right, and that God had spoken just to them, that the best I could hope for was pity for thinking differently. I'd tried a time or two to express a more global opinion, and Oscar had said he'd pray for me. I wondered if all Christians were like this. Kit was a Christian. He wasn't like this. I didn't remember Glory being so ... positive about her beliefs.

Oscar said my name, again, and I rejoined the conversation around the fire. He asked me, gently, if I remembered what it had been like, being a Jew in Russia during the war. I veiled my eyes, thanking God they were dark, and shook my head. "No," I said quietly, "It was right at the end of the conflict, and I was too small. I remember being scared. And I remember

... while we were prisoners, and traveling to the camps, I watched them take an elderly married couple and stand them up against the wall of their izba, and shoot them ... just because they were old. I remember seeing the blood splashing against the side of their house before they ever fell. It's about the only thing I do remember, but I remember it like it was yesterday. That, and what they did to my mother and me, but that, I won't discuss, Oscar. I just can't. I do know they killed the cattle in the fields and the dogs in the streets. The people starved, the very old and the very young first, and the fact that my family was wealthy and respected, availed us nothing in the end. It did not matter who we were, or what we had."

"How did you get away?" Dennis asked.

"We didn't. Through the kindness and courage of friends, we were able to make it through all but the last weeks of the war, but ultimately, we were found out. We were held ..." I paused, struggling for words. "Fortunately, my mother had been able to get word to my father by then, and because it was the closing days of the war, and the Third Reich was crumbling, and every man was in it for himself, documents were produced, officials were bought off, and Mother and I were put on a train for Switzerland, which was beginning to open its borders again. To walk out of that place ..." I shook my head free of that image, took a deep breath, and felt Philippa's hand, warm and soothing on the back of my neck. "Anyway, we were put in a Red Cross hospital in Lucerne, and when our health had picked up enough to travel, we were shipped to the States and my dad's loving arms. That's about it."

"Except for the nightmares," Phipps said.

"Except for the nightmares," I smiled, tossing a broken stick into the flames. "The worst nightmare of all is that kids are growing up today not really comprehending that it happened, and that it can happen again. Right here, if we let it. This whole 'religion as a platform for intolerance' thing, the resurgent White Supremacist movement, that whole group of lunatics next door in Idaho, gives me the willies."

"You really think the children should be subjected to that in school?" Adelle asked.

I looked at Sarah, nursing sleepily under an afghan at her breast, and at Kenny, who was trying, with Ruth's help, to pick the last of a marshmallow out of his hair, and said emphatically, "Oh, yes, I do! Far better in the classroom than at the feet of an invading army. Because I was little, and just wanted to be like everyone else, it took me a long time to face the fact that I had to remember, and not forget. Surprisingly, it was my best friend, Kristoffer Miller, who first pointed it out to me. He was wise, even when we were kids."

Adelle was no longer interested in the subject. I could tell by the look on her round eyed face. "Bud, do you mean the Kristoffer Miller? The actor?"

"Makes your heart go pitty-pat, does he?" I teased, and she glanced at her husband, who smiled and added another log to the fire. "Don't be embarrassed, Adelle, he does have that effect on women, always has. He was fighting them off in first grade. And yes, my Kit Miller is the Kristoffer Miller."

"Is he ... married?"

"No, Adelle, he's between wives and available at the moment. You'll meet him at the wedding."

"Really?" she smiled, blushing and awestruck, then glanced again at Dennis. "No more marshmallows," she said firmly, stood up, excused herself, and took Sarah into their trailer.

I waited until the door closed, and then said, "I'm teasing her, Dennis. I've known Kit a long time, seen him through some rocky romances and broken marriages, and I've never seen him look at a married woman. Which is more than I can say for myself."

"Phipps says she's the one who hit on you first," Dennis grinned, flipping a small pine cone her direction. "She says you were a dear friend, and the soul of honor."

"I was a dear friend and a darn good actor," I replied, squeezing her hand. "When she hit on me, as you put it, she had been carefully maneuvered into a position where she could do very little else, bless her heart."

"But not necessarily maneuvered by you," she said.

I kissed her, watching the firelight move against her skin and her hair, and the muted burgundy plaid she wore open at the throat ... as the candlelight had touched her in that restaurant by the beach that night. How long ago had that been? It seemed yesterday, and then, many years. Almost, I couldn't remember life without Philippa. Loving Philippa.

"Have you talked to your dad?" Oscar asked, and I came back to myself again. I must be sleepy that my mind was wandering so.

"Not since last I talked to you," I sighed. I was beginning to regret having ever mentioned my problems with Dad to Oscar. It had become a campaign with him, and a source of deep and enduring pain for me.

"You have to talk to him."

"Oscar, he told me that he had no Christian children. His eldest daughter, he said, had died tragically many years ago, and, recently, his only son. I have every reason to think he means it. He didn't wail or rip his clothing, he's too sophisticated. But he did turn his back and walk out of my house, and if I never see him again, I won't be surprised."

"Your sister turned Christian?" Oscar inquired askance, and I bit down hard on a grin.

"No. She died of heart failure. Literally died, not figuratively, like me. I'm figuratively dead in my Father's eyes, Oscar, but it feels much the same as real death. It's just as lonely."

"You have tried your best to talk to him?" Oscar insisted gently, re-affirming his stand during more than one anguished conversation by phone and in person over the last month.

"Of course I have, Oscar. I told you I would. But you do not understand the Jewish way of thinking about such matters. I tried. Philippa tried. Kristoffer tried. Glory tried. There's nobody left to try. I won't ask my mother. She's not well, and I won't catch her between us. Racheal, my baby sister, I hardly know anymore, not that I knew her in the first place, and she's very Jewish, married to a Jew, living in Chicago. She might as well be a complete stranger, living on the moon. I, have made my choice, and lost my father, period. I knew it was the price I would pay. I just knew it."

"What does it profit a man to gain the whole world and lose his soul?" Ruth said quietly. "You're in the right, Bud. Stick to your guns."

"I intend to," I smiled, "But I sure miss my dad."

The conversation drifted then – to people lost, people gained – the nature of loving and losing. I knew that if I alienated these people by word or deed, I would lose them, and because of that, I would lose part of someone I loved. The struggle within myself about what they believed and how they expressed it, had to stay right there. Not that my expression of faith was any more graceful at that point. It wasn't. It was just ... different.

I stared into the fire, smiling to myself, at myself, and my rigid, unbending pride. I could still see myself, thudding down on a barstool and glaring at that dear, kind woman who had prayed for me so many years. "I've decided to become a Christian," I'd snapped. "Not that I think you're all that right. I don't. I think the Jews have some very good points. But for me, in my situation, marrying a Christian, I think it's for the best. I have no intention of being gung ho, so don't push me. I'm a Jew at heart. I'll always be a Jew by heritage. Rag my ass and you're fired."

"Who pushed you into this?" she'd asked, setting aside her dish towel and facing me across the counter.

"Nobody pushed me. I ... promised God."

"Made a commitment, or just made a commitment to make a commitment?" she'd asked, pouring my coffee and using a tone she usually used to discuss the weather.

"I said ..."

"Heard what you said, Boy. You hear what I said back?"

"Yes."

"Then get your eyes outta that coffee cup and up here at me. Now, answer me," she said gently.

"I don't know what to say."

"That's a start right there. You sure 'bout this?"

"Yes. At this time, in this situation ... Dammit Glory, I made a promise, okay? I told God that if he healed Alex I'd ..."

"Go from bein' Shylock to bein' Antonio," she smiled. "You have said that a few times over the years, Aloysha. This been on you mind a long, long time. Have you told Jesus you accept him, not as history, but as the one who personally paid the price for you personal salvation?"

"Aw ... geez." I'd sat there and squirmed like a five year old. It still makes me squirm, as a matter of fact, and back then I was just a baby Christian, with few options for understanding my adopted faith. I'd shook my head no, and muttered, and ... blushed. I could feel it, just like Philippa blushed when she was embarrassed and uncomfortable. But Glory had persisted, as was her way, and I had come, as every Christian supposedly does, by the confession of sins and the professing of Jesus Christ, and gone back to staring at my coffee.

I shook my head and realized my eyelids had closed on me.

"Pretty chilly out here," Philippa smiled. "Still want to sleep under the stars, on the hard ground, and let the ants carry you away, kicking and screaming into the darkness?"

"Don't let her scare you," Oscar muttered. "They wouldn't carry you off. They'd just swarm all over you in great heaps, stripping your flesh from your bones."

Kenny squealed, and wiggled all over with horrified delight, and Ruth reached over and ran her fingers up his back making spooky sounds and ending with a gentle pinch on the back of his neck.

"Now I want to go home," I laughed, but I excused myself and opted for the fifth wheel, with Philippa close behind me.

"Soon, you'll be kindling," I smiled, putting my crutches up beside the bed, "And soon," I smiled, reaching for Philippa, "You'll be Mrs. Peter Aarons."

She sighed, and hugged me, and rubbed my back as I rubbed her shoulders. "You know," she said after a while, "maybe if we waited to get married until after you settle things with your father, he'd see how much you care what he thinks."

"He might also see that I'm willing to compromise my faith rather than lose my inheritance."

"Aw, you think so?" she asked sympathetically.

"I don't know," I sighed. "I have never gotten the feeling that my dad admires compromise." I let go of Phipps, unbuttoned my shirt, and sat down on the couch to untie my shoes. "Maybe I'm just guessing at what I would see if I was in his place. I don't know."

"Look," Phipps smiled, pointing down, "you have two shoes on. How do you feel?"

"Stiff ... so to speak."

"Not in a fifth wheel you don't," she said, teasing me, and I reached out and grabbed her.

"You don't what?" I asked, sitting her on my left knee, and she blushed. "None of that, now," I said. "You start something, you finish it. What don't you do in a travel trailer?"

"Anything," Dennis laughed in passing outside, which made it obvious he was right.

I took just enough medication to ease the throb in my leg and back, tucked Philippa into the crook of my arm, and I slept, with the fragrant whispering of those evergreens, better, more naturally, more restfully, than I could remember having slept in a decade of pain.

I was awakened at first light to go fishing. In the far north at midsummer, first light comes about four o'clock, and Oscar's none too gentle slapping on the side of the trailer next to my head, was not exceptionally well received. He persisted, and I crawled out.

I was sore from the base of my neck clear to my toes. In trying to bend that knee, I'd pulled every muscle in my body. I remembered this part from last time, but last time I'd been ten years younger. I hobbled forth, determined to be cheerful. A cup of Ruth's good coffee, a couple ibuprofen, and I was. The air was crisp and clean and smelled wonderful. The water looked like grey glass with a jagged white rim of sand. Best of all, the fish were hitting hard and often. We kept only enough for breakfast and released the rest. Another perfect day beginning.

Steve and Jan and the kids rolled in, and we laughed and visited, and napped, and fished – sat around the fire and told ghost stories – and those couple of days spent in peace and quiet helped brace me for another grueling week in the city.

More and more, I felt myself escaping to a simpler place and time.

What had been diversion was becoming polarity. Washington was becoming home. I had been so afraid Phipps would change, and I had changed instead. Problem was, my work, our work, was in Los Angeles.

The seat belt light went off, and I turned to get more comfortable. Philippa smiled and patted my thigh, but she was very little company on these flights. Phipps was terrified of flying. She took tranquilizers and slept most of the time. When she was awake she hardly knew her name. She receded into that person she had been after Frank's attack on her, dreamy and detached.

How long ago that, too, seemed. How long ago since I had picked that poor, bloodied person up off the floor and sworn vengeance on the man who'd hurt her. Truth was, I'd never even raised my voice to him. Whether or not that was to my credit I had no idea, but I guessed it was. He was another one like my father, who made me wonder what he thought of my reaction to him. Did Frank assume he had me cowed? Did Frank assume anything? Probably not. Frank Tyler was a stone wall of indifference. It started with himself and touched everyone he knew more than casually. Singularly odd, enigmatic person. I doubt he'd even have heard me yelling, poor man. Except as he related to Philippa and the girls, I chose to avoid him. Not pointedly, bodily, but mentally and emotionally. Almost, I could convince myself I'd done him a service in taking his high tempered little pistol of a wife. Even Oscar had mentioned that Frank seemed happier lately.

One thing I did feel guilty about, was that I was living in the house Frank Tyler had built with his talent and the sweat of his brow, and the fact that he had over a hundred thousand dollars of my money didn't really change the way I felt. I knew, very well, what it was like to be on the outside looking in. To be the displaced person, and I ached for anyone in that position, even Frank. I really didn't want to give him the run of the house when we weren't there, nor did I want to exclude him completely. What I wanted to do was chant a little incantation and have him disappear somewhere far away – hopefully somewhere nice – but mainly, far away. I wasn't comfortable with him, and I didn't want to be. What I had, I had paid for, in one way or another, and I wanted a clean break. That, of course, was wishful thinking.

About like wishing I didn't have to see Megan. We had managed, up until Alexander's accident, to maintain a tenuous but viable relationship. Friendship, was too good a word for it, but it worked. Now, I saw her at the hospital, and she did everything but spit on me. She looked at me like my father did, with the loathing reserved for dead snakes. I was ... dead. In their eyes, I was dead. I wondered if they'd had a funeral for me.

Funny, my father nor Megan either one had ever given Judaism as religion more than lip service until I had decided to pass on it. Now all of a sudden they were the outraged devout. Between the two of them they couldn't quote two passages from the Torah to back their own beliefs, but they could find a hundred passages to condemn me for mine. They. It had become, they. The insult added to injury. Megan had taken my place in my father's affections. Of course they'd always been close. As a matter of fact Dad had talked me into proposing to her. He was welcome to have her back. His dear, Jewish daughter-in-law.

Why then such a keen sense of loss on my part? Again, I had walked out of imprisonment and left people I loved behind. I spoke, and Megan looked through me. I was dead. My voice could not be heard from beyond the grave. I was dead. Even Alex looked at me strangely and asked what had come between Megan and me. I lied of course, because I didn't dare tell him the truth. How could I explain to a six-year-old that my family had disowned me for my beliefs? They weren't evil or harmful beliefs, but they were different. The people my family chose to deal with and socialize with every day might hold these beliefs, but I could not, because I was not born to hold them.

Philippa traced the lower edge of my eye socket gently with the edge of her index finger, and I watched a tear shimmer its way down over her knuckle to be caught by her lips.

"You need help," she said again, as she had for the last month or so. "Bud, you need to be with other Jews who have made the same decision you have. You need support from your own kind, and saying that you were never really Jewish, won't help. You're Jewish by half your blood and most of your heritage, if not by faith, and you need reinforcement in those areas.

Please. You're scaring me."

I nodded. The last thing I wanted to do was scare this dear friend. The fact that she knew what I was thinking because I was subconsciously weeping, only made her point stronger. Nevertheless, I felt like I was being asked to join a leper colony. I didn't want to seek out these people. I didn't want to feel any more ostracized than I already felt. I said so. Phipps smiled and disagreed. "You're ostracizing yourself," she said gently, knowing it would hurt. "Why do you think Washington looks so good all of a sudden?"

"Because it's beautiful, and clean, and sparsely populated, and those people who are our friends and neighbors are wonderful and kind and honest and open, that's why," I replied. "Not much of a riddle."

"They're also not Jewish. Most of them have never even known a Jewish person. Most of them don't know you're Jewish."

"Point taken," I snapped. "I like that piano better, too." I looked out the window for a minute or so at the endless, cloudless darkening sky and fought the words in my mind, but it was no use. "I think I've made the wrong decision," I blurted at last. "I'm afraid I've done the wrong thing."

"Remember telling me I'd been dragged into doing the right thing for the wrong reason?" Phil smiled. "Maybe you have, too. Couldn't hurt to ask."

"Whom?"

She grinned, and I just shook my head. She just was not ever as sleepy as she seemed. I said I'd look up the organization when we got home. Tomorrow. Tomorrow was Monday. I'd do it ... tomorrow. She nodded and held my hand.

We swung by the hospital on the way home from the airport so I could show Alex I'd gotten my leg back, then went on to the house. Kit was there waiting, and Tommy and his wife, Emily, and they'd added James to the mix, and we snagged Rafael as usual, and went out to celebrate having ten legs between us instead on only nine. The girls, opted to go elsewhere. Probably wouldn't have come with us even if we'd invited them. It had been a long time since I'd been out with the guys, and I was really enjoying it.

We went out for pizza and a couple of beers, then Kit dragged us all to a burlesque show on the strip. After that, deciding we'd better upgrade ourselves just a tad, we went to one of the nicer rooftop lounges near the studio. We were all laughing, and none of us appeared very sober, but one of us was. Me. I'd lost the toss for driver, and I was stone sober when Richard Stein's hand closed roughly over my shoulder.

"Hello," I said, cordially enough. "Care to sit down?"

"What I'd care to do is bash your fucking brains out," he grated, and there were five sober people sitting at the table.

I froze for a moment or two, trying to figure out what was happening. I hadn't seen Stein since that evening in my study. I hadn't seen Megan for several days. Alex hadn't said anything out of the ordinary.

"You have me at a disadvantage," I said, pushing my chair around to get his hand off my shoulder. "What seems to be the problem?" Now I was facing him, my chair in profile to the table, and I could see that he was staggering drunk. "Stein, I'm talking to you." I really didn't want to stand up and have the whole place see me. I really wanted this idiot to sit down and be calm, and I told him so.

Instead, he swayed belligerently and snarled, "Why are you trying to steal my wife?"

My mouth dropped open long before a thought entered my head. "Me?" I exclaimed. "Me? Stein, do you know who I am?" God, I am so stupid sometimes.

"Peter Aarons," he bellowed obligingly, and I'm sure they heard him in San Fernando. Hell, might as well stand up, now.

I came out of my chair, seized his shirtfront with both hands, and sat him down none too gently where I'd been sitting a moment before. Kit kicked a chair under me and I sat back down.

"Trouble here?" the bouncer asked. Tommy slipped him a bill and said no, but asked him to stay close, just in case.

Richard started back up, but I held him firmly in place, which surprised him. I could see it. "What's the matter with you?" I hissed. "Don't yell, just answer me. What's the problem?"

"Megan says you asked her to leave me, and take the kids and go back to you."

"You sure she said that?" I grimaced. "You sure you didn't imagine it, Stein? Read the gossip columns, you wife hates my guts!"

"That's what you want me to think, you asshole! You cradle robber!"

"Keep your voice down or I'll twist your neck, I swear I will. Stein, you have met Philippa Tyler, remember? I am engaged to Philippa Tyler. Six weeks from today I'm marrying Philippa Tyler. What do I want with two wives? Richard, I am in love with Philippa, not Megan. I'm fond of Alex and little ... what's her name, but I certainly have no desire to be raising children at my age. I have Phil's daughters to share, and Glory's boys ..."

"That nigger," he sneered. I saw Rafael's chair start to move, and Kit's arm reaching to stop him.

"Please don't tempt me. My hands are making me a lot of money right now. I don't want to break them on your face. And I don't want Rafael hauled off to jail for decking you. He's having such a good time tonight. We all were."

"The Nazi's should have gassed you when they had you ... Aloysha. You're not a Jew, you're a damned Russian. And your old man, slithering around my wife like a snake. Damned old fool."

"You're not going to call him a damned Jew?" Kit grinned, and Tommy hushed him.

"Richard," I said quietly, still trying to make him listen, still trying to avoid the cover of that rag for inquiring readers, "Richard, Megan won't even speak to me. Since the day I told her I was going from Judaism to Christianity, she has not said one, single solitary word to me. She has slandered Phil and me in every gossip column west of the Mississippi. If she and Dad are doing anything together they're planning my funeral. Please ... please hear me. If Megan says I asked her to leave you, she's either lying or hallucinating. She's under a tremendous amount of stress. She has a tiny baby, an injured son, and a troubled marriage. Go to her, talk to her, get her help if she needs it. She nearly had a mental breakdown when she was married to me, and she didn't have close to the pressure she does now. She's the mother of your children, and they need her. Don't ignore her."

I pushed my chair back and allowed Stein to get to his feet. "I'm sorry," he mumbled. "I should'a known it was her and not you."

"Don't approach her with that attitude," I said, and I could hear Philippa speaking in my heart. I smiled. "Are you here alone?"

"Of course I am. I'm always alone."

"Come on. We'll take you home. One of us will call you in the morning and tell you where you left your car." I plunked his keys down with the bartender and steered him on out to the elevator.

"Great finish to the evening," Kit groused, sprawled on my couch, and I shook my head.

"Could have been worse."

"Could have been better. You think Megan's really cracked, or is she just hounding for attention as usual?"

"I think, "I said slowly, "that if she's that desperate for attention, she needs it. I just hope Richard gives it to her." I thought a moment, picked up the phone, dialed a number. "Max, please ask the senior Mister Aarons to check on Megan in the morning. I'm worried about her. Thank you," I said, and hung up.

"At this hour you call your father's house?"

"At this hour I knew I'd get the machine, or someone too groggy to hang up on me," I muttered. "You ready for bed?"

"You're really not going to give me my car keys?"

"That is correct. You're here for the night my dear friend. I will give you the choice of any of the six vacant bedrooms, and loan you my favorite jammies, though."

"I assume you never wear them anymore, that you're always naked and well-oiled under the sheets."

"You know," I grinned, "I'd like to be there right now. Because, between the heat, and my nerves, and two nights in a travel trailer, and now this late night partying you lured me into ...."

"Poor Aloysha, you have my sympathy," he giggled. "That man who goes around Hollywood taking other men's wives. I never thought I'd see the day."

"Keep it up and you won't," I laughed. "Come on, I'm putting you to bed."

CHAPTER FIFTEEN

Because I am, however grudgingly at times, a man of my word, I looked them up in the phone book. Jews Accepting Christ as Messiah, JACAM. Terrible, tacky name. It made me cringe. I went right then, before my ego got the better of me.

They were kind and supportive, and informative. Apparently, they'd been expecting me, and had contemplated contacting me. I was beginning to wonder if the general public knew what I wore to bed, but I didn't ask. My life was changing nearly as much as Philippa's, and I can't say I was particularly enjoying it at the moment.

At JACAM I found kindred spirits from all different denominations and friends I have kept. People to laugh with, and cry with, and put the pieces together with. There were advocates among them who would try to reach my father. There were people among them with tattoos on their forearms, which made me feel less like I was turning my back on the suffering of my father's race.

They met five times a week. Meetings morning and evening Monday and Thursday, and for those who wished, church on Sunday mornings. I could choose an all-male meeting, or one that was mixed. I told them I'd be back that night.

I didn't want Phil to go with me. I wasn't sure how to tell her that, but of course I didn't have to. She knew. She told me she couldn't go and hoped that was okay. She needed to be back on camera in the morning, and she just had to work on her lines.

At last, I could let my guard down and talk about my conversion, or acceptance, or whatever it was. I really wasn't sure. I could talk in an open forum about how uncomfortable I was with my Pentecostal friends, though God knows, I loved them. Understood. They asked me what I believed aside from any religion about the nature of God, and I told them, feeling lighter with every word they understood. Oscar had not understood at all. Nor had Dennis. I had been asking questions of them, trying to evaluate information, and getting reactions rather than answers. I couldn't seem to make them understand that I wasn't challenging them when I questioned what they believed. I just wanted to understand why they believed it. They took the 'The Bible says it, I believe it, and that settles it' stance, which gave me as a learner no information at all about the logic of their beliefs. Glory talked to me, and Phipps talked to me, and they were wonderful ... women. Women believe differently than men. I needed to talk to men.

At JACAM, sitting in a comfortable chair with a cup of coffee in one hand, surrounded by guys who had been through the same process I was going through, I got answers – tons of answers, simple and direct. When I asked about churches that might be more suited to my beliefs, they began to explain to me just a little bit about all the different denominations, and how they viewed this same Jesus and his teachings, and I realized there was a place in Christianity for someone who felt as I did. Interestingly enough, when I discussed with them what Phil had taught me, and basically what she believed, they hiked their eyebrows a little and asked me if she was for sure an evangelical. I said I thought she was. And she thought she was.

When they asked me about being Jewish, I was really embarrassed. I had to admit, quite frankly, I'd paid it lip service only, and didn't know a thing about it, and for good or ill, I didn't think my father did, either. I thought he was using it as the closest weapon to pick up and swing at me. I admitted that I didn't realize there would be such far reaching trauma with my decision to turn Christian, considering I'd never really been Jewish by faith. That, got a laugh from everybody who'd ever had a matzo ball cross their lips. Jewish, was Jewish – by blood, by faith – the only religion that worked that way, and one of the most complex to understand.

With these people I could say anything I wanted, ask anything I needed to, and not be questioned as to my motives or my beliefs. They understood that I didn't really have any of those in place yet, and that I wasn't equipped to discuss much in the way of religion as a set of quotable rules. Faith, is what we talked about.

In the end, they suggested that I come to church with the core group on Sundays, until I had some general knowledge under my belt, and then, they suggested, I try going to church with Jacob, who was a Universalist Unitarian. It sounded like it might be a fit.

"Actually, I think your Gram's Psychologist friend, Steven Effendi, in the course of rehabilitating you after the war, converted you years ago," Jacob had laughed, "I think you're a Baha'i without benefit of their particular prophet. But my church is as close to faith and away from religion as you'll get with the Christian experience. You're welcome anytime."

Slowly, slowly, as we talked over the days, the nails began to come loose in my soul, and a glimmer of light, a widening crack, appeared around the black door of my frustration. Again they assured me, somehow, they would reach my father.

I had little time to be the dutiful, despairing son, though it tapped often at the back of my mind as I worked hour after hour at the keyboard. I wrote at the piano, arranged at the piano, occasionally ate lunch and slept there. That week, I pounded my Steinway twelve hours a day, and made two quick trips to the other studio to film with Tommy. I ached clear to my shoulders, but by the end of the week I was walking with a cane instead of a crutch, and diving into my swimming pool at the end of the work day. It felt so good. I felt so good! I'd swim, eat dinner, go back to my piano or my script until bedtime.

Phipps seemed to be as busy as I was, and I was relieved. I was worried she'd feel left out when I went into one of my crazy cycles, but it seemed we'd come mutually out of hiatus and back onto the fast track. Our health was in top form, and we picked up a new label around town. The Dynamic Duo. Hardly original, but accurate.

That next Sunday, because we were not up north, Philippa went to church with me and my ilk. She said she really enjoyed it, and I was comfortable enough to enjoy her company. She was the perfect stranger, and I got more than one envying glance. That evening she went to church with Glory, just to keep her lungs and her hands in shape. How comfortable she was anywhere God was present. Except in her own church. I wondered if I dared mention that.

Monday on the way home from work at a decent hour for once, I stopped to see Alex, and the nurse said it was wonderful I was there. No one had come to see him for two days, and he was terribly lonely.

"Nobody?" I scowled. "I thought his mom and dad and his grandmother were here all weekend."

She gave me the oddest look. "Usually," she smiled. It was the same nurse who'd come in that morning Alex woke up. "I believe Mister Stein is back in Mexico, or Central America? The grandmother went home, or so Alex informs me. I don't know where Mrs. Stein is, but she hasn't been here."

"Has she called?"

"Not to my knowledge."

"When did you see her last?"

"Um ... Friday, I think. Mister Aarons, you look very worried."

"Do I? I guess I am. Anyway, can I see him?"

"He's your son," she smiled, gesturing the way, and my eyes widened in surprise.

"Where did you get that idea?"

She looked puzzled and said, "Mrs. Stein confided in me. She said the boy was only using his stepfather's last name."

I rubbed my face and muttered something she didn't quite catch and I wasn't about to repeat, and asked again to see Alex. She gestured, still looking puzzled, and let me in.

Alex seemed fine. He blossomed as soon as he saw me, all excited hugs and big smiles that he was going home in a few days. We talked, and made plans, and he said I sure looked better without my crutches. He also told me Kit had stuffed HLM in a linen cart and smuggled him in. He wished his mom would let him be in a room with other kids instead of a private one. I said I'd see what I could do.

"No use," Alex sighed. "She hates you, Peter. If you suggest it, if you suggest anything, I'll never get it."

So, I was a handicap. Pleasant thought. She was burdening this little one with her hatred. Megan and I were going to have a chat if I had to pin her in a corner to do it. I phoned from the hospital lobby, but there was no answer. I drove over there anyway. Meg wasn't above turning the phones off when she had a mind to, and I was steamed.

I didn't need to punch in a code; the gates to the Stein mansion were ajar, which was unusual. The garage doors were open, the cars in their places. I parked the Benz and looked around. It was sweltering, but there were no sprinklers going. The lawn looked wilted and brown in spots, and Felix was a fastidious gardener.

I rang at the front, and no one answered. As I walked to the back I could feel the flesh on my arms and the nape of my neck starting to creep, and suddenly I wanted to run.

I gave myself a firm shake and told myself I was just dreading a confrontation with my ex. I rubbed the hair back down on my arms and looked around. Deserted. No busy gardener, no bustling staff. The door to the potting shed was partially ajar. There must be someone here. There must be.

"Meg?" I called. "Felix?"

No answer. I stood there wishing for a cigarette and thinking about leaving. I was really, truly afraid, and I couldn't for the life of me figure out why. Felix had been feeding the plants very recently. The smell of something unpleasant and organic hung in the late afternoon air.

On impulse I rapped sharply on the kitchen door and turned the knob. It opened. In Glory's kitchen that would have been no surprise. Here, it was.

"Mrs. Keen?" I called, stepping in. Silence. Utter silence. The house too, smelled very unpleasant. The kitchen wasn't clean. As a matter of fact ... there was food prepared that was obviously days old.

Right then I should have grabbed the phone and called the police, but fear for Megan had taken over my common sense, and it didn't occur to me. Instead, I charged blindly into the dining room and there was poor Mrs. Keen, lying face down in a puddle of dried blood. She was dead. She was very dead.

I did not move. I did not move, because I had ceased to function – all but my eyes, and my nose. And I stood there. When my brain did kick in an eternity later it was in high gear, and it took my body with it up the stairs three at a time, yelling for Megan.

When I went through the bedroom door I was going too fast to stop myself until I was right on her, and I gagged, and clapped my hands over my mouth and spun away ... because Megan ... had blown her brains out.

Oh God... Oh God... I was paralyzed. I couldn't turn back around. I couldn't go forward. I couldn't ... anything, but vomit onto Megan's lavish white carpet.

Then, I heard a tiny, pitiful whimper. Octavia. I cracked myself in the forehead with the heel of my hand to make myself move, grabbed a blanket and flung it, trying not to look, over the mess in the bed. I looked into the bassinet in the corner of the room, fearing what I'd find. At least, at least, she wasn't dead, but she desperately needed help. At that point it occurred to me that I could call somebody.

Thank God it's a standard three digit number. A female voice answered, and I said, "I need police assistance and I need an ambulance…" I swallowed hard and said it again and that time all of it came out. I told her what I thought had happened, that there was a baby involved, gave her my name, Megan's address, and let her hang up first. Luckily one remembers such things.

I called the house and Philippa answered. "Megan's killed herself," I said, trying not to run screaming up the draperies. "Phipps, Megan has killed herself."

"Peter, where are you?"

"At her house," I said, "Please come," and Philippa hung up.

The baby! I had to do something for the baby. The room was like an oven. Water. A little water. I grabbed a glass from the bathroom, and went back into Megan's room. It occurred to me to wonder, as I touched the baby's cheek with my finger, why her mother had spared her. I wondered what those baby ears had heard, what horrors had been implanted in that little brain to surface later.

She was starved and stinking and pale as death. I held her close, kissed her, gave her a few drops of water with the tip of my finger, and she sucked greedily at it. She was weak, I didn't want to make her sick. Should I try to clean her up? Should I not try to clean her up? Would she die in my arms just from the handling? What should I do? How should I react? All I could see in my mind was the horror under that blanket just a few feet away on the bed. God, Megan had killed herself. God, Megan was lying there with her brains splattered all over the wall and the lampshade! I adjusted the blanket back away from the baby to cool her, and a chunk of Megan's skull fell out of the folds.

That baby and I went back down those stairs the same way I'd gone up – three at a time. I shot through the front door and I didn't stop until Octavia and I were safe and sound in the front seat of my car. My car. Familiar smelling car. By then, I could hear the sirens.

The police pulled up, but I was too numb to move. I saw them. I heard them. It just didn't motivate me to do anything. I felt like I was half asleep in front of the television set. I hadn't shut the car door. An officer touched my shoulder and said my name, then called the paramedics, and I realized I was lying on the lawn in the shade.

"Aw ... damn," I said quietly.

Someone has said heroes are born and not made. Well, I may be a survivor, but I will never be a hero. I don't think heroes faint. I rubbed my face and managed, with assistance, to sit up. At that point I realized what I'd done to my knee and never felt a twinge until now.

"Are you all right?" the Paramedic asked, her arm still firmly around me, and I laughed without humor.

"Young lady," I nodded, trying to be polite. "Yes, I'm fine. How is the baby?"

"Kids are amazingly tough," she said, and a thought went through me like an electric shock.

"Alex!" I exclaimed. "Please, call New American Hospital and tell them what has happened. If Meg's little boy sees this on the news ..."

"Done," she said, patted my shoulder, and left me.

I pulled my good knee up, folded my arms across it, and let my head drop down toward oblivion. I heard a sports car, big engine, coming fast and shifting down. It slowed dramatically, then came on up the driveway – a Benz by the sound of it. My head came up enough to see blue out of the corner of my eye. The sporty little coupe I'd given Philippa as an early wedding present. I took a deep breath to steady myself, and by then Philippa had brushed by the police and sprinted across the driveway, long hair flying, to kneel beside me and wrap me in her arms.

"I'm very, very sorry," she murmured, rocking me gently, and I knew she was. "Is there anything I can do for you?"

"Another body out back in the potting shed," one officer said to another.

"Just hold me," I said through my chattering teeth. "Just hold me. I'm really … I feel like I stuck a fork in a socket."

An officer sat down in the shade beside us and asked, "Are you Peter Aarons?"

"Um hm."

"And you made the call?"

"Um hm."

And what is your connection with the deceased?"

"Mrs. Stein is ... was, my first wife."

"And why were you here?"

"To talk to her about her son, Alexander."

He contemplated me for a minute or so, and I could see by the movement of his eyes that he was making some mental connections. "The little boy who was hit by a car some weeks ago," he said slowly, "running away to live with you, if I remember the stories correctly."

"Dirty pool," I said under my breath. "Megan blamed everything she caused on somebody else. That incident was no different."

"And when did you last see the deceased?"

"Alive?"

The officer nodded patiently. "I know you just saw her dead, Mr. Aarons. Please answer the question."

I thought a moment. "I'm not sure. Wednesday, I think. I was coming to see Alex as she was leaving. We passed in the hall."

"Did she say anything to you?"

"No. We weren't on speaking terms." I felt Phipps pinch me gently, and I paused, wondering why. Then I realized, chillingly, that if this was questioned as more than a murder suicide, I could well be suspect number one. Apparently that had already occurred to Philippa, and possibly to the press milling about in ever increasing numbers.

"I should think," Philippa said quietly, with an edge in her voice, "that if you're going to pursue this line of questioning much further, you'd better Mirandize Mr. Aarons."

The officer looked genuinely startled. "He's not a suspect."

"You're treating him like one," she said quietly, and I could sense her hostility. "If he's free to go I'd like to have our doctor look him over."

"I'm fine," I said, patting her hand, but she insisted. She stonewalled the press, put me in her car, and drove me to Dale Layman's office at New American.

"I love my little car," she smiled by way of conversation as she shifted down and moved into traffic. "Thanks again."

"I love my little horse," I replied. "And don't worry, my friend. We may be impacted by this, but we're not entangled."

"But we will be, Peter," she said in a reasonable tone of voice. "We have to be. We'll have to go to bat for Alex. He's supposed to be coming home in five days. Home to where?"

I just shook my head and rubbed my face. My hands smelled terrible, and I wondered if that smell was death. I reached into the glove compartment for a moist towel packet. "You're right, of course. I'm just not thinking."

"You're in shock," Phil said.

Layman agreed, and I felt like a pantywaist. I just wanted to be left alone so I could cry my eyes out, and that made me feel worse yet. He made me take my shirt off, rolled the EKG machine up beside me and asked, "What time did you get up this morning?"

"Four."

"What'd you do at work today?"

"Shot a concert scene." My fists suddenly doubled up and I caught my breath. I bent my knee, put my foot flat on the table, and the pain subsided a little. "Why do you care what I did at work today?" I snapped.

"I'm nosy. Why'd you go over to you ex-wife's house?"

"To talk to her."

"You told me you two weren't speaking."

"It wasn't going to be a conversation, Dale. I was going to pin her in a goddamned corner ..." I caught myself and my tone, and forced myself to settle down. "I was going to give her a piece of my mind." No pun intended. She'd certainly given me a piece of hers. I closed my eyes for a moment and that chunk of Megan's skull fell past. My eyes flew open and I ground my teeth to keep from screaming.

"Why?"

"Why what?" I gasped.

"Why give her a piece of your mind?"

"Because the way she treats Alex is unforgivable. Treated Alex."

"So, what did you find?" he asked, and I just looked away. I felt like my heart was stuck in my throat and choking off my air supply. "Bud, answer me."

"I ... aw, dammit, Layman, watch the news!" I exclaimed, jerking a hand through my hair. "Look, someone I had close ties to, someone I cared for once, is dead, and I'm sad. I'm shocked. I'm worried sick about Alex and Octavia."

"Lost a girlfriend that way a couple years ago, didn't you? You had a falling out, she met a violent death, and you witnessed it. Nasty pattern forming here."

"Dale, you are a miserable bastard. Why are you telling me these things at this point?"

"I'm vocalizing what's forming in your mind now, or will be when it gets dark." He began sticking electrodes to my chest, and very gently patted my right hand, which was closest to him. "Relax," he said. "Bud, Relax." He slapped it a little harder the second time, and I realized my hands were both knotted into white knuckled fists.

"I just don't want you thinking it's an original idea. What I want you to remember, when this thing starts getting twisted around, is that you cared enough to be angry. Half the people in the civilized world know Stein jumped you in a bar, and over what, and that you calmed him down, took his car keys, and drove him home. You cared, for him, for Megan, for Alexander. You have the right to grieve. You cared enough for Megan to confront her husband. You cared enough for Alex to confront his mother."

He said it again, very slowly and emphatically. "You have the right to grieve. I think ... you have the right to try taking custody of those children away from Stein, if you want my unprofessional, very personal opinion. Okay, lie real still and let's see what the old thumper's doing. Just relax. Think about Philippa. No, cancel that, your heart rate just went up. Think about your good housekeeper, serving you coffee and her famous pancakes. I assume she makes great pancakes."

"God, you're a racist. I suspected it and now I'm sure."

"There is nothing racial about pancakes," he said, unperturbed. "Think about your roses, think about how much better your golf swing's going to be with that new knee."

I thought about all the things Dale had told me. I pondered, as Glory would say. Layman said the EKG was acceptable, checked my blood pressure, gave me something mild for my nerves and the pain in my knee, and told me to check back in twenty-four hours. I promised I would, and Phipps took me back to get my car.

The police were still there, and some of the press, so I got out and sent her on. My cane, I discovered, was on the front seat of the Benz, and I got the sinking feeling I'd left my car sitting there unlocked.

"Found that in the dining room," an officer said. "From the trouble you had getting that leg under you earlier, I thought it might be yours."

"It is, thanks," I smiled. "Wonderful stuff, adrenaline."

The officer nodded. I leaned against my front fender and waited for the question in his eyes to come out his mouth.

"Do you have any idea, why?" he asked at last – he and the press – and I had no answer.

"Terrible price to pay for post-partum blues," I muttered. "But why? I just have no idea. Why did she kill her staff? Why did she leave that helpless baby? Why didn't she kill the baby, too? Did she leave a note?"

"I was about to ask you that same question."

I shook my head. "This just is not like Megan. It just isn't. Number one ..." I looked around. "Say, can we get away from the front page, here?" I scowled, and the officer nodded.

"We can go in the house."

"Not a chance."

He opened a palm toward the squad car and I nodded. We got in, closed the doors and he said, "Go on with what you were saying."

"I'm puzzled, is all. Megan was firmly convinced that the world would stop spinning the day she died. Megan wouldn't have done anything that messy. She would have laid herself out in a white negligee and taken sleeping pills, but not too many. She, would have left a note! Megan wanted everybody to know what she was thinking every minute." I paused, nearly biting my fingers for a cigarette, and rubbed my aching forehead.

"I'm no expert," I said, very quietly, very unwillingly. "But something is not right here. I think, maybe …."

"She was murdered?"

I nodded. "Um hm, I do. But I'm no detective, either. Maybe she just lost it all of a sudden. I know she was sliding that direction, or Stein said she was." I choked and looked at the man beside me. "Stein said she was," I echoed, mostly to myself. "Jesus, I wish my father would speak to me. He knew what she was thinking."

Again I found myself downtown, sitting across a table from an officer, answering questions about another man's wife. This time at least, it was voluntary. All I could tell them, really, was what I knew of Meg's personality; what I'd gleaned in our years of marriage. What I knew of Stein, and what he'd told me.

"My dad," I said again, "is the man to talk to. He and Megan have been spending a lot of time together the last few weeks. Since neither of them spoke to me, I have no idea what was being discussed."

A stereotypical detective with a paunch and bulldog jowls asked me for the umpteenth time why, if we weren't speaking, I was over there. I ground my teeth and, for the umpteenth time, gave him a civil answer.

The door opened, the younger detective across from me looked up at someone and said, "Thank you for coming," and my father sat down, pointedly leaving a chair between us. "Mister Aarons, your son ..."

"I have no son."

I rolled my eyes back slightly and motioned with my head, and he arched an eyebrow, almost imperceptibly, in acknowledgment.

"Pardon me, Sir. I'm Kyle Bohannon. I assumed, since you look alike, and have exactly the same name, that you might be related. Anyway, this gentleman, whose name is also Peter Aarons, says you might be able to help us sort out Megan Stein's death."

"Does he?" my father said, and his voice was rough with weeping. "He assumes much."

"He seems to care much."

"He's an Emmy winning actor. He can make you believe anything he wants."

"Be that as it may, the younger Mister Aarons seems to think his ex-wife may have been murdered."

I felt Dad's keen black eyes burn a hole in the side of my face. "Murdered?" he gasped. "A daring assumption considering his feelings toward her. Have you established his whereabouts at the time of my daughter-in-law's death?"

Bohannon jumped noticeably, and fought to control a nervous laugh. This imperious and powerful man was accusing his son of murder. "Well, we haven't been able to pinpoint down to the hour a time of death, yet, but on Friday your son ... I mean, Mister Aarons ... the younger Mister Aarons …"

"Bud," I said wearily. "It'll simplify things."

"Bud seems to have been first at the studio filming in front of a dozen people, and then with a physical therapist in Van Nuys."

"Van Nuys?" Dad grimaced. "He had to go to somebody in Van Nuys? You can be mugged in Van Nuys." I saw his eyes flicker downward toward my knee, and just for a moment his hand twitched, palm up. His usual questioning gesture. The same gesture I used. The one I'd undoubtedly learned from him. I just wanted to fling myself in his arms and beg him to hug me and tell me all was forgiven. I was so tired at that juncture, and I missed him so much.

I resisted the urge to do anything but smile, and said, "That therapist in Van Nuys, is a crackerjack. Another month, I'll be good as new. Thanks for asking."

Bohannon was still sucking on his cheeks. "Mister Aarons, when last did you see Megan Stein?"

"On Thursday. The day before she ... supposedly committed suicide, or so the officer who telephoned informs me."

"And how was she?"

"Fed up. With Richard, his women, his drinking, his lifestyle and hers."

"Fed up enough to kill herself?"

"No." he said quickly. "To leave him, yes. To foolishly beg her foolish former husband to take her back, yes. To kill herself, never. Not Megan."

"Now see, that's what your ... Bud says. We probably would have written this off as a suicide and closed the books on it if it hadn't been for your son. Now we're not so sure. Also, that baby would be dead if not for your son. Busy schedule for a man who doesn't exist."

"Bohannon, don't bait him," I murmured. "He has enough grief in his life right now." I didn't add that, sufficiently provoked, Dad could probably have that young man fired or transferred to someplace that used dogsleds as squad cars ten months out of the year.

Dad didn't look at me. He just snorted. "Charitable. He takes his

Jesus more seriously than most, I see."

"Someone you both care for has died," Bohannon said reasonably. "Perhaps she was murdered. Can we put our differences aside long enough to maybe figure out who would do such a thing?"

My father was motionless for a moment, then nodded. "What can I tell you?" he asked, and half an hour later they put out an APB for Richard Stein. Wanted for questioning.

"What about the children?" my father asked. "What about them?" It twisted me inside to hear his tone. He adored Alexander as much as I did, and had been with Octavia on an almost daily basis. This was overwhelming. He was losing everyone he'd ever loved. I wanted to cry.

I looked at Bohannon. "Tell the elder Mister Aarons that I'm working on it," I said. My knee bit me, which it had every right to do considering how it had been treated this long day, and I sucked air through my teeth, and leaned back in the chair, slowly straightening my leg out in front of me. Dad's hand moved toward me, halted, and returned to the table in front of him. "Megan has no family except in Boston, and, this time of year, on the French Riviera." I continued. "Stein, I dunno. But Phil and I have pretty much decided we're going to try to get the kids placed in our custody for the time being. They need a stable environment, even if it means putting some plans of our own on hold."

"Phil?" the jowled man barked. He looked like HLM, he really did, only not as cute, and I almost laughed. "Phil? Are you queer, pretty boy?"

"Philippa!" my father snapped before I could open my mouth. "I assure you, she's female. My ... they are very capable ... of caring ... any good Jewish … any good family is capable of caring for two small children." And by that time he'd gotten himself shut off. "I must go, if you have no further questions," he said stiffly.

The detectives thanked him, said he was free to leave. Said they'd be in touch. Dad turned away, paused, turned back, and stared at a nondescript photo that was at shoulder height and to one side of me.

"My wife is not well," he said quietly to the photo. "Nothing I can do seems to help."

"I know."

"She may not be with us much longer. Her heart, suffers further from the strain of a broken family."

"I know," I whispered, and I thought, so does yours.

"It is her wish ..." he paused, searching the photograph for what he wanted to say. "She sits, often, in the garden in the afternoon and speaks of the old days in Russia before the Nazis came. Of the good times, the relationships she had there. I think, having someone to visit with who speaks Russian, would lift her spirits, and perhaps, her health."

I nodded. He turned on his heel and left without ever meeting my eyes.

"You're free to go," Bohannon said as the door closed behind my father.

"In a minute," I smiled. "I'll let him make a clean getaway."

Bohannon nodded. He studied me for a few moments, then walked to the window, parted the venetian blinds and looked into the street below. "Chauffeured limo?"

"That's Dad."

"Just pulling away. He's quick on his feet."

"I'm just as dead to him as Megan was to me, and probably just as hideous. He has no desire to view the corpse longer than necessary."

"I did hear him invite you over, at least as far as the garden."

"He loves my mother," I sighed, "that doesn't mean he loves me. Detective Bohannon, it's been a pleasure. I'll look forward to hearing from you." I forced myself up, palms heavily on the table, and laughed in spite of myself. "My doctor says pain builds character."

"From the color of your face I'd say you're well on your way," Bohannon laughed, but I could see concern in his eyes. "Can I walk you to your car?"

"I must really look like hell," I muttered, but I thanked him, said no, and took myself out with some semblance of grace.

When I got to the street I realized it was dark and had been dark. I looked at my watch. Nine-thirty. By the time I got home, soaked my knee, had dinner, practiced tomorrow's music, got to bed, it would be after midnight. Four hours to sleep. On the bright side, maybe I wouldn't sleep.

All the way home there were ... things, lying on the back seat of the car. The stereo didn't scare them away, and they lingered, chilling the back of my neck like I was six years old. Six years old – like Alexander. How frightened he was going to be, and how sad, and who was going to be there to hold him and kiss his tears away and rock him to sleep?

I parked the Benz between Philippa's car and Glory's. So good to be home – even in that stuffy, junk lined garage. I got out, leaned on the open car door, put my head on my arms and closed my eyes, just for a minute.

"Hello, sailor." That resonant, well-deep alto I treasured so much. Kind face, gentle hands, warm hug. So much love exuding from one person. "If you just want to get back in the car I can bring you your supper and a blanket," she grinned.

"I'll pass," I said, forcing myself to take a deep breath and shake off my creeping psychosis. I held Phil at arm's length and admired her. "You look especially beautiful this evening, my love."

"It's my garment," she laughed, modeling the sleek, sleeveless blue jumpsuit. "My fiancé bought it for me, and he has exquisite taste in clothing, among other things. You'll notice the jumpsuit matches the new car."

"You'll notice most everything he buys for you is blue," I smiled. "What isn't blue, is pink. You're his baby." Baby. Again, I moved that blanket, and shuddered.

Philippa just smiled, lighting me with her eyes, even as she saw me droop. That strong left arm came around me and we meandered toward the house, seeming to be in no hurry, as though she was setting the pace. I bent down and kissed her as we walked. So little. I never got over the feeling that she was as much my child as my lover and that I had to protect her at all costs. It was odd. Other small people didn't affect me that way.

"I've made a career decision," I said, dragging my legs up onto the back patio, "I, am going to join the Bolivian Navy."

"Good place for you in your condition," Philippa laughed. "Very little chance of seeing any action. Say, how about your rubber ducky instead?

You could sail all around the tub with him. Would that make you happy?"

"Oh, all right," I sighed, following her into the house. "You know, if we bring children to live in this house, there'll be a fight over that duck, and that duck is mine. Not even Saffron plays with my ducky. My Dad ... gave me that ducky for my fortieth birthday."

Phil unbuttoned my shirt, pushed me gently onto the downstairs bed and bent to untie my shoes. "Is this where the conversation was supposed to end up?" she asked. "With a discussion of the children?"

"Why do you ask?"

"Well, I can see something's weighing heavily on your mind. I just thought it might be that. Soak first, or supper?"

"Neither," I said. "I need a shower. I stink of fear, and sweat, and death, not to mention wet babies. Then, I'll soak. Then, maybe a bite to eat. And I do need to practice. If you're tired go on to bed."

"No, I'm fine, Peter. You haven't answered me."

"About the children? May I ... think while I shower? I'm not really sure what to say right now."

The shower made me smell better, but it didn't do a thing for my brain or my communication skills. We went to soak in the spa, and still I couldn't figure out how to phrase what I wanted to say.

I wanted to let Phil know that, even though I loved Alex, she was more important to me. Even though I would welcome the children into our home, my marriage was more important. Sounds straight forward enough, doesn't it? Now, try saying it out loud. I'd practiced it in the shower. It came out sounding like the kids could go to the pound, for all I cared. I tried rephrasing it, and it came out sounding like Philippa, if she loved me, should give up her plans for a freewheeling existence and raise the children. Worst of all, the more I ran it through my head the more I wasn't sure I wanted any part of it. I didn't want to give up the plans Phil and I had made for the two of us.

I finally just blurted it out, feeling lousier with every word. Phipps floated me over to lean against her chest, kissed my temple, and told me to have a little mercy on myself. Quit blowing things out of proportion. I took her advice as best I could, and found myself wishing Glory and Rafael were home to talk to.

Supper, wasn't much of a success. I tried telling Phil about the episode with my dad, thereby sneaking a little food into my stomach as I talked, but whatever makes me swallow, was not easily deceived. It remembered all too vividly the smell of that house and the screaming, shattered face in that bed. I gave up. Gave up any semblance of self-composure, and crawled upstairs to rest, praying my sight reading skills were good enough to get me through tomorrow's shoot.

I did manage, finally, to fall asleep. My brain let up for just a second – the same second my knee called time out – and I was gone, wrapped in Philippa's comforting embrace.

I awoke at some point, I'm not sure when, in an ice cold sweat, nauseated almost beyond making it to the bathroom. I just spewed up the meager contents of my stomach. My guts twisted in agony, my bowels ran like water, the cold sweat rolled off me. The heaving threatened to take my eyes out of their sockets – like Megan's had been. Meg's beautiful, hazel eyes. God. I heaved again – too dry after a while even to sweat. I half sat, half collapsed onto the floor, back against the bathtub, knees pulled up to ease my cramping middle. Hot, cold, shaking like the big aspen trees on the front lawn up north.

Vaguely, as though perhaps I'd slept, I could hear the alarm going off in the bedroom. Even as I became aware that it was not a dream it was silent and I heard Philippa saying my name. She rapped gently on the bathroom door, then pushed it open and knelt beside me. I hadn't even raised my head.

"Aw, Peter," she whispered. She got my bathrobe and put it over my bare shoulders, and by then I was groaning my way back to life. "Can you stand?"

I just nodded and began scaling the side of the vanity. "Come on," Philippa said, "Let's get you back to bed."

"I have ..." I choked, shook my head, and stood up straighter to get a drink of water. The coughing stopped, and I tried again. "I have to go to work, Sweet Face."

"Are you insane?"

"Probably. What I'm not, is a hothouse plant. Winos go to work feeling like this every morning." Then, I made the mistake of looking in the mirror. I looked like I'd been carved, and not particularly well, out of library paste and wet concrete. The thought ... of the smell of library paste ... just the thought, threatened to turn my stomach.

I refused coffee – and not just because Philippa had made it – sent that lady back to bed, took a blazing hot shower, scrubbed my teeth for about ten minutes, convinced myself I looked immeasurably much better, got dressed, and went to work.

David Swift, who was directing this one as well as producing it, glanced up as I walked in, then stared, and I wondered if there was something frightening close behind me.

"Sweet Jesus," he exclaimed softly, "Bud, what are you doing here?"

"I work here."

"Well, after the news last night we certainly didn't expect you this morning. Do you feel any better than you look?"

"Blessedly, David, I don't know how I look. What's on tap?"

"We hadn't counted on you, and I should know better," he smiled, studying me and apparently deciding I was beyond repair. "Let's just film your hands today," he said. "We'll rehearse and record the Chopin Mazurkas, and work on the background track. Are they ready?"

"Right here," I smiled. I cuffed up my shirtsleeves, opened my briefcase, and got out my sheet music.

Chopin, compared to Rachmaninoff, is easy to play. Chopin is more structured. Not as full, not as driving. Chopin, I could manage. It got me over the hump of sitting down, and playing world class music. At nine O'clock that morning we recorded Chopin's *Scherzo in B Minor, Opus 20*, one of his best loved short works, and I'd never played Chopin as well. Haven't since. I think, perhaps, it was the slight weakness I could feel in my wrists, giving me rebound off the keyboard that I didn't usually have. I got a standing ovation from the crew, and the coffee I had afterward settled pretty well.

I don't suppose it is to my credit that I could lose myself in my work one day after losing my ex-wife, but I did, and felt better for it; more able to cope with the problems she'd left me.

At eleven O'clock, we broke for lunch, and I slept for an hour. David brought me a sandwich, and it looked good, but when I smelled the meat and the mayonnaise in it, something punched me hard in the gut. I dropped the thing, pushed it away, and when I could pry my jaws apart I said I wasn't hungry after all, and thanked him for the thought.

"You used to like my sandwiches in the old days," he said, removing the thing from my sight. "You do need to eat something."

"I know that. Convince my body. My brain is starved, believe me. I just ...." I let the rest trail off.

"I am sorry, you know that," he said, and I nodded, knowing he was sincere. David and I went back a long, long way. We'd acted in our first movie together when he was six and I was twenty-six, and his dad was the assistant director. David had directed me the first time when he was still a teenager taking Hollywood by storm, and now he was at the height of his creative powers. "Is there anything at all that I can do?"

"Just give me time for the shock to wear off."

"That, I can do," he replied, blue eyes twinkling against his fair, Swiss complexion. "As a matter of fact, I want you to take the rest of the week off and just work at home. We're going to be doing the rest of the casting, and some set work, and we're still trying to find a house for the location shooting. I can't believe we're still trying to find a house. There must be one estate left somewhere in Russia, don't you think?" He paused, watching me shuffle through my music, and I knew he had something else on his mind. Blue eyes are not so easily veiled as brown.

"Bud, does Bellwether Productions give its actors and actresses a free agent clause in all cases?"

"So far."

"Do you suppose ... your lovely mistress would read for the part of Natalya Satin?"

Past the word, mistress, I didn't even hear what he said. It was like he'd jabbed me with a pin. "She's not my mistress!" I snapped.

David jumped nearly as high as I did. "Sorry! I didn't realize she was renting her own room and buying her own food."

"You know damned good and well she's not."

"Then you know damned good and well she's your mistress. If you don't like the term, disassociate yourself from the action it describes. You're supposed to be a man of faith and high morals."

"Says who?"

"Everybody," he said gently. "They always have."

I thought about what he'd said instead of continuing to chew his head off, and after a minute I said, "You're right. I'm sorry. I guess it's hard for me to think of our relationship in those terms. Phipps deserves better than what I'm giving her."

"Give her something better then. It'll be one less thing on your mind. When's her divorce final?"

"What's today?"

"July first, you old patriot. Three days before Independence Day."

I just shook my head and smiled at him. Surely, even in my sorry state, I should have known what day it was. David was right. I had too much weighty, depressing stuff on my mind.

"Her divorce is final on the sixth, we hope. Anyway, David, You asked me if she'd read for Natalya?"

"Um hm. I'll admit it freely, she's hot property right now, and the public hasn't even seen her act yet. But those clips I saw ..." he smiled in wonder and moved his white-blond curls slowly from side to side, looking into space toward something I could only imagine, speaking slowly as he created a visual framework in his perspicacious mind. "Funny, she's not a pretty woman in the usual sense. But her voice ... it just rumbles out of the depths of her soul. The way her personality, and the power in her, comes across on film, I want her to balance you. The pair with the velvety voices. We could win an Oscar!" His beautiful face lit up with the finished picture, and his voice went up suddenly with his slender hands. "When she's passive, she's enchanting and hypnotic. When she's active, she's explosive.

She's the kind of real woman a real, honest to God man would give his whole future to spend one night with, and I want her!"

His voice had risen to a crescendo, along with his arms, and I think at that point he remembered who he was talking to, because he looked right at me, then slowly lowered his arms and his voice, and looked a little embarrassed. "That wouldn't be in the literal sense, of course. As you know, my sexual preferences run in other directions, so don't expect me to apologize," he muttered. "But you are one lucky bastard, as heterosexuals go."

"Exceptionally astute," I laughed, waving away his apology. "But not so much for the nights as for the days. Not so much for the passion as for the wisdom. The fire, and the tenderness, are such a delectable trade off. And none of it is practiced. It's funny. One of the last things Megan ever said to me – our last conversation – was that Philippa was plain and dumpy, and middle aged. Someone who would be an endless embarrassment to me. Poor Meg."

David's hand closed over my forearm. "Peter?" he said, and I jumped.

"Oh yes, about Philippa." I stammered, "It doesn't sound like you want her to read, you just want to cast her, and I'm not sure I want her on this picture. I wanted her to help me enrich my character, not her own."

"Selfish snot."

"You bet. She's awfully busy. How big a part is Natalya?"

"More stage presence than lines. Perfect for a busy woman like Philippa." I knew by the look in his eye he was quite probably lying to me, but it made me chuckle anyway.

"In any case, it's her decision and not mine. I'll relay the message," I smiled, and we went back to work.

I didn't have much time to wonder whether I wanted Phil playing Natalya Satina Rachmaninoff. I had to concentrate on what I was doing, and that got harder as the afternoon progressed. An hour before we usually quit I had to admit I was whipped.

If David was annoyed he hid it well. He thanked me a thousand times, praised my work, and sent me home with his blessings until Monday.

Would that I could have gone. Instead, obediently if reluctantly, I placed myself in Dale Layman's office as he had requested.

"Why is it," he asked as he sat down across from me, "that you weighed a hundred and ninety pounds yesterday, and today you weigh a hundred and eighty-four pounds?"

"Rough night. I'm fine now."

He pinned my palm to his desk with the side of his hand, and picked up on the skin between my knuckles and my wrist. "You're not fine, Bud. You're dehydrated as hell. Can't make yourself swallow?"

"How do you know these things?" I growled. "It unnerves me that you know so much."

"Always so charming, Peter. I know these things because I'm a doctor who deals with trauma. Shock follows trauma. Dehydration follows shock. I'm going to send an injection home with you, and when you get there have Mrs. Ruiz take your car keys and then give it to you. You won't have a care in the world for about eighteen hours. Then ..." he scribbled something down on a pad "... start taking these. Take them until they're gone. If they affect your ability to drive, or to concentrate, let me know immediately. In one week I want you to walk in here weighing a hundred and ninety pounds."

I nodded. "I'm better at dropping weight than gaining it, but I'll give it a shot. Got a minute you can spare?"

"Got five. What's on your mind?"

"Alex and his baby sister. Richard Stein is being hunted right now, and I'll bet even money he's not in Mexico making a movie. I'll bet he's far, far away, somewhere that has no extradition agreement with the US."

"I'll bet you're right," he nodded. "Megan's autopsy showed a slight bruise across the back of her hand where someone else quite possibly held the gun in place and made her pull the trigger. It was very clever of you to suspect murder."

The image made me cringe. It brought tears to my eyes and I blinked them away. "Dale, I don't want to talk about Megan. I want to talk about her children. Alex is scheduled to go home Sunday, isn't he, or do you know?"

"I know all, see all, hear all, and smell all that goes on in this hospital. He is, or was. Now, they'll probably hold him a few more days. His sister will be released when he is." Dale leaned back and smiled at me. "Been thinking about what I said?"

"Of course I have. The more I think about it, the more confused I get, and that's before I start talking to Philippa. Right now I'd like to take a couple days and run away somewhere simple and not think at all."

"Excellent idea. Speaking of running, how's the knee?"

"Didn't even swell up."

"Good. Have you really talked to Philippa about the kids? Have you talked to your staff?"

"Phipps, yes. Glory and Rafael, no. They took a few days off and went to visit their oldest boy. I haven't seen them since I found Megan and Mrs. Keen."

"And the gardener."

"Didn't find Felix, thank God."

"What says your good woman?"

"The same thing I do. This is going to play absolute havoc with our lives, and if we were in our right minds we wouldn't even consider it. But this is going to be hard enough on Alex as it is, without having him institutionalized. He loves me and I love him. If immediate family does not come forth to claim him – which please God they don't because they're a bunch of booze swilling idiots – I want him with me, at least temporarily. If it means hiring more on-site staff so Phipps and I can keep up our schedules, I'm willing to do that. We, are willing to do that."

"Somehow I figured you would deign to keep them a bit at this point," Layman smiled.

It didn't sound like a compliment, and I flared in his face. "What kind of a crack was that supposed to be, Doctor? What am I supposed to do, wash my hands and turn away and allow two innocents to be swallowed by the system? I can't do that. I realize even if it meant risking Philippa, I couldn't do it. My father shot his reputation all to hell to save me, and he didn't even know me. He really didn't even know I was his, for sure. If nothing else, he loved Megan, and I owe him."

Layman continued to contemplate me. "My, my," he said at last. "That really popped. Must have been festering for some time."

I stood up abruptly, resisting the frightening urge to reach across his desk and slap the smile off his face. "Do you have any constructive suggestions, Layman? If you don't, I'm leaving."

"People, as in somebody somewhere, is going to fight you on this, right from the word go, I guarantee it."

"Why did you suggest it in the first place then?"

"To save you the trouble of thinking it up," he grinned. "You know, Bud, you haven't really smiled once since you walked in here, and you're usually very pleasant, even when you hurt. I think your perspective has been blown completely to hell. You don't have a clue where Alex leaves off and your dad takes up. You can't begin to figure out where your duty lies, can you? When your focus was on Philippa you were happy, and you were in control. I'd suggest you go back there. Mentally, you're racing around like a rat on speed, and if you don't find someplace to back off a little and gain some peace of mind, you're going to be a very sick man. Yesterday you looked forty-five, today you look sixty-five."

"That's it. I'm leaving. I'm going up to see Alex."

"No!" Layman said sharply, rising out of his chair toward me. "Please don't! Please, Bud. He'll get one look at you and know something has happened that you can't handle. You're his rock. Don't do it to him. Send Glory. You go home. Eat, sleep. Sleep some more. Then come see him. In the meantime I'll make some phone calls and try to convince people you'd make a good foster ... grandparent."

"Thanks," I snickered, "I mean that."

"I know you do," he grinned. "You think about what I said." He sealed a plastic tube with the syringe in it and gave it to me along with the prescription and a warm, one armed hug as he sent me home.

I did make one more stop, a small jewelry store wherein worked a sorcerer with gold and precious stones. He smiled, gestured with fingers and palm, held it up on the end of a slim velvet cylinder – the ring for Philippa. It was exquisite. Diamonds in the eyes of golden daisies, small ruby hearts outlined in gold. Narrow in back, the two hearts in an overlapping but unattached embrace in front. "Perfect," I smiled. "Perfect."

I walked through the back door, and Glory dropped what she was doing and turned to me. "Hi," I said, "How's Royal?"

"He's fine, brought you some soap from Haiti," she said, and I could see tears welling up in her beautiful brown eyes. "You should'a called me."

"Aw, I didn't want to spoil your visit. But I suppose the damned newscasters did that, didn't they?"

She nodded.

"Come here," I said, and I folded her in my arms and held her, and soothed her, as she had done for me so many times, and wept with her, and we both felt better. We could weep for someone we did not love, because she did not deserve to die. That was something to offer two young children. I looked around at this warm kitchen with its good smells and familiar outline. This was home. If nothing else, I had that much to offer Alex and Octavia.

But I had more than that. I had myself, and Glory, and Rafael. And Philippa. After supper I took that small one walking, and turned her toward me in the light of the antique glass lamps around the swimming pool. Jeans, cowboy boots, the open throated pink shirt she'd been wearing the first time I'd brought her to this place. I reached behind her head with both hands, unclipped her hair, and let it spill through my fingers and down across my bare arms in a fragrant caress.

"So, how was your day, Sweet Face?"

"Busy," she smiled, touching my cheek. "As I've told you twice already. Peter, what's on your mind?"

"After that shot? Very little," I chuckled. "Papers still going to be signed next Monday?"

She looked away toward the pool. "I signed them this morning. Free at last, free at last, thank God Almighty, I'm free at last. Or words to that effect. I can't remember the exact quote." She smiled then, but only with her mouth. Her eyes were sad.

"Philippa, look at me," I said quietly. "Look at the greying hair and the gravity lines and tell me you're sure you want to marry someone this much older than you are."

Her chin tilted up toward me and she reached with her fingertips to touch the grey at my temples. "I have no need to look," she said, and David's words came back to me. Her voice did indeed rumble from the depths of her soul, velvety and soft. "I can close my eyes and see every beloved aspect of your countenance. In every good thought I have I hear your wisdom, in every happy thought your laughter. If I had to give up the rest of my life to spend one more day with you, I would do so and be happy."

"Don't cry," I whispered, kissing the tears on her cheeks. "We have many days yet together, you and I. And many nights."

"Come what may?"

"Come what may."

"Promise? Promise I can share your life. Don't ever seek to spare me by separating me from your problems. Any separation for any reason would be more than I could bear, Peter."

"I promise," I said, and kissed her – tenderly, lingeringly – tasting the essence of my life. "Philippa, I am so in love with you."

"I hope you don't want sympathy," she said, pulling back a little and twinkling up at me.

"No. What I want, is to marry you. Now. Day after tomorrow. I know we'd planned a wedding for the ninth of August, but living unmarried together when there's no reason to seems wrong somehow, and it's annoying a lot of people who are special to us. I want you to be my wife. Will you marry me?" I held up my left hand in the lamplight, and on the end of my little finger, the only place it would fit, was the wedding ring.

"Oh, Peter!" she breathed, catching my hand between both of hers. "Oh, Peter ... That's the ring Mark Kincaid gave Jean Whiteside. Aw ... Peter." Again the tears welled up in her eyes.

"Seems long ago, doesn't It? But it hasn't been. I met you on January seventh. I've known you almost exactly seven months. Not even long enough to have a baby."

"Long enough to acquire some, it would seem," she smiled, turning her attention from the ring to me.

"You sure? Are you absolutely sure about them?"

"Of course. We wouldn't be in this position for no reason. But I warn you, If we should happen to get them, and I'm not at all sure we will, and for however long we have them, be it a day, a month, or ten years, I'm strict, Bud."

"Oh, yeah, I'll bet you are," I laughed, and kissed her again for a long moment. "But we have the cart before the horse, Madam. First comes love, then comes marriage, then..."

Philippa laughed. "I can just see you with a baby carriage, Peter Aarons." She looked at the ring on my finger, kissed the palm of my hand, and said ... yes.

CHAPTER SIXTEEN

"All hail the handsome Bridegroom!" Kit laughed. He grabbed me, hugged me, gave me a kiss and released me to the ongoing congratulations of our closest circle of friends. They were gathered near my piano at one end of the big living room, out of the way of the mix of dancers. "Where's Mrs. Aarons?" he asked, knowing it made me grin like an idiot.

"Out there somewhere," I laughed, jerking my chin toward the crowd. I turned back to Kit and the guys, and said, mostly to Kit, "Now this, is the kind of party my grandmother built this house for, and I want to have more of them. Lots more of them." I sighed, and felt myself grow silent despite my best efforts. "I do wish my parents were here. This is one of the happiest days of my life, and I can't share it with them. I always thought I understood how you felt when your mom died. Now I know, I didn't."

He just nodded.

My wife danced into view in the arms of David's handsome partner, Connor Lockhart, her old fashioned white dress swirling gracefully about her calves, and Rafael said, "You guys should have seen his face when Philippa came down the aisle wearing that gown."

"Oh, geez," I whispered, and I could feel my eyes sting with tears.

"Remember?" Kit said softly, "I do. I remember like it was yesterday, how your grandma would tell us the story." He raised his voice a little to include the others, and went on. "How her parents had moved with her to this country from Italy. Her father had been an antiquities dealer, and an art dealer, and in their home had hung a beautiful painting of a girl in a white lace dress."

"That painting," I added, nodding toward the staircase.

"And when your grandmother was a young woman and decided to marry your grandfather, she had that painting taken down, and studied it, and copied the dress. She and her mother had crocheted the lace, remember? And your gram would take the box down with the dress in it – that old dress – and she'd look at our hands to make sure they were clean, and she'd let us touch the lace."

"And when my bride came down the aisle on Rafael's arm, baby's breath and roses in her hair, candles lighting that beautiful face of hers, she was wearing my grandmother's wedding dress." I wiped my eyes and laughed.

"Always stone cold," James Horse grinned. "You know, we've been so busy wrapping up our shoot and you've been so busy with Rachmaninoff, that we haven't really had time to discuss your wedding, or much of anything else, for that matter. You guys were back from Vegas on Sunday night and back on the set Monday morning – Philippa over our way with Petroglyphs, and you with David most of the time, and then the other way around."

It's been a hectic month," I agreed, "for a lot of reasons."

One of those reasons came squealing in at a remarkable pace despite being on crutches, accompanied by Kenny John – both dressed to the teeth in black tuxedos – Adelle in hot pursuit. I stepped out, crouched, and caught them, one in each arm, as they came past. I'd probably not have been quick enough under ordinary circumstances, but I could see that Kenny was pacing himself so as not to leave Alex behind.

"Thanks," Adelle said, taking Kenny firmly by the hand and Alex by the shirt collar. "You'd think they'd want out of their nice clothes and into their swim suits, but no, not these two."

Kit chuckled. Adelle looked up, blushed, and hurried away with the boys in tow.

"Alex, you behave yourself," I called after them. "Kit," I said quietly, "you really must flirt with Adelle sometime this evening. She thinks you're just ... it."

"I'll talk nicely to her. I won't flirt. She's married," he sniffed.

Long legged Kelly slid by in something vaguely western and very tight, and Kit said, "Now, if I'm going to flirt ..."

"You'll have to go over her stepfather," I growled. "You're way too old to be dating either of my stepdaughters, Mister Miller."

"You love that, too, don't you?" Kit smiled. "You love the whole husband and dad thing. Hell, I have kids of my own, and I don't even know them." He pulled his eyes off Kelly's departing figure, and said quietly. "I am, we all are, very sorry you didn't get custody of Alex and Octavia. It was a raw deal. You and P.K. would have been great for those kids."

I just shrugged. I was still shaken by the whole, unsavory process they'd put us through. "It shocked the hell out of us," I said, forcing a smile. "The furniture was ordered and the paint was sitting in the garage when CPS made their ruling against us." I stood turning my wedding band and admiring the diagonal flash of diamonds across its face. I slid it off my finger to look again at the inscription, and James Horse said, "What does it say?"

I handed it to him, and he smiled and nodded as he read it. "'We two form a multitude.' It suits you," he said. He handed it back, and I put it on my finger.

I was forcing myself to take it off from time to time, knowing I'd have to for various roles. And I liked looking at what it said inside. The statement it made to me about my marriage had been such a comfort in these past, troubled days. I'd studied it often. I could remember pulling it off and looking down at that inscription during the endless hours we'd met with child protective services while they sat there telling us all the reasons we wouldn't be good parents, and Dale Layman had sat there telling them they were idiots. We had tried everything. Our lawyer, Marion Goldberg, had tried everything. We had gone home more than once and cried, both of us, over the thought of those children going to an institution when we loved them and wanted them and had the means to make them a good, secure, and loving home.

Then, the tide had turned in our favor, and they'd said we could have them both. We were ecstatic. Alex was ecstatic. We'd ordered furniture for them, and picked out paint for the rooms upstairs where we planned to put them, and CPS had called to say they'd changed their minds. Information regarding my sexual behavior had come to their attention that was too disturbing to put aside. The children were going into foster care with someone else, a couple they didn't know out in the valley. They were nice people, had other foster children already. They were good Jews, and could provide a more stable environment that we could.

I'd panicked – no other word for it. Megan was dead and I couldn't save her. Now her children, my precious little Alex and baby Octavia were going to strangers. I had called my father, tears streaming down my face, and said, "Please don't hang up on me. Please. For the love of God, Dad, do something to save the kids. Call somebody! Call in some favor from somewhere, please!" I could still hear the anguish in my own voice, and feel the tears stinging in my eyes ... and hear the silence, and the click at the other end of the line.

I gave myself a good mental shaking and realized the silence surrounding Kit's kind statement and my lame reply was still hanging around us like an elephant suspended by sewing thread. Best talk it out openly and have done with it.

"At least Alex is here, and I get to see him often," I said, trying to sound perky. "And I know he couldn't possibly be safer or happier than he is with my dad and mother. They adore the baby. It could have been a lot worse."

"It was still a shitty deal, the way the system fought you," Tommy said. "Nobody in Megan's family fought you, nobody in Richard's family fought you, but the damn CPS people did."

"The press didn't help our cause any," I said, and it was true. By ever so politely saying I really had no reason to want Megan dead even though I felt she had taken a son who was obviously my flesh, and betrayed me with Stein, meddled in my career, embarrassed me in the press, slandered Philippa and me, criticized our religion and our lifestyle and our treatment of Frank ... and, gee, what person with more than two brain cells wouldn't have wanted her dead ... I didn't, because I was such a darned nice guy. Polite speculation. They wished me all the best. Mostly they wished me newsworthy. "I hope they're happy, the bastards."

"Well, it was CPS that came up with all that crap about you and me," Kit growled, "and I'm still thinking about suing their asses for slander."

"What?" James scowled.

"You missed it?" Kit laughed, but his eyes were smoky. "You must not have been on the set that day. CPS wanted to know if Bud and I had indeed been sexually involved."

"What?" the scowl deepened.

"When Kit and Cherry were getting their divorce a couple of years ago, Kit was having some adjustment problems," I began, trying to remove that puzzled look from James' face.

"I fell in a bottle," Kit said, matter of factly, "and Bud moved me in with him to help me get healed up inside. And those damnable people stood toe to toe with Bud, and accused him of being gay. They had evidence," Kit was snorting fire by now, "After all, he didn't marry until he was forty. Lived with his grandmother his whole life. Never fathered any children. And, and, he plays the piano! Now if that isn't the kicker I'll put in with you!"

I saw David Swift flinch and put my arm around Kit. "Cool off, Kit, it's over," I said, kissing his temple. I really didn't want him talking about the gay thing with David standing right there. "For good or ill, it's over. The fact that we are Christians and the children are Jewish, weighed very heavily against us, and the fact that we are an active part of the film community weighed heavily against us. The fact that my father and I aren't speaking weighed against us. I'm just grateful, and amazed, that my dad stepped in and asked for the children. I never would have guessed he'd do that."

"He did it because he loves you, very much," a voice said at my elbow, and I turned to give my wife ... my wife ... my wife ...Mrs. Peter Aarons ... Philippa Kate Aarons, a kiss. "Why the gloomy faces over here on this side of the party?" she teased, putting her arms around my waist. "Look around you. This is a wedding reception. It's a time for talking about all the good things, and the good times. Like, how much fun we had making Petroglyphs in Sunlight. I'm sorry it's over, in a lot of ways."

Everybody nodded and agreed, but said there would be other films, and maybe a new series coming up pretty soon, and Tommy said, "Congratulations to you, Mrs. Aarons, on being cast as Natalya Satina in your husband's new movie."

David Swift cleared his throat with some exaggeration and Tommy laughed. "Pardon, your new movie, Boy Wonder."

There was polite applause, and she dropped a graceful curtsy. The lace on her hem touched the floor ever so lightly, and I wondered, for the hundredth time, how, with only two days to prepare, and with as tall as my grandmother had been, Phipps and Glory had gotten that dress to fit my diminutive wife. "Thank you, thank you," she laughed. "I was going to be there with Peter anyway. I thought I might as well be doing something other than helping him with his part. I didn't want to smother him. Besides, when we didn't get the kids, I felt like there was a little empty spot I needed to fill with some activity."

She answered a hail from Glory across the room, and started off in that direction. "And now we get to honeymoon in that loveliest of all places," she threw over her shoulder in a deep, accented voice, "Mother RR-RRussia."

"Russia is beautiful this time of year," David said defensively. "The house we've found to film in is exquisite. Its gardens are magnificent, it has a lake and bridle paths. They could do worse for a honeymoon spot. I only wish I was on my honeymoon." He caught himself and looked sheepish. "Just kidding. We're not to that point yet. I wish we were, but we're not. I mean, I wish the two of us could even get married ...." He blushed and looked away.

"And I wish we'd found some Russian-looking estate in Wisconsin, or Quebec, or Alaska," I muttered. "I've never been back to Russia, and I can't say I'm crazy about the idea of going now."

"But you're going anyway, and taking your insecure little bride," Tommy said, not unkindly. "How is she going to react when she can't get out and garden, and the hay's not in the barn on time, and that current won't run her sewing machine, and she doesn't have Glory to lean on, and you're busy all the time?"

I thought about that as I watched her mingling with our guests, the folks from up north, my friends from JACAM, the cast and crew of three or four movies and a couple of TV series, church friends, Philippa's editor, hand-picked members of the press, Glory and Rafael and the boys – two eclectic lifetimes worth of friends, and I said, "If I didn't admit that I have some concerns, I wouldn't be being honest. But, you know, she survived on her own all those years with Frank, and she got herself down here and found us, and so I'm not too worried about Russia. Besides, she'll have her share of filming to keep her busy."

"I'd watch her, though," Kit said. "Can't you just see P.K. in her little Cossack outfit thundering across the tundra on a pony?"

"There's no tundra where we're going," David said with some annoyance, and all of us burst out laughing.

We were still laughing about the joys of the tundra, when there was a gentle touch on my arm, and I turned to see Wennie standing beside me.

"Gentlemen," I said, dropping an arm around her shoulders, "I'd like you to meet my oldest stepdaughter, Wenonah. Wen, this is James, Tommy, and David ... and Kit, you already know."

The two of them looked at each other, started laughing like crazy, and James and David both said, "What, what?"

I said, "Kit, You've got to tell me this story again. Tell the guys. Listen to this, this is amazing."

Kit shrugged modestly, and his eyes twinkled, and I could see he was still right up there on cloud nine with me. "Well, here goes. I come home late on a Wednesday night from San Diego, and there's a message from Buddy to call him. So Thursday morning I call, and he says, 'Hey, I'm getting married tomorrow night at nine O'clock in Vegas, will you come?' Would I come? Do you believe that? So I said I'd go on ahead and make all the arrangements and call him and Phil at noon, just before they caught their flight. I mean, he's done the same for me more than once."

"Get to the good part," I prodded.

"I am, don't push me. You're married to a master storyteller. You should know these things take time to do right. Anyway, I was trying to think of what would make this special. So I got on a plane and flew up the coast, and rented a car, which, on the Fourth of July weekend, was an experience in itself."

"Excuse me," Wen smiled, "But one thing I haven't figured out yet, is how you knew where to go."

"Connections," Kit winked. "Glory knows where your mom keeps her address book. So anyway, at seven O'clock at night I go beating on a door. This pretty little duck right here comes out, and I knew this was the place because she had her mother's smile, and I said, 'Hi, my name is Kit Miller, and I'm not a crazy man.' 'Oh,' she grins, 'you don't have to admit that. We let crazy people in here,' and she lets me in! What beauties," Kit sighed. "What beautiful girls inside and out. I tell you, Bud, you really drew to a great pair in these two. Anyway, I said, 'your mom is marrying my best friend tomorrow, and we've got a wedding to put together. Grab some clean underwear and your makeup, we'll buy you dresses when we get there. Call work and tell 'em you won't be there in the morning, and put down food for the dog. We're flying to Vegas.'"

"And they went!" I laughed. "The amazing part of the story is, they went with this guy. This perfect stranger. I had a talk with both of them."

"Actually," Wen smiled, "I've seen some of his movies, so I knew who he was, even before he introduced himself. Lest you think me completely stupid."

"Grabbed their stuff, made their calls, jumped in the car. I've never heard girls laugh like those two until I heard 'em with their mother. We were in Vegas and in a hotel by one O'clock or a little after. Up at eight, had breakfast. By noon we had it in a sack. We called Buddy and asked him what kind of flowers he wanted Philippa to carry ..."

"And at that point he blew it, because he said 'we', but I didn't tell Phipps, and to see her face light up when we got to the hotel ... Kit, Wennie, I owe you both. Having you two girls there with Glory to help your mom get dressed, and make a fuss, meant so much to her."

"You owe me nothing," Kit smiled. "I've never seen anyone as happy as you were, have you, Wenonah?"

"I never have," she said, and she and Kit looked at each other again and Wennie laughed.

Wenonah Pearl has the most beautiful laughter I've ever heard. Most people have kind of a crazy laugh, but hers is like an artesian well bubbling out of the depths of her. She laughs often, and her whole face lights up.

She suddenly got quiet, looking across the room, and I bent close to her ear and said, "You have an admirer."

"That's actually what I came over here to ask you about," she said, trying not to look his direction. "Who is that gorgeous young man who keeps staring at me?"

"And smiling?" I teased. "That's one of the finest young men I know. Would you like to meet him?"

"I'd love to," she said, and I put an arm around her waist and steered her over to where Titus was leaning against the banister, listening to the orchestra. He straightened up as he saw us coming, and took a few steps our direction.

"Wenonah, I'd like you to meet my honorary nephew and youngest God-son, Titus Ruiz. Titus, my stepdaughter, Wennie."

He flashed his big, white teeth at her, took her hand and kissed it and said, "Charmed," with just a hint of his mother's southern drawl. Wenonah laughed as she responded, and I knew I could give up my day job. I was ordained a matchmaker.

"Titus is a lawyer working with Southern Poverty Law Center," I said helpfully.

"I hear such good things about them," Wen responded. "What do you do?"

"Work on issues of equity and justice, piss people off, occasionally get arrested or beat up. It's lots of fun."

"Good for you!" Wenonah exclaimed. "Got a place in your organization for an outspoken Social Services major with a quick right hook?" She made a jabbing motion with her right hand, Titus caught it in both of his, and tucked her arm through his own.

"My dear," he smiled, "Let us talk. Uncle Angel, if you'll excuse us, just for a bit." He apologized for stealing my companion while looking not the least contrite, and escorted her toward the front door and the sunshine beyond.

I watched them weaving their way through the guests, out toward the nature trails, and gave the guys a thumbs up. I realized Glory was coming my way, so I walked to meet her, put my arm around her, and turned her so she could see Titus and Wen as they walked. "Five years or less, grandkids, I guarantee it," I said. "And when we're dead and gone and they've inherited this place, they can turn it into some sort of a wonderful sanctuary for people."

"It's always been a wonderful sanctuary," Glory said, momentarily laying her head on my shoulder. "For you, when you was little and so scared, and for Rafael and me when we was outcasts, and for Philippa. You Gram put all that healin' in the stones of this place, Boy."

She turned to straighten my tie, and I held her out at arm's length and said, "You look absolutely stunning, Mrs. Ruiz." And she did. She was wearing the kind of vibrant yellow that only very black skins can wear with any success – cut smoothly, but not tight, around her ample figure. "Did you and Philippa whip this little number out in your spare time?"

"Honey, you been workin' too hard to notice, but nobody got any spare time around here these days. No, I bought this."

"It's beautiful."

"Thank you, Aloysha. You lookin' as bright as a new penny youself this day." The ensemble stopped playing and put their instruments down for a break, and Glory said, "Now see, we was visitin', and now they've quit, and I was gonna grab you and dance that two step we practiced."

"Grab me after the break," I smiled, "I'll save the first dance for you."

"Hey, Aarons," several voices called in unison, and I turned to the group standing near the piano. "Time to earn your keep and play something for your wife," Kit hollered.

There was applause, and lots of encouragement, and I said, "I need my wife if I'm going to play for her."

The guests parted, and Philippa appeared on Royal's arm. He handed her to me, and I tucked her arm through mine and walked her over and sat her down on the bench beside me. "Remember," I said quietly, just to her, "That day you sat here and asked me to help you figure out what you were worth?"

"Yes," she whispered, "I do."

"Have you figured it out yet?"

I believe I have," she smiled, and there was an infinite gentleness in her voice. "I believe, in terms of luck, I am the richest person on earth."

"Next to me," I whispered in her ear, gave her a kiss on the temple, and played, *Unforgettable*, for her.

I played for a while – Broadway and ragtime, hymns and classical, and all the time I was playing I was thinking about those parties Megan used to throw, and how sterile and cruel they had been by comparison, and wishing Gram were alive to see this one in progress. Wishing my parents were here on this happiest of days for me. Almost, I wished my sister Racheal were here ... but not quite.

I looked up from time to time, seeing Wenonah and Titus enter, still arm in arm, Oscar and Ruth, Jan and Steve, David and Connor, James Horse visiting quietly with Kelly. Mostly, my senses were full of Philippa.

"This," I said at last, "I wrote for my wife. It's called, *Sweet Face*," and I began to play a piece that had come out of my fingers the day I'd given Philippa her diamond earrings. I'd saved it, hoping and praying this day would come. From over my left shoulder Glory's beautiful voice soared into the lyrics, and Philippa and I both started to cry. What a pair of old softies. A few years later I put that song in a movie we wrote together, and won an Academy Award. Amazing.

When I gave up the keyboard and took a bow, there was applause, then Glory said, "And now, if youall will come in the dinin' room, you have a duty to perform." Philippa and I followed her in, trailed by our friends, and found a beautiful wedding cake, decked with real roses, on the dining room table.

"Didn't want to have the caterers bring it out too soon," Glory grinned, "I was afraid we'd dance right over it."

She handed me a silver cake knife, whispered, "Phil's bit is just behind the cake," and stepped back into the crowd.

We cut the cake amid cheers and well wishes enough to last a lifetime. Philippa fed me a small piece, then I picked up the morsel Glory had pointed out, and fed it to Phipps. She tasted it, and laughed, "Frosted cream cheese. My indulgence for the week."

Then Tommy raised his champagne glass, rang it with a spoon and said, "I'm taking credit where credit is due! I told you she was nice! I said you'd like her!"

It was much later, when the guests had gone, the caterers had left, the mess had been cleaned up, and the four children had taken their collective selves elsewhere in my Benz, that Philippa brought a package out to where I was sitting blue jeaned and barefooted on the balcony, and handed it to me.

"What's this?" I asked.

"I honestly don't know," she said, "but it came from up north, and it's addressed to you. Open it."

I took my pocket knife out of my jeans and carefully cut the tape away, to find a note, part of a calendar, and, wrapped in tissue paper, a child's jump rope with little red handles and bells. I laughed with delight and read, "Aarons, when you have marked off all the days on this calendar, and I do mean every single damned day, you can go back to using this wretched thing. You may use it for one minute the first five days, two minutes the second five days, three minutes, and so on until you're as sweaty as you want to be. If it hurts, stop. Happy Wedding. Merrick Denton."

"Things are looking up," my wife laughed, and I caught her to me, and kissed her hair, and took her walking out beside the pool with me.

"You all packed to go to Mother RRRRussia on the twenty-first?" I teased, imitating her earlier voice. "I see you have some kind of big trunk that you're stocking."

"That's my mystery trunk. It's being packed based on reliable information coming out of Russia via Pappy Shepherd and Russell O'Halloran."

"And are your clothes packed? Your babushkas and such?"

"Getting there," she chuckled. "I wonder if there will be horses to ride just for pleasure, I mean besides the ones we're using to film. If there are, I want to take riding clothes of my own, not just my costumes. Not that I don't adore riding sidesaddle. I really hope they don't make me ride sidesaddle."

I laughed and told her what Kit had said, and she replied that it was hard, having a reputation like hers. People expected to find her riding the mechanical horses outside the supermarket, and she just wasn't all that horse-nuts. She really wasn't.

I said I believed her, and there must have been something in my tone of voice, because she punched me, and made me laugh some more. We strolled across the bit of lawn toward the roses, not saying anything, just enjoying one another's company, and then something occurred to me, and I asked, "Are you in a mood to give up a couple of secrets, wife of mine?"

"I might be," she grinned. "What did you have in mind, husband of mine?"

"The dress. How, with two days to prepare, did you get that elegant, very complicated dress to fit your little self?"

She grinned up at me. "There are a couple of secrets, right there in the answer to that. First, it's a flapper-style dress. It wasn't cut off, it was tucked up at the spot where the bodice meets the skirt- carefully, mind you, but tucked up. If one of our girls wants to wear it, at least if Tall Girl wants to wear it, it can be let back down. And the seams were basted to make it smaller, but that can be ripped right out again, I promise."

"And?"

"And," she twinkled, "When's the last time you checked on that dress?" The light dawned, and I just shook my head and chuckled. "Not that I want you to think I took our marriage for granted, or that I thought nothing could possibly go wrong," she blushed slightly, "but Glory knew how dearly you would love it if I wore that dress, so we kind of got it out and gave it the once-over… more than once." She shrugged and looked shyly away and asked quickly, "What else do you want to know?"

"Remember when we first met, and you said Tommy had prepared you for what I would be like?"

She looked up at me and wrinkled her nose, "Um hm."

"You said you'd tell me when I was older."

"Um hm."

"I'm older. I'm an old, married man. What did he tell you about me? Whatever it was, it doesn't seem to have scared you off."

She took my arms and turned me to face her, and studied me for a bit with her heart in her blue eyes and then said, "He told me ... you were nice. He said I'd like you."

ABOUT THE AUTHOR

Showandah S. Terrill is an award winning speaker, storyteller and writer. Born into a ranching family and raised in the Wild West, she has traded her horses for kayaks, and her trails for the rivers and lakes of Western Pennsylvania, where she resides with her husband and their beloved Jack Russell Terriers.

***She is currently writing two extended series: the fictional autobiographical* Peter Aarons*' novels and the epic science-fiction* Dragonhorse Tales.**

www.ingramcontent.com/pod-product-compliance
Lightning Source LLC
Chambersburg PA
CBHW030428310726
48979CB00009B/1674/J

* 9 7 8 1 7 3 2 8 0 5 2 6 2 *